PRAISE FOR AVA MILES

SEl

MW01110396

"Ava's story is witty and charming."

— BARBARA FREETHY #1 *NYT*
BESTSELLING AUTHOR

"If you like Nora Roberts type books, this is a must-read."

— READERS' FAVORITE

"If ever there was a contemporary romance that rated a 10 on a scale of 1 to 5 for me, this one is it!"

— THE ROMANCE REVIEWS

"I could not stop flipping the pages. I can't wait to read the next book in this series."

— FRESH FICTION

"I've read Susan Mallery and Debbie Macomber... but never have I been so moved as by the books Ava Miles writes."

— BOOKTALK WITH EILEEN

TAKE A TRIP TO DARE RIVER.
READ THE ENTIRE SERIES.

"Ava Miles' books just make you feel good. They're like a printed hug. They're characters you'd want for friends and neighbors. Love them all, but especially Dare River!"

— A VERY SATISFIED READER

THE DARE RIVER SERIES

Country Heaven

A down-on-her-luck cook uses food's magical properties to tame a beastly country singer after he hires her under false pretenses to restore his image.

The Chocolate Garden

An inventive gardener creates a magical chocolate garden for a sexy songwriter only to be swept away by the magic of their love.

Fireflies and Magnolias

A steel magnolia turned crusading law student must face a haunting family secret while falling in love with a cynical country music manager who's lost his faith in magic.

The Promise of Rainbows

A military vet overcomes the shadows of his past with the help of country music and a woman he's hired to remake his new home.

The Fountain Of Infinite Wishes

A determined businesswoman searches for her long-lost father while helping a tough private investigator believe in wishes again.

The Patchwork Quilt Of Happiness

A sassy quilter invites a long-lost family member to her quilting class only to fall for the sexy single dad next door.

OTHER AVA TITLES TO BINGE

The Paris Roommates

Your dreams are around the corner...

The Paris Roommates: Thea

The Paris Roommates: Dean

The Paris Roommates: Brooke

The Paris Roommates: Sawyer

The Unexpected Prince Charming Series

Love with a kiss of the Irish...

Beside Golden Irish Fields

Beneath Pearly Irish Skies

Through Crimson Irish Light

After Indigo Irish Nights

Beyond Rosy Irish Twilight

Over Verdant Irish Hills

Against Ebony Irish Seas

The Merriams Series

Chock full of family and happily ever afters...

Wild Irish Rose

Love Among Lavender

Valley of Stars

Sunflower Alley

A Forever of Orange Blossoms

A Breath of Jasmine

The Love Letter Series

The Merriams grandparents' epic love affair...

Letters Across An Open Sea

Along Waters of Sunshine and Shadow

The Friends & Neighbors Novels

A feast for all the senses...

The House of Hope & Chocolate

The Dreamer's Flower Shoppe

The Dare River Series

Filled with down-home charm...

Country Heaven

The Chocolate Garden

Fireflies and Magnolias

The Promise of Rainbows

The Fountain Of Infinite Wishes

The Patchwork Quilt Of Happiness

Country Heaven Cookbook

The Chocolate Garden: A Magical Tale (Children's Book)

The Dare Valley Series

Awash in small town fabulousness...

Nora Roberts Land

French Roast

The Grand Opening

The Holiday Serenade

The Town Square

The Park of Sunset Dreams

The Perfect Ingredient

The Bridge to a Better Life

The Calendar of New Beginnings

Home Sweet Love

The Moonlight Serenade

The Sky of Endless Blue

Daring Brides

Daring Declarations

Dare Valley Meets Paris Billionaire Mini-Series

Small town charm meets big city romance...

The Billionaire's Gamble

The Billionaire's Secret

The Billionaire's Courtship

The Billionaire's Return

Dare Valley Meets Paris Compilation

The Once Upon a Dare Series

Falling in love is a contact sport...

The Gate to Everything

Non-Fiction

The Happiness Corner: Reflections So Far

The Post-Covid Wellness Playbook

Cookbooks

Home Baked Happiness Cookbook

Country Heaven Cookbook

The Lost Guides to Living Your Best Life Series

Reclaim Your Superpowers

Courage Is Your Superpower

Expression Is Your Superpower

Peace Is Your Superpower

Confidence Is Your Superpower

Happiness Is Your Superpower

Children's Books

The Chocolate Garden: A Magical Tale

THE PROMISE OF RAINBOWS

DARE RIVER ★ BOOK 4

AVA MILES

www.avamiles.com
Ava Miles

To Kati: friend, sister, blessing. Thank you for helping me remember there's always the promise of rainbows and for shining so brightly in my life.

ACKNOWLEDGMENTS

Team Ava blesses me beyond belief: for Angela and all her insights on my stories; for Kathia, for her creative vision; for Lori, who helps spread the stories worldwide; and to a whole bunch of others who elevate my messages to the world.

Dr. Richa Thapa of the Central Arkansas Veterans Healthcare System, for being the kind of psychiatrist you wish every veteran could work with.

Gary Tabke, private investigator, whose counsel helped my imagination cook up all sorts of good stuff for our Dare River family.

Lastly, to you wonderful readers, who love these beautiful people in our Dare family and for reaching out to me and telling me how much they impact your life. You are a blessing and a treasure.

1

A thick blanket of dust stung Jake Lassiter's eyes. His vision blurred, and his heart rate kicked up to jackhammer speed. He couldn't see anything. And that was when he was vulnerable to attack. He couldn't shoot what he couldn't see.

Was there someone in the alley with him?

On the face of it, the narrow, bullet-pocked area looked clear after the dust faded, but his gut was quivering. After two tours in Iraq, he'd learned to trust it.

Someone was lurking.

Perhaps more than a mere someone. Though he'd grown to hate it, his job was to find out. To clear the area before the other men passed through. And he was good at it. Too good.

When he looked in the mirror in the morning, he didn't recognize himself anymore. His mouth was stretched in a permanent tight line, and his blue eyes reflected a new hardness from all he'd seen. Friends killed, and equally horrifying, women and children dead—sometimes out of brutal necessity. He looked older than his twenty-eight years, and ten years in the Army had turned him bitter. He hated that too. Sure, his father, also in the Army, was the one who'd pushed him into the service, but he could only blame himself for not standing up to the old man.

Not that it mattered now.

He could die in this alley if he didn't focus.

Another gust of wind blew dust over him. He pressed against the wall as a new swath of dust blinded him. His men were nearby, but that didn't guarantee his safety. All it took was an unprotected second for an enemy bullet to put a man down.

His pack felt like it weighed more than usual, and he knew it was because of the brutal heat wave sweeping through Basra. When they'd left the Humvee to go on patrol, the temperature had registered one hundred and twenty-one degrees Fahrenheit. They'd all been chugging water enhanced with salt to keep hydrated—a trick suggested by one of the medics—but it was a losing battle. He was dripping sweat, which burned his eyes differently than the dust.

His best friend, Booker Harris, gave him the signal to cross the street. From the minute they'd met, they'd trusted each other. Felt that whole "band of brothers" thing. Perhaps it was because they were both from Arkansas. They watched Razorback football together and reminisced about going to watch the horses race at Oaklawn in Hot Springs. In a hellhole like Iraq, talk of home kept a man from coming out of his skin.

Jake took a deep breath and let it out before darting out from his position. As he cleared the opening in the alley, he heard the whine of bullet fire at his back. Pressing into the wall, he listened to the ricochet. Two bogies from the pattern of the bullet fire, sitting at three o'clock in the building across the narrow alley.

His gut quivered. Other militants would come this way after learning Americans were in the area. They were in for a shit storm if they didn't move fast.

He signaled to Booker to cover him and waited for his friend to start firing in the direction of the militants. After the first discharge of bullets, Jake squeezed his eyes shut for a second and then pushed off the wall, running flat out. It was only twenty feet, but his heart was pounding in his chest, so loud he feared the enemy could hear it. And this damn alley was so narrow that it didn't have any hidey-holes he could duck into for cover.

Bullets punctured the alley, kicking loose stone, which jettisoned off the wall like projectiles. Looking up, he saw one of the militants peering over the edge of the third-story apartment building. The man disappeared from view after taking a hit from one of Booker's bullets.

Jake waited to see if there were any combatants hidden in the opposite building. He didn't think so, but he made himself wait. Listen. Watch. When he was sure there weren't, he signaled to Booker to run. They needed to clear that damn building fast.

He angled his rifle in the position where he thought the second gunman was hunkered down and fired. He kept his eyes trained on the spot where Booker had taken out the other militant and continued to squeeze the trigger in methodical bursts. Jake never wasted ammunition. Not after he ran out on his first tour, when he was still young and stupid, and had to take some from a dead soldier.

No one fired back as Booker raced across the space, but that didn't mean anything. The enemy would know they'd blown their position. They were likely regrouping.

Booker reached him and pressed his back against the wall. "We need to take out those fuckers," he whispered harshly.

Jake nodded and signaled for Booker to follow him. His gut told him the building's entrance was to the west, around back. He briskly stepped over pieces of trash and bullet casings in the alley. When they reached the end of the building, there was a flash of something above them. Another combatant. Jake pressed back with Booker.

He radioed in their location and situation and was relieved to hear some of their guys were only a block away. Of course, in this situation, a block might as well have been halfway around the world.

An unnerving quiet fell in the streets, and he braced himself. He'd only learned the true meaning of "the calm before the storm" in Iraq.

A spattering of bullet fire in their direction made him duck, praying all the while the bullets wouldn't travel down the wall. The bullet fire continued as he crouched down. He heard his friend's whoosh of breath and the horrible sound of bullets entering flesh.

He's hit.

Rifle ready, Jake popped up, knowing their position was blown. He had no choice.

He narrowed in on the man shooting at them in the street and took him down. A part of his brain registered that the combatant looked about fifteen years old.

With his rifle in ready position, he checked the area for more combatants.

"Booker," he rasped out, not daring to look at his friend while he surveyed the area. "Talk to me, man."

There was no response, and he forced himself to go numb. Secure the area first. Then take care of his friend.

When Jake knew the area was clear for the moment, he knelt beside Booker. His friend was slumped against the wall, a streak of red gore tracking his descent. Blood was gushing from his friend's mouth. A bullet had punctured his neck. Jake's gorge rose as he set his weapon aside and reached into his pack for a cloth. He pressed it to Booker's torn flesh. The carotid artery spurted blood in his face, and Jake shivered from head to toe.

"Jesus," he said, wiping at the blood on his face. "Booker. Booker! Stay with me, man."

His friend remained unresponsive.

"Booker's down," he called in. "I need a medic. Right now, dammit!"

Then he heard the distinct scrape that told him another combatant was coming for him.

His hand tightened on the cloth, but his instincts kicked in. Releasing his pressure on the wound, he grabbed his rifle and readied himself.

When the combatant peered around the edge of the alley, Jake took him down with two taps to the chest. He listened to hear if any more were coming, his fingers itching to stop the blood gushing from Booker's wound.

When he felt it was all clear again, he set his rifle aside, grabbed the cloth, and pressed on the wound to stop the gush of bright-red blood from his friend's neck. There was enough blood to soak the cloth and his hand.

"Booker," he ground out. "Dammit! Don't you dare die on me."

A weak hand grabbed his, and he jumped. Booker's brown eyes, filled with fear, met Jake's. He tried to speak, but all that came out was a horrible moan and more blood.

He's not going to make it, he thought, *not unless the medic comes stat.* He pressed harder on the wound, feeling power-

5

less. Men had died in his arms before, but it wasn't the kind of thing that got easy.

Jake turned to the only Person he knew who could change it—one he'd mostly stopped talking to amidst all the carnage and senseless killing of this damn war. "God! Do you hear me? Keep Booker alive until help arrives. Please. I'll do anything you ask. I swear."

His friend gave a horrible choke and then his eyes went glassy.

"No!" he called out. "Dammit, no. Come on, God. Help us!"

Jake pressed harder on the wound, his fingers searching for a pulse. Maybe Booker wasn't dead. Maybe he'd only fallen unconscious. Maybe God was keeping him alive until the medic could reach them.

But Jake knew it was a lie.

When he needed God the most, the Almighty had let him down. *Again.* How many times had he prayed for a fellow soldier to be saved? Too many to count. It was like God didn't care enough about any of them to lift a finger. And if Jake hadn't taken his hands off the wound to save himself, Booker might still be alive.

Unable to locate a pulse, he slumped against the wall beside his friend and put his head in his hands. *It's not fucking fair. It should have been me. How am I going to face Booker's wife and tell her I couldn't bring her husband back? Darren, Randy, and Monty are going to be so upset when they find us.* His close friends were only a few blocks away, clearing other buildings.

His commander radioed him for an update. Jake made himself relay the news that Booker was gone. Another team was coming his way, he was told. He just needed to hang in there.

Hang in there? What did it matter? Booker was dead.

His hands were bathed in blood, and he couldn't take his gaze off the torn flesh of Booker's neck. He made himself close his friend's eyes.

Then he reached for his rifle like he knew he should. Like he'd been trained to do.

But he didn't care if anyone took him out.

———

JAKE AWOKE IN A RUSH. HIS SKIN WAS CLAMMY. HIS HEART WAS pounding. And then he felt it. The horrible greasy nausea in his belly.

He rolled out of bed and stumbled to the bathroom. The inside of his mouth was dry, and though he knew it was a trick of his mind, he could *taste* the dust in that alley where Booker had died.

When he turned on the bathroom light, he soaked in its warm glow. Even though he was thirty-three now, and Booker had died five years ago, he still couldn't sleep in the dark after one of these nightmares.

He turned on the cold water and leaned over the sink, plunging his sweaty head under the faucet. *I'm not going to throw up. I'm not.*

But he did.

There was no stopping it tonight. After it was over, he leaned his head on the toilet seat, praying the dry heaves would stop. They always hurt his throat, and as a country singer, he didn't like anything harming his voice.

Singing was his salvation. His music had healed him in a way he'd never imagined. He just wasn't healed all the way yet.

Tonight he wondered for the millionth time if he ever would be.

He'd done everything he was supposed to do, from therapy to meds. And it had worked...to an extent. He wasn't afraid to leave his house any more; he didn't break into a cold sweat whenever he heard a loud noise; he no longer felt compelled to ignore phone calls and texts from worried friends; and he didn't flash into a rage if someone cut him off on the highway.

But nothing seemed to permanently stop the nightmares.

This time, he'd gone six months without the dream of Booker coming back to haunt him.

He'd been so hopeful the nightmares were gone for good... And that hope had given life to a new one.

A few months ago, he'd met Susannah McGuiness, his friend J.P.'s sweet and beautiful sister. He'd fallen for her in the space of a few minutes. Her voice had wrapped around him like a cool breeze after a hot day, and her moss-green eyes had seemed to reach all the way into his tattered soul.

She was as magical and creative as the fairy tale pictures she'd painted in a tree house for her niece and nephew. And she'd taken the photos of abused women and made them into a work of art for the charity concert he'd headlined with another country singer and friend.

And then there was her smile. It was like a warm slice of apple pie, the kind that made everything good in the world after a backbreaking day. She was beautiful and funny too, and he was so crazy about her he could barely string together complete sentences in her presence.

But because he hadn't trusted himself to be completely cured of all his shit, he hadn't asked her out on a date—

even though he'd wanted to do that more than he'd wanted to win another Country Music Award.

They'd worked on that charity concert together, and he'd even held her hand once. What a shock of attraction that had been! He'd never been so affected by an innocent touch. Still, he'd played it safe and asked her to redecorate his new house in Dare River, right outside Nashville. This way, he could see if he could be in her presence without risking a return of the nightmares. Because the strange thing about them was that they always came back when he was happy, when he started to let himself think he could form a full life for himself.

He'd called off two relationships in the last five years because of the nightmares. There was no way he was going to do what his daddy had done to his mama. He'd seen the cracks in their relationship at an early age. The wild mood swings his Army colonel daddy blamed on anything from the dog barking too loud to the extra traffic in Little Rock, Arkansas as he drove home from work had been manifestations of his own PTSD, a topic rarely discussed at that time and never acknowledged by his tough-as-nails daddy.

Then there was the way Daddy had treated his two sons, not giving them much choice about following in the family footsteps by going into the Army. Jake's older brother, Aaron, was still serving, and he was just like Daddy.

No, Jake wasn't going to let himself carry on that tradition.

But with Susannah, he'd dared to let himself think things might be different. As each nightmare-free night had passed, the hope in his chest had bloomed bigger and brighter. An invitation lingered just behind his lips each time he and Susannah saw each other, and the look in her eyes told him that she wished it would voice itself.

Now that was over. Another dream turned to ash.

Susannah was supposed to come over to the house for her first consultation this morning. That must have been the trigger for the dream. When Jake was able to stand, he rinsed his mouth out and looked into the mirror. The jagged bullet scar on his shoulder seemed uglier in the light —his daily reminder of what he'd seen and done.

"I vow I will never get involved with a woman again until I'm totally okay," he reaffirmed to the harsh image of himself in the mirror.

He put his hands under the faucet to wash them. But even though the water ran clear, to him it looked like Booker's blood. His gut surged anew, and he stumbled to the toilet and dry heaved until his stomach muscles trembled.

"God," he said when he finally was able to push away.

He hadn't even gotten a brief interlude to believe in the possibility that he and Susannah could be together. It was over before it had even started, before he'd been able to push her long brown hair back behind her ear or kiss her sweetly on her rosy-red lips.

His heart broke. It was like being doomed to a life of darkness.

He was never *ever* going to be okay again.

2

S usannah McGuiness schooled herself not to go gaga over Jake Lassiter on their first consult. Sure, he'd held her hand a couple of times, and when he looked at her, he made her feel like she was the only woman in existence. But he'd made it clear he wasn't interested in her romantically. If he had been, he would've asked her on a date instead of asking her to decorate his home in Dare River.

Still, she found herself checking her image in the rearview mirror to make sure her brown hair wasn't frizzy. Even though it was mid-January, there was more than average humidity in the air. And it was fifty-two degrees outside. In the South, weather was as unpredictable as an elderly relative—the kind who perched on the front porch and held court, spouting wisdom or crazy notions.

She was checking her lipstick when she caught sight of Jake coming down the front steps. His creamy-white three-story house boasted dormer windows, black shutters, and a red gabled roof. Like most of the houses in Dare River, it featured a traditional wrap-around porch. She wondered if

Jake ever sat on the red-cushioned porch swing or the oak table in the right corner of the house and played his soulful country music.

As she stepped out of her Audi, she forced herself to meet his cobalt blue gaze. He'd stopped six feet away from her—almost as if he'd intentionally decided not to come any closer. Today he had on a simple button-down navy shirt and faded jeans that hugged the defined muscles of his legs. His signature silver belt buckle engraved with a stag winked in the sunlight.

The punch of attraction that rocked through her was unwelcome. Why did she feel so drawn to him? It was so unfair given the fact that he didn't seem to like her that way.

His sandy blond hair curled at the ends, giving him a softer look. She had a hard time imagining what his hair must have looked like when he was in the Army. The military cut would have made him look fierce and likely unapproachable. Then there was the way he moved—like the brave soldier he'd been. No sauntering or strutting for Jake. There was purpose and grace in each movement he made.

"Hi," she made herself say.

"Hey," he answered, his smile completely open and engaging now. "Welcome to Redemption Ridge."

Her brow winged up. "I didn't know you'd named your property."

He lifted a shoulder. "Some people around here do, so I decided why not me? I just didn't put a sign out front."

Redemption. The word settled over her as she studied him. What did he feel he needed redemption from? Having heard his music, she guessed it was from the war. There were still shadows in his eyes when he sang about it.

"I like your place," she said, turning to scan his property. "Tammy did an incredible job with the grounds."

"She did," he agreed, and with that, he finally came to stand beside her, though he maintained a good amount of distance between them. "She pushed pretty hard to plant everything before the first frost. I can't wait until everything comes up out of the earth and blooms in spring. It's going to be spectacular. You're lucky to have her in the family."

Even though Tammy hadn't yet officially married Susannah's brother, John Parker, or J.P. as they called him, she and her two kids were already family. "Yes, we're incredibly blessed by them."

He took a few more steps until he was standing closer to her, almost as if the family talk had made him more comfortable. "You have a wonderful family."

"I do indeed." She looked him straight in the eye. There was something in his voice. Up close, she noticed the dark smudges under his eyes. "You look tired. Were you up late working on a song?"

He kicked at the ground, breaking eye contact. "Maybe. I didn't sleep too well last night."

She knew a forbidden subject when she heard it. "Why don't you show me around?"

He extended his hand to her, and her gaze lowered. His palm looked so open and inviting, but his hand clenched an instant later, as if he'd only then realized what he was doing. She looked up to meet his eyes.

What is he thinking?

The memory of how that hand had felt wrapped around hers washed over her. He'd held her hand during the preview of her art for the concert to benefit abused women, and in that long, delicious moment, she'd been unable to tell where his hand began and hers ended. Never before had she felt like she'd melded into someone else. Afterward, she'd hoped he would ask her out, but he hadn't. And he'd reached for her hand again after asking her to be his decorator.

Obviously, there was some sort of connection between them—one he wanted to fight, for whatever reason. He lowered his hand slowly, and her throat squeezed down to the size of a pea. The laugh he uttered was as strained as a preacher confessing his sins to his congregation.

"The whole 'hold your hand thing' between us is weird, right?" he asked and then coughed, looking away from her.

"Jake—"

"Ignore what I just did—and said." He turned on the heel of his caramel-colored cowboy boots and took off in the direction of the house. "Let me show you around."

Suddenly it was difficult to breathe, but she slung her purse and the strap of her thin leather briefcase over her shoulder and followed him, schooling her features and praying her heart rate would calm down. She took her time, walking in slow, easy steps, trying to mirror her breathing.

He was waiting for her by the side of the house, and from behind, she could see how tense his back muscles were through his shirt. Since it clearly wasn't an option to talk about what had just happened, she gave him a simple smile when he glanced at her.

"Tell me what you have in mind for the house," she said in her best professional tone. "I'll share my thoughts later, and we can forge a joint vision."

"You sound like your brother when we write songs together," he said, rubbing the back of his neck.

It was undoubtedly easier for her brother, a lawyer and songwriter, to collaborate with Jake—he didn't have to balance his professional duties with this...*tension*. "J.P. knows how to collaborate. I'd like to think it's because he grew up as the only boy in a family with four women."

They started walking down a flagstone path lined with copper garden lights. Tammy had created curved beds that hugged the path before opening up in the backyard. A stone fountain dominated the open space, surrounded by a ring of stones flanked by dormant rose bushes.

"Your daddy wasn't around growing up, as I recall," Jake said when they reached the fountain.

"No," she replied, wishing he wouldn't breach this topic. It was too personal, particularly given this strange tension between them. "He left when I was four. I didn't expect you to have a fountain."

Jake shrugged. "I really like water. I think it's from all the time I spent in the desert."

He didn't need to tell her what desert he meant. She wouldn't press; if he wanted to talk about it, he would.

"I'm surprised to see the fountains working in January," she commented.

"I turn them on when the weather heats up, like it has lately. So long as it's not freezing at night, I can't bust the pipes. And we don't often hit freezing temps anyway."

That was certainly true. Ice storms or snow showers were as rare as a blue moon here in Tennessee. "Would you like a water feature inside the house? We could incorporate something if you'd like."

Looking back in the direction of the house, he narrowed his eyes in thought. "I hadn't thought about that. I'd love to hear what you have in mind."

"Consider it done." She added that item to her mental list.

More beds lined the sides of his property to break up

the expanse of lawn. Even though she didn't know all the names, she identified some Cypress trees and Japanese maples. Adirondack chairs and wooden benches rested in strategic locations to allow enjoyment of the marvelous views. Unlike her brother's property, the expanse of Dare River was visible from Jake's house.

"You're lucky to have such an amazing view of the water," she said as they continued walking across the cushiony lawn.

"I mentioned that I like water," he joked. It was still there, though, that thread of tension in his voice.

She almost reached out to rub his back, but she knew it would be the wrong move. Her job was to help him with his house. Not help *him*.

"Have you seen enough outside? There's not much to see on the inside. That's why I need your help."

She glanced around at the rest of the grounds. Tammy was meticulous when it came to meeting her client's preferences. There was a fire pit and another water feature in the distance. Mini-rainbows seemed to dance and tumble in the air above the bubbling spray.

"My mama always says there's the promise of rainbows every morning when you wake up," Susannah said with a small smile.

He looked over at her sharply and then off in the distance, as if searching for them.

"There're a bunch of rainbows over by the water feature," she added.

He squinted. "I don't see them."

"You don't?" They were so obvious to her. "Maybe if we go closer you will."

They walked in the direction of the fountain, and by now, he was frowning.

"I don't see anything," he mumbled with an edge of frustration.

This time she did put her hand on his arm—he needed it, she could tell—and it was hard not to react to how hard, hot, and muscular it felt under her fingers.

"Don't worry," she said in a cheery voice. "Maybe it's just the way the sunlight is hitting the spray from my vantage point. Let's go inside so you can show me the rest of your place."

When she moved off in the direction of the house, she realized he wasn't following her. She stopped and retraced her steps. A scowl had spread across Jake's clean-shaven jaw, and there was a surprising amount of desperation in his eyes.

"I can't see the rainbows," he muttered. "You know, I've never seen one in my whole life. Can you believe that?"

That caught her off guard for a moment, but rainbows weren't exactly a common occurrence. It made sense that not everyone had been lucky enough to see one. But his desperation clearly went above and beyond rainbows, so it seemed best to table the subject. "I don't know, Jake, but I know it's upsetting you. Maybe you'll see them later."

He kicked at the grass under his feet. "Okay, let's go inside."

When they entered the house, she had to school her reaction. He hadn't been exaggerating one bit. The house *did* need her. There was nothing on the walls, and most of the rooms were actually empty. With her busy client schedule, she'd fit him in as soon as she could, but if she'd known he was living this way, she would have done something temporary to dress up the place back in November.

"I did tell you that I was going to have my former decorator remove all her stuff," Jake said, picking up on her reaction. "Especially the dead stuffed animals. Man, that decorator lady really misread me."

Yes, she had. He wouldn't want anything dead around him after being surrounded by so much death as a soldier. Had the woman not listened to his music? Susannah had. In truth, she couldn't stop listening to it. His songs were all about losing friends in war and longing for home. The thought sparked something in her. Jake wanted a home here in Dare River, a safe sanctuary after everything he'd experienced.

"Let's talk about colors," she said, glancing over at him. "Since you're an artist, I know you have a sense about what you like. You certainly create a mood at your concerts."

"I like warm colors. And blues. The white walls aren't working for me. I tried to tell that to the decorator lady. She thought it gave the house clean lines. Gave it a contemporary look."

"She didn't listen to you." Susannah fought the urge to ask who in the world he'd hired. "Some women think men don't know a thing about color or decorating. Or that they like contemporary because it's minimalist."

"Minimalist." He rolled his eyes. "It's like you know her."

"I know decorators like her," she said cautiously. "I have a different approach."

"Good," he said, nodding. "This place feels like a tomb."

That pretty much summed up her opinion of the place. "We'll make it everything you want and more."

"I want art and color and magic." He rubbed a hand on his face, as if embarrassed, and then said, "When we first met, I told you that I really liked the wall paintings you did in your niece and nephew's tree house. I want people to have that feeling when they come in here. I want them to feel happy and at home."

That day was forever crystallized in Susannah's mind. She had arrived at J.P.'s house as Jake was leaving. Everything in her seemed to slow down as she looked at him, taking in his massive shoulders and muscular body. Then she realized he was waiting to talk to her.

He'd been charming and sweet, and she'd felt a shocking promise of possibility between them. But something had changed since then—something she didn't understand.

"I told you I can paint for grown ups," she joked, shaking the memory away.

"There's no shame in what you painted for those kids." He tucked his hands in his jeans. "It's real and pure and from your heart. That's what I want here. Something real. Something...something that has meaning."

"We'll do that," she assured him and then let him take her through the house.

"There's a lot to decorate. My place is over six thousand square feet. I have six bedrooms, including my recording studio on the lower level."

"That's fine. I've decorated large houses for other country music clients."

"Good," he said, leading the way.

Every room he showed her was bare bones, including his bedroom, which was empty but for a set of queen mattresses on the floor in the corner with plain white sheets meticulously tucked into the corners. There wasn't even a dresser in the room. Or a lamp. The sparseness hurt her heart, but it shocked her too. Jake was a famous star on the rise. How could he be living like this?

"I'm...ah...still more comfortable in smaller beds after

sleeping in Army barracks and on the tour bus," Jake said, his ears turning bright red.

"Any opposition to me finding you something else to sleep in?" she asked, schooling her voice. "Maybe get you off the floor?"

She was not going to think about anyone else being in bed with him—especially not herself.

"No," he said, his cheeks beet red now to match his ears. "The other decorator put in some antebellum bed with curtains. I felt like I was suffocating."

Again, she wondered who in the world he'd hired. "I won't select anything that will make you uncomfortable, I promise."

Then he did it again; he grabbed her hand. "I know you won't." His eyes shot down at their linked hands, and he dropped hers like it was a hot potato. "I'm grateful, is all."

"I know you are, but we're only beginning." She turned to face him, and because they were standing so close together, she had to crane her neck back to meet his eyes. "How about we visit a showroom so you can pick out some of the bigger items? That way we can shape the rooms around them."

With the clients who truly cared about making a home, she'd discovered it was the most efficient approach.

"I like that idea," he said, leading her out of his bedroom. "I imagine things better when I see them. I hate looking at color swatches and stuff. I'm not good at that."

"Most people aren't," she told him, walking down the walnut hardwood floors with him.

When they reached the entrance of another bare bedroom, he stopped and leaned against the doorway. "You must think I'm bat shit crazy to be living like this."

"Why would you say that? I don't think you're crazy at

all. You just happened to hire a terrible decorator, and you needed to wipe the slate clean. But that's finished now. We're going to make this place feel like a home in no time." She would do her all to make it come together quickly.

His mouth bunched up like he was fighting powerful emotion, and it took her every strength not to reach her hand out to him again.

"J.P. mentioned you have a beautiful recording studio here," she said instead, doing the only other thing she could think of to help him re-balance: change the subject. It was quickly becoming her go-to strategy with him.

"I didn't let the other lady touch it," he admitted. "There's no way I could write or sing a song with a dead deer looking at me. Let me show you."

When they entered it, she finally saw the man she knew. At least a dozen antique guitars were arranged on one wall. The paintings scattered around the room displayed music scenes, everything from jazz in New Orleans to folk singers in the mountains. A clay jug with a cork stopper that might have once held moonshine rested on a nearby table. A bear hide covered the hardwood floor in front of the fireplace, positioned so he could rest his feet on it while sitting on the brown leather couch. A blue and white handmade quilt was draped over the arm of a matching loveseat. There was a flat screen TV in the corner in the sitting area. And behind her was the recording studio outfitted with the live room, the control room, and the isolation booth.

He didn't just write and record music in this place. "You spend most of your time down here, don't you?"

"It's cozier," he said, straightening the quilt on the loveseat.

So he liked cozy. Huh. It surprised her, but now she was

starting to see how to bring his home to life. No wonder he liked her paintings in the tree house.

"You like folk art," she commented, pointing to the wall. "Is that man playing the spoons?"

"Yes," he said, coming up beside her. "I bought that painting in a small town in the Ozarks. I don't need fancy art. It's not that I don't like it, but I'm a simple man."

She wasn't so sure about that. But simplicity seemed to comfort him, so that's what she was going to give him. "Tell me where you found these other pieces."

As he spoke, more layers of the rising country music star peeled away. He loved to drive his truck to small towns and visit antique shops or old country stores. Beyond the stories he told her about the treasures he'd found—including the guitars—he spun captivating stories about the shop owners who'd sold the pieces to him.

"No wonder your music is so real," she said finally. "You talk to people. And you listen."

"I don't talk to everyone, and I probably don't listen to everyone either."

She gave him a look.

He held up his hands. "I'm telling the truth."

"You're being self-deprecating. No wonder you and J.P. get along so well. He would probably say the same thing about himself."

"Is that a bad thing?" he asked, studying her face.

Unable to look away, Susannah gazed deep into his blue eyes. He had a light dusting of freckles on his nose. And his eyelashes? She could have skied the long jump off them. But his lips threatened her restraint the most. They were lush and full and made her want to feel them move over her own.

"Susannah?" he asked in a deep tone, one octave lower than usual.

Her eyes flew back to his, and she felt a blush spread across her cheeks. "Sorry...I was...thinking about J.P. I was supposed to...ah...call him."

As if her blatant staring wasn't bad enough, now she'd added insult to injury and broken one of the Big Ten, her mama's nickname for the commandments. She'd just made a liar of herself to cover up her infatuation.

"Maybe you'd better call your brother then," he said, his lips twitching. "You seem flustered all of a sudden."

Was he flirting with her? Dag nabbit, he was so *not* supposed to do that, not when he clearly didn't intend to ask her out.

"If you'll excuse me," she said, as much to save face as to screw her head on straight.

"You can step outside through the French doors if you want some privacy."

"Thanks," she said and took off in the direction he'd indicated.

She did make a call to her business manager to keep up the pretense. When she returned to the studio ten minutes later, feeling more in control of herself, Jake was sitting on the couch strumming a guitar.

"I like that melody," she commented. "I don't think I've heard it before."

"I'm working on a new album," he said, setting his guitar aside. "So you know my music?"

"Please. I live in Nashville, and you write songs with my brother. Of course I know your music. And if for some reason I didn't, I would have listened to it as research for this job."

"I don't want to be a job to you," he said, scanning her

face. "I'd...like us to be friends...too. Your brother is one of my friends, so it only seems fitting."

Fitting. Is that what he thought? "Friends then. But I'm still working for you as your decorator. That's an important distinction to me."

He rose from the couch and came over to stand in front of her. Again, she had to crane her neck to meet his eyes.

"I respect that. So why don't we do what I do with you brother? He works for me too, technically."

But he's not attracted to you, she wanted to add. "What's that?" she said instead.

"We work together, and we...talk like friends. You're going to be decorating my house, and unlike the last lady, you're going to want to do it right. That means we're going to have to be friendly."

"Okay, so tell me more about your favorite small towns."

"Well, the first one that comes to mind is Booger Holler in Arkansas. It's famous for the town sign that said *Population 7...countin' one ol' coon dog.* The town is closed now, but it even had a two-story outhouse at one point."

She laughed. "You're making that up."

He crossed his heart like the good Boy Scout he'd probably been. "Nope. Even my lyrics couldn't be that original."

"A coon dog?" she asked. There was no way she was discussing an outhouse with a man. She was too Southern for that.

"Mountain folk set a high price on their coon dogs," he said. That made him laugh too, and the laughter seem to loosen up his whole body.

"You don't have a dog."

He immediately tensed up again. "No. I had one when I got back...when I left the Army. But he got hit by a car."

"I'm so sorry." What must that have been like? To lose friends in combat, only to come home and lose your dog?

He shrugged. "I forgot my manners. I didn't offer you anything to drink."

"You don't need to be concerned about that."

"But I am," he countered, "so what can I get you?"

"Do you have a beer?" she asked jokingly, hoping to lighten the mood.

His face went blank.

"I was just kidding. How about some ice tea?"

Jake was studying her again, like he wasn't sure how to read her all of the sudden. "Sweet?"

"Of course," she said easily. "What other way is there?"

"Do you actually like beer?" he asked, readjusting the guitar he'd left sitting on the couch.

"On occasion."

"Hmm...I didn't take you for a beer kind of girl."

Susannah almost gave him a playful whack, but it would be too flirtatious. "I prefer wine, but I'll drink beer if it's offered." Her brother teased her and her sisters sometimes for liking their white wine. And they teased him for liking pretty much anything that came out of a jug—which really wasn't true. But it's what siblings did.

"Is your kitchen as bare bones as the rest of the house?" she asked him.

"Pretty much," he said and led her back to the steps leading to the first floor. "My mama didn't believe in men cooking growing up, so I never learned. And being in the Army and then on tour didn't help much."

"I'll teach you some basics, if you'd like," she said before thinking about it. So much for keeping it professional.

"I'd like that," he answered after a long pause. "I'll bet

you're good at cooking. In fact, I'll bet you're pretty much good at everything you do."

A while back, Jake had told J.P. he thought she was charming. Apparently she'd been upgraded to proficient.

"My mama is a good cook, and we needed to help growing up."

"I expect so," he said quietly. "I met your mama at one of your brother's parties, but I'd like to get to know her better. She sounds like an incredible woman."

"You should come to her church," she said brightly. "And hear her preach. She's in her element there."

From the way he closed down and physically backed away from her, she knew she'd made a terrible mistake.

"I don't go to church any more," Jake said, looking down at his boots. "Not that I don't believe or respect other's beliefs."

"Of course," she said immediately. This topic was a powder keg. "Why don't you get our tea? I'm going to wander around, if that's okay, and let some ideas form."

His chest rose as if expelling a tortuous breath. "Take as much time as you'd like. I want you to have a feel for the house. I'll be in the kitchen."

She made herself smile. "Good. I'll find you."

When he left, she stared at the plain, bare walls. And wondered over the pain in her heart how such a loving and gentle man had been reduced to living in an empty house and closing himself off from church.

3

J ake wet a paper towel with cold water and dabbed the back of his neck. He hadn't expected Susannah's invitation to church—although he should have. She was rightly proud of her mama's preaching. And inviting people to services was the Southern way. Heck, J.P. had already issued that same invitation.

But it had filled him with shame to tell Susannah church wasn't for him anymore. What must she think of him now? She would want to be with a man who would go to services with her every Sunday and raise their kids in some kind of faith. Even her continued attraction to him couldn't compensate for that.

How was he supposed to tell her he'd lost all his faith when God hadn't answered his prayer to save Booker? That he didn't understand God or the way things worked anymore? He'd prayed in the beginning, sure, but prayers had done nothing to save Booker and a few of his other friends. Wasn't his friend, Monty, walking around with a prosthetic leg after stepping on a landmine? There had been a few near misses for him as well, and he had a scar on his shoulder to prove it.

The more senseless carnage he'd witnessed, the harder it had become to pray. What kind of God would allow such atrocities to happen? Growing up in a country that had a constant supply of food and water and a system of government that dealt mostly—albeit imperfectly—with things like violence and disorder hadn't prepared him for the chaos of war. Unspeakable things happened in battle.

Since there weren't any ready answers to his questions, he'd decided to do the respectful thing and stop pretending to believe in a God that allowed these things to happen. He honored other people's beliefs—was even heartened by their prayers for him and their own stories of how prayer had changed their lives—but it wasn't his story.

Jake felt like he'd been abandoned by God, and maybe it was true. Forgiveness was all well and good, but wasn't there a line whereby a person simply couldn't come back? Maybe he wasn't redeemable after everything he'd done, and that's why God hadn't saved Booker when he'd cried out. God sure acted like He didn't love Jake anymore, if you asked him.

"Are you okay?" she asked, making him jump.

The damp paper towel fell from his hand and plopped on the floor. He snapped down to retrieve it. "It's a little warm in here, don't you think?" he asked, hoping to cover up his moment of weakness.

She rubbed her arms. "Actually, it feels a little cool to me. Maybe I'll need that sweet tea warmed up."

The sweet tea. He'd forgotten all about it. "I can warm it up. And I'll turn up the heat while I'm at it."

"Don't bother on my account if you're warm," she said, her moss-green eyes soft.

So she knew he was unsettled.

"I'll get you one of my jackets," he replied, liking the idea of seeing her wearing something of his.

Then he had to remind himself that they could never be anything more than friends.

"That's not—"

He darted out of the kitchen before she could continue to protest. His favorite jean jacket hung in the front closet, and truth be told, it would look nice with her red blouse and navy skirt. Country professional, he decided, and then frowned. His daddy would have called him a sissy or worse for having an opinion about women's clothing.

Daddy didn't understand that as an artist Jake knew about things like color and textures, the same way he knew how to pair words with musical notes. But according to Daddy, "real" men weren't attracted to the arts. But then he and Daddy had never seen eye to eye.

When Jake had returned from his final tour and announced he was leaving the Army, Daddy had been more than disappointed. His brother, Aaron, hadn't voiced an opinion about his choice, which made Jake suspect he wished he could get out too. None of them spoke to him anymore, but perhaps that was in part because there was so little to say.

His decision to pack up his one battered suitcase and his guitar and head to Nashville had been his salvation. He'd played on street corners and in honky tonks, singing songs that simply wouldn't be silenced. The more real the songs, the greater the audience's response. His whole life had changed after he was discovered at Nashville's famous Bluebird Café.

For the better.

Well, mostly. He didn't like to think about where he'd

be if he'd stayed in the Army. Or if he'd taken up a job at the bank like his mama had encouraged him to do after he left the service.

He'd forged his own path.

Even so, the past still had its hooks in him. He could make music, but it appeared he would never make real love with a woman and raise a family.

But as he walked back into the kitchen and helped Susannah into his jacket, he simply couldn't make peace with that death sentence. The light in her eyes was like the North Star, and she looked so sweet and small in his jacket. There had to be a way out. There had to be something he hadn't tried.

Maybe it *was* going back to church. Maybe if he could figure out why God had stopped answering his prayers—what made him so unlovable to the Almighty—he could find his way back.

"I've changed my mind about your offer to go to see your mama preach," he said before he could chicken out. Sweat was already beading on his back, and his heart had jumped to attention like a new recruit, pounding hard in his chest.

What if God struck him dead when he tried to walk through the doors of the church? If he hadn't been so tense, he would have laughed at himself.

"You want to go?" she asked, her moss-green eyes wide. "I'm so happy to hear that."

"This Sunday," he said, forcing himself to swallow the bile in his throat. Vomiting in front of her would be beyond humiliating.

She took the damp paper towel he'd set aside and dabbed his neck with it. "Are you sure?"

He wasn't sure of anything, but he had to do *something*. "Absolutely."

Silence descended as she studied him, and even though the cloth she was holding to his neck was cool, her touch was hot. He almost yanked her hand away. The control he forced himself to have around her was slipping again, and his gaze dropped to her lips.

The fingers applying the cloth to his neck tensed, and so did his whole body. His hand immediately rose and cupped hers. Her gaze flew to his. He could hear her breathing change from normal to agitated in the same instant his heart rate went from accelerated to manic. His fingers tightened around her wrist, and she leaned into him, and the first notes of something floral drifted to him. Man, she smelled good, woman good. And he wanted to get closer to all that goodness...

His other hand reached for her waist, but when he brushed the hourglass sides of her body, his brain kicked in. *What are you doing?*

He dropped her hand and stepped back, wishing he could take a deep drag of air into his lungs without being conspicuous. But he couldn't. So he suffered through a tight chest and limited oxygen as she took a few steps back. Her eyes refused to meet his, but he told himself it was probably for the best.

"I should go," she said finally, depositing the damp towel on the counter. "I'll have some ideas for you soon. Given...the size of the job, it might be a week. Then we can talk about scheduling a time to look at some furniture."

"I didn't get you that sweet tea," he said, not knowing how to make things right between them.

Neither one of them could ignore what had just

happened. Then again, neither one of them could really talk about it either.

"It's all right," she said, stripping out of his jacket so quickly it might have been on fire. "I'll be in touch."

"Let me walk you to the door."

He set the denim jacket down on the counter and followed her long strides. She was halfway to the door when he caught up to her. Who could blame her for making a speedy exit? He slowed to a walk a few steps behind her and tried not to admire the curves of her waist.

When he opened the door for her, she stopped at the threshold. "You don't have to walk me out."

"I want to," he replied, locking his jaw at the change in her voice.

She was so professional and cold now, but he knew it was his doing. "Susannah. If you don't feel like we should work together on my house, it's okay. I realize..." What the heck was he supposed to say? That they were attracted to each other? That he was too much of a mess to ask her out?

"It's okay," she said, fiddling with the purse and satchel she'd retrieved on her way out. "We'll manage."

He didn't want to manage. He wanted to tell her why things were the way they were. Why they had to be. But he couldn't force the words out.

"Can I still go to church with you?" he asked.

Her rigidity dissolved like water poured out from a canteen in the desert. "Of course. You're always welcome."

"Should I meet you..." Did they call it the vestibule? He was fresh out of church words.

She worried her lip. "Why don't you simply find us inside the church? We sit in the front if one of our family members arrives early enough to save us all seats. If we meet...people might think..."

There was no need to finish the rest of the sentence. He knew what people would think if they showed up together. This way it could look like he was joining his friends. Friends like J.P.

"I don't have to sit with y'all. I don't want to make you uncomfortable or cause unwanted speculation."

This time she did lay a hand on his arm, but only for a moment. Her touch shot up his arm with as much power as a rifle's kickback.

"My family would be happy to have you sit with us."

Walking back into church would take some courage, and if he couldn't sit with someone he knew, he might chicken out. Since it was only Wednesday, he still might. "Wonderful," he replied, forcing false enthusiasm into his voice. "Which service do you attend?"

"The ten o'clock. It's Grace Fellowship. On Country Lane Road."

"I know it." He nodded, fighting the urge to shift on his feet. Nerves. The kind he'd locked down each time he took the Humvee out for patrol. Or performed for a sold-out arena.

"We'll see you then," she said, playing with her purse strap.

"Thanks, Susannah," he said as she started to walk away.

Turning, she gave him a smile that brought out the dimples in her cheeks. "You're welcome, Jake."

He watched her until she'd disappeared from sight in her sporty Audi. Then he sank down onto his front porch steps.

Was he really going back to church?

For a moment, he wondered what he'd do if that failed to cure him as well.

4

S helby McGuiness cruised into the parking lot of Cream and Sugar in her new convertible BMW. Her sister Susannah was standing near her Audi, waiting for her. She waved as she blew by her sister and, braking sharply, swung into a parking space. When she checked her hot pink lipstick in the rearview mirror, she blew herself a kiss. Then she hopped out of the car, slammed the door behind her, and leaned against the frame.

"What do you think of her?" she asked, running her hands along its body. "I've named her Pearl."

"I think you still drive like a bat out of hell, and this convertible is bound to make it worse." A slow smile stretched across Susannah's face as she ran her hand over Pearl's white body. "But I love her. Your Christmas bonus really *must* have been hefty."

"It was," she said grandly, buffing her nails on her teal jacket and blowing on them. "My boss loves me."

Shelby counted her blessings everyday. For the last five years, she'd been the personal accountant for Gail Hardcrew, one of Nashville's leading entrepreneurs. Gail had inherited the money from her daddy and first husband and used it to create places she'd want to patronize involving her three favorite past times: food, clothes, and personal grooming. Now she owned two restaurants, three fashion boutiques, and four hair salons.

"You make me want to get a convertible," Susannah said, running her hand along the frame.

"You should," Shelby said, "but not like mine. We can't be car twins."

Her sister snorted as she finally stopped admiring Pearl and pulled her into a hug. "I love you, but not that much."

"It's too chilly to pop the top today, but I had it down yesterday. It's been warm for January."

"It has," Susannah agreed as they linked arms and walked to the coffee shop. "I almost brought out the open-toe shoes, but I'm behind on my pedicures."

Shelby laughed. "What have I told you about trailer-park-trash toes? They're just not done. Mr. Sex-On-A-Stick wouldn't go for it."

Her sister slanted her a glance. Just like she'd expected. Heck, she'd been waiting for this moment ever since Susannah had told her about the scheduling of their first consultation. Nudging her, Shelby gave her a saucy wink. "So...how was Jake yesterday?"

Susannah nudged her back and led the way to an open table in the corner. "You can ask, but I may not answer. He's a client, Shelby. No more calling him Mr. Sex-On-A-Stick. That stops now."

Since her pout was her signature, Shelby gave it her all. "Oh, poo. You're no fun!" Knowing full well that Susannah wouldn't respond, she plopped down onto an open chair and placed her purse in the adjacent seat. Southern women never put their handbags on the floor.

"Let's order," Susannah said, still standing. "You're going to make me get the drinks, aren't you?"

"Yep," she answered with an extra bit of sugar in her voice. "If you're not spilling on Mr. Sex, then you're buying."

"I'm buying," Susannah said and rummaged through her bag for her wallet before setting it down next to Shelby's.

"Cappuccino." Shelby kicked her feet up on Susannah's chair.

Her sister narrowed her eyes. "Don't get too comfortable."

"I won't, honey," she drawled.

When Susannah walked off, Shelby almost laughed. Her sister's chin was in the air, almost as if she were an aloof queen. It suited her as the oldest girl in the family. Susannah had a royal way about her, while Shelby considered herself to be more of a Southern belle.

A paper coffee cup snapped down in front of her.

"Are we really not talking about Jake Lassiter?" Shelby asked Susannah, removing her feet from her sister's chair.

"We're really not." She seated herself grandly.

Sisters could be so annoying sometimes. "But he's *adorable.* And he likes you. It's obvious."

"Shelby, I swear," Susannah said with an aggrieved sigh. "He hired me to be his decorator. He wouldn't have done that if he wanted to ask me out."

Opening three packets of sugar, she dumped the contents into her cup. "I've noticed the way he looks at you. I know things."

"You *don't.* We're not talking about this."

There was an edge in her voice, one Shelby recognized all too well. "But you *thought* he was going to ask you out, right?"

There was no sign of her sister's usual warmth in her green eyes. "I'm going to take my tea on the road if you're going to keep this up."

That wiped the pretend pout off her face. "Susannah. Level with me, and then I won't bother you about this again. You're upset, and I hate seeing that." In truth, she was worried about her sister. She'd seen the way Susannah looked at Jake—it was rare.

"I'm not upset," her sister said with little conviction. "*Really.* I won't deny that his place is going to be a big job though."

"*And?*" Sometimes Susannah needed to be prodded like a cow.

"Oh, fine!" she said, setting her tea aside. "He seemed troubled. His home is bare, like Army-barracks bare. I invited him to come to church with all of us to hear Mama this Sunday, and after initially saying no, he agreed."

Now *that* was interesting. Why would he have said no at first? Maybe he wasn't a church-going man, in which case he might not be right for Susannah after all.

"I'm glad he's going," Shelby said diplomatically.

"This doesn't mean he's interested in me. He just needs...I don't honestly know. He's lonely and still hurting from his time in the war."

"And you want to help him." Then the light bulb went on in Shelby's head. "Like J.P. helps in his own way by writing songs with Jake. You're going to do it with your heart and your talent of making a house into a home. Are you finally going to admit you like him that way?"

Susannah took her time brushing her hair over her shoulder.

"You know you can't hide anything from us, right?"

"I don't want to admit it," Susannah said quietly.

"Why not?"

"Because I can't tell how he feels about me." She pressed a hand to her forehead. "I didn't tell you and Sadie because I didn't want you two to make fun of me."

Or pressure her. She knew Susannah, who was thirty, had been receiving plenty of pressure from the old biddies at church. Shelby was glad she had a couple of years left before the big three oh—not that people didn't still comment about her being single. Her usual reply was that she wasn't even thirty yet. She was going to need a new excuse then.

"I'm sorry we made fun of you," Shelby said, grabbing her sister's hand. "In the beginning, we didn't know you liked him. Now that we know you do, and that you're unsettled about it, we won't tease you anymore. I promise."

Susannah studied her to see if she meant it and then sighed. "Okay. I appreciate it. He reminds me of some of the veterans at church. He's hurting, Shelby. I mean...he's sleeping on a mattress on the floor with nothing but white sheets. No dresser. No lamp. It was horr-i-ble. In all my years of decorating people's houses, I have never seen anything like it. And it's not like he doesn't have money."

Sleeping on the floor? Poor Jake. She never would have guessed he was hurting that much, particularly since he looked so confident on stage. But her focus right now was on Susannah.

She knew that tone.

"It's not your job to save him, you know."

"I only invited him to church..."

Everyone knew where that kind of thing led. You didn't invite a man to church if you didn't have a glimmer of hope you might save him. It was so *Walk The Line*.

"Can we talk about something else, please?" Susannah asked.

Shelby nodded. "So, I like your new dress," she said, gesturing to her sister's navy sheath. A brown leather belt cinched her tiny waist. "I wish I could wear something like that, but it would make me look like a hippo wearing a girdle."

"Oh, hush," Susannah said with a frown. "I wish I had your curves. I'm like an ironing board."

"No, you're not."

"And you aren't that curvy," her sister added to be sweet.

"I know," she said because it was expected. She did know she wasn't *horribly* curvy. She just wished her boobs and hips didn't stick out so far.

Susannah took a sip of her tea, so Shelby decided to change the subject.

"Have you thought about passing on the job with Jake? If it's going to bother you this much, maybe you should bow out." Not that her sister would.

"I thought we weren't talking about this anymore," Susannah said.

"Just a thought." She picked up her cappuccino and took a healthy sip.

They fell into silence. Susannah started making faces at the baby at the next table, getting the little one to laugh. Shelby grabbed her phone and checked her voicemail. She knew the infant ruse well. Children always took a shine to Susannah—and vice versa—so playing with them was her favorite and most used delaying tactic. Her sister would answer her when she was ready.

"I can't say no to him now," Susannah finally said when the baby went back to trying to steal her mama's spoon.

"If you could say no, would you?" Shelby pressed, setting her phone aside.

"No."

"Well, that cinches it. You'll decorate his house, be his friend, take him to church—and maybe, just maybe, his spirit will mend."

She didn't dare give voice to the rest of her thought—that Susannah and Jake might fall in love and give in to their obvious attraction to each other—but it pleased her to imagine it. Since she wasn't interested in anyone right now, she had to enjoy life vicariously.

"Be his friend," her sister mused, wincing when she drank her tea. "It's cold."

Shelby rose. "I'll have them heat it up."

Her sister looked horrified by the notion.

"You're such a novice," she said with a wink. "They'll offer to make you a new one for free. It's good business."

As she took off for the counter, a little girl with pigtails and a pink dress shouted, "Daddy," and darted across the coffee shop, nearly colliding with Shelby. A well-dressed man beaming a smile as bright as sunshine snatched the girl up off the floor.

The pinch to her heart dredged up something she'd been stewing over for a while now. Should she find out what had happened to her father? No one else in the family seemed to want to know, but she'd never stopped thinking about it. Maybe it was because she barely remembered him. She always found herself wondering what he looked like now and where he was living. Was he even alive? In some of her fantasies, she spun a tale of how he'd died of sorrow at a young age after leaving them.

How could no one else be curious?

But curiosity killed the cat, Mama was fond of saying. And the rest of her family might be hurt if she went through with it and tried to find their daddy.

She was between a rock and a hard place.

Flirting with the barista took her mind off her troubles, and she was smiling again when she returned to Susannah with a steaming cup of tea.

"You're terrible," her sister said, fighting a smile.

"I don't see you pushing it away. I could probably drink another cappuccino."

Susannah took the cup. "You're too hyper as it is. It's a wonder you haven't been pulled over for speeding in that new car."

She breezily waved the air. "I was yesterday, but I talked my way out of it. All you have to do is bat your eyelashes and say in the sweetest tone ever, 'Oh, Officer, was I speeding? I didn't know what the limit was. I was thinking about my poor mama.'"

"Did I say terrible? You're the kind of trouble that gives the word a bad name."

"Trouble isn't bad," she said easily. "I *like* to shake things up. Life would be so boring otherwise."

While Susannah drank her tea, Shelby tried to keep from watching the family sitting on the other side of the coffee shop, but when it came time to leave, she gave them one last look.

The daddy was holding his little girl on his knee as she colored in a coloring book. When he kissed the top of his daughter's curly blond head and tugged playfully on her pigtail, she had to bite her lip. Had her daddy ever done anything like that with her?

"She's a cutie, isn't she?" Susannah said, nodding to the little girl.

"She is indeed," Shelby replied as they left.

Susannah liked to watch other children when they were in public and dream about having her own.

Shelby liked to watch other daddies and wonder what had become of theirs.

5

J ake was sweating like a sinner in church and none too happy about it. Especially since Susannah was sitting right beside him. Her fragrance reminded him of honeysuckle on a hot summer day, and it was so enticing, he found himself grateful for the demure neckline of her simple green dress. Not that he would let his eyes stray today. He might not have darkened the door of a local church for some years, but he still had manners.

J.P., Tammy, and her two children were nestled to his right. The little blond-haired girl, Annabelle, had climbed over J.P.'s lap at the beginning of services to nestle in between the two men. She'd whispered to him in her church voice that she was in kindergarten.

He'd given her a wary smile and tried to edge away. He was sweating, after all, and she was so sweet in her pink dress stitched with little white hearts. Of course, she'd only scooted closer to him, which he couldn't do much about lest he end up nestled closer to Susannah. People were already watching them with unguarded interest, and he didn't want to add fuel to that fire. No siree.

His friend and fellow country music star, Rye Crenshaw, sat in front of them with his wife, Tory. Rye had given him a welcoming hug when he'd arrived five minutes before the service.

The temptation to chicken out and skip the service had been almost overwhelming, but in the end, Jake had promised Susannah he'd come, and he wasn't the kind of man to go back on his word. Especially to a beautiful woman.

Correction. Decorator. She was his *decorator*.

Of course, no one believed that. Rye's sister, Amelia Ann, had given him a knowing smile before cuddling close to Clayton Chandler, her fiancé and Rye's manager. They'd gotten engaged over New Year's after a rough start, and the family couldn't be happier for the couple.

Then there were Susannah's sisters, Sadie and Shelby, whom J.P. had tried to protect him from on occasion. They had a little too much of the "fan girl" thing going on. He hoped they wouldn't ask for his autograph after services, although he expected others might. The whole autograph thing still embarrassed Jake. It didn't make sense to him why anyone would want his messy scrawl on a piece of paper—or, worse, a photograph.

The church's hymns were mostly familiar, although there were some upbeat ones he rather liked. In fact, the church seemed downright modern if you asked him. The choir had played "It Is Well" and a song by Toby Mac called "Speak Life." He'd blended his voice to harmonize with Rye's, and J.P. and Clayton had joined in. He'd liked singing with his friends. Of course, it had only attracted more attention to their little section in the church.

He wanted to squirm in his seat.

When Reverend Louisa appeared at the pulpit,

Annabelle rose up on her knees so she could whisper in his ear, "That's my grandmamma."

As he nodded to her serious little face, Jake felt Susannah turn her head toward him. The pull to look at her was impossible to resist. Her moss-green eyes were liquid and soft when their gazes met, and he almost broke his vow and asked her out then and there.

But suddenly he heard, "Grace can save," and he swung his gaze back to the pulpit.

Susannah's mama had silver hair that bobbed under a strong chin, the kind that conveyed she wasn't merely a sweet ol' Christian lady. No, he expected she could be tough when it came down to it. If that chin didn't do its job, the red suit she was wearing would.

"I met a man this week who'd lost his wife a year ago," she began in a voice that was as powerful as it was soft, rather like caramel candies.

"He was wondering how he could ever get on with his life," she said, and then paused to scan her congregation. When her gaze came his way, Jake felt like she was staring straight at him.

"His wife had died in a car accident, you see. She was only thirty-two years old. God had seen fit to take her young, which made it all the more tragic. This couple had only been married for two years—not even close to long enough."

Jake couldn't help but think about how little time Booker and his wife had been given together. How was Diane even doing? He'd tried to call her a few times, but her voice had told him all he needed to know. It pained her to talk to him. His Army buddies Darren, Monty, and Randy had tried to reach out to her as well, but she'd been no more inclined to talk with them. Jake took a little comfort in the fact that he'd been able to help her out financially.

"I told the man I was so sorry for his loss," Reverend Louisa continued, "and I asked after his name so I could pray for him. His name was Tommy, and he used to work in construction. Made a good living at it, but he felt like all his dreams for a family had died with his wife."

Is that how Diane had felt? He knew Booker would have wanted her to find someone else to love. But had she? It really wasn't any of his business, of course, but he hoped so. Monty had tied the knot over a year ago to a sweet-as-pie waitress after finally getting a handle on his own PTSD. He was the first of their group to get hitched after receiving his disability discharge, and Jake hoped it would turn out okay for him and the rest of his friends. But it still wasn't fair Booker wouldn't get his happy ending.

"Tommy said he'd lost his faith," the Reverend continued, "like some of you have out there, I expect."

Now he *knew* she was talking about him. Jake returned his focus to his surroundings. His heartbeat was increasing in speed, and he was sure those around him could hear the pounding. He recognized the signs of his PTSD returning. Anxiety. Disassociation from the present. Anger.

"I told Tommy that the only thing with the power to get us through tragedy was grace," Reverend Louisa said, scanning the church anew.

Jake sat up straighter. Grace, huh? He couldn't remember what the word even meant. Where was this *grace* thing the day Booker had died? Hadn't he asked God to save his friend? The scar on his shoulder burned as anger spiked through his system.

A small hand nudged its way under his own large one,

jarring him out of the familiar spiral. He looked down to see Annabelle grabbing his hand.

"It's okay, Jake," she whispered, her doll-eyed baby blues staring at him. "You just listen to Grandmamma."

His throat closed in shock. How had she known he was upset? He wasn't sure if he should keep holding her hand. She was so little, and he might hurt her without intending it. But when he tried to free himself, she squeezed his hand with all her strength and gave him a look that conveyed she meant business.

He turned back to listen, but felt Susannah watching him out of the corner of her eye. Would she follow the little one's lead and take his other hand? Every time he was around her, he wanted to hold it. Somehow he always felt weightless when they held hands, almost like he was swimming in ocean water, which was totally crazy.

"Grace means a lot of things to a lot of people, and certainly the Bible talks about it more than its fair share. When I think of grace, I think of those moments when I'm struggling, and someone appears all of the sudden to help. Or when I'm hurting over a loss and my heart eases. Grace steals over you like the night wind. You don't know where it's coming from, but it's welcome."

Jake fought down his cynicism. There hadn't been many moments of peace associated with Booker's death. For all that he'd relived it over and over again in his stint with therapy or his lingering dreams, he'd never once said, "I'm okay with this." Maybe he never would. Deep down, he wondered if he even should. When someone died tragically, no one could Pollyanna that away—at least not without making Jake want to punch them in the mouth.

He lowered his head, prepared to tune out Reverend

Louisa. But Annabelle shifted beside him and crawled into his lap, keeping his hand clutched in hers. She stared into his eyes again—and he nearly jumped out of his seat. She didn't look like a five-year-old now. More like a wise woman in the body of a child.

"Listen to her, Jake," Annabelle whispered, patting his chest with her other hand. "She'll comfort you."

The whole thing was sweet, he tried to tell himself, but the back of his neck was hot with embarrassment. He hadn't stopped sweating. And really...he didn't know this little girl well enough to have her perched on his lap.

J.P. tried to remove her, but Annabelle swatted his hand away and shook her head, her little face mulish. Jake glanced at J.P. for help, but his friend only shrugged. Noticing that even more people had eyes on him, Jake nodded. He even gave a tight smile. This child had gump-tion, and she had it in her head she was going to help him, it seemed.

He turned back to Reverend Louisa, who was still spouting off about all that grace stuff. The words "hog swallop" passed through his mind, and anger crested in his blood. He wanted to walk out of the church and never come back, but Annabelle laid her head back against his chest, caging him in. Keeping him there.

He shifted again and caught Susannah looking on with a wrinkled brow. Who could blame her? It was like everyone knew he was coming apart, and over something as simple as a sermon on grace.

He should never have come to church.

"Some of you may be thinking I'm making grace out to be more powerful than it is," Reverend Louisa said, and it was like she'd hit a bulls-eye on his chest. "You think that

I'm a foolish old lady who doesn't know what loss means. Well, I've cried over things I never thought could be put right again. Cried until I couldn't cry anymore. I've even yelled at God and asked, 'Why?' And then, each time, I would remember the problem wasn't for me to fix, whether I'd had a share in creating it or not."

Jake stilled in the pew. It was like the woman was reading his mind.

"I decided it wasn't always for me to understand why something had happened to hurt me and mine. God's ways are mysterious, and I can honestly tell you I'm not always comfortable with the mystery, with the unknown whys and what-fors."

Someone gave an "Amen," and another person echoed it.

The Reverend tapped the lectern. "Those questions drive me plumb crazy sometimes. Why in the world would a thirty-two year old woman die in a car crash? What purpose could that possibly serve in the grand scheme of things? I told Tommy I didn't know why he'd lost his wife, but I did know there was a power greater than himself that could help him heal from the loss and move forward with his life."

Jake felt a familiar rush of sadness rise within him, one which made his rage seem small in comparison. He missed his friend. He couldn't even watch the Arkansas Razorbacks play football anymore because of all his memories of watching games with Booker.

"To move forward, we sometimes have to stop asking why. Stop shaking our fists at the heavens. What's done is done. It wasn't fair. It likely wasn't our fault. But now is the time to dig deep into ourselves and find out why we can't move on if we're stuck in the past like an old truck in a ditch."

Anger spurted inside him again. Was Reverend Louisa saying this was his fault? That since he hadn't been able to move on, he was wrong? His skin prickled.

"I asked the man what scared him most, and he told me he feared he would never find another woman who could hold a candle to his wife. He was afraid he'd never marry again, never have children. He was afraid he'd die alone."

Booker hadn't died alone, and that was one thing for which Jake felt grateful.

"I told Tommy that grace might surprise him some day. That as he continued on with the business of living, he might be surprised by how events unfolded. But he had to be willing to *keep* living. Some of us wall ourselves off from the world after a tragedy. Even if we're out and about in the world, running our errands and going to work, we stop living and merely exist. We stop connecting to people out of fear. And when that happens, my friends, we might as well be made of clay and not flesh and blood."

It was as if she had written the words for him alone. Other than when Jake was on stage singing his heart out, he felt like he was mostly drifting through life. His music was his purpose, but when it came down to it, he knew it wasn't enough. He wanted love and laughter and family. Should he simply stop beating himself up and ask Susannah out on a date? Get on with the business of living and trust that the nightmares and the guilt and the horror would one day stop? The temptation to look at Susannah was strong.

"Fear takes us in the opposite direction of love, friends," Reverend Louisa continued. "And love is all there is when it comes down to it. Take a minute with me. When you lay your head down on your pillow after a hard day at work, what brings a smile to your face? The way you helped a colleague? The kind word a stranger had for you on the street? A phone call from a good friend? A kiss from a loved one?"

Jake knew all the mumbo jumbo about happiness. Had even read some books about it. Deep down, he knew that everyone wanted to be happy. He did too. It just wasn't always that easy.

"What makes you really happy?" the Reverend asked again. *"Who* makes you happy?"

Locking his muscles so he wouldn't turn to Susannah, Jake thought about how seeing her, holding hands with her, sitting next to her—even here in this church—made him happy. Despite the fact that he wanted to run away from all this grace stuff and this Reverend who seemed to see into his very soul.

"If you're sitting next to someone who makes you happy, go ahead and tell them," Reverend Louisa called out.

Jake felt rooted to the spot when Annabelle turned and gave him a kiss on the cheek. "You make me happy, Jake."

Well, slap him upside the head with a 2-by-4 because he couldn't imagine what he'd done to make this little girl happy. Rye turned around and grinned at him, making a heart over his chest like a teenage girl might. The silly grin on his friend's face tore a reluctant laugh out of Jake's mouth, but it cut off the instant he felt Susannah brush his hand.

He couldn't have stopped himself from turning to her then. She didn't say the words to him, but he felt her emotions in the soft way she looked at him. There were stars in her eyes, surely, and he felt transported to a place that...well, if he'd been writing a song, he would have called it paradise.

For a moment, it was hard to swallow, and when the choir started playing "Amazing Grace" as the Reverend walked to her seat, Jake couldn't look away from Susannah's moss-green eyes.

6

As far as Susannah was concerned, Annabelle was a little miracle worker. She'd watched her soon-to-be niece work her magic on her brother's tough-guy friends, Rye Crenshaw and Clayton Chandler.

But her heart had swelled fit to burst when Annabelle climbed onto Jake's lap during Mama's sermon and whispered that he needed to listen to her grandmamma... Even though they'd given each other plenty of room in the pew, Susannah had felt him go rigid beside her. The urge to reach out to him had been so great, but she'd suppressed it.

People were watching, after all, and it wasn't appropriate.

Now, he was joking with her brother and the rest of his friends in the church hall. His hand brandished a glazed donut dripping with sugar, and while his smile seemed full, it was forced. She knew his smiles now, she realized, and her heart pounded harder in her chest with that knowledge.

"He became pretty upset during my sermon," her mama whispered to her.

Reverend Louisa had finished greeting the members of her congregation after church before joining Susannah.

"I know. It might have touched home."

"It might have just," her mama simply said, looking over at the men standing in the corner. "I'm glad no one has asked for his autograph. We want him to feel welcome here even though my sermon might have made him want to head for the hills."

Indeed it did, she thought, but refrained from saying it. "You were pretty clever to scoot Sadie and Shelby along so you could talk to me about this. Asking them to pick up more donuts indeed."

"I'm also keeping people from overtly asking you if you're dating Jake," her mama said with a knowing look. "You recall the older women pestering you about getting married."

Yes, she did. For a Southern woman, being unmarried at thirty was akin to becoming a spinster. She'd stopped attending fellowship after services because of it. But her brother had talked her into coming back by promising to keep the well-intentioned old biddies at bay. So far, he'd done a good job.

"Are the men keeping people from bothering Jake about coming here with me?" she asked.

"What do you think, honey?" her mama replied.

A soft sigh floated out. It was kinda sweet of them.

"Let's go chat with the men before Sadie and Shelby return," Mama said. "They know they're on a fool's errand, but they won't complain."

"Much," Susannah said, which made them both laugh.

Her mama took her hand and led her over to the area where J.P., Rye, and Clayton stood huddled around Jake. It was pretty interesting, watching the men protect one of their own. She and her sisters sometimes did that sort of thing at a bar when they went out to listen to music in Nashville.

"Well now," her mama began as the circle opened to welcome them. "How's everyone doing this morning?"

"Good," everyone answered, almost speaking in tandem.

Well, everyone but Jake. His shoulders had turned to stone again.

"We're mighty happy to have you here, Jake," her mama said, eyeing the man with that compassionate gaze for which she was rightly famous. It held a person. Most people melted. Jake's eyes only narrowed at the corners.

"Thank you, Reverend," he said easily—a bit too easily. "Susannah was kind to invite me."

"We'd love for you to join us at Sunday dinner this afternoon," her mama said, bold as brass. "And I won't take no for an answer."

Whoa. Mama definitely had something on her mind. Susannah had to force herself not to intercede and give Jake an out. J.P. met her eyes and shook his head only once. He knew Mama's ways too. She was not a woman to be reckoned with when she had a notion in her head.

"I wouldn't want to intrude on a family affair, ma'am," Jake replied, clearing his throat.

"It's no intrusion." Mama patted his forearm. "We'll see you at two. J.P. can give you the details." And then she sauntered off with an extra sway in her hips, more than pleased with herself.

Jake looked at Susannah. "I'm...that's...a family affair."

J.P. was biting his lip to keep from smiling. "You heard

my mama. She won't take no for an answer. We're having dinner at Rye's house. That's why Tory left right after the service with Amelia Ann, Tammy, and the kids. They're preparing something special for us."

Jake didn't look convinced, but he nodded crisply.

Rye slapped him on the back. "Don't worry, bubba. The Reverend won't baptize you out in Dare River unless you ask her."

Clayton barked out a laugh, but he cut it off when Jake shot him a look.

"Mama hasn't baptized anyone in Dare River yet, Jake," her brother murmured, "so I think you're safe."

"I've already been baptized," Jake said, looking off in the direction of the exits, like he was planning on making a break for it.

Susannah wasn't sure how best to comfort him—whether she should walk him out or simply hold his hand.

"I have an idea," Rye said, wrapping his arm around Jake's shoulder. "Why don't you come on over now? We can play some music together. After that charity concert, our fans have been begging us to write a song together. Perhaps it's time now that the holidays are behind us."

"Perhaps it is," Jake said, smiling a sight more easily now. "A collaboration would be fun."

Rye drew J.P. to him by slinging a meaty arm around her brother's shoulder. "This one can help us write it."

"Sounds like a plan," J.P. mused, stroking his chin. "We'll need a theme."

"How about family?" Rye suggested. "We seem to be growing by leaps and bounds."

Clayton's grin was pretty dazzling. "Like pond frogs in springtime."

At first, Susannah hadn't been so sure Clayton was a

good fit for her friend Amelia Ann. But his signature tough-ness had melted away like butter on hot cornbread. Now he seemed like the perfect match for the determined law school student who championed women's rights by volun-teering in one of Nashville's leading legal clinics.

"Family, huh?" Jake said, tightening up again. "We can brainstorm ideas later. I need to...bring some flowers or a bottle of wine to the dinner."

"You don't need to bring squat, bubba," Rye said, rolling his eyes. "Do I look like the kind of man who enjoys wine and flowers?"

Everyone laughed, and Jake gave Rye a playful shove. "You always struck me as the yellow roses type. Maybe a lover of white wine."

Rye released both men and clutched his heart. "You know me too well. Feel free to bring some by. I'm going to head out now that I've had my donut quota for the day. Tory might need me to lift something heavy for her."

Susannah gave Rye a look. "You are such a pig sometimes."

He leaned in to kiss her cheek. "But you love me anyway."

"True." She kissed him back.

"Besides, I'd lift something heavy for you too, if you needed it," Rye said with a wink before turning on his heel and taking off toward the front of the church. "See y'all later. Clayton, I'd like red roses from you."

"In your dreams, Crenshaw," Clayton replied. "What I'd say if we weren't still in a church."

"But you are, so you'd better keep it clean," J.P. said with a grin. "Save it for later. I'm off too. Rye might offer to lift heavy items, but he hates kitchen duty. I'm pretty good at chopping vegetables myself."

"A champion," Susannah agreed. After their daddy left, J.P. had taken on some of the housework duties to help their mama.

"I'm going to head out too," Clayton said. "Jake, we'll see you later. Don't fuss too much about coming. It's only terrifying for the first twenty minutes or so."

"Oh, stop that," Susannah said, making a shooing motion at him.

He pretended to fall backward and then shot them a charming smile before taking off.

"You really don't need to bring anything," Susannah told Jake.

"Bring what where?" Sadie asked, rushing up to the group with Shelby in tow. Mama's task hadn't taken them near long enough.

"Mama invited Jake to join us for dinner today," J.P. said in a steady voice, one that matched the steely look in his eyes.

Their sisters both playfully batted their eyelashes at him since they knew J.P. was issuing a warning. After all, her brother had once overheard them calling Jake Mr. Sex-On-A-Stick.

"How *lovely*," Shelby said in a voice that could have beat Bette Davis out of the Best Actress Oscar for her role in the Southern classic, *Jezebel*.

Susannah wanted to pinch her. Sadie bounced in her heels, and J.P. put his hand on her arm to calm her.

"Too much sugar in the donuts? *Sugar?*" her brother asked her.

"Oh, poo," Sadie commented. "You're so mean sometimes. We'll look forward to seeing you later today, Jake."

"I'll walk out with you," J.P. said, giving their fan-frenzy sisters a pointed look.

"That's mighty kind of you," Jake said. "Ladies. I'll see you later, it seems."

He looked at each of the sisters in turn, his eyes meeting Susannah's for a tad longer, and then inclined his head and walked off with their brother.

Sadie put the back of her hand to her forehead. "*Ladies.* Oh, my heavens. The way he says that one word. It makes me want to—"

"Put a sock in it, Sadie," Shelby ordered. "We're not talking like that anymore, remember?"

She gave a pout. "Oops. Sorry, Susannah. I'm still getting used to the new agreement."

Shelby gave Susannah a gentle nudge. "*See* how good we're playing. We ran that silly errand for Mama even though we knew it was a ruse."

"What did Mama say?" Sadie asked, fingering one of her curls. "I mean, did she ask you if she could invite Jake to the family dinner?"

If only. "No, she told him that she wouldn't take no for an answer."

"That's Mama for you," Sadie said, her head bobbing. "I'm glad she's on our side. When she's like that, you don't mess with her."

"Besides," Shelby added, "anyone with eyes could tell how upset Jake was during her sermon. Could you believe it when Annabelle climbed onto his lap and comforted him? That child. It brought tears to my eyes."

"I would have comforted...ah...offered to *pray* for him," Sadie said, quickly correcting herself.

Susannah knew her sister was only teasing. Well, perhaps not completely. But she was happy Sadie and Shelby were making an effort not to talk about Jake like he was a sex object anymore and not to tease *her* about her interest in him.

"So, what do you think Mama plans to do once she has him at Sunday dinner?" Shelby asked.

Susannah stroked her chin. If she knew her mama, she was fixing on bringing Jake under her wing.

That man didn't have a chance.

7

J ake was seriously considering dropping off the flowers and the wine he'd bought and making tracks back to his house in Dare River. Sure, it was often lonely on Sundays when he wasn't on tour, but that's what his four-wheeler and fishing gear were for.

Distraction was a useful tool for the lonely heart. He'd learned that as a young boy growing up without his daddy around much. Sundays had been about going to church, and when they returned home, his mama would make a roast or grill a chicken. Sometimes she would even make a pie, his favorite being cherry.

But they'd never felt like much of a family. His older brother had sat across from him while his daddy's seat would sit empty more often than not.

Now Jake was going to a real family dinner, and on a Sunday to boot. How in the world had that happened? Reverend Louisa might look like someone's grandma with her gray hair, but she sure as shooting didn't act all sweet-like. No, that woman could have given Annie Oakley a run for her money. Instead of lassoing horses, the Reverend lassoed souls. Apparently, she had her sights set on his.

He rubbed his heart as he drove down Rye's driveway. He only had to stay a few hours. Maybe it wouldn't be as bad as he feared it would be.

Then he saw the little girl waiting for him at the end of the driveway in a pale blue coat decorated with sunflowers, and he had to pound his heart to ease the sweet ache of it. He'd once dreamed of having a daughter like Annabelle. Perhaps a few of them. He'd never wanted a son. Not when the boy might have to go off to war. Jake didn't want that for his kin.

Holding Annabelle in his arms this morning—even though she'd pretty much plopped herself there without asking—had moved him something fierce. And the wisdom that had come out of her mouth? Well, that old saying was true. Kids did say the darndest things.

No one else was with her, and he wondered if she'd told them she was going to greet Jake all by her lonesome. Her blond curls weren't in the perfect ringlets from this morning, suggesting she'd been playing outside.

When he pulled his truck to a stop beside the other vehicles and opened his door, she ran over to him.

"Jake!" she shouted and then launched herself at him like he was a dear, long-lost friend. "I'm so glad Grandmamma invited you to Sunday dinner. You need a home-cooked meal."

He needed a home-cooked meal? Who *was* this child? "It's good to see you too, Annabelle." Reaching inside the truck spontaneously, he grabbed one of the yellow roses from the bouquet and handed it to her.

She tilted her head to the right and gave him a soft smile, one that melted the last of the fear hovering around his heart. "I *love* flowers. So does my mama. When spring comes and the flowers reach out of the ground again, can I come see the gardens my mama planted for you?"

Talking with this child was like talking to Yoda. "Ah...sure."

She took his hand as he tucked the flowers and wine against his chest and shut the door to the cab. "Yay! I'll talk to Mama and make sure you have some chocolate plants so the chocolate fairies can come live with you. You like chocolate, don't you?"

Tammy had joked about using chocolate plants in his garden, but the last thing he wanted was for the press to get wind of any eccentric star behavior on his part. He liked to stay out of the news when he could help it. "Never had a thing against it," he answered to be polite.

"You can have some of my chocolate in the meantime," she told him, leading him to the front door. "Uncle Rye keeps extra candy here for me and Rory. I'll have to let go of your hand to open the door since I have my flower in the other one."

She was pretty much clutching the rose to her chest. Thank God he'd bought the type with the thorns removed. "Okay."

Two adorable dogs were waiting at the door, barking. The sight made his muscles lock up. Dogs always made him think of the one he'd lost.

"It's okay, Jake." His little friend immediately reached for his hand again. "Rory, you're going to have to hold Barbie for me just a little longer. I need to show Jake where to put the flowers and the wine."

"*Annabelle*," her brother said, holding two leashes in hand, "you're supposed to call him Mr. Lassiter."

She shook her head. "He's Jake to me, Rory, but you

should call him Mr. Lassiter. Jake, that's Barbie, my dog, and the other one is Rory's. He's a labradoodle, and his name is Bandit. They don't bite or jump, so don't be scared. Aunt Tory used to be afraid of dogs, so Uncle Rye went to extra trouble to train them to behave around her. Even Bullet and Banjo are good now. But don't worry a bit. Uncle Rye put them in the mud room since we have company."

She was soothing him about the dogs? How had she guessed that the sight of them caused him grief? "I'm not scared of them, Annabelle," he said to reassure her.

"Maybe you should get a dog," she said. The scary determined look in her eyes reminded him of Louisa. "They're man's best friend, you know."

"Maybe sometime," he said, hoping that would satisfy her. After all, he couldn't tell her what had happened to his dog. The poor girl would cry. Man, he was already getting emotional, and he was only a couple of inches inside the door. Jake focused on the smell of home-cooked food drifting from the kitchen, hoping to shift his inner turmoil.

"I see you have a new friend, Jake," Rye observed as he walked into the foyer. "And there's no better friend than Annabelle. Unless we're talking about Rory," he said, chucking the little boy under the chin. "They're both pretty special sprouts. Good to see you, bubba. Welcome."

Jake had been to Rye's house before, but never for something as personal as Sunday dinner. "Thank you. I did bring yellow roses—your favorite—and wine. You can have a rose if you'd like."

Rye gave a soft chuckle. "I'll let you save them for the ladies."

Annabelle held her flower out to her uncle. "Jake gave me a rose, Uncle Rye. Isn't that the sweetest thing? Of course, I can't have any wine. I'm too young to drink spirits."

She was so serious, Jake didn't dare laugh. Rye's mouth twitched, but he didn't laugh either.

"You are at that, sugar," Rye said with a twinkle in his eyes. "But soon enough I'll have to chase off all the boys because you're way too pretty for words."

Annabelle looked up at Jake. "J.P.—my daddy once Mama finally agrees to marry him—will have to chase them off too when I get older."

"I'll help them, Annabelle," Rory said, frowning now. "No one messes with our women. Right, Uncle Rye?"

Rye nodded. "Right, bubba. Come on in, Jake. We've been talking your ear off by the front door. Where are our manners?"

"In the barn with the cows," Annabelle said, earning her a kiss from her uncle.

"Moo," Rye added, making the kids giggle.

Annabelle gripped Jake's hand. "Come on. We need to get these flowers in some water. They're thirsty."

"I'm surrounded by women who seem to hear flowers talking," Rye said, rolling his eyes.

"Uncle Rye, you're not supposed to make fun of us," Annabelle said, waving her rose at him. "Aunt Tory doesn't hear the flowers talking yet, but she's gonna some day soon. Mama said."

"Your mama had better be wrong about that," Rye responded, putting his hands on his hips. "Jake, if I ever start hearing flowers talk to me, put me down, will ya?"

"Oh, Uncle Rye," Annabelle said in a much aggrieved tone. "You're incorrigible. Isn't he, Rory?"

"He is, Annabelle," her brother said, earning him a noogie from his uncle.

"Rory, go on and put the dogs in the mudroom for a while. Annabelle, honey, you'd best take those flowers off to get their water," Rye teased.

Annabelle nodded and skipped down the hallway to the kitchen with Jake in tow, humming a tune he recognized as "Amazing Grace." It made him think back to the sermon this morning, to the Reverend's advice about moving on with life. But this wasn't the time for making decisions. He could set his mind to it when he was alone later.

The kitchen was brimming with activity. Some of the stainless steel pots were steaming. Others were sizzling. He hadn't been in this room before, but it didn't surprise him to see that it was a chef's dream. Rye's pint-sized Yankee wife was a chef, after all.

"Hello, Jake," Tory said, wiping her hands on a towel and crossing the kitchen to greet him. "You brought wine and flowers. How kind."

She took the gifts from him and gave him a brief hug.

"All of the ladies get a rose," he said, trying not to feel embarrassed. But his ears grew warm anyway. He wasn't used to giving multiple women flowers, although some of his female fans threw them at him. It was still beyond him to understand why.

"You should get us flowers more often, Uncle Rye," Annabelle added.

"I might if y'all stopped hearing them talk," he muttered. "Freaks this good ol' boy out."

"Are you complaining about the flowers talking again, sugar?" Tammy said, stepping away from cutting a heap of peppers. "Hello, Jake. I see Annabelle has taken you in hand again. Literally. Let go of the man's hand for a bit, honey, so Jake can greet everybody."

"Indeed she has," he commented, leaning down to kiss Tammy's cheek as the little girl stepped back.

This quiet Southern lady had always charmed him, and he couldn't be happier that his friend had found such a perfect partner. She'd listened to Jake's vision of the land surrounding his home and helped him plant his roots there. Come spring, he couldn't wait to see Redemption Ridge in all her glory. He hoped to feel more settled by then.

As if summoned by his thoughts, his beautiful decorator strolled into the kitchen with her two sisters and thrust out her hand for what seemed like a professional handshake. He shook it lightly, aware of the eyes on them. Susannah's skin was so soft and warm against his that he didn't want to let go. She hadn't changed clothes from church and looked more beautiful than ever.

"You should kiss him on the cheek, Aunt Susannah," Annabelle suggested. "It makes a person feel more welcome."

Susannah's cheeks turned pink, and Jake fought the urge to clear his throat.

Tammy gave him a strained smile. "She gets that from school. Annabelle, shaking hands is just fine for some people, and it's best to let them decide how they wish to greet each other."

"But kissing is *always* better, Mama. Uncle Rye says so."

Tammy gave her daughter a look before turning to Rye. "Your uncle was mostly talking about family members, and you know he's a kidder."

"But sometimes Uncle Rye is right," Annabelle said with a stomp of her foot.

Rye swung her into his arms. "Thank you, darlin'. Now, let's go find a vase for your rose so it won't die of thirst."

"Oh, Uncle Rye," she drawled, waving at Jake as her uncle carried her across the kitchen.

Jake shook Shelby and Sadie's hands too. It would seem awkward to hug them after being so cool and professional with Susannah.

J.P. strode into the kitchen, accompanied by a gray-haired man wearing a green polo shirt. "You remember my stepfather, Dale."

"Yes. Good to see you, sir."

"And you," the older man said.

Then Reverend Louisa appeared right beside her husband, and after a quick glance, Jake noticed she had a cat-who-got-the-cream smile on her face.

"I'm happy you could join us, Jake," she said, leaning in to hug him without so much as a warning.

He tensed up as she patted his back. "Ma'am... Reverend." He was getting flustered. "What would you prefer I call you?"

"Louisa would be lovely," she commented.

Tory appeared with the bouquet of yellow roses he'd brought. "You mentioned that each woman was supposed to receive a flower."

Had he? He must have been demented. "I...ah...thought it was more...symbolic-like."

Annabelle jumped out of her uncle's arms. "Hold that vase, Uncle Rye. Jake. Here. Let me help you." She set her flower on the kitchen counter and proceeded to hand him the first rose.

The Reverend—Louisa—held out her hand while he stood there like an idiot. He extended the first flower to her, and the rest of the women lined up to take theirs. Susannah was the last one to take a rose. Giving it to her felt more than symbolic. It felt *right*.

He wished he could give her a wheelbarrow full of them, enough to perfume her home and make her dream of him when she rested her head on her pillow at night.

Susannah's moss-green eyes met his, and for a moment, he didn't feel his feet. His clumsy fingers almost let the rose fall.

"Careful, Jake!" Annabelle shouted beside him.

Tammy immediately shushed her.

"But Mama," she protested. "He almost dropped it. He wasn't paying attention."

Not only were his ears burning now, but his cheeks had to be bright red too. Imagine a little mite like her calling him out for not paying attention. Even though it was true. Smiling just a bit, Susannah took the rose from him.

Moments later, Rye appeared by his side and pulled him toward the door to the family room. "We're going down to the recording studio. Y'all holler if you need anything."

"Like I haven't heard that before," Tory called out, going back to stuffing large mushrooms with a mixture made out of what looked like butter and herbs.

"Can I come, Uncle Rye?" Annabelle asked, rushing over.

"Not right now, half-pint," Rye said, which put an instant frown on her face. "Jake and I are going to write a song with your daddy."

Tammy looked over her shoulder. "I can hear your hints from a mile away, Rye."

"Marry the man, Tammy, for the love of God," Rye said in an aggrieved voice.

J.P. leaned down to kiss Tammy's cheek. "Don't let anyone pressure you, sweetheart. I know you'll marry me when you're ready."

"But *when?*" Annabelle called out in a half wail. "I want to go back and live at his house."

"Enough of that," Tammy said, hugging her daughter. "It'll all happen in good time. Now, why don't you help your aunts peel potatoes?"

"But I hate peeling potatoes," Annabelle said with a wider frown.

"Then run on outside and play," Tammy said in a crisp tone, a little shorter than usual.

Annabelle raced out of the room. "See you later, Jake. I'm going to find Rory."

Jake met Susannah's eyes as he left the kitchen with J.P. and Rye. She was still holding her rose pressed against her chest. The moment stayed with him as he followed his friends downstairs to Rye's recording studio.

His contribution to their song was a string of lyrics involving giving the woman you love a passel of roses. Rye got a bit misty-eyed when he offered up a couple of lyrics about giving red roses to his wife when she gave him a baby. J.P. gazed at him thoughtfully before suggesting they write a song about all the times a man is supposed to give a woman flowers, which they agreed would be a powerful message.

Clayton joined them for a time, and they broke out a single batch bourbon that warmed his belly. Some time later, Tory called out that dinner was ready, and they all headed back upstairs.

Jake greeted Amelia Ann, who was now helping the others in the kitchen. Then he shook hands with Rye's parents, who had arrived while they were downstairs. In the few times Jake had met Rye's mama, she'd seemed like a harsh, bitter woman. But tonight she was holding hands with the husband who'd separated from her months ago, and she glowed with a renewed radiance he recognized as love.

Rye pulled him aside and led him into the dining room. "My parents seem to have reconciled for the moment. It came after Christmastime. They're not back to living with each other yet, and if that's not the weirdest thing you'll ever hear, I don't know what is. But they seem to be happy, so I'm happy for them."

Jake knew Rye had been estranged from his family for many years after becoming a country singer. His reconciliation with them was recent, fostered in many ways by his Yankee wife. Jake doubted he would ever reconcile with his own family. Sometimes estrangement was sadly for the best.

"I appreciate you letting me know about your folks," he said, not knowing what else to say.

Rye snorted. "Shoot. I sound more like a greeting card than a man should these days, and it's only going to get worse. Excuse me for a sec."

He walked over to his wife, whom he hugged like a gentle bear. She patted him on the chest and nodded.

"Everyone," Rye called out. "Grab a seat, please."

Annabelle appeared beside Jake like a homing pigeon and took his hand. "You're sitting beside me and Aunt Susannah."

The little girl led him to the other side of the table, and sure enough, there was one lone seat open for him. Reverend Louisa was sitting way too close to him for comfort, but he forced himself to give her a weak smile.

Rye put his arm around Tory as they stood at the head of the table. "Usually we buffet the meal, but today demanded something special. These family dinners have come to mean a lot to all of us, and I'm happy Jake could join us today since he's a good friend to many of us here."

Jake coughed to dislodge the emotion clogging his throat, and Annabelle reached for his hand again. Susannah patted his arm, and suddenly he felt like he *was* a part of this family—the sort of family he'd always longed to have.

"Tory and I have some special news, and because she's going to have to do more of the work, I think she should be the one to tell you."

A huge smile stretched across Tory's face as she looked at the rest of the family. "Rye and I are having a baby."

The entire table erupted with whoops and exclamations. Chairs scraped the floor as people lurched to their feet and ran up to the happy couple. Jake watched as Annabelle ran off and wiggled her way through the crowd.

"Yay!" the little girl shouted. "I'm going to have a cousin."

"You sure are," Rye exclaimed, throwing her up in the air.

Jake hung back to let the family have its moment. When everyone started to take their seats again, he finally headed over to give his well wishes.

"I wondered if this was your news, given the lyrics you suggested downstairs," Jake said, grabbing his friend in a hug and pounding his back.

"You're writing a song about the baby?" Tory asked, tears popping into her eyes.

Rye wiped at his own eyes. "Don't I write songs about you? I have to include our baby, right?"

"Oh, Rye," she said, and they embraced again.

Jake made tracks to give them privacy and took his seat between Annabelle and Susannah. The little girl was bouncing in her seat from the news, but it was Susannah who drew his gaze. She was brushing aside the tears streaming down her face. Her eyes met his, and she shrugged.

"I'm so happy for them," she said as more tears rolled down her face.

Without thinking, Jake picked up his cloth napkin and blotted a few of those tears before he had the presence of mind to stop. When he looked away from her, her mama and sisters were all staring at him. He grabbed his water glass and chugged the contents. Good Lord. Could he be any more obvious?

When Rye and Tory finally found their seats, Louisa—there, he'd remembered not to call her Reverend like she'd asked—led them in grace. Of course, all it did was remind Jake of her sermon again. While he feasted with the others on the beef and pork roasts and the heap of sides, he made sure to keep his mouth full so no one would say much to him.

Well, no one save sweet little Annabelle. She talked to him throughout the meal, never needing him to reply. For a small thing, she sure did have a lot of words inside her. Susannah's mouth curved often, so Jake could tell she was amused by the situation. Beyond that, she said little, except to Shelby, who sat on her other side. But he couldn't get comfortable because he'd caught Louisa watching him more than once. She was stewing something fierce, was all he could think. He made a vow he would leave as soon as dinner ended.

After the platters and bowls were scraped clean from the men's second and third helpings, Rye carried in the biggest chocolate cake on the planet. Atop it was a plastic Elvis, which made everyone laugh.

"Uncle Rye dressed up as Elvis once," Annabelle told him. "He's so silly sometimes."

And Rye was in fine form—laughing as he ate cake, talking about all the changes he was going to have to make to be a good daddy. For some reason, Rye thought he was going to have to wear jeans that weren't so form fitting, and this made everyone, including his wife, break into laughter.

"Your career will tank for sure if you can't show off your assets," Tory teased him.

"What's assets?" Rory asked seriously.

Tammy wiped her mouth to hide her smile. "It's like the gifts God gives you. Eat your cake."

Annabelle rose onto her knees and said, "Uncle Rye! Now you're really going to have to start talking to flowers. Especially if you have a baby girl."

The man visibly shuddered. "I hadn't thought of that."

Tory rubbed his back. *"Breathe.* You're going to be just fine."

And so the famous country singer took deep breaths as everyone around the table polished off their cake and offered parenting suggestions, serious and otherwise.

"Susannah," Rye called out finally when his color returned to normal. "Why don't you show Jake my patch of Dare River? I would, but I'd like to stay with my lovely wife here and finish my cake."

Jake could smell a stink bomb when it was dropped. Anyone could have shown Jake the river. As a suggestion, it was plumb crazy. Besides, didn't he live upriver as well? But that didn't mean he wasn't grateful for the excuse to spend time with her.

"I'd like that," he said, rising from his chair. "I don't think we'll even need a coat it's so pleasant out."

"Mama made me wear a coat earlier, but I was hot," Annabelle said.

Tammy put her hand on the little girl's leg and gave her a look when she started to scoot out of her chair to follow them. Was *everyone* intent on setting them up? When he caught Clayton's gaze, the man was biting his lip. Yeah, it pretty much seemed to be a group conspiracy. Shucks.

Susannah gave Rye a knowing look, but even so, she let Jake help her out of her chair. As they walked out, all conversation in the room seemed to cease until Annabelle called out, *"Ah,* don't they look sweet together."

Someone shushed her, and Jake increased his pace to the French doors at the back of the house.

"Goodness me," Susannah said, fanning herself like she was a mite warm. "That was terribly awkward."

"You think?" he asked with a laugh. "I've never known a room to grow so quiet."

"We don't need to walk to the river, you know," she told him as they walked down the path through the garden. "We can hang out here for a while and then head back inside. Maybe they'll stop pushing. Rye just wants everyone to be as happy as he is."

Jake suspected it was more than that, but he refrained from commenting. "I wouldn't mind a walk to the river after that meal." He wished he could say he would do anything to walk to the river with her every night.

She turned to look at him, and he saw the flush of embarrassment on her cheeks. "Okay then. We'll walk."

They meandered through the garden, past a well-used tree swing, and then angled over to the river's edge. The sun was bright, and the weather was mild for January. Still, Jake took off his denim jacket and put it around Susannah's shoulders because he...well, he wanted to make this moment into something...more.

"I'm not cold," she protested even as she wrapped the jacket around her. "But I like this jacket. You gave it to me before."

"I did," he said, heartened she remembered.

Her soft sigh warmed his heart, and he gestured to the bench beside the river. He sat down next to her when she took a seat, but still maintained the distance he'd imposed earlier at services.

A heron took flight from the trees across the river and circled the water, its mighty gray wingspan awe-inspiring. A white egret struck at something on the shore across the way. Jake settled his back against the bench, relaxing for the first time all day.

"I'm glad you came," Susannah said softly, scooting over a fraction.

Her hand was so close to his on the bench. He wanted so badly to reach for it and wrap it around his own.

"I'm glad I did too."

The sunlight caught her hair, highlighting the reds and golds wrapped in the brown of her curls. The urge to ask her to dinner swelled in him again. Instead, he made himself bite his tongue. Hard.

"I'm sorry if my family was...implying things," she said, wringing her hands in her lap.

He didn't ask her to clarify what she meant. They both knew. "They're looking out for you. Don't concern yourself. In fact, I'm honored they would think I was good enough to walk out with you."

Her body shifted on the bench, enough that her shoulder brushed his. He turned his head to look at her. The moss-green eyes he found so enchanting were luminous. The air around them seemed to suddenly still.

To bring them both back to earth, he said, "I was ah... serious about you painting a mural in my house. I would love something in the dining room."

She immediately broke eye contact, fussing with her dress. "I don't usually paint for clients. I could commission someone much more talented."

This time he had to touch her hand. She jumped at the connection, her gaze flying to his.

"You *are* talented," he said roughly. "Don't sell yourself short. Ever."

Her flesh was suddenly hot to the touch, and her fingers were shaking. He made himself remove his hand.

"What kind of a scene would you like me to paint?"

He kicked his legs out in front of him and put his hands behind his head. Better to keep them occupied after that brief, alluring touch. "I'd like a scene from Dare River. Maybe with a canoe and some birds. And a dock." He was making it up on the spot since he didn't have a clue. All he knew was that he wanted something personal from her, something from her creative place—like one of his songs that would never fade. "You'll come up with something."

Her knee started jumping, and her foot tapped the ground. He counted the beats. *One-two-three. Four. Five-six-seven. Eight.* There was anxiety in the music she was making —and excitement.

"I'll work up some sketches for you to look over," she said, her eyes glazing over.

He knew that look. People said he got that look when he was stringing a melody together for a new song. It was reserved for that special land of imagination, a place he loved to visit.

"That sounds fine."

Then she laughed, coming back to herself. "You do realize this is going to take a while, right?"

"I do," he answered, trying not to grin. The longer the better, as far as he was concerned. Perhaps he should build a guesthouse at Redemption Ridge as well. That way he'd have another project for her to work on when she finished the main house.

"We should probably walk back," she said, rising from the bench and fussing with the silver buttons on his denim jacket.

A heron flew over the water and alighted in a pine tree across the way as Jake stood as well. "Maybe you can paint me one of those birds."

She looked out across the river. "They are pretty majestic, aren't they?"

Her steps were slow as they walked back, and he matched her stride. It was as though neither one of them wanted their time alone to end. And wasn't that crazy? He was going to see her often as she helped decorate his house.

But he knew better. Being with her now—in the sunlight by the water, with the light shining off her hair— well, there was romance and magic here. It made the man in him want to sweep her up and never let her go.

When he opened the door to the back of the house for her, she gave him a shy smile that made his heart race. God, she was so pretty. He wanted to curl her hair around his finger to see if it felt as soft as it looked. Heck, he wanted to *tell* her she was pretty.

"Thanks for walking with me," he said quietly instead.

She nodded, and he touched her back as she went through the door. The muscles there jumped. He quickly removed his hand.

"How was the walk?" Tory asked them as they reentered the family room.

"Jake! You're back!" Annabelle pushed off the floor where she was playing with her dog. Barbie, was it? The poor thing. He felt worse for it than a turkey trussed up for Thanksgiving, what with the hot pink bow around its neck and the rhinestone collar. To his mind, no dog should be dressed up like a mini debutant. His own dog would never have allowed it. Not that he would have tried.

"The walk was pleasant," Susannah answered for him, her tone more than a little pointed.

"The weather seems so nice," Rye commented, and Jake shot him a warning look.

He'd known Rye a spell, and the man wasn't the type to converse about weather.

"I need to get on home," Jake said, and Annabelle ran over to him and tugged on his pant leg.

"You can't leave!" she cried. "I need someone to push me on the swing."

No one hated to disappoint a little girl more than he did, so he sank to one knee in front of her. "Perhaps we can do that another time."

"Promise?"

He'd given up on making promises years ago, knowing he wasn't always able to deliver on them. Sometimes forces bigger and greater than he was had a way of changing things out from under him. "I'll do my best."

J.P. picked Annabelle up and threw her in the air, causing her to giggle. Barbie barked, and Rory's dog joined in the chorus.

"Let's all say goodbye to Jake and thank him for coming today," J.P. said, tickling the little girl. "He probably has things to attend to."

Jake didn't, but that wasn't the point of him leaving. He walked over to Rye and shook the man's hand. "Thanks for having me over, and congratulations again to you and Tory. You're going to be wonderful parents."

"Thanks," Rye said, putting his arm around his smiling wife. "I have more learning to do on that score, but I have the best teacher. I never imagined I'd be a father, but now I'm as eager as a kid waiting for Christmas. The next six months are going to be endless."

"And then the baby will be here," Tory said, patting his chest. "The time will go fast. Even the famous Rye Crenshaw can't hurry nature along."

"More's the pity," Rye said with a snort. "If I could shorten the time a woman needs to be pregnant, my female fans would love me even more than they already do."

That earned him a playful punch in the stomach from his wife.

Jake said his goodbyes to everyone, and J.P. held Annabelle up so she could kiss his cheek.

"Bye, Jake. Do your best to remember about pushing me on that swing."

Oh, what a sweetheart she was. "I will. And you make sure to remind me if I forget."

"I'm good at reminding people," she declared, making everyone laugh.

Shelby and Sadie kept their faces composed, but he could see the grins they were fighting. Both of them smelled something in the air between him and Susannah—like everyone else apparently. Jake was going to have to be careful here. His friends were involved, and so was this family. These were relationships he treasured. He wasn't going to mess that up.

Someone linked arms with him, and he looked down to see Susannah's mama. He tensed up again.

She simply smiled. "I'll walk you out."

Susannah gave her mama a narrow-eyed look, but Jake nodded to her to assure her he'd be fine. She gave him another soft smile, which made his heart feel like it weighed less than a sheet of music.

"I'll see you soon, Susannah. We have a lot of furniture to buy."

He almost winced at the lame goodbye. What he really wanted was to kiss her cheek and smell the honeysuckle fragrance of her hair as he whispered how much he'd loved being with her down by the water.

"We do indeed," she said, a smile flickering on her face.

He made himself turn away, and with her mama's determined arm linked through his own, he walked out of the room. Later, he'd tell Rye that it wasn't like he thought between him and Susannah. Well, it was. He *was* attracted to her. He just couldn't act on it until he was okay. Yes, he'd gone to church—a huge step for him—but it didn't guarantee he'd be cured.

At the front door, Jake turned to say goodbye to Louisa, but she ignored him and kept their arms linked. She was one determined woman.

When they reached his truck, she stood beside him in the silence. The sun was beginning to set, and the sky was alight with a swath of blue streaked with orange and pink.

"Something on your mind, ma'am?" he finally asked.

"My sermon got you all stirred up," she said as bold as a red barn in a green pasture. "Are you still recovering from your service to our country?"

It was difficult to keep her gaze, but he made himself.

"Pardon me for saying so, ma'am, but that's an awfully personal question."

"It's Louisa," she told him, releasing his arm and crossing hers over her chest. "And it *is* personal. As personal as it gets. The question I'd like you to consider is this: do you want to recover?"

For a moment, his tongue felt too thick to answer. "That seems like a ridiculous question."

Her eyes narrowed. "That's not an answer."

"Yes," he ground out. "More than anything."

She gazed at him thoughtfully, and suddenly all he could feel was her compassion. "I see some veterans for counseling. I'm assuming you've tried everything else."

"I have," he answered crisply.

"Veterans don't see me as their first choice, but I've managed to help a lot of them in my church. If you'd like, I'm sure a few of the men would be happy to speak with you about our time together."

Did he really want to open that box of horrors all over again? And with her? She was Susannah's mama, after all.

"Are you sure you want to make the offer? It's not exactly...pretty."

"I'm not especially fond of 'pretty' myself. Life is about experiencing the full spectrum, don't you think? It's what being human is all about."

"I wouldn't wish this spectrum on my worst enemy, ma'am," he told her. "War isn't what I want for this world."

Her smile was brief. "It's not what I want either, but it exists, and you experienced it. Others have, and others will again. I don't like divorce or child abuse either, but they exist too. Grace is how we overcome it and then do what we can to help others heal."

Heal. There was that elusive word again. "I'm afraid some things can't be mended."

This time she shook her head at him. "I don't believe that. I won't say it'll be easy, but if you want healing badly enough, you'll find it. Showing up today at my church told me you want it. Badly enough to sit through my sermon and not walk out like another might have."

He grimaced at that.

She laughed. "I've had people walk out, Jake. I know it's not about my words."

He felt that way about his songs, so he understood. Sometimes people were just haters, and that was on them. "I *do* want to be okay again. More than anything." And dammit, if it wasn't hard to admit it to her, both as a preacher and Susannah's mama.

"Anything we discuss will be completely between us. I know you have relationships with people in my family. You can trust me, Jake."

He realized he was fidgeting, and he forced himself to stop. "It's not that I don't trust you, ma'am."

"It's Louisa, and you don't have to be completely sure of me yet." She patted his chest again. "Give me your number, and I'll text you the names and numbers of some of the men I've helped. You can talk to them and see what you want to do. Come once and try it. You might be surprised. Some men don't think I'm tough enough to hear their stories. Those men are wrong."

"The steel in your spine isn't in question...ah...Louisa." He dug into his pocket for his phone. "Give me your number, and I'll call you right now so you have it." If he didn't, he might just up and leave. Maybe when he talked to some of the other vets she'd helped, he'd be more sure of her.

She dictated her number, and he let it ring twice before hanging up. Her smile was open and generous, and he found himself smiling back at her in spite of his now greasy stomach.

"You want to date my daughter," Louisa said suddenly.

"Are you always this tenacious?" he asked, his head darting back. "No offense, but you're like a pit bull."

Her smile only widened. "Why, thank you. I like being a pit bull for God. Trust me, I've dealt with enough men to know some of them have to be poked, prodded, and pulled along to get them to open up. You open up in your music, but not many other places. Am I right?"

"I...don't like talking about my time in the Army." He paused. "I don't much like talking about myself period. Even for my career. I just want to sing."

"J.P. was a lot like that," she said, her gaze tracking back to the house. "It's why he left the stage and decided to write music with artists like you. The other stuff was starting to spoil the thing he loved."

Jake understood. Sometimes he found himself considering whether the price of fame was too high. But every time he thought about what else he might do, nothing came to mind. He was a singer. Going back to the Army would never be an option.

"I should go," he said, walking to the driver's side of his truck. "I'll talk to the vets and let you know what I decide."

"You still didn't answer me about Susannah," she said, and darn it all, if she didn't step right up to him and look him straight in the eye. "You're afraid to date her because you're still suffering from PTSD. Hiring her as your decorator was to keep her close to you. As a move, it's not a wise one, but I understand it."

He kicked at the ground. Had he said a pit bull? She was

as fierce as a fire-blowing dragon intent on finding a chest of gold. "Is this between us?"

She nodded crisply. "Confidentiality kicked in the minute we left the house."

"Then, *yes,* I really like your daughter. She's amazing... but I'm...well, I'm broken."

He took a few steps off and clenched his fists. He wanted to hit the frame of his truck, which wasn't at all like him, but she was stirring up so many deeply buried feelings. More than she had with her sermon.

"You're not broken, Jake," she told him, putting a hand on his back and rubbing it in soothing circles. "You just need to remember that you're whole. I want to help you remember, and I hope you'll let me. I'll send you those names."

And with a last motherly pat on the back, she left him alone in a silence brimming with hope.

8

Susannah was still reeling from Sunday's embarrassment of being nudged by Rye to walk out with Jake. Tory had taken her aside and said it wouldn't happen again. Her sisters had wisely remained silent, but her mama... Well, that woman was on a mission to help Jake, and she knew to stay out of her way.

When she arrived at Jake's house the following Tuesday, Susannah put on a smile and walked to his front door. Jake was opening it as she reached the top step.

"Mornin'," he said in that sexy way of his.

His smile was slightly crooked, as if he too was feeling uncomfortable about Sunday. In a nod to the fifty-degree weather, the sleeves of his white button-down shirt were rolled up, showing off his forearms. Somehow that was sexy too. And the way his jeans fit his legs was slightly indecent if you asked her, since it made her think about running her hands down them. His stag belt buckle was way too compelling to ignore, which meant her eyes flashed to the bulge there before darting back to his face. God, had he noticed she was checking him out? Pink stained her cheeks.

"Good morning!" she said way too brightly. "Are you ready to buy some furniture?"

"Yep," he said and then patted his behind.

For a moment, she feared he'd read her mind, but then he said, "Got my wallet right here."

Oh. Lucky wallet. "Would you like me to drive?"

"Nope. I don't mean to be sexist, but when I'm with a woman, I like to drive. It's a courtesy."

Actually, she couldn't deny that she liked gentlemanly courtesies like that. There was something nice about it as far as she was concerned. And sue her if that made her less modern. She also liked men to pump the gas.

"Works for me."

"Good. I made sure my truck was clean."

They walked over to it, and sure enough, the vehicle looked like it had recently been detailed. "Are you this...ah... tidy because you were in the military?"

He hooted. "Heavens, no. It was my mama. She didn't like a mess. I don't either."

She stored that information away for decorating his home. He wouldn't want lots of knickknacks around. "What's your mama like?"

His shoulders tensed as he opened the truck door for her. "She's a quiet woman. Just does what she's told mostly. We...don't speak now. My daddy was none too happy with me for leaving the military, and since she goes along with him, we lost track of each other. My brother too."

It seemed there was more to the story, but she knew better than to dig. "I'm sorry to hear that. I'm sure you miss them."

He shrugged. "I stopped missing them when I went to war. I realized we weren't really a family. We were only related to each other. I found my true family in the military."

"I'm glad you found people of like minds," she said as she got into the truck. "It's important. Do you keep in touch with any of the men you served with?"

"Yes." After closing the door behind her, he walked around the cab and got settled in the driver's seat. "Only with three of them, but they don't live in Tennessee. Monty got married this year and lives in Georgia, but Darren and Randy are still single. They live out West. We try and get together every year, and I see them on tour if one of my concerts is nearby."

"I'm happy to hear you have such good friends," she said, adjusting her seatbelt. "Are they still serving?"

"No, they got out like I did. Monty had to, but that's another story. Too many tours. It...puts pressure on a person." He shook himself as he put the car in gear. "Now, you...well, your whole family is what it's all about. It's clear y'all would do anything for each other."

"We would," she said cautiously, sensing the change in his mood. "And that brings up a sensitive topic."

He turned his head to look at her as he drove down his long driveway. "What's that?"

"My mama can be a determined woman." She made a grimace.

"Amen," he said, making her laugh.

"I don't want you to be uncomfortable about her wish to...ah..." Gosh, what was she supposed to call it?

"Help me get in touch with my feelings?" Now he did laugh, but it was bitter. "Many have tried. It only seems to work with my music. But I talked to some of the vets she's helped, and they all sang her praises. They called her a miracle worker."

Her mama had given Jake references? Well, well. She'd only mentioned her offer to counsel him. "She is that, but I don't want you to be uncomfortable while we're working together."

He turned onto the country road that would lead them to a highway. "Is your mama planning on helping us pick out furniture today?"

Her brow knit. "Ah...no."

"Then I don't see a problem." He slowed down when they came across some turkeys from a nearby farm scooting across the road. "That farmer really needs to do something about those birds. Every time I see one of them on the road, all I can think of is Thanksgiving."

Her lips twitched. "They weren't out when I went by. It's a good thing this is a quiet road."

"They like to taunt me," he said, stopping the truck as three more ran across the pavement.

She leaned forward to watch their flight. They were rather adorable with all their...what did you call it? Gobbling? She felt his eyes on her, and suddenly it was impossible to ignore him. Her body tingled in response.

"Susannah," he said quietly.

Even though she knew it was a mistake, she looked at him. The blues in his eyes were darker now, and there was tension in his jaw.

"You need to know that I *need* a miracle," he continued in that same soft tone.

The gobble of the turkeys in the background disappeared, and all she could do was fall into his eyes.

"If your mama can help with that, then I'd be forever in her debt." He took a breath and let it out. "There are things that I want. Things I can't let myself have until...something like that happens."

In that moment, she knew he was talking about her. She'd always been able to read between the lines. When he rested his hand on the back of her seat, right above her shoulder, it was close enough that she could feel the warmth of his skin.

"I want you to have the things you want, Jake," she whispered. "You deserve them."

He swallowed thickly. "I don't know about that, but it doesn't stop me from wanting them."

At the agony she heard in his voice, she turned in her seat and reached for his hand. He took it without hesitation. The spark that shot up her arm at his touch was nothing compared to the tingling in her heart.

And then he stared straight into her eyes again. In those blue depths was a vulnerability she hadn't seen before.

"You deserve good things too," he said in that same hushed tone.

"There are things I want," she admitted quietly. "When you want them—the wishes in your heart—you have to do everything you can to get them. And to pray for them to come. We don't have to do it all alone."

His sigh was audible. "I don't know if I believe that anymore."

She stroked the back of his hand with her thumb. "There's always the promise of rainbows, right?"

"Right," he admitted, although she knew he didn't believe it yet.

His thumb joined hers in the caress, and though it was such a simple touch, it felt like an erotic dance—all the more surprising for its simplicity. From day one, the power of their connection had redefined her experience with men. She fought the urge to nestle close and lay her head on his shoulder.

A car honked, and he looked over his shoulder. "I guess we ought to mosey. Lost track of time there...with the... um...turkeys."

Susannah wanted to bless those turkeys for giving them this moment. His fingers traced the inside of her palm one last time before he released her hand and resumed their drive.

She sat back in her seat and kept her eyes on the road, awash in sensation. Those confused signals she'd been getting from him made sense to her now. She would have to trust her mama to help him as he helped himself. And she'd pray—harder and longer than she'd done before.

When he parked in the lot of the furniture megaplex, he turned in his seat to face her. "I'm going to see your mama, Susannah. And then...we'll see what happens."

The breath froze in her chest. He planned to ask her out! She just knew it.

"Okay," she said, giving him what she hoped was an encouraging smile.

It must have been because he opened his palm to her again. She didn't hesitate. She took it and felt her heart explode with joy. They held hands for several moments longer, gazing into each other's eyes until the corner of his mouth finally tipped up.

"I guess I'm back to holding your hand."

"I guess you are."

And when he let go of it to leave the truck, she pressed it to her happy heart and waited for him to open the door for her.

9

J ake hadn't expected furniture shopping to turn into a date, but darn it all if it hadn't. As he and Susannah walked around the old mill that had been converted into a fancy showroom, he pretty much flirted with her unmercifully. And wasn't it a delightful surprise when she flirted right back.

"Who in the world would ever buy this?" he asked, tapping the head of an alligator smoking a cigar.

"Someone who misses Florida?" she quipped.

So far, she'd had a witty reply for every comment he'd thrown out. Seeing this side of her only made him want to kiss her pretty smile. She was having a good time, and he couldn't be happier. Especially after their moment in the truck.

"And what about this?" he asked, gesturing to a trio of pewter mice who were obviously running in place.

"An angry cheesemonger? Maybe he wants to send a message."

"Don't mess with my cheese," he finished for her in an ominous voice.

They both laughed, and he fought the urge to reach out and take her hand again. But they were in public now, and even though the sales person was giving them space after delivering a brief greeting, he was still hovering in the showroom.

"Okay," Susannah said, putting her hands on her hips. "Let's get serious. We've established what you don't like. Now, we need to find what you do. How about we start with a couch?"

"A couch," he said, stroking his chin. "Why don't you show me some of your favorites?"

"Do you want leather or cloth?"

"Let's give both a gander," he said, following her as she headed off to another room.

The old mill was built with red brick and had scuffed-up walnut wooden floors. He liked the look of the place, which Susannah had praised for preserving the past while curating the largest furniture collection in the area.

When they entered another showroom, his mouth dropped clear open. "It's a couch potato's dream."

The smile she gave him was sweet as honey with a touch of spice. "Let's find your couch."

She set off with a determined stride, scanning the rows upon rows of couches. He tried not to watch the way her backside swayed as she walked, but he couldn't help himself. She was gorgeous all around, front, back, *and* sideways. Oh, and if that wasn't a great lyric. He drew out his phone to write it down. He was always jotting down phrases that came to him. Many ended up in his songs.

"What about this one?" she said from a few rows up.

The leather was the color of a caramel apple, which made him long for Halloween. Growing up, he'd loved him a caramel apple—more than any other candy. "Is it comfy?"

She sat down and bounced on it, making him hot all over. Good Lord, it wasn't very gentlemanly of him, but he could watch her bounce up and down all day.

"It is," she said in a cheery voice. "And it's long enough to fit all of you. Do you like to veg on the couch and watch TV like other couch potatoes?"

"Is there anyone who doesn't?" he fired back, sitting next to her and giving it a matching bounce for good measure. "Hey, this *is* pretty comfy."

"It's one of my favorite brands," she said, running her hand over the leather in a way that was far too arousing for a public venue.

He needed to get a hold of himself. A man shouldn't get hot and bothered from watching a woman sit on a piece of furniture.

"What about the color?"

"I like it," he said, touching the leather, but not caressing it like she had. He needed to draw the line somewhere. "Let's keep it in mind."

"I thought a dark brown might not work for you. The one downstairs is a lighter shade. You're earthy, but not dark."

If she knew everything about him, she wouldn't say that. "What an interesting observation. Do you get them often?"

She kicked her feet out, more relaxed than he'd ever seen her. "Yep. It's how I see clients. Although I don't always tell them my way of thinking."

"What other observations do you have for me?"

She turned and faced him on the couch. He could easily imagine watching a movie with her on this couch. And then after it finished, he'd lie down beside her and kiss every inch of her gorgeous body until she sighed out his name.

"You're not showy even though you're in show business," she said, studying his face. "You like earth tones, but you also like metal."

His head darted back at that, and the corners of her mouth tipped up even more.

"The belt buckle," she said with an arched brow.

He looked down. "This old thing? I've had it since I first arrived in Nashville. I thought...well...I thought it was something a country music star would wear." Darn it all if that wasn't a bit embarrassing to admit.

"Do you like to hunt?" she asked.

He thought of the times his daddy had taken him and his brother out as boys. Before his voice had even changed, he could shoot a deer with a gun or a bow-and-arrow. Later, he shot men.

"Not anymore," he said gruffly and watched her smile fade.

"I'm sorry to bring up a bad memory," she said softly.

Scrubbing his face, he steeled himself to shake off his change in mood, but the taste of dust and sand was in his mouth. Oh, how his subconscious delighted in torturing him.

"It's okay." He stood up and extended his hand to help her up. "Let's keep looking, but I think this one goes on the possible list."

He helped her up, but then quickly released her hand. People could misinterpret things, and he didn't want to bring that talk to her door. The part of fame he liked the least was having his picture snapped against his knowledge and posted on social media, but he'd made his peace with it. Part of his job. But she didn't need that crap. At least not until they were more sure of each other.

"Like I said, I'd like to outfit the larger pieces for your

house before we talk about things like lamps and more personal items," she said as they walked through the showroom.

"I can't imagine having much of an opinion on lamps."

"You might feel different if you find a chandelier or a special light fixture. You can build a room around a piece like that, but I don't think that's your thing."

Build the room around a light fixture? "Ah...no."

She shrugged. "Some people prefer to start with color and supporting pieces like a piece of art or a light fixture. But most of my male clients prefer to start with furniture."

Jeez, he couldn't imagine looking at all that color swatch shit again. "The old decorator lady tried to make me choose colors first, but it didn't work for me. I'm a simple man with simple tastes."

"So you've said." There was a little smile on her lips as she said the words. "Let's go by function." She placed her hands behind her back as she walked. "Where do you plan to hang out with your friends?"

"In the den. Now that you mention that, I'm pretty sure I want that couch."

"Noted." She scanned the showroom. "Do you play pool?"

Her suggestion brought back memories of his early military days when he and the guys would go out on the town. Those were good times. "Sometimes Randy, Darren, Monty, and I play pool when we get together. We rotate years. I suppose I could put one in the room on the lower level for when they visit."

He'd hosted the get-together two years ago at his old house in Lebanon, Tennessee, and they'd ragged him good about all the boy toys he'd purchased now that he was a country music star. But they'd enjoyed driving around on the four-wheelers. Their mouths would gape like catfish when they saw Redemption Ridge.

"I'll add it to the list. A game room would be nice," she said to him, all business again. "What else do you like to do with your friends?"

Most of his friends were musicians. He wasn't much of a partier, but he'd had Rye, J.P., and Clayton over for a casual beer. Sometimes they went four-wheeling or took out his boat to fish on Dare River.

"We like to write or play music," he said, trying to help her. "Have a beer. Go off-roading or four-wheeling. Watch sports or an action movie."

Her eyes gleamed brighter, which was how she looked when she had an idea. "Movies! We need to get you some more TVs. One for the den upstairs. How do you feel about having one in your bedroom?"

When he thought about getting home late after a busy day, the idea of crawling into bed and watching the news appealed to him. Often, he fell asleep in his studio and awoke in the middle of the night to infomercials. "That would be great."

"I can put TVs in a few of the guest bedrooms as well, if you'd like." She was already drawing out her sleek leather notebook.

"I'm sure my company would appreciate that," he replied to be friendly even though he didn't have many overnight visitors. Truthfully, the house was empty except for him more often than not.

"Would you like to pick out the furniture for the guest rooms?" she asked, searching his face again.

"Not really," he said, laughing to shake off thoughts of Monty. "I don't think I could stand outfitting six bedrooms. Can you...infer my tastes from the main furniture I select?"

There was a flash of something in her eyes.

"I'm sorry. That was a stupid question. Of course, you can. It's your job."

"Not stupid at all. I'm starting to get a sense of your taste. Let's go look at bedroom furniture for you." Pink suffused her cheeks in the most charming way, and she increased her pace to the next room.

He gave her some time. Given the building heat between them, it wasn't hard to imagine what she was thinking. Selecting a bed with a man you were attracted to had to be awkward. Not that he wasn't fidgety himself. He would try to make it easy on both of them.

"I'd...ah...like a king bed," he told her when he reached her.

She was already scanning the showroom. "How about the sleigh bed over there? It's simple, but makes a statement."

There were at least a dozen bed frames set up around them. He scanned them all, making sure to study the one she'd recommended. The sleigh bed was pleasing to the eye. "I like it. Is there another one you fancy?"

She cleared her throat. "Well, I like the one over there with the carved footboard. It's still simple, but the design adds something extra."

He walked over and studied it. There was a simple carving of a tree on the frame, nothing too fussy. "What kind of bedding would you recommend?"

"Something blue since you seem to like the color," she told him, tracing the grooves on the footboard. "Navy, perhaps?"

One of her inferences again. "I like navy," he mused, now running his fingers over the carving as well.

Their eyes met, and in them, he could see a heat that

matched his own. His mind conjured up an image of them tangled in navy sheets, his body pressing hers into the new mattress.

"The sleigh bed is a great choice too," she said softly, looking away.

But her hands lingered on the one with the carving. This bed was her favorite. Maybe if he bought this one with her, he could change his fate. Maybe one day, he would be whole enough to come to her as a man and make love to her in it.

"Let's get this one."

Her mouth tipped up into a smile that faded the instant she caught him staring at her. He needed to pull it together.

"I'll add it to the list."

He told her to buy the other sleigh bed for one of the guest rooms, and they fell into a quiet lull as they walked through the other showrooms. When he caught sight of another statue of an alligator smoking a cigar, he crouched down beside it.

"Just so we're clear," he said, his shoulders shaking with silent laughter. "I'm not looking for anything like this."

"Duly noted," she replied, fighting a smile. "I hate to tell you this, but I happen to know that statue is one of their bestsellers."

"No kidding?" he said, rising and patting the reptile's head.

"I shouldn't mention it, but I believe Rye has one in his game room," she said, trying not to smile.

He snorted out a laugh. "Somehow I missed that. I'll have to rag on him the next time I'm over."

"Feel free. How about we look at some desks for your office?"

He did need an official office, he supposed. "Right now, I do most of my business stuff in the kitchen." Paperwork didn't belong in his studio.

"We need to get some bar stools for the island in the kitchen," she said, flipping the pages of her notepad. "Then we should look for a couple of dining room tables."

"A couple? Isn't one usually good enough?"

She laughed—the same natural laugh he'd heard around her family. "You need one for the kitchen too. You have a nook to fill."

"A nook? That's like a nook and cranny, right? I might have to use that in a song sometime. It has whimsy."

"Whimsy," she said with a sigh. "I love that word. It's magical."

His gaze traveled across the lovely planes of her face. Her cheekbones made his fingers itch to trace them, and the outline of her lips tempted him to kiss her right then and there.

"You are so beautiful," he told her quietly, unable to hold back the words. "Especially when you're like this, talking about whimsy and magic."

"Jake..." she said in that same soft tone he was coming to love, full of both uncertainty and allure.

The urgent beat of his heart reminded him that he was still a flesh and blood man even if he wasn't a whole one. "I'm going to visit your mama next week. I wasn't forthright before, but I want...no, I need to be."

She let out a long breath.

"When I have a handle on...my past, I'd like to ask you out. Is that all right?"

Looking down for a moment, she fussed with her nails. "You're a client right now, and I shouldn't..."

"What if I wasn't?" he asked, wishing she'd meet his gaze. "Would you go out to dinner with me?"

She finally glanced up, but it was brief, as if she were shy. "Yes. Yes, I would."

He made himself step back. "That's all I wanted to know. We'll complete my house, and I'll work with your mama." He ignored the part of his mind that said maybe her mama couldn't help him.

To believe that would be to lose all hope.

10

Belle Meade Boulevard was a feast for the senses. Shelby loved driving down Nashville's famous street, and now that she had Pearl, the trip was even more enjoyable. She passed one Southern mansion after another before pulling up to the wrought-iron gate of her boss' palatial estate. When the gate opened after she rang the call button, she sped down the lane to the wide circular driveway.

Situated on four acres, the two-story brick mansion was over ten thousand square feet and sported six bedrooms, eight baths, and five fireplaces. It always took her breath away. After exiting her car, Shelby rummaged for a penny from her coin purse to throw into Gail's massive Italian stone fountain, something that had become her good-luck tradition. She'd first done it years ago, back when she was a scared twenty-three year old with only one year of accounting experience under her belt. Her wish on that first visit had been for a successful interview.

The water sparkled in the sunlight as she rubbed the penny between her fingers. Three cherub-like children were frolicking in the spray as one mighty angel watched over them.

"I wish for..." Shelby had to think for a minute. "Something amazing and wonderful to happen today."

She threw the copper coin, and it sank to the bottom with the hundreds of other coins she'd tossed on earlier visits. Though Shelby was the one who'd started the tradition, other visitors had continued it. It drove Gail's butler crazy, but her boss had insisted the coins remain where they were. Gail loved the idea of people throwing money and wishes at her doorstep, especially the accountant who looked after her finances.

The two-story white wrap-around porch seemed to glow in the bright morning light, and Shelby skipped up the brick steps to the front door and rang the bell, feeling renewed from her wish.

Jeffries—the bona fide English butler Gail's daddy had brought over from London to serve the family—opened the door. Nearing seventy, she imagined, he had a fine head of short white hair, permanently narrowed eyes from the haughtiness he wore like a prized cloak, and a lean frame that likely came from never sitting down. She had a talent for thawing his uptight demeanor, but he'd yet to crack a full smile in her presence.

"Hello, Jeffries," she said as she entered the foyer. "The house is looking beautiful as always. Every time I visit, I don't think you can make it more presentable, but you somehow manage."

"I try, Ms. McGuiness," he said, bowing slightly.

Fighting the urge to bow back to him like Carole Lombard might have done in an old movie, she turned and scanned the room. Orchids wound their way around bamboo stalks in eye-popping lavishness on the center table.

"The orchids are particularly stunning. Where is Ms. Hardcrew at the moment?" she asked formally.

"In her office, miss," Jeffries said in that stiff upper-class accent, turning in his black butler's uniform that looked like an old-fashioned tux and tails. So *Downton Abbey* of him.

She followed Jeffries down the long hallway to the office. When she entered, Gail was bent over on her desk, her black hair fanned out around her face. Alarm shot through her, and then she heard a sob. Was Gail *crying*?

"Maybe you should return at another time, Ms. McGuiness," Jeffries suggested in a quiet tone, completely nonplussed by the scene.

"I've got this, Jeffries," Shelby told him. Then she shut the door in his deadpan face.

Moving quickly across the white silk rug to where Gail was seated, she put her hand on the woman's back.

"Gail! Good heavens. What in the world is the matter?" Gail wasn't named Hardcrew indiscriminately. She was the toughest woman Shelby knew.

Her boss shook a weak hand in the air. Her ruby, amethyst, and sapphire rings all glittered in the sunlight streaming through the floor-to-ceiling windows.

"Give me a minute, Shelby. In case you haven't noticed, I'm having a moment."

Leave it to Gail to set a person down even when she was crying. Shelby took a seat in the tapestry chair across from the antique cherry desk. Silence hung between them for a few long minutes.

"Do you have a mirror?" Gail finally asked, pushing herself upright.

Leave it to Gail to address personal grooming first and foremost. Shelby handed her a makeup mirror from her purse, hoping that request was a positive sign her boss was coming back to herself.

Gail wiped at her kohl-lined eyes, which were smudged, and tidied her curly black hair. "Oh, take that thing away. I look like an old crone."

"I'm sure Jeffries can find you a wet washcloth," Shelby suggested, hastily stowing the mirror.

"It will take more than a good scrubbing to alter this damage." Gail heaved out a sigh. "Crying does age a person, doesn't it? I will have to ensure I don't do it often."

If Shelby hadn't been so worried, she might have smiled.

"Shelby dear, why are you here? I can't seem to remember at the moment." Gail opened a desk drawer and drew out an object that took Shelby a moment to recognize.

"Is that a garter flask?" Shelby asked with a gasp.

Gail waved it in the air, and sparkles shot across the room from the crystals etched in the glass. "Yes. My first husband, God rest his soul, presented it to me on our first anniversary. I should have buried it with him. He made me drink quite a bit until he passed. But it's too lovely for words. It's from Paris, and it's covered in Swarovski crystals. Of course they rub your thigh raw if you actually put it in a garter. Not a smart design."

"It is beautiful." Maybe she needed to get herself one, minus the chafing. "I'm here for your signatures on payroll this month." Gail always signed the checks personally, saying it was her way of showing her employees she cared about them. Shelby rather respected that.

"Of course! Payroll! Lord have mercy. I must be having a day if I can't remember something as regular as that." She tipped back the flask and took a long draught. "Bourbon. Reserve barrel. Damn good. Would you like some?"

"No, thank you," she said politely. "Do you want to talk about what happened?"

Fresh tears darted into Gail's eyes, and she reached into her desk for a hand-stitched blue handkerchief embroidered with her initials. "I had a call this morning from my doctor. He tells me I have something called familial hyper... hyper." She grabbed a notepad by the phone. "Hyper-tri-glycer-i-demia. Good Lord! Where do medical people come up with these names?"

Shelby had no idea what the term meant, but it sure didn't sound good. Besides, tears and a garter flask implied something serious. "I'm so sorry to hear that, Gail," Shelby said, her stomach swirling with nerves. "Is there anything I can do? Anything you need?"

"Hell's bells, Shelby, this disorder isn't going to kill me," Gail muttered, taking another deep draw from her flask. "I won't let it. But I am pissed I didn't know about it earlier."

"Umm...I'm not familiar with...what you have," Shelby said, wishing she'd taken Gail up on her offer to have a drink.

"Neither was I," Gail sighed, holding the flask to her ample bosom. "I went in for a checkup because a friend insisted I should. I'm only forty-five. You'd think I was in danger of being put six feet under if you asked Eunice. But that woman turned out to be an angel in disguise. Even though I exercise and watch my weight like a belle out for my first season, my triglyceride thingies were off the charts. The doctor asked if anyone in my family had heart issues at a young age, and I honestly didn't know. I immediately called my aunt because my daddy—God rest his soul—

never talked about his health. I hung up with her shortly before you arrived."

Shelby immediately thought about her daddy. He'd be going on fifty-five years now—about the time when many men started to experience health troubles.

"True-blood Southerners don't flap their gums about their health," Gail continued. "It's bad taste. Like talking about money."

Shelby only nodded.

"Well, after having my aunt hem and haw about how it wasn't polite to discuss anyone's health, she finally shared that *she* had coronary heart disease. And of course my daddy died of a heart attack, but I always attributed that to him being with that gold digger of a woman half his age. He died in her bed, but I covered it up. The scandal would have rocked Nashville—although I think some people suspected."

Mr. Hardcrew had died in someone's bed? Good heavens! Shelby tried to school her features.

Gail waved her handkerchief in the air. "The doctors tell me I have this family disorder, which no one ever knew about because no one talks about their health. Well, I'm done with that provincial way of thinking, not that I'm going to pass my bad genes on to any children. I think that ship sailed when I divorced my cheating asshole second husband two years ago and took back my maiden name."

Calvin Henderson had cheated on Gail? Shelby had always disliked him, but even though she and Gail were close in their way, her boss usually didn't get this personal.

"My doctor wants to put me on Lipitor and suggested I eat more kale and sprouts," Gail moaned, throwing her handkerchief on the desk. "I suppose I should be grateful he caught it, but the news was like a splash of cold water in the face. I've been carrying this genetic thing inside me my whole life and no one knew." Then she shot up straighter in her chair. "*Shelby McGuiness.* I know your daddy left you when you were a baby, but what do you know about his family's medical history?"

Suddenly Shelby found it hard to breath. Every time she went in for her annual gynecology exam and filled in her medical history, her daddy's information and that of his kin amounted to a bunch of white space on the paper.

"Nothing really."

Now Shelby was more than nervous. Didn't people inherit genes for cancer from their parents? Like Angelina Jolie? Everyone knew the actress had gotten a double mastectomy for cancer prevention.

Shelby put her hand on her stomach—her body. What if she had something inside her from her daddy that could hurt her?

"Shelby," Gail said in that tough-as-nails voice she was known for. "You listen to me. Don't make the same stupid mistake I did. I was ignorant, and I'm not proud of it. You don't need to be. Can your mama tell you anything about his family's medical history?"

"We...ah...don't discuss my daddy." Mama didn't like to talk about the past, and Shelby had never felt the need to ask her about family diseases. She was only twenty-eight, after all.

"It may be none of my business," Gail continued, "and you can ignore me if you want, but I highly encourage you to find out as much as you can about your father's family's medical history from your mama. My doctor said they can prevent many conditions if they're armed with knowledge upfront. He's doing a full work-up on me now that we know I have this disorder. I'm *praying* they don't find anything else."

Shelby thought back to her last doctor's visit. It had been for a pap smear, and they hadn't talked about much beyond the fact that she was healthy, ate well, and exercised. But what if Gail was right?

"The same is true with cancer," Gail said, echoing Shelby's earlier thoughts. "My doctor couldn't scare me enough about all the new tests they possess that can detect a family propensity for breast cancer."

She handed Shelby the flask, which she took without hesitation this time. Cancer? Who wasn't scared of that? Her mama's sister had died of breast cancer. She took a deep draw of bourbon and coughed at its potency.

Gail leaned her elbows on her desk and stared at her. "I can't imagine how difficult it might be to talk about this with your mama, but you should bite the bullet and get it done. Your health is important, Shelby. Trust me when I say I will no longer be ignorant about mine. I'm calling all my kin this coming week and asking them enough personal questions to send the women into vapors and the men off to their bourbon, mistresses, or both."

Her head was pounding now. "All I know about my daddy's people is that they were from Memphis, not close, and didn't have much in the way of money."

"*Hmm...*" Gail said and held her hand out for her flask, which Shelby passed to her. She took a deep drink and extended it back. "How did your daddy come to be in Nashville?"

Talking about her daddy was stirring Shelby up something fierce. She took another drink of the bourbon, hoping it would burn away the lump in her throat. "He came to Nashville in the hopes of becoming the next country music star. Instead, he became a washed-out musician who couldn't land a gig anywhere in town. He ended up volunteering for the church choir to keep his music alive, and that's where he met my mama." For a time, they'd been happy, and that's all Shelby knew.

"Why did he up and leave y'all?" Gail asked, her eyes intent.

"No one seems to know," Shelby said, fighting the urge to cry suddenly. "Mama never talks about it. She won't welcome me asking these questions. I haven't asked about daddy's medical history before, but I've asked plenty of other questions. She always tells me to leave the past in the past."

"Sounds like my family," Gail murmured, taking a hold of the framed photo of her daddy and mama on her desk and showing it to Shelby. "One thing I learned from the school of hard knocks is that there's always more than one way to get an answer to a question. Hell, when I suspected my ex-husband was cheating on me, I up and asked him. That son of a bitch lied to my face. Do you know what I did? Hell, I hired a private investigator and had his ass followed. You can bet I had photos of him with some blond-haired slut half his age to toss in his face the next time I confronted him."

Shelby couldn't imagine what a scene that must have been. "Good for you."

Gail's nod was crisp. "You'll figure out something, honey. No one is more enterprising than you. Why else would I hire some fresh-faced kid with a one-page resume? You have fire and wit, girl. Like me. Use them."

Awash in fear and hurtful memories of the past, Shelby didn't feel very fiery or witty. In fact, she felt all too human.

"I'll see what I can find out," she assured Gail, but mostly she was assuring herself.

"I know you will," Gail said, reaching for the flask and draining its contents. "Well, that conversation was very Yankee of us, wasn't it? How about I have Jeffries make us a proper drink to drive that foul taste from our mouths?"

Another drink sounded like heaven about now, even if it was just shy of eleven o'clock. "Jeffries does make the best drinks."

Gail waggled her brows. "The doctor told me to watch my alcohol consumption, and I probably should, but right now, I just don't give a damn."

Shelby didn't really give a damn either. She decided then and there that she was entitled to something as important as her daddy's medical history.

Somehow she was going to get it.

11

J ake had already sweated through two shirts by the time he showed up for his counseling appointment with Reverend Louisa the following Tuesday. All the motivation he needed to get well was his near-daily work with Susannah getting his house in order. Nothing was going to stop him from being the man who could take her out for a date and kiss her goodnight.

Nothing.

Not even himself.

Louisa stood up from her desk when the church's receptionist showed him into her office. The room was a cheery yellow, and there were pictures of her family and inspirational sayings scattered around as decoration. The Reverend was wearing a pink blouse paired with a gray skirt. Stepping forward, she gave him a hug.

"Congratulations on showing up," she said, shooting him an encouraging smile. "That's sometimes the biggest step."

"What's the other one?" he asked, trying to balance his nerves.

"Coming back," she quipped, reminding him of Susannah. "What would you like to drink?"

Joking about wanting a bourbon would be in bad taste, what with her being a preacher lady and it being only one o'clock in the afternoon. "How about some water?"

"Water we can do," she said, crossing the room to a small tray table that held glasses. She opened the mini-fridge below it and drew out a bottle of water.

"I don't need a glass," he added quickly, wanting to wet his whistle. He could taste the dust and sand already, and they hadn't even started talking yet.

"Humor me," she said, pouring the water out slowly.

A picture on the far wall caught his eye. A rainbow stretched across a storm-clad valley. "The promise of rainbows," he said aloud.

The Reverend looked up. "I see one of my children has told you one of my favorite sayings. Was it J.P. or Susannah?" Then she laughed. "Of course it was Susannah. You like my daughter quite a bit, don't you?"

"Yes, ma'am," he answered truthfully, gazing back at her steadily.

"It's Louisa, and it's a hang-onto-her-every-word kind of like, right?"

Goodness, this woman was either going to cure him or kill him. "That would be correct."

"Correct? No need to stand on formalities here, Jake." She brought over his water. "Not when you're about to pour out your heart and soul."

His hand clutched the glass to keep from dropping it. "Only my heart and soul? I should have brought my guitar."

Her eyes scanned him again, and he felt like a lab rat headed off for tests. "Maybe you should bring your guitar next time. When we spoke at Sunday dinner, you said music is the way you're able to communicate what's inside. I've been listening to your music lately. There's a lot you're communicating."

"Yes, ma'am," he answered, taking a hasty sip of the water and spilling some down his chin. "I mean Louisa."

She handed him a tissue, and he wiped his mouth, shuffling his feet a little. He'd worn his best cowboy boots today, not just because he was going to church—well, sort of—but also to make a good impression. She was Susannah's mama, after all. Then he realized making a favorable impression was pointless. The ugly truths of his past would crack any smooth terrain between them.

"Let's sit down," she said gently, gesturing to the tan couch.

For a moment, he wondered if Susannah had decorated her office, but he refrained from asking. Louisa would see through his small talk. She sat in the matching arm chair perpendicular to him. He hoped she wasn't expecting him to lie down like he was in a shrink's office.

"Where...ah...do you want me to start?" he asked, thinking back to the other therapy sessions he'd endured. "Do you want to hear about my military background?"

She shook her head. "There's no need, really. I expect you've already done that with the specialists you've seen."

If she didn't want his military background, he felt compelled to share his treatment background. He didn't want her to think he hadn't been trying to overcome his PTSD.

"When I left the Army, I had a severe case of PTSD, although the symptoms started while I was serving."

"Anxiety," she said, crossing her hands in her lap. "Depression. Insomnia. Paranoia."

He nodded. At the time, his inability to do normal

things without fear had made him feel like a coward. "I wasn't myself. Sometimes...it was like I was a different person. Going to a bar or talking with my buddies was beyond me at first. Simple conversations made me feel like I was walled off in glass and couldn't get out. I...God...sorry. I won't swear again."

"Don't worry about swearing around me," she said with a soft smile. "I don't mind it, and it's important for you to voice how you really feel, curse words and all. Please finish what you were saying about feeling like you were in glass."

A preacher lady who allowed curse words? Well, well. Maybe this would work after all. "I couldn't function, and I knew something was wrong. I immersed myself in my music since I needed gigs to pay the rent when I first came to Nashville, and it made me feel a little better to play my music for people."

"But the symptoms didn't go away."

"No," he said. A memory swept over him—stumbling into an alley for a break during a set and falling apart. Dry heaves. Heart pounding so hard he feared he was having a heart attack. Pure primal fear. Looking side to side for an enemy even though he knew logically he was in Nashville.

"I had meds at first to get me over the hump, but I didn't see them as a cure," he explained, not knowing how she felt about the use of medication.

"Isn't it interesting that in this day and age no one has discovered a medicine to treat PTSD?" she asked with a wry incline of her head.

"Yes," he answered. "Ah...from there I tried Cognitive Processing Therapy, which was supposed to desensitize me to events, but only seemed to re-traumatize me. I completed all twelve weeks prescribed. I even did the homework they gave me." He gave a hollow laugh. The doctors had asked him not only to describe the events that had traumatized him, but also to write about his issues with safety, trust, control, self-esteem, and intimacy. Seeing all his problems scrawled on paper had only depressed him. He'd never felt more broken.

"That's a hefty amount of treatment," Louisa said, picking up his water glass and handing it to him. "Why don't you take a drink?"

His mouth was bone dry even though sweat was dotting his brow. The water felt cool in his mouth, and he drank the whole thing before realizing it. She simply took the glass from him and refilled it. When she handed it back to him, she also gave him a tissue.

"Think I'm going to cry?" he asked, his solar plexus tight. He'd cried before, but the thought of crying in front of her made him queasy.

"I thought you might want to wipe your brow," she said, compassion filling her eyes. "But if you need to cry, go right ahead. Many have. What you've experienced deserves its day. Tears are God's way of helping the body get rid of painful feelings."

He still hated crying. "Yes, ma'am," he answered immediately. "Sorry. Louisa."

"You'll get the hang of it," she said gently. "And after Cognitive Processing Therapy?"

"I tried some Prolonged Exposure Therapy, and I have to admit, the homework was a life saver. The doctors asked me to go to busy concerts to face the loud crowd noise. My career was just starting to take off, but I hadn't played for a big arena yet. By the time I did, I was mostly prepared. I don't think I would have succeeded as a country music singer if I hadn't undergone that therapy."

"Then some of it was a blessing for you," she said. "That's good to hear."

"Yes. I tried to focus on that, but when you're in the grip..."

"It's hard to do," she answered. "I know."

For a moment, a flash of sadness crossed her face, and he remembered that this woman had grappled with her own demons. What must it have been like for her to raise four children on her own after being abandoned by the man who'd pledged to love and care for her? He couldn't imagine.

"Everyone seems to have at least one hardship in life, don't they?" he said.

This time her smile was but a trace on her face. "I keep waiting to meet someone who's never experienced one. I'm going to dance on that day to celebrate their providence."

"I'd like to hear about that too," he told her, giving her an answering smile before clearing his throat to continue. "From there, I did some EMDR, but again, reliving my trauma didn't work for me. I know the therapy is supposed to replace traumatic memories with positive ones, but mine seemed to stick like black tar."

"That's a good way to describe it," she told him. "You certainly have a way with words."

"Thank you," he said, crossing his ankles, trying to get more comfortable even though he knew that wasn't going to happen. He always got shifty when he talked about the past.

"Would you like to change seats with me? Some people are more comfortable in the chair."

"It's...ah...not the furniture," he said, ducking his head. "There's another therapy I should mention."

Her eyes never left him, and she didn't take notes like other therapists and doctors he'd seen.

"When I started touring, it was harder for me to meet with my psychiatrist, so he recommended a service dog for me."

"Those aren't easy to come by," she said. "I wish more of the men I see could receive one."

"I was lucky," he added, remembering how thrilled he'd been. Not just to have an animal trained for emotional support and companionship, but a real dog. He'd always wanted one. To this day, he still supported the organizations that provided them: America's VetDogs, Canine Companions for Independence, K9s for warriors, and New Horizons Service Dogs, Inc.

"What happened to your dog, Jake?" she asked quietly.

He pressed his fingers to his brows. "I...ah...had a concert in Jackson, Mississippi. There was a lot of activity in the parking lot. TV crews. Fans. It's still not clear what happened. My manager was supposed to be watching him. One of the TV crew's buses ran him over."

Losing that dog had darn near broke him, and he'd almost cried in front of everyone.

"What was your dog's name?"

"Hercules," he said in a hoarse voice. "No dog was better named. He was a...hero."

"I'm sorry you lost him," she said in that same gentle voice, causing tears to burn his eyes.

"Me too," he said with a catch in his throat.

That black Labrador had even learned to bark and whine in accompaniment to his songs, which had made Jake laugh. Until then, there hadn't been much laughter in his life. "I wrote some of my best songs with Hercules by my side."

She was quiet for a moment. "You didn't think about finding another dog?"

"No," he simply answered, remembering how Annabelle had suggested it. He didn't think his heart could take the pain of losing another, but a part of him longed to try. A dog would be happy at Redemption Ridge.

"I see. Is there anything else you want to share with me about what you've done?"

Frustration grew inside him as he thought about his regimen. "I've tried art therapy, mindfulness meditation, and relaxation techniques. All of them have helped to a point, but honestly, writing or playing songs has been the single best therapy for me."

"After hearing your music, I believe that," she added. "It's from your heart. There's no denying that. Or your honesty."

"If you're not honest in your music, people know it," he said, shifting to cross his ankle over his knee. "Oh...and I've exercised...a lot. To release the endorphins. That probably helped me get over my depression too."

Her mouth tipped up. "Yes, it's pretty obvious that you work out. I believe my youngest daughters have referred to you as Mr. Sex-On-A-Stick."

He rolled his eyes. "I don't keep in shape for my image." Despite what his agent said about it driving the female fans wild.

"Of course not. So after all of these different treatments, what continues to plague you?"

Were they finally getting to that? He realized he'd been giving more detail about his treatment in an attempt to delay the real reason he'd come here today. "I still have flashbacks, and sometimes I can taste the sand and dust in my mouth, but I can manage those. It's the nightmares that torture me. One in particular has never gone completely away. Nothing seems to fix it. Nothing seems to fix *me.*"

"As I've told you before, and I'll tell you again, you're not broken." She sat up even straighter in her chair. "Jake, there is nothing in you that needs fixing. Yes, you suffer from PTSD, but there's no reason you shouldn't have a happy life. You're already doing amazing if you ask me. You left the military, which I expect wasn't the easiest decision for you, and now you're a famous country singer doing what you love. That's pretty incredible, don't you think?"

He wanted to curse, but refrained. "It is...and I know it. I don't mean to be ungrateful. I just want..."

She leaned forward in her chair. "What do you want?"

"I want the nightmares to stop," he said in a voice harsher than he intended. "I want to share my life with a woman without fearing I'll drag her down into the dark with me like my father did to my mother."

"I did some reading before you came to visit me. I know your father was in the military. And that your brother is as well."

"He'd already done four tours in Afghanistan when we stopped speaking," Jake said. "He's already turned into my father."

"And what is your father like?" she asked in a neutral voice, one that helped him rein in the messy emotions that were rising up in him.

"Cold. Dominant." He thought of all the times his father had beaten him with his belt for "defiance"—anything from looking at him wrong to asking a question for the second time. "I know he has PTSD. He and my brother both do. But they aren't interested in getting help."

She folded her hands prayer style in her lap. "Then your decision to seek it out is all the more admirable."

His chest was so tight now, he rubbed the base of his diaphragm. "I want them to *want* to get better."

"I imagine you do. It might have made your childhood easier. But that's in the past, son. Forgiving them and moving on is your only way forward."

He'd heard this line before, and his anger surged to the surface. "How are you supposed to forgive someone who's not even sorry?"

"I can only tell you what I did. When my husband left me, I simply prayed over and over again for God's grace in letting go of all my anger and hurt. It took years, and sometimes when I sense my children's hurt, I get angry all over again. I pray more. Some acts like forgiveness are a life-long process. Eventually it gets easier."

"I've been out of the military for five years," he said, depression lacing his voice.

"I've met men who still have PTSD from their service in Vietnam," she said kindly. "There's no time limit on hurt and trauma. I wish there was."

He hung his head for a moment. "I just want to get better."

"You are," she said, laying her hand on his arm. "But that's no comfort right now. All you can see is your hurt and your frustration, which is completely understandable. You've been at this for a long while."

"Sometimes it seems like forever," he said, forcing himself to look up and stop being so pathetic.

"You've told me about all you've done to get over your symptoms. Why don't you tell me what the nightmare is about?"

He glanced at the clock on her wall. They'd been talking for almost forty minutes. The bible verse of John 14:27 was inscribed in the clock's face. It was a verse he didn't know, not that he knew many by heart. He might be able to recite a few lines of Psalm 23, "The Lord is my shepherd." But that was pretty much all he remembered from his Bible school days.

"Are you sure we have the time?" he asked, wishing he wasn't such a coward.

"We do if you want to tell it," she said softly. "Do you want to tell me, Jake?"

"Honestly, Louisa, I really don't." He laughed harshly. "But if you can help me, it's worth any embarrassment."

Her narrowed green eyes looked so much like Susannah's it gave him a jolt. "There's nothing to be embarrassed about, Jake. *Ever.*"

He shifted on the couch again. "Do you mind if I stand?"

"Not at all," she said patiently, folding her hands in her lap again.

"You're pretty good at waiting people out, aren't you?" he asked, rising to his feet.

She lifted a shoulder. "It's not easy for people to talk about what hurts them. It's not easy for me either, although I've gotten better at it. Love and compassion have a way of encouraging us to bring our hurts out into the light. While I know you don't know me well, you can trust me with your hurts."

"I know I can trust you," he said, running a hand through his hair. "I wouldn't be here if I thought otherwise."

"Then just start telling me," she said, leaning back, likely because he was towering over her. "It doesn't have to be pretty or even linear. Who's the nightmare about, Jake?"

His muscles locked. "How did you know it was about someone?"

"From my experience, most of the nightmares that

haunt people are about someone. Other memorable events, like the destruction of buildings, don't make the same kind of impression."

Yeah, he'd seen his fair share of buildings and vehicles blown up. It wasn't anywhere near as awful as seeing people blown up. In a sick way, he was glad Booker hadn't gone that way. Monty had almost met that fate, and now his missing leg was a constant reminder.

"The nightmare...it's about my friend." He could barely draw in a breath. "Booker."

"Go on," she encouraged.

He could barely draw in oxygen. "He...he died in my arms."

His foot started tapping as he told her about the nightmare. Everything from the dust in his eyes to the bitter end when Jake stopped applying pressure to his friend's wound to shoot the enemy combatant.

Somewhere in his recitation, he'd started pacing, completely numb to his surroundings. He tried to draw in air and focus on being present, like his psychiatrists had taught him. He patted his chest to feel his body. To come back.

Louisa was watching him steadily when he finally met her gaze. "I'm sorry about your friend, Jake."

"Thank you," he whispered harshly, wiping at the tears in his eyes.

"Other than the obvious, why do you think his death still haunts you?" she asked.

"You mean besides survivor's guilt?" he rasped. "He was my best friend. I failed him."

She rose and stood before him. "I know you believe that, but that isn't what happened."

He wanted to lash out. *You weren't there. How could you*

know? But he locked his jaw so the words wouldn't spew out like bile.

"You're angry with me for saying that," she said, watching him carefully. "Tell me why."

"Everyone keeps telling me that it's not my fault."

"And yet from the time you joined the military you were trained to protect your brothers in arms and never leave one of them behind. Is it any wonder you feel so conflicted?"

His eyes narrowed. "No one has ever said that before."

"No? Well, then at least I've helped you see one thing differently." She tilted her head to the side as she studied him.

He could feel that illogical emotion surging up like a wave he was powerless to halt. He bit his tongue—hard enough to draw blood—but he couldn't stop the words. "Logically, I know I didn't kill Booker, but I can't seem to accept that. When it comes down to it, I let my best friend die."

"Even if you hadn't taken the pressure off his wounds, I have a feeling he would have died," she said softly. "The bullet hit the artery—"

"You don't know that!" he shouted. "God...I'm sorry I yelled."

"It's okay, Jake," she said quietly. "I know you're not yelling at me."

His nod was crisp. He needed to get his control back. What must she think of him for standing over her and shouting like that? He was no better than his daddy. "There's something else. When I realized how bad it was, I...I asked God to save him. To keep him alive until the medic arrived."

She pressed her fingers to her mouth briefly. "So when

124

Booker died, you concluded God didn't answer your prayer. That you and Booker didn't matter enough."

He pinched the bridge of his nose. "Yeah. Pretty much any of us over there."

The Lord might be everyone else's shepherd, but He had turned a blind eye to them.

"You're not the first person to come to this conclusion." She shook her head. "Jake, I see things differently than you do, so will you let me share my thoughts? They might be a little different than what your psychiatrists shared with you if they talked about God at all."

"They didn't. They were government shrinks. They were bound by that whole church and state thing."

"Why don't you sit down?" she suggested, gesturing to the chair this time. "I'll take the couch."

"Okay." He sat down heavily, but didn't find the chair any more comfortable. If only he'd worn a T-shirt instead of his button-down shirt. He was blazing hot and sweating like a pig.

"You aren't going to want to hear this," she said, "and I have to admit that I can't be one hundred percent certain of anything. That's where faith comes in. I don't know why your friend had to die, but he did. It doesn't mean God doesn't love you or your friend. I don't know why God couldn't answer that one request. It's one of those mysteries we can't understand. It was Booker's time. Otherwise, he wouldn't have died."

Jake's anger burned hot and red. "Who decided that? Booker was a good man. The best friend a man could ever have. He had a wife... Dammit, he was only twenty-six."

"I told you that I don't know why he had to die that day in the alley, but he did." She leaned forward and rested her hand on his knee. "You haven't forgiven yourself for believing you let him die, but you also haven't let go of your anger against God for taking him and not answering your call for help."

"God shouldn't let good people die like that," he choked out. "What the hell good is prayer if He doesn't listen?"

Her chest rose as she took a breath. "Everyone dies, Jake. I wish we could all die in our beds having lived good lives. But that isn't the way it works. I can't tell you why it works that way, but it does. You're having trouble accepting the world for what it is. That's what's causing your hurt."

"People have said I need to accept Booker's death," he lashed out. "Do you think I haven't tried? How am I supposed to accept it when it's so unfair? I saw so much senseless destruction over there."

"Grace," she simply said. "Have you prayed since that last prayer by Booker's side?"

He lifted his shoulder. Great, they were going to talk about the status of his soul now. "No. I...just couldn't." Not even while he and his buddies carried Monty, screaming and bleeding, to the Humvee after he stepped on that landmine.

"People's actions bring the hurt into our world, but there are angels everywhere to help. They helped you live. That's an answer to prayer in its own way."

What good had that done? "Then why didn't they help Booker when I asked? We needed them!"

"I wish I knew." And from her tone, he could tell she meant it.

"So, what am I supposed to do?" he asked, reaching for control again. "I've tried to let it go. I've worked *so* hard to move on."

She rose and poured herself a glass of water, sipping it in the silence. Then she said, "You don't have to believe in

THE PROMISE OF RAINBOWS

God to move on, but I think you *do* believe in God. You just don't want to talk to Him anymore."

No, he really didn't.

"You think He failed you and Booker because you'd fallen from his favor. I understand the feeling even though our stories are different. For a time I felt like God had failed me and my family. That maybe in the whole scheme of things I had done something to deserve it."

"I feel that way too. I figure it was all the killing we did over there. Even though it was our job."

She shook her head. "There's nothing you can do to stop God's love for you. I believe that. I've seen it time and time again. Trust me when I say that you are more loved than you realize. We all are. You need to remember that somehow, and that starts with loving yourself. Have you forgiven yourself for all the people you've killed?"

Her question struck him like a lance to the heart. "Jesus, you don't shy away from anything. Mostly. I wish they hadn't gotten in the way or shot at me. I never killed someone who wasn't putting me or my men in danger."

"Of course you didn't," she said softly. "God understands that."

"Does He?" he asked, feeling like that kind of belief was beyond him.

"You don't need to take my word for it. You just need to ask God to show you He loves you and that you're whole and complete just as you are. You might try praying again for a start. It's really only talking anyway. I've seen it work miracles in people's lives."

Miracles? He didn't know if there were any of those left for him. "I'll try it." Maybe.

"Good," she said with a smile. "Next time—if you

choose to come back—we can talk about why you can't forgive yourself. Oh, and I have some homework for you."

Great. More homework. "What is it?"

"I want you to write down all the things that wouldn't have happened if you had died in the war. The ones that have made a difference in the world and in the lives of the people around you."

"Kinda like *It's a Wonderful Life?*" he asked, arching his brow. "I'm no George Bailey."

"We're all George Bailey, Jake." She gave him a smile so wide it reminded him of Donna Reed in the movie. "Every one of us matters in this world. We all have a purpose if we choose to listen."

"And what is that?" he found himself asking.

"To love and be happy," she answered easily, patting his knee.

"Well, that's not hard at all," he said with a trace of sarcasm.

"It's only as easy or hard as we make it. Most of the suffering in the world stems from people *not* choosing love and happiness."

The simplicity of her view was hard for him to accept given what he'd seen of politics, greed, and violence. "How do we know if we've made the right choice?"

She smiled. "If you're doing what makes you happy, you express the most love in the world. Rather like you do with your music."

He couldn't deny that he *did* feel a calling to his music. "What about my time in the Army?"

"Did you join the Army because you wanted it or because your daddy wanted it?"

He sighed and shook his head. "I didn't feel I had a choice."

THE PROMISE OF RAINBOWS

"Then there's your answer." She extended the water glass to him again. "Some soldiers love what they do. Not that there aren't hardships, especially if they see combat."

He hung his head. "I hate this. I hate feeling guilty about Booker, I hate being angry at God, and I hate being too weak to move past it."

"What's stopping you from moving forward? From sharing your life with someone?"

"Every time I get close to a woman," he said in a harsh whisper, "the nightmare about Booker comes back."

"Ah... So you don't think you deserve to be happy with someone since Booker's dead? He was married, I believe you said."

Was that the reason? Had he decided he couldn't be with a woman if Booker couldn't be with his wife? "Yes, he was."

"Are you still in touch with her?" she asked.

"I tried to be...at first," he said, feeling his throat burn with emotion. "But it was hard on both of us. I could tell she wanted me to stop calling. I have a feeling she blames me for what happened."

"Well, if she does, she's wrong. That's not for you to take on, Jake."

She rose and extended her hand to him. He didn't know what she wanted, so he simply stood. She stepped in and hugged him.

His muscles locked. "*Whoa.*"

"None of your psychiatrists probably hugged you, but like I said, I do things differently."

Her arms were firm but relaxed. He knew he could step away at any time.

"You're a good man, Jake, one who experienced a horrible loss. Your friend wants you to forgive yourself and be happy. God does too. I know it's impossible to understand why God didn't answer that particular prayer that day, but He still loves you. And I do too."

He stood in her embrace for a few more awkward moments choking on emotion before patting her on the back. She took it as the sign it was and stepped back. There was a gentle smile on her face.

"I'm glad you came today, Jake. Thank you for sharing your story with me. I hope you come back. And if you do, remember to bring your homework."

Nodding, he reached into his back pocket for his wallet.

"There's no charge," she said, biting her lip as if she suddenly found him amusing. "It's my job to help."

"But I'm not in your church..."

"Doesn't matter," she said, shaking her head. "The prisoners I visit aren't either, and I don't charge them."

Dear Lord. "If you visit inmates, you really are a pit bull for God."

She smoothed back her hair and gave a soft laugh. "Thank you. I hope to see you again soon."

He walked to the door, trying to think of some way to compensate her since she wouldn't take money. Surely, her church could use something. His hand was on the doorknob when he heard her say, "Jake, if you want my opinion, one of the ways to move forward with your life is to ask my daughter out on a date. Companionship between people can move mountains."

He turned around. "You still feel that way after everything I've told you today?"

"Absolutely. We heal in community."

Holy—

"But I'm still messed up," he protested.

She gave him a killer wink. "We're all a little messed up, Jake. Have a good day."

His legs were unsteady as he let himself out of her office and walked through reception.

If you asked him, there was messed up and then there was *messed up*.

But her suggestion—heck her blessing—to ask her daughter out on a date echoed in his ears as he drove home.

What if Louisa was right about moving forward by dating Susannah?

Then another thought intruded: what if she wasn't?

12

When Susannah arrived at Jake's house, she made sure to compose herself. He'd met with her mama yesterday afternoon. Her mama would never say anything about a private meeting, but she wondered if Jake would.

Whatever happens. I just won't ask after it, is all, she told herself.

She'd prayed for him this morning upon waking—just like she'd done before going to sleep. He'd been added to the circle of people she prayed for daily.

He had the front door open before she could alight the steps, and there was a smile on his handsome face. Some of the tension in her belly loosened even as she took in the jeans hugging his muscular legs, his signature stag belt, and a hunter green dress shirt. She caught a whiff of his cologne as she neared. The clove and pine scent was almost as alluring as the man.

"Hey there, pretty lady," he said with a twinkle in his cobalt-blue eyes.

Pretty lady? Good heavens, this man was going to give her the vapors, as her Aunt Ella would say.

"Hey, yourself," she answered, taking care not to add the word handsome. She needed to maintain some professional distance. Didn't she?

"How much time do you have for me today?" he asked, letting her inside and then closing the door behind them.

Since it was only eleven o'clock, she pretty much had all day. "As long as you need," she answered, scanning the house.

So far they'd bought the main pieces for most of the spaces Jake used, minus the dining room table. Since he was a VIP, the furniture had been delivered promptly.

"Everything is looking great," she commented. "How does it feel to have real furniture?"

He gestured to the enormous flat screen TV in front of his new caramel-colored leather couch. "I watched an old Clint Eastwood movie last night. Even made myself some popcorn to celebrate."

"Good for you," she said, smiling now.

He seemed lighter. Had her mama worked her magic? She sure hoped so.

"I was looking online for towns with good antiquing," he commented. "Thought that might be the kind of place we could go to find some of the other pieces. Um...if that's okay. I kinda wish the 123 Sale was going on right now."

Color her surprised. "Have you been to the 123 Sale?"

"When I first moved to Nashville, I heard about it from a friend. I outfitted my first apartment at the sale. I'd never seen anything like it."

A woman friend, she expected, but refrained from asking. The 123 Sale had been around for almost thirty years.

Held for only four days in August, it covered six hundred and seventy-five miles, stretching from Lookout Mountain Parkway into Tennessee and then winding its way along the Cumberland Plateau into the Bluegrass Region of Kentucky.

"I kinda like flea markets," he said in a hushed tone. His shoulder shrug was adorable. He was acting like he was confessing a dark secret.

"I like them too," she said, happy he'd made the suggestion. She'd taken him to all of the furniture places she used in the greater Nashville area.

"Have you been to the sale?" he asked.

"Yes. I've been a couple of times with my mama and sisters. The traffic can drive you crazy with everyone craning their necks to see what people have for sale in their front lawns."

He laughed. "It was pretty intense when I went too, but I liked hearing people tell stories about how they'd come to own certain things. A few of the pieces I bought are in my studio."

That explained its homey feel. "Which town do you have in mind?"

"Sweetwater, if that's not too far."

"That's a little over two hours from here." Now she understood why he'd asked about her plans for the day.

"I'd insist on driving," he said, clearly biting his lip to keep from smiling.

He still hadn't let her drive anywhere they'd gone together, and she liked to tease him about it. If she were honest, it was more than simple teasing. They were flirting.

"We can't have you break your driving record now. I'll just use the bathroom before we go." It still felt awkward to mention when she needed to use the facilities, but she just had to get over that.

"Good idea. I'll see you in a jiffy."

When they met again in the entryway, she was juiced. Somehow taking a road trip with him was exciting. Even though she kept reminding herself this wasn't a date or a social outing, it certainly felt different from her shopping trips with other clients.

They settled into his truck, and Jake made sure she was buckled-in and comfortable before heading off.

"I've heard Sweetwater is lovely," she said, stretching out and taking in the fallow fields as he turned onto Interstate 40. "I've only been to Athens."

"How was Athens?" he asked.

There was rain coming in, she decided, eyeing the puffy gray and white clouds billowing in the direction they were headed. "It was nice. The downtown is historic and filled with antique shops. I found an antebellum sterling silver serving spoon with a flower engraved on the handle once."

He looked over and waggled his brows. "Maybe we should go to Athens too. Tammy and Annabelle might like a spoon with a flower on it."

Well, wasn't that sweet? "Let's see how things go."

By her recollection, the two towns were about twenty-five miles apart. They'd likely arrive in Sweetwater sometime after one o'clock if the traffic cooperated. She expected they would have a spot of lunch and then hit the shops. Depending on how much Jake liked to hear the owners' stories, they might be in Sweetwater for a while.

"All right," he said, his voice octaves lower than usual. "But I insist on buying you lunch...and dinner...if we stay late."

The husky way he said the words made her think of smoke, and as they said, where there's smoke, there's fire. She wanted to fan herself.

"Okay."

"Now, what kind of music do you want to hear?" he asked.

"Anything you'd like since you're the one doing the driving. That's how it works in my family."

He fiddled with the radio, and they both laughed when they heard one of Rye's songs.

"He's everywhere," Jake commented. "I couldn't be happier for him. And now with the baby coming... He's a changed man."

J.P. and Rye had been friends for years, so she'd seen Rye in his wilder days. "It's good to see him settling down. Tory's an angel."

"She seems to be. How about we not listen to country music for once?"

Turning in her seat, she scanned his face. His jaw was clean-shaven, and her fingers itched to caress his skin. "Don't tell me you're secretly a fan of rap?"

He laughed as he selected Nashville Public Radio. "Is the news okay? I like to keep up with what's happening in the world."

Of course he would. He'd fought in wars that were headline news. "Sure."

"To answer your question, though, I do enjoy quite a few rap artists. I have a real respect for their lyrics, although they're a tad spicier than my own."

Spicer was being kind. Some of them were downright vulgar, if you asked her, especially the ones that talked about women in a derogatory way.

"Do you get embarrassed when your songs come on the radio?" she asked, knowing some singers did.

"Actually, no. I usually crank up the volume and sing

my heart out, marveling that I'm on the radio...and that I even created the song in the first place."

His gratitude was as sweet as could be. "Do you find the fame part difficult?"

"Sometimes. At first, I had a hard time with everyone staring at me when I was doing mundane things like going to the grocery store or the gym. But it's part of what I love, so I've accepted it."

"That seems wise. J.P. could never make his peace with those aspects of fame."

"He seems pretty content with his choice," Jake answered, turning on the blinker as he changed lanes.

She'd noticed that he never drove more than five miles per hour over the speed limit. Whenever they went out together, he obeyed pretty much every traffic sign.

"Are you being a good driver for me or is it your norm?" she asked him.

"I'm never in a hurry to get anywhere, so it's pretty much my normal." He rolled his shoulders like he was tense again.

"Well, if you want me to take over at any point, I'm happy to help."

"I've got it. I'm pretty used to being on the road.."

"Yeah, but normally you aren't the one driving the bus," she mused, fussing with her nails.

"I...ah...wanted to tell you that my appointment with your mama went real well yesterday," he said, ending his sentence by clearing his throat.

When she looked over, his hands were clutching the steering wheel so hard they were almost white. Now she understood his tension.

"I'm happy to hear that," she responded, waiting to

hear what else he planned to say. "I hope you know Mama would never breathe a word to me."

His laugh was harsh. "I do."

Rain began to spit on the windshield, and Jake turned on the wipers. The clouds in the west turned a menacing gray, but there was still a splash of sunlight coming through—almost like the heavens wouldn't let everything go dark.

They continued to talk about the music she liked—he was very curious about the artists she enjoyed—and she made sure to ask him what his favorite cities were to tour.

By the time they reached Sweetwater, she was thirsty and needed to use a bathroom again. They agreed to have lunch at a little place called Hunter's Bakery and Café, nestled in the corner of a large brick building.

"I'm a sucker for places like this," she said as he parked in front of it. When they reached the black and glass door, he opened it for her to enter.

The chandelier gave the red interior a warm glow. The hostess did a double take when she looked up from the seating chart to greet them. Her strawberry blond hair bounced when she jumped in place.

"Holy heavens! Jake Lassiter! Oh, my God." She took a couple of deep breaths, staring. "Oh, my *God!* Are you eating here?"

The restaurant wasn't full by any means, but every conversation died. There were some priceless looks in the dining room. One woman put a hand to her bosom as if Jesus himself had just walked through the front door while a teenage boy dropped his spoon into his soup, showering his T-shirt.

She could tell Jake was fighting a smile as he said, "I was planning on eating here, yes. Are you still serving?"

She looked to be all of nineteen years old, and from the stunned expression on her face, it was clear she'd lost all ability to think. "Ah...what?"

"I asked if you were still serving?" Jake repeated, the soul of patience.

"We sure are." She danced in place. "And if we weren't... well, of course we would be open for *you*. You're Jake Lassiter."

"I am that," Jake said, a polite smile on his face.

"Do you mind if I get your autograph? I'm your biggest fan. I mean...you're Jake Lassiter."

Leaning over the hostess podium, Jake grabbed a take-out menu and a pen. "What's your name?"

"Beth," she breathed out, crowding him as he wrote.

Susannah found it interesting Jake didn't call her "honey" or "darlin'" like she'd seen Rye do with fans. But then again, Jake was as different from Rye as chocolate cake was from strawberry pie.

Beth clutched the piece of paper to her chest for a moment before reading it aloud. "To Beth. Thanks for believing in my music. All the best, Jake." Then she pretty much melted. "Wow. I mean, *wow*. This is the best day of my life."

"I'm glad you're happy, Beth," Jake said, still acting like he had all the time in the world. "Which table do you recommend? This is a mighty pretty town. Perhaps one by the window?"

There was an open one in the front. Smart of him to steer Beth in the right direction. The poor girl needed it.

She gazed up at him adoringly. "You can sit *anywhere,* but the window does give you the best view of our town. Not that it's anything like Nashville or anything."

"Why don't you show us on over to that table then? I'm getting hungry, and I expect my friend is as well."

Beth gave her a measuring look—one filled with a touch of envy and inquiry. Susannah responded with a neutral smile.

"Sure thing, Jake," the hostess said as if they were best friends. "Come this way. I'll take real good care of you."

Susannah noticed Beth didn't include her, but it didn't bother her. She'd seen Tory become invisible to Rye's fans —almost like they didn't want to acknowledge her. Frankly, she would rather not be the recipient of that kind of adoration. It was a little freaky.

When Jake pulled out her chair and helped her get situated, she smiled at the other patrons in the restaurant who were watching them. A few were being discreet, but they had their phones out. Taking pictures, most likely.

"I'll be right back." Jake stood with his back to the restaurant, whispering so only she could hear him. "Best get this out of the way, or we won't eat in peace."

She simply nodded, and he gave her a wink.

He turned around and walked into the center of the restaurant. "Howdy folks. As some of you know, I'm Jake Lassiter. I've come to your town to go shopping with my decorator for my new house, and I'd really appreciate y'all making us feel welcome. If you're a fan, I'm happy to give you an autograph or take a picture now. That way my food won't grow cold when Beth brings it out for me. Seems a shame for good food to be treated that way."

People slowly rose, some blushing while others flat-out cooed like turtledoves. He smiled at the women who clutched him during pictures and listened attentively to everything his fans had to say. At one point, he called out to

Beth and said, "Can you get my friend a beverage? I expect she's thirsty from the drive."

His regard for her warmed her heart, and Susannah ordered a soft drink from a frazzled Beth, who couldn't take her eyes off her favorite star. By the time Jake returned to the table, he'd been gone for twenty minutes. Her stomach was growling.

"Sorry about that," he said, taking a seat. "If I hadn't indulged them, we would've been interrupted every five minutes.

"I didn't consider how challenging it might be for you to come here. Why didn't you mention it?"

"Because I don't let it stop me from doing what I want to do. I'm hoping people aren't texting their friends to tell them I'm in town, though. Otherwise, our shopping trip might be a bit challenging. But we'll make it work."

Beth appeared with menus, and Jake ordered a soft drink as well.

"Anything look good?" he asked Susannah.

The list of options was pretty impressive for a small town. "The burgers sound good. What about you?"

"A burger sounds good to me too," he answered, smiling when Beth brought his drink.

"Are you ready to order?" she asked, as eager as a cheerleader at Friday night football.

"We sure are," he said, handing her their menus.

They selected the same burger, and thankfully Beth didn't linger at the table although Susannah could tell she wanted to.

"I'm sorry I didn't introduce you by name," he said so only she could hear. "I didn't want to intrude on your privacy. You never know with people..."

"I appreciate that," she said, trying to ignore the

discomfort of being watched. "But you don't need to protect me."

"I know you can handle yourself. I just don't want anyone...saying anything or doing anything that might make you uncomfortable because of me. Most of my fans are great, don't get me wrong. But there's always the possibility of one rotten apple in the bunch making things difficult."

"J.P. used to say the same thing," she told him. "Not that he ever got to be famous like you and Rye."

"He would have if he'd pursued another record deal. Rye and I agree on that. Look at me. Not everyone needs to wiggle their butt to sell records. Not that I'm implying people only buy Rye's records because of his...ahem...sex appeal."

Her lips twitched. "But it helps."

He shrugged, and she found it interesting that he didn't seem to recognize his own sex appeal. Or perhaps he did, but he didn't like to talk about it. Well, neither would she. That was as clear a path to trouble as could be.

"Beth makes Shelby and Sadie seem like lukewarm fans," she mentioned. The girl was pretty much drooling from her perch at the hostess station. She obviously did double duty in the restaurant—either that or she'd insisted on waitressing their table.

"Yes, but I have a feeling your sisters might have given her a run for their money if J.P. hadn't talked to them."

"You're not wrong there," she said, chuckling. There was no way she was going to mention she'd also given them a talking-to.

Their burgers came, and the char and juiciness of the meat made her close her eyes in ecstasy.

"They certainly know how to cook a hamburger," she commented when she could finally focus.

He was staring at her with his cobalt blue eyes, and her hand froze mid-reach for a fry.

"You really are beautiful, you know."

He'd said it before, but she was still startled into speechlessness for a moment. "Thank you," she finally said.

"Had to be said," he mused, breaking eye contact and reaching for his hamburger. "This is real good. Let's hope the ice cream across the street is of similar quality."

She composed herself by eating another bite of her burger before responding. "Are we having ice cream?"

He gave her a lop-sided smile before popping a fry in his mouth. "I am. You're welcome to join in."

The rain wasn't overly unpleasant, but it was still cold out. A high of late forties if the weather report this morning had been right. "I'll pass. It's wintertime."

"Winter? Nah. We don't have winter down South. This is more like spring."

She narrowed her eyes at him. "Everything looks pretty dead to me, and I'm wearing a winter jacket." This morning she'd selected a lined rain coat in a rich plum that reached mid-thigh.

"We can find you something warm for dessert then," he said, seemingly obvious to the people watching them.

Had he learned to tune them out? Probably. Otherwise, it would drive him crazy. Heavens knew, it would drive her crazy if and when they started going out more. Of course, she would have to find a way to handle it to be with him.

"Maybe some hot apple pie," she suggested, imagining the caramelized apples and flaky crust. "I scanned the dessert menu."

"I like a woman who thinks ahead. Maybe they can add some ice cream to mine."

"For you, I bet Beth would find a cow, milk it, and make you homemade ice cream."

He leaned forward conspiratorially. "Best not say that too loud. She just might."

Laughing, Susannah resumed eating and polished off her plate before he did. Jake was right. He didn't hurry through much of anything.

Susannah spotted a young woman emerging from the kitchen. She was tall and curvy and had dishwater blond hair. Her hands were fisted against her stomach as she looked at Jake.

"I think you have another fan coming your way," she told him.

To give him credit, he didn't wince, but he didn't shift in his seat either. The woman made her halting way over to their table.

"Mr. Lassiter? I'm sorry to interrupt your meal, but my boss let me leave the kitchen since we're closed for lunch now."

"What can I do for you?" he asked, finally turning to face her.

"I'm Mary," she said, extending her hand, which Jake took without hesitation. "My brother is serving in Afghanistan. He's in the Army like you were. I was wondering if you'd be willing to give me an autograph that I can give him when he next comes home."

His smile immediately changed from polite to earnest. "Of course, Mary. What's your brother's name?"

"Howard, Mr. Lassiter. He's a huge fan of yours."

Her apron had a couple of oil spots and food stains on it, making Susannah guess she was one of the cooks.

"How many tours has your brother been on so far, Mary?" he asked.

"Three, sir," she said, extending a blank piece of paper and a pen.

God love her, the woman's hand was shaking something fierce. Jake wrote a longer note than he had done for anyone else in the restaurant.

"When was your brother home last?" he asked, handing the paper back to her.

She read the note, her eyes tearing up. "Oh, thank you, Mr. Lassiter. This means the world! Um...Howard was here for Thanksgiving this year. It was a blessing." She folded the paper, treating it like the finest china. "You should know that Howard says your music has helped him carry on when he's missing home or the friends he's lost over there. He says if you could get through it, so can he."

Jake's face crumbled, and an extra shine appeared in his eyes. "I'm mighty happy to hear my music inspires him. You tell him to make it home to y'all."

A lone tear streaked down her face as she nodded. "I know you're a famous country singer, but to me, you'll always be a great American hero. Thank you for serving our country, Mr. Lassiter."

Jake paused for a moment before saying, "I was only doing my part, Mary, just like Howard and everyone else."

The woman sniffed and wiped her nose. "He's a good man, sir. Like you are. Can I hug you?"

Jake didn't hesitate to push his chair back and stand. The young woman's arms wrapped around him, and Susannah heard her whisper, "Thank you. Thank you so much. This will give him another reason to come home to us."

Susannah fought tears herself as she watched them

embrace. She said a silent prayer that Howard would make it home unscathed.

"Thank you, Mary," Jake finally said, dropping his arms and stepping away.

The woman brushed at her tears. "God bless you, sir."

"And you and your brother," Jake said in a rough voice.

He didn't sit down again until Mary disappeared into the kitchen, and when he did, he let out a huge sigh.

She wanted to reach for his hand, but everyone was watching. "What does it feel like to be a hero to so many?"

He visibly shuddered. "I'm no hero, Susannah. I'm just a normal guy who served my country and has grown famous writing songs about it."

Her heart hurt, hearing that, but she knew there was no use arguing with him. "It's a blessing that your music touches people. I'd love to be in the room when she gives that autograph to Howard. What did you write to him, if you don't mind me asking?"

Clearing his throat, he reached for his soda and downed the remainder of it. "I told him to stay strong and know that people were praying for his return." His ears turned red. "I know you don't think I'm much of a religious man, but...it comforted me when I was on tour, hearing people were praying for me."

She dug her hands into her lap. "I don't know why you think I'd believe that of you."

"Because it's true," he said, the earlier light gone from his eyes. "Susannah, I have done things...unspeakable things. I'm no hero."

She didn't know how to help him see what was so obvious to everyone else. "I think you are, and so do a lot of people. I can't imagine what it must have been like over there, but I know you wouldn't have done any of those things if you'd had the choice. That's the difference between a good man and a bad one if you ask me."

He rubbed his forehead. "We should probably get shopping." Turning around in his seat, he waved at Beth, who ran forward. "Can we get the check?"

She beamed as she shook her head. "The owner said it's on the house. For serving our country."

Jake blew out another breath. "Well, at least let me leave you a tip then for your kind service." Digging into his wallet, he drew out a wad of twenties.

Beth picked the bills up and squealed. "Oh, Jake, you're just the best!"

There was a polite smile on his face as he rose again and walked over to assist Susannah out of her chair. He helped her on with her coat, which made her feel cared for. She wasn't going to mention they'd discussed having pie when he clearly wanted to leave.

"Thanks again for the autograph," Beth said, trailing after them as they walked out.

Jake waved to the remaining patrons, who'd lingered over their meal. Mary stood in the doorway to the kitchen. She gave him a teary-eyed smile, and Jake stopped for a moment. They shared a look, and Susannah wondered if they were both thinking about what it meant for someone to return home from war.

Then Jake seemed to shake himself. He held open the door for her and closed it firmly behind them after they left. There were more people outside, waiting for him. So someone had squealed.

He took her elbow. "Let's make a beeline for one of the shops. Maybe they'll give me a break for once."

For a man who professed not to be in a hurry, he picked up his pace. She had to rush to keep up with his long legs.

They entered Cooney's Corner, which was housed in another old brick building. The green awning gave a welcome respite from the drizzle wetting her hair. The shop was warm inside, and it sold everything from bureaus seasoned from use to antique medicine bottles. Jake leaned down to pet the black Labrador that greeted them at the door as he perused the Coca Cola signs on the wall. He let out another breath, and she wondered why he was edging away from the dog so quickly. The owners watched them surreptitiously but gave them space.

Even though Jake made a show of looking at the wares, she knew his heart wasn't in this shopping trip any more.

When she walked past a ten-foot stuffed brown bear with super scary claws, she nudged him in the ribs. "If I were your other decorator, I would have this paid for and put in your truck before you could blink."

But her joke didn't even prompt a smile.

He studied the old records on the wall and picked one up. Holding it out to her, he forced a smile. "Hank Williams' classic album, *Ramblin' Man.* I like the idea of having a cluster of these on display."

The shopkeepers had arranged the vinyl albums on the wall minus the album covers. "We could do that," she said as he wandered off again.

He made a valiant effort of selecting a few things, but when he paid, he didn't engage the shopkeepers in their stories before pocketing his wallet and picking up the carefully-wrapped packages.

"Would you like to call it a day?" she asked as she hurried after him toward the truck.

Glancing over his shoulder, he gave her a puzzled look. "Why?"

"You don't seem as enthused as you were when we

arrived," she said cautiously. "We don't have to keep going. Or at least you don't have to on my account."

"I'm fine," he said tersely and unlocked the truck and stored his purchases.

From there, they visited Bobby Todd's Antiques, which was more upscale. Jake walked through the shop after nodding to the shopkeeper, but he didn't find anything he liked, so they moved on to the next shop, The Robin's Nest. Susannah loved the old hardwood floors and wood paneling, made all the warmer by the soft light coming from the shop's well-executed lighting.

"I have a feeling you're going to find something here," she said with extra enthusiasm.

Jake had said very little since they'd left Cooney's Corner, and she couldn't help but wonder if he was mad at her for suggesting they cut the day short. Had it been wrong of her to point out his obvious distress?

"Let's see if you're right," he said, walking through the shop, not waiting for her.

He moved with determination, his usual mode of lingering over items a thing of the past. She gave him space, her solar plexus tight. She wished she could ask him why his interaction with Mary had upset him so.

He pointed to a gleaming oak farm table. "I like this for the dining room. It's not stuffy."

"It's a beautiful piece," she said, eyeing the well-varnished planks. "And it expands if you have company."

"Can you find some chairs?" he asked crisply.

She fought the hurt she felt from his tone. "Of course. I'll add it to my list of things for the house."

He stalked away, and she stayed where she was a moment to take in deep, calming breaths before seeking out the shopkeeper to arrange for the table to be wrapped up to protect it from the rain. Jake's truck would accommodate it, but she didn't know if he had a tarp handy. Not that he needed to fuss with any of that right now. He selected a rocking chair that he said reminded him of his grandmother's favorite chair, and she could tell from the softness in his voice that she was gone and he'd been fond of her.

With quick efficiency, he paid for everything and helped the shopkeeper heft the goods out to his truck after pulling into a parking spot in front of the store. People were still milling around on the street, taking pictures of him.

She watched him secure the pieces with bungee cords.

"I don't think I can fit much more in the back," he said to her, not meeting her eyes. "We'd best head back."

"All right," she said quietly and went around to the passenger door. It was going to be a long drive home.

He slammed his door behind him and shoved the car into gear. Then he backed up with more force than needed and punched the gas, taking them out of the town limits. When he reached the interstate, he turned up the radio, making conversation impossible. Not that she wanted to converse with him right now.

She had no idea what to say.

13

J ake stared out the windshield, dimly aware of the vehicles driving alongside him. The roads were slick, so he was present enough to keep to the speed limit, but that was about it. He'd felt himself slipping after lunch. Meeting Mary and hearing her call him a hero had shaken him to the core, and then Susannah had gone and agreed with the woman. The glass wall of past regrets had entombed him again. Though Susannah was just inches away from him in the passenger seat, she might as well have been on the other side of the world.

He couldn't reach out to her.

He couldn't even reach himself right now.

The rain began to pelt the truck, so hard it sounded like a million bullets were hitting the top of the cab. His pulse started to race, and his breathing accelerated. The noise buffeted his ears. He slowed down and fumbled with the knob to increase the speed of the window wipers, keeping a vigilant eye on the tail lights ahead.

The need to protect Susannah kicked in. She was in his

care, and he couldn't let her down. The image of Booker dying in his arms flashed into his mind, and for a moment everything went black.

"Jake," Susannah said urgently.

He shook his head like he was shaking off the rain and noticed the car ahead of them had braked to a halt. He hit the brakes hard, jarring them both in their seats. Someone honked from behind, ratcheting up his nerves.

His heart thundered in his chest. Susannah was speaking to him, but he couldn't hear it over the din of the rain pelting the truck's topper.

Then a soft hand touched him.

The gentleness of the gesture made the noise recede in volume some. Then her hand rubbed his forearm in easy circles.

"Jake," she said, her voice urgent again.

Another honk punctuated his consciousness, and he swung his head around toward the sound.

"Stop honking at me!" he yelled.

"Don't worry about him," Susannah said, still stroking his arm. "Stop the car now. Jake, look at me."

There was an unusual quality of steel in her voice, and he responded to the order without question.

"Pull over and let me drive the rest of the way." She flipped the hazards on.

He slowly processed her request. She wanted to drive. Now that her hand was stroking his arm, he could feel some of his body, but not all of it. She was right. He was in no condition to continue.

"You need to be safe."

"I am safe," she said softly, a balm to his ears after the honking. "You just need a break. I'll tell you when the lane's clear so you can go to the shoulder."

THE PROMISE OF RAINBOWS

She kept her hand on him as she watched the cars. That simple touch made the glass feel thinner, but he was still scared to move from the lane. The paralysis tore through him. What if he crashed into another car and killed her? What if another car crashed into them when he wasn't looking?

"I...can't do this," he rasped out, gripping the wheel.

After adjusting the seatbelt, she rose onto her knees and put her hands on his shoulders, looking straight into his eyes. "Repeat after me. I can do this."

Her hands grounded him, and more glass fell away, crashing to the ground in broken shards. "I can do this," he repeated hoarsely.

"Okay," she said in a strong voice, her green eyes never leaving his face. "When I tell you to move over, you do it. Okay? I won't let you down."

No she wouldn't. He would go through an enemy door with her at his back.

"Now turn on your right blinker and wait for my signal."

He did as she bid. Another car honked as it went by, and he shuddered at the noise.

"Stay with me, Jake. Ignore them." She was on her haunches, scanning the lane next to them. "Okay, ease over."

"*I can do this.*" He had to get her to safety.

"That's it. Just keep edging over," she said in that same tough voice. "They're going to let you over."

The rain was coming down harder now. He wanted to wipe the sweat dripping in his eyes, but he couldn't take his hands off the steering wheel.

"Keep going, Jake," she said, her hand returning to his shoulder. "You're almost there."

He inched over, and it felt like an eternity had passed by the time he put the truck in park. He slumped in his seat as emotion rolled through him.

She heaved out a breath, rubbing his shoulder briskly now. "Good job. Now, I'll switch with you."

His body refused to move as she left the truck to come around to the driver's side. When she opened the door, she had to lean over him to unbuckle his seatbelt. His hands still had a white-knuckle grip on the steering wheel, and she rubbed them until he released it.

"I'm sorry," he said in a hoarse voice. "*I'm so sorry.*"

She wrapped her arms around him. "Don't be. Not for a moment."

Raindrops fell onto him, and he realized the door was still open. "You're getting soaked."

"I'll dry," she said, holding him like a mama bear might. With all her strength. God knew he needed it now, even though he was awash in shame. The cold air helped clear his head, and he realized how close he'd come to the edge again—after all this time.

God, he'd almost gotten them both killed.

He dug deep for the strength, but she didn't let go of him. She wouldn't. It was like she knew their connection was the only thing keeping him from falling back behind the glass. It took effort to swing his legs out of the truck, and he found his knees were weak from the adrenaline fall-out. God, he was such a baby.

He stomped the ground to feel his feet—something one of his psychiatrists had suggested—and blood seemed to surge into his legs. He strode around the hood of the truck, dimly aware that Susannah was holding his arm and walking beside him as he made his way to the passenger side.

His hand fumbled with the door, so she brushed it aside and opened it for him. He took his seat. The seatbelt might as well have been child proof, it took him so long to secure the buckle. Somewhere in the back of his mind, he noticed Susannah situating herself in the driver's side, adjusting the seat and the mirrors. All he wanted to do was disappear.

Soft skin touched his cheek, and he looked up. She was gazing at him again with those luminous moss-green eyes, concern etched on her face. The warmth of her palm was a comfort. More glass shattered and fell away.

"It's going to be okay," she said softly, breaking the last of the glass surrounding his heart.

Pain shot through his chest. "No. No, it's not. I almost got you killed."

"Don't you dare say that. You got upset. It happens to everyone."

Shaking his head in disagreement, he said, "This does not happen to everyone. Welcome to the horrible underbelly of PTSD. I'm so sorry you had to see me like this."

Strong hands lifted his face until they were once again eye to eye. "Jake, I was not in danger of dying. Neither were you. We were only going thirty miles an hour. If anything had happened, it would have been a simple fender bender. But nothing did happen."

His mind conjured up dramatic images like the fuel tank exploding on impact or a semi ramming into them from behind and crunching their vehicle.

"I let you down," he said with a burn in his throat. Just like he had done with Booker.

"Jake," she said, a steely command. "You listen to me. You did not let me down or put me in danger. Part of this is my fault. I knew you were upset, but I didn't know what to say. That won't happen again. I'm going to listen to my instincts."

"There won't be a next time," he ground out, knowing it had to be that way. "You need to run away from me. Someone else can finish the house. I'm only going to drag you down."

"That's total bullshit," she said in a tone angry enough to break through his funk.

"I didn't know you swore."

"Only when the situation demands it," she said, her hands coming to rest on his shoulders. "I am *not* letting anyone else decorate your house. And I sure as hell am not running away from you because you had a bad moment. And Jake, you are *not* going to drag me down. I wish you'd stop believing that. I'm a hell of a lot stronger than that."

The fire in her voice cleared his head even more. She was dead serious, and he was relieved. This situation wasn't going to make her run, although God knew it should.

"I'm going to drive us back to your house," she told him. "You can either sit there and count all the blessings you have in your life or you can call my mama and talk to her about what happened."

He couldn't call her mama in front of her. It was one thing for her to see his shame. It was another to have her know the reasons behind it. "I'll sit here."

She ran her eyes over him, as if conducting a final inspection on the state of his health. Then she cupped his cheek again. Her green eyes were wet with tears, he realized.

"Don't you ever tell me to run away from you again or that you let me down," she whispered.

His throat closed, and darn it all if tears didn't pop into his eyes too. He nodded, but as she put the car in gear, he wasn't sure if he could keep that promise.

14

Susannah prayed the whole way back to Jake's house. He pretty much stared out the window. She turned on NPR at one point to fill the silence, but he mumbled, "Sorry," and flicked it off. Only then did she remember reading that people with PTSD were sensitive to noise.

When they arrived at his house, he told her to take them around to the back. He hit the garage door opener on the windshield.

"Go ahead and pull in," he muttered.

There were three four-wheelers inside the garage, and a line of fishing poles were suspended from one of the side walls. A tackle box rested on a counter beneath them. She turned off the engine and watched as Jake pushed himself out of the car with the energy of an old man. Taking a breath, she unbuckled her seatbelt and left the truck. He was standing at the rear, looking at his feet.

"Let me help you carry these things inside," she said, feeling at sea again.

"I can get them later," he said, still not looking at her. "You go on home. Thanks again for your help earlier."

The words sounded as if they were being rolled across sandpaper. He turned to walk away from her, and that's when she realized what she had to do.

She lurched forward and grabbed his hand.

He jumped a foot, but she only gripped it harder. He shifted on his feet until they were facing each other. His tired cobalt blue eyes fixed on her face.

"If you think I'm going to just get in my car and leave you, you're crazy."

His hand went lax in hers, like he was trying to let go, but it only made her more determined. If there was one thing she'd learned, it was that holding his hand connected them. Right now he needed to be connected to someone.

"I'm fine, Susannah," he said, releasing a giant gust of air. "You can go."

She shook her head and stepped closer to him. His whole body tensed, whether from fear or rejection or touch, she couldn't be sure. She only knew she needed to reach him, and if touching him was the only way to remind him that he was whole, then she would touch him but good.

Gripping his one hand so hard he couldn't let go, she lifted the other and traced his jawline. It locked, and he closed his eyes.

"Don't," he whispered, agony lacing his voice. *"Please."*

Her heart felt crushed under the weight of his despair. "Look at me, Jake."

He squeezed his eyes shut, like he was fighting her, but she only cupped his cheek—like she had done when they were in the truck. He swallowed thickly.

"Look at me," she repeated more forcefully.

Finally he looked at her, but he ducked his head. "I don't want you to see me like this."

Her heart broke clean in half. She nestled close to him and rose on her tiptoes to press her cheek against his. "There is nothing wrong with you. You don't have *anything* to be ashamed of."

Their hold was awkward, but he finally clenched the hand she'd so determinedly clutched. They held each other that way as the rain continued to fall outside. His heart pounded against her chest, a sure sign of his distress. Then he pressed his face into her neck in surrender, and she was lost. The tears she'd been fighting since Sweetwater started to fall.

He must have felt the wetness on his skin because he darted back. "I made you cry."

"I'm crying for you," she said, baring herself to the truth —a truth he needed to hear right now. "I can't imagine what things must have been like..."

"That doesn't excuse what happened."

She disagreed. He couldn't hear that right now, but maybe the truth of it would penetrate if she said it enough. "Let's go inside. We both could use something warm after all that rain."

His steps were reluctant, but he let her lead him to the side door to the house. She kept a hold of his hand as they entered the mudroom and walked down the hallway to the kitchen.

"Do you want tea or coffee?" she asked him, leading him to the pantry.

"I don't have any tea," he said, his boots scraping the kitchen tiles.

Of course he didn't. Not many single men kept a supply of it. "Coffee then."

He had an Italian coffee maker in the corner of the counter closest to the stainless steel sink. She kept hold of his hand as she crossed to it.

"Are you ever going to let go of my hand?" he asked, following her.

Since she wasn't sure he would stay with her if she did, she shook her head. "Not yet. Making coffee is going to be a two-person job this time."

He didn't fight her. The process was awkward, and it took a bit longer than it might have otherwise, but soon they had coffee percolating.

"Now for the mugs," she told him.

This time, he led her to the cabinet over the dishwasher and removed two plain white mugs one at a time. She nearly smiled. While she thought it might be safe to release his hand now, she found that she didn't want to. He was still vulnerable, and if she were being honest, so was she.

When the coffee reached the end of the brewing cycle, they walked over to the station, each holding a cup. Taking turns, they poured the coffee and then walked over to his new kitchen table. It was a simple mahogany with a beautiful grain. It had immediately caught his eye in the Nashville showroom she'd taken him to. The taupe upholstered chairs kept things casual and comfortable, like he preferred.

They didn't release their grip on each other's hands as they sat beside each other on those taupe chairs. Susannah's hand was starting to cramp, but she didn't care. She brought their connected hands to rest on her thigh. There was nothing sexual in the gesture. She only wanted to be close to him, and since he wasn't as tense as he'd been before, she knew he didn't want to be far from her either.

They drank their coffee in the quiet kitchen. Usually she took cream and sugar in hers since black was too strong, but there was no way she was going to lead him across the kitchen again like a chain gang.

She could feel him gathering himself beside her, and she prayed for the right words when he broke the silence.

He set his mug aside and squeezed her hand. "I'm fine now. Really."

He *was* better, but he was far from fine. "I'm glad, but I think I'll just keep you company a while longer." A dark thought entered her mind—one she was scared to voice. Would it be safe to leave him alone after what had happened? She'd asked her mama for a little reading on PTSD, but none of the materials had prepared her for today.

Was he feeling equally at sea? She expected he must be since he'd told her to all but run. She might as well put it out there carefully because if she didn't, she didn't know how to help him.

"So this has happened before..." she said gently.

He pushed the mug forward a couple of inches, playing with the handle. "Yeah, but not for a long time. Mostly I suffer from nightmares, but they...don't come all the time. This...I feel like I'm back to square one again. Every time I have an episode like this, I'm afraid my PTSD won't ever go away."

The despair lacing his voice pierced her heart anew. "You're not back to square one," she said, hoping she was saying the right thing. "Do you know what triggered it? It seems...um...related to the young woman from the restaurant."

"So it would seem," he agreed, his jaw tight.

Best to look him straight in the eye. She put her mug down and swiveled in her chair to face him, rearranging their joined hands to rest on her knees. He stared at their hands while she scanned his face. His mouth was pressed firmly together, like he was struggling with himself.

"Tell me what I can do to help you. I want to, but I don't...well...want to make things worse by saying or asking things that will dredge up more pain."

He took a couple of deep breaths before answering, "You've already helped, Susannah, and for that, I'm grateful. Not many people would have hung in there with me. Not that you had much choice, what with us being in the center lane on the highway."

"It wouldn't have mattered if we'd been in the center lane or on..." She tried to think of something more outrageous. "A submarine. I still would have stayed with you. It's what..." She trailed off. She'd been about to say, *It's what friends do for each other.* But he was so much more than that. So, she said instead, "It's what you do when you care about someone."

"You shouldn't say that to me." He lowered his head and rested it on their joined hands on her knee. "I'm messed up, Susannah."

She would have to trust her mama to help him, but right now, she could do her part. Leaning over, she pressed her cheek against his back. "You're *not* messed up. Not to me. What you've done is heroic, fighting over there and then coming back here to start over in a completely different profession."

"I couldn't fight anymore," he whispered harshly. "The cost was too high."

"It's okay," she said, knowing it wasn't—not for him, not after today. She still wanted to ask why he didn't see himself as a hero, why that young woman's request for an autograph for her brother had triggered him. But she didn't. She'd leave the questions to her mama, who was better equipped.

That didn't mean she couldn't provide comfort. She was good at comforting, and right now, he needed it. She raised his head and kissed his cheek, feeling a trace of wetness there. Was he crying? Her whole body tensed. Men crying simply slayed her.

"Come here," she said, nestling closer.

He leaned back until they were only inches apart. She pulled on her left hand, and he let it go. She traced his jaw. Something like wonder flashed in his eyes, almost like a falling star flashing across the heavens. A current of power surged between them, adding to the warmth created by their connection. She found herself touching his lips with her fingers. Their eyes locked together.

"There's *nothing* wrong with you," she whispered.

The pull between their bodies grew heavier, and she found herself closing the final distance between them. She kissed his lips softly, hearing his surprised inhale of breath and feeling the jump of his muscles under her fingertips.

"Susannah," he uttered harshly, his grip on her hand almost painful now.

Unable to resist the need to comfort him, she flowed into him, kissing his mouth again, his jaw, and his cheek—first the right one and then the left.

He nestled closer. "You shouldn't touch me."

Since his actions were at odds with his words, she continued to rub the back of his neck with her free hand and press gentle kisses to his jaw. When she returned to his mouth, he turned his head, and their lips met full on. The softness of them had her sighing.

And just that simply, they were kissing each other.

He finally released her hand and wrapped both arms

around her, pulling her onto his lap. His mouth took hers in heated passes, and for a woman who hadn't been kissed much, she was stunned by the power of this connection. Their hands had been one thing, but their lips...

His body heat surrounded her. His hands came up to cradle her head as he kissed her and kissed her and kissed her. She lay against his arms, her legs trailing over his thigh like she was lounging on a sofa bed. She had a moment to be thankful she wasn't straddling him. That would be too much, too soon. For both of them.

Her hands smoothed the tense muscles of his back as he flicked the seam of her mouth with his tongue. She knew what he wanted, and she opened for him. This kiss punched through her system, heating her blood, tightening areas of her body that were unaccustomed to passion. Then he softened his kiss and led her in what she could only decipher as a passionate dance, one she willingly followed.

When he gripped her hip, she found herself moaning into his mouth. A jolt passed through him, one she felt down to her toes. Her lips softened under his, and then his mouth was gone. She opened her eyes, which had fluttered shut some time back from the onslaught of sensation, only to discover his beautiful face in agony.

She touched his cheek, hoping to comfort him, and he met her gaze. The look in his eyes was like lightning striking a tree, summoning an answering fire in her.

"This wasn't how I wanted our first kiss to be," he said harshly, shifting her on his lap.

She realized he must be uncomfortable, but she was terrified to allow more distance between them. He settled her onto his knees, and she could feel him retreating again.

"It was a beautiful first kiss," she said, stroking his face.

He let out a harsh breath. "It shouldn't have happened

after today. Heck, it probably shouldn't have happened at all."

"Don't start all that talk again," she said, cupping his face. "Look at me."

Those cobalt blues had lost some of their heat, but they still radiated a powerful vulnerability. "This isn't a good idea. After today...I'm worse off than before."

"You let my mama be the judge of that," she said, putting some steel back into her voice since he seemed to respond to it. "You'll go see her, and you will overcome this, Jake. Look how far you've come."

"How do you know how far I've come?" he asked with suspicion in his voice.

"I've read a little about PTSD, and if you've had any of the symptoms—"

"I've had *all* of them, Susannah."

The way he emphasized that word sent ribbons of fear through her belly. Had he considered suicide then? She was too afraid to ask. "But you've overcome so much. To make your living by going on stage night after night is an incredible feat for someone with PTSD."

"You have no idea," he ground out. "I used to throw up before I went on stage, at break, and when I walked off. The crowd noise was pure torture at first, notwithstanding the crush of people. It was..." A shudder ran through his frame.

"And yet you do it all the time now," she said, trying to encourage him.

"I still have a recurring nightmare, Susannah. A horrible one. One that makes me throw up. One that makes me keep the lights on at night."

Her chest tightened from that revelation. What must it be like for a grown man, a military man, to admit to having to keep the lights on after a nightmare?

"You haven't asked me out because of all this," she concluded. "Am I right?"

"I promised myself I wouldn't drag you down. My daddy and my brother have PTSD, but they won't get help. I've seen the toll it takes on a family."

She was starting to see the light now. He'd been exposed to PTSD as a child, and now he'd experienced it personally. "But you *have* been getting help. You're different than they are."

"Sometimes I wonder about that," he admitted in a harsh tone. "Susannah, I don't want to hurt you with all this. I'm broken."

"Stop saying that. I care about you." She ran her hands up and down his arms. "Don't turn away from me. What's between us...when you first held my hand..."

"I felt it too," he admitted, his eyes narrowing. "From the start. But that doesn't mean I'm good for you."

"You are good for me, Jake." She knew it in her soul.

He waved a hand at himself. "Not like this."

His heels were digging into the ground again. "Does my mama feel it's okay for you to date me?"

For a moment, the kitchen was completely silent save for the ticking of the retro wall clock he'd selected last week on one of their shopping sprees. She waited for him to answer, praying he would.

"She did before today," he finally said.

Susannah took a deep breath. "Would you call her right now to see if she'll meet with you tomorrow? I...don't want to meddle...but I think it would be a good idea."

"I'll call her in the morning. It's late. She's not in the office."

Since he didn't argue about making the call, she knew today's attack had scared him. "I have her cell."

"Okay," he said with a sigh. "She gave me her cell number at Rye's house, but I don't like bothering her after office hours."

"My mama doesn't keep office hours, she's fond of saying. When people need her, she's there for them."

Digging out his phone, he made the call. He gave a brief and apologetic greeting and then launched into a quick version of what had happened earlier. "I'm with your daughter," he added. Then he said, "Yes, ma'am" about four times, and a short while later he ended the call.

"I'm seeing Louisa at eight in the morning." He set his phone on the table and pushed it away.

"Good." Mama had moved her prayer breakfast back just like Susannah had thought she would. "When you meet with her, I want you to ask her if she still thinks you should go out with me. Will you abide by her wisdom?"

"I don't know if it's wisdom or folly," he muttered.

"*Jake.*"

His mouth tightened. "All right. I'll ask her, but there are some things you don't know."

Her belly quivered in fear. There was no doubt he had many secrets, ones she probably didn't want to hear. But if he wanted to share them, she would listen. "Does my mama know them?"

"Some of them," he admitted after a time. "Not all."

"Then you tell her what she needs to know, and you tell me what you think I need to know. I trust you both."

"You shouldn't place yourself in my hands," he said, looking away from her.

"You should trust yourself more," she said softly. "*I* do."

"That's a mistake." He exhaled sharply. "PTSD strips away all the trust you ever had in yourself and then some. It's like..."

When he broke off, she caressed his face. "It's like what?"

"It's like I become a different person," he admitted harshly. "Someone I hate being, and I can't make him go away."

She'd seen shades of it today, from the man who'd closed down emotionally to the one too paralyzed to change lanes on the highway. "That's not your fault."

"And yet it puts you at risk. You and anyone else close to me."

"That's crap," she said boldly. "Have you ever, in all your time of dealing with your PTSD, thought of hitting another person? Be honest with me. I think we're past the point of telling tales."

He sighed. "Not a woman. My shrinks called me one of the protective types. I want to defend the people I care about more than I want to lash out at them. When I first got out, I had the urge to hit a guy for talking smack to a girl I was seeing. But I didn't."

"Then I don't see why you should be worried," she said calmly. "I'm not."

"You don't know..."

"Jake, I'm not scared of you." And she meant every word.

He gently set her down on the opposite chair and stood. "Well, I'm scared enough of the other Jake for both of us."

She was silent for a moment, and so was he. Now that he had an appointment with her mama, she could leave. But there was no way she was going to do that just yet.

"You don't have to babysit me," he all but growled.

She decided to ignore that. "How about we order in and watch a movie? It's suppertime."

"I'm not hungry." His mouth flattened. "You should go home."

She decided to try another tactic. "Didn't we just have our first kiss? You'd think you could buy me dinner and watch a movie with me."

Part of her was surprised at herself. Where was she getting all this boldness?

"This is the worst first date on the planet." His dramatic eye roll punctuated his feelings on the matter.

"So there's room for improvement."

He pointed his finger at her. "I need to do some thinking after today—independent of what your mama thinks about us dating. It's been...intense."

"That's a good idea." Intense seemed a tame word if you asked her. "What would you like to order?" she asked, standing up.

"Are you really hungry?" he asked, scanning her face.

She didn't think she could force down a bite, but maybe if she ordered something, he would eat. That would be a step in the right direction, wouldn't it? "I could eat. How about BBQ?"

"Fine," he said without enthusiasm.

She extended her hand to him, and he took it after a few moments, making her breathe a sigh of relief.

"Are you planning on holding my hand for the rest of the evening?"

"You can bet on it," she answered, making herself smile.

15

When Mama called at eight o'clock at night and said, "Text your sister, Susannah, and tell her that you're praying for her," Shelby listened. Those words meant it was time for their family to circle the wagons around one of their own.

Of course, Mama didn't give one teeny weensy hint about what she knew, but Shelby expected it had to be something with Jake. What in the world was going on?

She immediately texted Susannah. And then she stewed. Had Mama called anyone else? She wished she'd thought to ask.

Worry wedged under her breastbone as she fiddled with the papers on her office desk. She'd worked late after a long business lunch with Gail, who seemed to be doing better. She'd brandished her rust-colored pill bottle of Lipitor in one of Nashville's finest restaurant and announced rather loudly she was taking care of her cholesterol. Since Gail was a well-known figure in Nashville, plenty of people had taken notice, and she'd left with a pleased smile on her face.

Her fiddling didn't help much. Most days it looked like a tornado had blown across her desk. Shelby liked it that way. Her numbers were all around her—like they were swirling inside her head. Sometimes she felt like she could dance with them, she saw them so clearly.

Of course she'd never told another soul about that. It would make her sound as loony as Lavender May, their old neighbor growing up who liked to wear real bird nests in her Sunday church hats because she said, "Jesus liked him some birds." Personally Shelby thought the woman was taking Matthew 6:26, the Bible verse about God caring for the birds, way too far.

Tidying the mess gave her something to do as she watched the clock. She was closer to Susannah's townhouse from her office, so if she didn't hear from her sister in twenty minutes, she could head over. She was mostly finished anyway.

But tidying her desk got old real fast, so Shelby's thoughts turned to the one that had been pressing on her heart and mind. Since her conversation with Gail in her office, Shelby hadn't been able to stop thinking about her daddy's medical history. For all she knew, she was a ticking time bomb like Gail had been before her diagnosis.

During lunch with Gail, Shelby had asked for the woman's opinion on her using a private investigator since it had been her idea. Gail had immediately recommended Vander Montgomery, assuring Shelby he was the best P.I. in the city and easy on the eyes to boot. She'd used him on more than one occasion, but refrained from explaining why beyond the issue with her ex. It had been hard not to press her out of curiosity. Gail could be mysterious sometimes.

After clicking on Vander's website link, Shelby had to admit Gail was right about him being dreamy. Good Lord, with a name and a face like that, he could play a starring role in a TV show. He didn't sport a mustache like Magnum P.I., thank God, but he had the same thick, dark curly hair. His eyes were a shade between green and blue. She'd call them aqua if she had to pick, rather like the Caribbean waters in all those vacation ads. His lips were full. Yum. But he didn't smile. In fact, he was downright serious.

She remembered she was supposed to be fussing about Susannah and immediately felt guilty.

Then she saw one of his endorsements was from the now-mayor of their fine city. Another was from Donald Blanders, the CEO of Giant Inc., whom she respected. No wonder Gail used him. *Vander* wasn't just a pretty face. Not that Gail would hire a moron.

She wasn't ready to hire him today, so she clicked off his website, rubbing the tightness in her chest with her free hand. This would be a big step, and she wanted a little more time to make sure it was in the right direction.

She jumped when her phone rang. Snatching it up, she saw that it was Sadie.

"Hey, girl," she answered.

"Did Mama call you?" her sister asked, her voice full of intrigue.

"You mean about prayer texting Susannah?"

"Yes. Goodness, it gave me a fright, having Mama call me like that. She hasn't used the Sibling Hotline for a while now."

"No," she said. The last time it had been used was after someone broke into Rye's house while Tammy and the kids were staying there.

"I'm driving over to her place now," Sadie said. "I left my date early. Not that it was much of a date."

She could ask her sister about the guy she'd seen later. "It has to be about Jake, don't you think?"

"I used my phone to search for news on him while my date took care of the bill. Nothing popped up, but I found a few tweets about him having lunch and going antique shopping in Sweetwater today. Susannah must have gone with him, right?"

Who needed to hire a P.I. when there was Sadie? "I expect she would."

"I also found some pics on Instagram, and Jake didn't look himself. I mean, he was smiling in some, but he looked downright weird in a few of them if you ask me."

Had something happened on the trip? "Sweetwater's pretty far away," Shelby said, tapping her foot. "Susannah didn't tell me they were taking a road trip. You don't think they were in a car accident, do you?"

"No, Mama would have told us that," her sister immediately assured her. "Do you think Mama called J.P.?"

"Let's find out." She dialed her brother on her office phone and put both siblings on speaker.

"Hey, Shelby," he said, picking up on the first ring. "Do you know something about Susannah?"

"So Mama called you too? Sadie is on my other line, by the way, listening."

"Hey, J.P.," Sadie said. "I'm more than a little worried here."

"Me too," her brother said, his voice heavy with concern. "I texted Susannah. And then I texted Jake to see if he knew anything. Neither of them responded."

Right. J.P. would have Jake's cell number since they worked together. "I bet it involves Jake. Mama doesn't cause alarm for nothing. What did she tell you?"

"To text Susannah and to ask Tammy and the kids to send up some extra prayers," he told them.

Goodness. "Sadie, tell him where they went today."

She fiddled with a pen while her sister recounted what she'd discovered on social media. Why hadn't she thought to look there herself?

When Sadie finished, her brother said, "Do you think we should swing by her house?"

"I'm turning onto her street now," Sadie said. "Her car isn't here, and the lights are out."

"J.P. Do you want to swing by Jake's house?" Shelby suggested, worry racing through her now. "Maybe she's there."

"I thought about it," he said, "but I wanted to call y'all first to see what you were thinking. I had a hunch Mama must have called you too. I'm not sure I should go over to Jake's if Susannah's there. Whatever happened...well, they might need to be together uninterrupted."

If she hadn't been so worried, Shelby would have fanned herself. *Together. Uninterrupted.* Two words guaranteed to inflame a girl's sensibilities. Heavens to Betsy, but Mama wouldn't text them about prayers if they were together in *that* sense. Mama frowned on that sort of thing before marriage.

"But what if she's not with him?" Shelby asked, playing devil's advocate.

"Then she'll text us when she can," J.P. said calmly.

"I don't like waiting, especially if she's in trouble," Sadie said. "Plus I texted *and* called her."

Sadie could be such a stalker. "How many did you leave?"

"Three voicemails and five texts. I even used Philippians 4:13."

Shelby gasped. "Not Philippians 4:13." You didn't bring out *I can do all things through Him who strengthens me* unless it was an emergency. "We need to find her stat."

"Now, y'all settle down," J.P. said in his sister-soother voice. "No need to get riled up when we don't know what's going on."

Sometimes she hated how he was the sole voice of reason. "J.P., I know you mean well, but Mama riled me up something fierce. Do you really expect me to simply kick up my heels and wait for Susannah to get back to me?"

"Yeah," Sadie shot out in solidarity. "Do you?"

He sighed on the line. "I'll meet you in front of the road to Jake's house. We can walk down the lane until we can see his driveway. That way we won't interrupt them if they want to be alone together."

"You want us to walk down his lane in the dark?" Sadie asked. "It's winter. J.P., you must be plumb crazy."

"If we drive all the way to the front of his house and she's not there, what do you plan to tell him when he sees us? Because I can guarantee you that he'll hear a car approaching. It's one of the benefits of living in the country."

"Maybe you can tell him we were going for some ice cream and wanted to see if he'd like to join us," Shelby suggested.

"Didn't I just say it's winter, Shelby?" Sadie said with a tsk. "It's too cold to eat ice cream."

Sadie could be so literal sometimes. "Fine. We're going for a drink. Good heavens, Sadie, it doesn't need to be as serious as the writing of The Declaration Of Independence. Stop overthinking things."

"Stop being ugly to me," her sister fired back.

"Girls," J.P. said. "I'm not going anywhere near Jake's property if you don't stop your squabbling."

Squabbling, huh? Shelby crossed her arms, but she did take a few deep breaths to calm herself. Sadie could work her up something fierce.

"I'm going to call Jake again," J.P. said, "and if he doesn't answer, I'll swing by his house and see if Susannah is there. I'll call you and tell you what I find out."

"You mean you're going without us?" Sadie asked.

"I live two miles away from the guy," J.P. said, his tone as aggrieved as it ever got.

"But she's our sister too," Shelby said, proud of the pouty voice she was able to roll out on command.

"All right," he said with a sigh. "I know when not to argue with y'all. I'll wait for you by the road to his house— like I said. But if this turns into a spectacle, and we embarrass Jake, I'm going to hold you both personally responsible."

"I'll text you when I reach Dare River," Shelby said, eying the clock on her computer. "I'm leaving the office now. Be there in thirty."

"I'll be there in twenty," Sadie added.

"Wonderful. I'll see you then." He paused. "Don't worry about the security alarm guarding his property. I'm sure he only turns on the system when he goes to bed."

He'd dropped the call before Shelby could sputter, "His alarm?"

"You don't think we could go to jail for this, do you?" Sadie asked, ever the fraidy cat.

"Only if we're caught," Shelby said to get her goose. "All the better to let J.P. do the driving. I think Jake's warming to us, but trespassing on his property might officially put us in the stalker category if we're caught. See you soon, Sadie."

"You too," her sister said and hung up.

Shelby grabbed her purse, her phone, and a couple of files she planned to bring with her. She all but ran to her car. No one was in the office to see. Goodness, she was out of breath. By the time she reached her new convertible she was huffing and puffing like a dragon with emphysema.

Her new car got her to the meeting spot in twenty-four minutes flat since there was no traffic this time of night. Okay, and she'd sped a little. Well. More than a little.

Sadie jumped out of J.P.'s truck and ran to her. Her hug was fierce, and Shelby knew she was scared too. Hadn't she prayed the whole way, fighting the urge to call Mama and flat out ask her what was going on? But if Mama hadn't said earlier, she wasn't going to. That's what made people tell her things they'd never share with another soul.

J.P. didn't get out of his idling truck, but when Shelby scooted into the cab, he leaned over and kissed her cheek.

"Good to see you, darlin'," he said. "Now, buckle up and let's get this done."

Sadie awkwardly leaned across her to kiss their brother, and because Shelby was worried, she didn't nudge her in the ribs for crushing her.

She and Sadie reached for each other's hands as J.P.'s headlights illuminated Jake's long driveway.

"Do you really think his alarm is going to go off?" Sadie whispered.

"Maybe it will be all right since he knows J.P.'s truck," Shelby said.

"I was joking about the alarm," J.P. said, clearing his throat. "He may have one, but I doubt it. He's a pretty good shot from his military days. He doesn't need an alarm."

Shelby punched him since she was closer. "How terrible

of you to joke like that. You nearly scared us to death, making us worry about the police showing up."

"I would look terrible in an orange jumpsuit," Sadie said with an edge in her voice.

"You do look terrible in that color," Shelby said, keeping her eyes on the road—not that they could see much else. "Goodness, it's dark out here. I sometimes forget what it's like outside of the city."

Something ran in front of their car. The tail was long, and the pointed head was disgusting.

"Was that a possum?" Sadie asked.

"Yes," J.P. said, his aggrieved tone back. "Hush now. We're getting closer."

They both shushed, and then Shelby punched him in the arm again. "Don't tell us to hush. No one can hear us outside this car."

She looked over and saw his mouth twitching. "My mistake."

The house inched slowly into view. Lights were shining in a few of the windows, but the front porch lights weren't on, so they couldn't see much else.

Her brother drove into what looked like a circular drive-way. "Get the ice cream story ready."

"It's drinks," Shelby reminded him.

Sadie gasped when J.P.'s headlights illuminated her sister's Audi.

"She's here!" Sadie called out, messenger of the obvious. "What do we do now?"

J.P. put the truck in park. "Well, seeing as how they likely know we're here, we should go on up to the front door to deliver our lame excuse for why we've shown up for a visit after nine o'clock on a school night."

Shelby saw a muscular frame appear in the front window.

"He's seen us," Sadie declared, panic lacing her voice. "Where is Susannah?"

How *was* Susannah going to react to them showing up unannounced? Hopefully, she'd feel supported by her family.

"Of course he's seen us," J.P. said, shaking his head. "Let's get on out of the truck."

"You do the talking, J.P.," Sadie suggested. "He knows you best. We can see to Susannah."

"Unless Jake is seeing to her," Shelby said, but she doubted it. Susannah was a certified mother hen, and if Jake was seeing their mama for therapy, he needed one.

The air was cool on Shelby's cheeks as she followed Sadie out of the truck. She nestled close to her sister, and her brother slowed his steps so they could keep up with him in their heels. The front door opened, revealing Susannah next to Jake. Thank God.

"Evenin'," her brother called out. "I know it's late, but we wanted to see if y'all wanted to join us for a drink."

The request was as lame as they came, but at least it wasn't an out-and-out lie. As they neared the door, Shelby could see her sister's pale face in the light from the entryway. The look on Susannah's face made her desperate to run up and hug her. Then she noticed that Jake was holding her sister's hand. His own face seemed carved out of stone today. Something had definitely happened. Mama had been right to call for prayers.

Susannah leaned close to Jake and whispered something. When he turned to look at her, Shelby saw the corner of his mouth tip up. He mouthed something to her, but it was impossible to make out the words. What *was* possible

THE PROMISE OF RAINBOWS

—heck, undeniable, if she had to use a word—was the sheer power of their connection. Something had definitely grown between them since she'd last seen them together.

"Why don't y'all come in?" Jake suggested.

The McGuiness siblings entered the house, each of them hugging Susannah fiercely in turn. Her return squeeze told Shelby all she needed to know. Unexpected or not, she was happy to see them.

J.P. gave Jake a man hug, and Shelby decided to be bold and give him one too. Heavens knew the man looked like he needed it. Sadie followed suit.

His entryway featured a curvy staircase leading to the second floor. A painting of a man playing his guitar stood on the wall opposite the doorway. At any other time, Shelby would have taken in every detail. But this wasn't the time.

Jake led them into a den and gestured for them to sit on the couch. They all took a seat there, and Shelby crossed her legs out of awkwardness. Susannah stood by Jake, and if she hadn't known better, she would have thought her sister was protecting him.

"Thanks to your wonderful sister here, I have a bar caddy now," Jake said, rolling his shoulders like he was about to step into a boxing ring. "What can I get you to drink, ladies?"

"Wine would be fine for me," Shelby said, noticing how Jake reached for Susannah's hand again.

Sadie gave Shelby a knowing look. "Me too."

"I'll get y'all some," Susannah said softly. "Would you like a beer, J.P.?"

"That would be mighty fine," he answered, setting his hands calmly in his lap. "Can I see what you have, Jake?"

Jake and Susannah shared a look.

"Sure," the man answered. "Come this way."

"I'll find a bottle in the chiller and pour them some wine," Susannah told Jake, putting her hand on his arm.

His chest seemed to rise like a mountain's shadow at night. "Thank you, J.P. Let's get you that beer."

Shelby bit her lip, watching as they left the room. Jake was obviously upset, but he was making a brave showing. Sadie ran over to Susannah, and Shelby followed suit. They wrapped their arms around their sister.

"Mama called," Sadie whispered harshly. "She said you needed prayers. We got scared."

Susannah was gripping them back with all her strength.

"Are you all right?" Shelby asked.

"That poor man," Susannah whispered and then pressed back. "He needs prayers too. What he must have gone through..."

"What happened?" Sadie asked, cuddling closer.

"I can't talk about it now," she continued, "but I'll tell you later. I know it must have been weird for y'all to come over here and check on me, but I'm so glad you did."

Someone cleared their throat, and their heads swiveled. J.P. had his hands in his pockets. He walked forward slowly, his lips pursed in thought.

"Jake doesn't feel much like a drink tonight, after all," he told them. "He wanted me to give his apologies."

Susannah's face fell. "You need to go. I'll stay a while longer."

J.P. shook his head. "Jake asked me to stay behind and chat. Susannah, can you see the girls to their cars?"

"Where are y'all parked?" Susannah asked, staring in the direction of the kitchen with a concerned look in her eyes.

"Ah...at the end of Jake's lane," Shelby said, twisting her hands.

Her sister didn't seem to hear her or find anything strange in that comment. "Fine. I'm ...going to say goodbye to him." She walked a few steps and then turned. "Are you sure you're all right to stay, J.P.?"

He nodded. "It'll be fine, Susannah. I'll take good care of him."

Tears welled in her eyes, but she shook her head as if to deny them. "Be right back."

As soon as Susannah left the room, Sadie reached out and clutched Shelby's wrist. "Oh, she's crying. J.P., do you know what happened?"

"Did Jake say anything?" Shelby shot out.

"Nothing more than what I told you," her brother said gravely. "Y'all take good care of Susannah, you hear?"

They both bobbed their heads. Susannah came back, wiping tears from her eyes. They rushed toward her.

"It's okay," she said, patting the hands they'd stretched toward her. "Let's go." She paused and wrapped her arms around J.P. "Thanks for taking care of him for me."

"Don't worry, sugar," he said, kissing her cheek. "I've got him now."

The sisters held hands on the way to Susannah's Audi. She drove them to their cars, but when she put the car in park, silence descended.

"We're coming over to your house," Shelby said.

"Don't even think of putting us off," Sadie added.

Susannah only nodded.

As Shelby walked toward her convertible, she pressed a hand to her heart. Her sister was in love—all the way in love.

And from the look of it, Jake was a much more troubled man than any of them had thought.

16

"I told my sisters to go on and head out," J.P. told Jake when he wandered back into the kitchen.

Jake loosened his grip on the edge of the kitchen sink. He'd been staring out into the blackness. Susannah's touch and their connection had kept him from being enveloped by the familiar void, but he could feel it on the edge of his consciousness. One of his favorite writers on fear and anger—Pema Chodron—had a saying: *Don't Bite the Hook.* And he was doing his best not to get sucked back into the story of today or the past. He was trying to be present. But honestly, he was exhausted, the kind of bone-deep fatigue that came from facing all your demons and crawling away to survive one more time.

Susannah had been exhausted too. He'd known it was time to send her home because of the way she'd clutched her sisters like they were life vests. Asking J.P. to stay a while would help ease her worry, so he'd gone ahead and done it.

"You can head on home to Tammy and the kids any time," he said, turning around.

The situation could hardly be more awkward, but J.P. was the embodiment of calm.

"They're at their other house tonight since Annabelle has a cold."

"Sorry to hear that. She's a sweet girl." Even thoughts of her didn't ease him.

J.P. reached into the refrigerator for the beer Jake had never offered him. "Would you like a beer?" He popped the top using the edge of the countertop—a move Jake had never mastered. Yeah, he couldn't remember where his bottle opener was. His mind was mush.

"Best not," Jake responded, leaning back against the counter to support himself.

"I want you to know that my sisters and I don't usually show up unannounced," J.P. said after taking a sip. "Our mama called us and asked us to let Susannah know we're praying for her, which is code in my family for something big being wrong. Mama wouldn't say what, of course. When Susannah didn't pick up her phone, Sadie drove by her house. After some discussion, we decided to see if she was out here with you. I did try contacting you to ask."

He was relieved to hear Susannah's siblings didn't know the full scope of the situation. The sound of the truck approaching had put him on high alert. No one came to his home unless he knew about it, like with the BBQ delivery man earlier.

And then the McGuinesses had stepped out of J.P.'s truck. Susannah hadn't made any calls, so for a horrible moment, he'd imagined that her mama had asked them to come get her. It was one thing for him to be messed up. Perhaps it was another thing for him to be messed up with her daughter. Talk about the paranoia that comes from PTSD.

"I appreciate you sharing that," Jake said, studying his boots. "You really don't need to stay."

"We've known each other for a spell now," J.P. said, easing back against the opposite counter. "I know a friend in need when I see one. Do you want to tell me what's going on?"

Shame flushed his cheeks. He'd told J.P. some stories about his time in the Army to help inspire some of the songs they wrote together. But this? It involved his sister. If he told him everything, J.P. might not want him to be involved with Susannah. Perhaps it would be good to find out. He wasn't too sure what to do right now. He wanted Susannah, but he was more scared than ever to be with her after today.

"I know you won't say anything to anyone," Jake said, bracing himself, "but I'd still like to ask for your confidence."

"You have it," J.P. said, resting the beer against his chest.

And so, Jake told him about the day's events. His friend listened without interruption, watching him all the while.

"Your sister...she wants to be involved with me despite all this. Even though I deeply care for her..." Care was a tame word, but he wasn't prepared to use the word "love." That had too much power. "I don't know if us being involved is a good idea. Your mama thought it might be. Before today."

"When are you seeing my mama again?" J.P. asked, his brow knit in deep thought.

"Tomorrow morning." His mouth was suddenly bone dry, so he refilled his water glass.

"That's good. That's real good. Why don't we sit a spell?"

The chairs scraped the floor as they sat at the kitchen table. J.P. set his beer down and leaned back, crossing his arms over his chest.

"My mama has plenty of experience with people who have PTSD, so she's got a good head on her shoulders. See what she says tomorrow. But I'm your friend, and I've also fallen in love with someone who had PTSD."

Jake was sure his mouth about dropped open. Then it hit him. "Tammy." Funny, he saw PTSD as a man's problem, but the disorder wasn't exclusively for people serving in the military. Plenty of women had PTSD too.

Nodding, J.P. continued, "I met Tammy right after she'd left her ex-husband, but I waited almost a year to ask her out. I wanted her divorce to be final, obviously, but I also wanted to give her enough time to heal from it."

J.P. certainly had been patient, which was more than honorable, if you asked him.

"Some might say, I shouldn't have gotten involved with a women who was still recovering from domestic violence," J.P. said with a shrug. "Frankly, the thought never occurred to me. Tammy is the most wonderful woman in the world. Nothing would have stopped me from being with her."

Was that how Susannah thought about him? Her behavior certainly suggested it. His heart squeezed in his chest. But how could she want to be with him when he had so much baggage?

"Maybe Susannah is like me in that regard," J.P. said, pausing for a moment. "She doesn't see any reason not to be with you when you both obviously care about each other."

Jake shifted in his chair. "I *do* care about her. I have from the beginning. I didn't ask her out—"

"Because you were concerned about your PTSD," J.P.

finished for him. "I guessed as much. I was hoping your worry might fade, or Susannah's feelings for you would grow enough that you'd cave like Tammy did with me. She resisted at first. Heck, that woman still hasn't agreed to marry me yet. But I support her and love her just the same. And she will marry me. Love always wins out."

Jake liked to believe that, but he knew firsthand that the world didn't always work out the way it should. "Susannah is like you, and for that I'm grateful. More grateful than you could know. How she acted after what I did today... Well, it's a sheer miracle, and I don't believe in them much anymore."

"There's always the promise of rainbows, Jake."

Those words again. "What? You too?"

J.P. chuckled softly. "It's not just something my mama says. She used to say you could wish for a rainbow after a storm with your whole heart and one might appear. It might sound crazy, but I believe it to be true. Not all rainbows are visible to the naked eye. Tammy and the kids are my rainbows, and I'm theirs."

Jake's mama had told him to hush his mouth whenever he'd talked about things like magic and stardust when he was a boy. "That's really beautiful, man." And he meant it as both a friend and as a fellow artist.

"Tammy won't mind me saying so, but she thought she was messed up too. We've talked before about some of the problems you faced after you left the Army. Things have gotten a heck of a lot better for you, Jake, if you ask me."

All that was true, and he'd tried to hold onto that thought like a drowning man would hold onto a piece of driftwood. He ran a hand through his hair. "The thing is... except for the nightmare I still have on and off, I felt like I had my remaining symptoms under control. Flashbacks and mental tricks like tasting sand in my mouth. Now I'm afraid—"

"That you've backtracked," J.P. finished for him, picking up his beer and taking a swig. "When you start to care about someone, it has a way of bringing other things up. Rather like deep water fishing, if you ask me. It sounds like being with Susannah is doing that for you."

Jake rubbed his forehead. There were dried salt crystals there from all the sweating he'd done today. God, he needed a shower. "I'm worried it's getting worse again. While there's a lot written about PTSD, the experts don't know if it ever completely goes away." And didn't that fear drive a stake in his heart?

"So you're supposed to go your whole life without the love of a good woman and family?" J.P. said. "In my opinion, that's bullshit."

His lungs seemed to deflate in his chest. "The rational part of me wants to agree with you, but Susannah doesn't deserve the problems I'd bring to our relationship."

J.P. rested his elbow on the table, thinking for a spell, and then said, "Do you think Tammy deserves to be with me even though she's still healing from what happened to her?"

He hung his head. The hole he'd dug himself was big enough for a dinosaur. "Of course she deserves it."

"Then why don't you?" J.P. asked, watching him closely.

"Tammy was a victim of what happened to her." Jake's throat burned. "I wasn't a victim. I killed people, and when it mattered the most, I let my best friend down."

"When you wrote 'Man Down' with me, I wondered who you had lost. I knew it had been someone close to you even though you wouldn't talk about it." J.P. rested both forearms on the table. "You killed people because it was your job, Jake. I can't even imagine what that would be like, but if I had to kill someone to protect my own, I would do it and live with it. Not that I wouldn't be sorry and pray for forgiveness and hope it never happened again."

J.P.'s matter-of-fact attitude was oddly soothing. It *had* been his job, one he'd signed up for. And the man was right. If he had to defend someone he loved or cared about, he wouldn't hesitate to do it.

Something clicked inside him.

"As for your friend...you didn't kill him," J.P. said, "and from everything I know about you, I'd bet anything that if you could have saved him, you would have. Right?"

His throat grew thick with emotion. "Yeah."

"Then are you going to punish yourself for the rest of your life because you weren't God?"

"You sound like your mama," Jake said, shifting in his chair again and drinking some water to wet his dry mouth.

"Thank you," J.P. answered, his mouth tipping up at the corners. "There are times when I've wanted to be God. Especially with Tammy and the kids. But I don't want to be God full-time, and I'm pretty sure it's a full-time job."

"If it's a full-time job, where was God when I asked him to save Booker? Or my other friends?" He still couldn't make peace with that.

J.P. rubbed his chin thoughtfully. "That's not easy for me to answer. Some of my prayers haven't been answered; some of them have. I don't always understand God's rationale. Again, I'm not God, and last time I checked, neither are you."

Jake found himself fighting a smile too, and wasn't that a miracle all its own? "You make it sound so easy," Jake said, and he meant that as a compliment. "You're not a Pollyanna, but you're not sugarcoating it either."

"I know none of this is easy." J.P. gave a heart-felt sigh. "Some things reach inside and rip out your heart. Plenty of prayers are never answered. It doesn't mean God doesn't care. I believe that."

And from his sincerity, Jake knew he meant it.

"Where there's love," he continued, "there's grace. And that's when the miracles come. Some prayers *are* answered, Jake. Sometimes a miracle shows up without us even asking. Maybe Susannah is your miracle. Maybe she's God's way of restoring your faith in Him and in His mysterious order of things. Maybe she's God's way of showing you that He loves you—despite all you think you've done not to deserve that love."

He broke out in gooseflesh as his friend's words washed over him. "You humble me."

J.P. shook his head. "No, bubba. I'm only telling you the truth."

Silence descended. Jake's mind was reeling from their talk. Could it be that Susannah *was* his miracle? Could she help him break through this pain and love him through it? "It's a lot to put on someone."

"Don't misunderstand me. I'm not Tammy's savior. I love her—totally and completely—for all that she is. Perhaps I've helped her remember she's lovable and strong and sexy. But she did the healing all by herself, and she's still doing it. She took the risk to love me and be with me. The question for you, my friend, is whether you're willing to do the same with Susannah?"

His temples were pounding now. "You've given me a lot to think about."

J.P. rose and slapped him on the back like a brother might. "I suggest getting some shut-eye first and then rising with the dawn. Things always look different at sunrise. If my friend Rhett Butler Blaylock were here, he might even say, 'After all, tomorrow is another day.'"

Jake sputtered out a laugh. He'd met Rhett on occasion. The man should have his own reality TV show called *Southern Eccentrics*. "I hate that movie."

"Don't breathe a word about that around my sisters," J.P. said, giving a pretend shudder. *"Gone With The Wind* is up there with *Steel Magnolias."*

"Good Lord," Jake said, standing as well.

"Do you want me to bunk here tonight?" J.P. asked. "There's no shame if you need a friend. We all do sometimes, and I know you'd be there for me."

"No, I think you're right. I need a shower and some shut-eye. Your mama's agreed to meet with me in the morning."

J.P. put his hand on his shoulder. "You're a good man, Jake. I wouldn't let just any man be with Susannah. In fact, I can't think of anyone better. She's got good judgment. You can trust that if you find yourself doubting your own."

More humbling words to cap off the night. "Thank you, J.P."

"You're welcome, bubba. Get some rest. I'll give you a call tomorrow."

His friend headed out. Jake was too tired to follow him. He sank down at the table again and rested his head on his forearms.

Was J.P. right? Was Susannah his miracle?

Remembering that first sweet caress of her lips over his after he'd poured his guts out to her, it was hard to believe otherwise.

17

Susannah had just parked in the driveway of her townhouse when she spotted Shelby and Sadie hurrying toward the car. Both of them drove faster than they should, but tonight she didn't mind. She exited her vehicle and closed the door, waiting for the double embrace she knew was coming. Sadie smelled like butterscotch from her favorite lotion, and Shelby had on her signature Jo Malone Peony & Blush Suede. She inhaled deeply, hoping her aching heart would ease.

"Come on, Susannah," Shelby told her. "Let's get you some tea. Then you can tell us what happened."

Sadie grabbed her purse and rummaged for her keys while Shelby took hold of her hand. She wanted to call her mama, but she didn't want to influence her mama's assessment of Jake tomorrow. His needs were more important than hers right now, and besides, she had her sisters.

Her body was so tired from the strain of the day, she slumped onto the couch as soon as her sisters led her inside. Forcing herself to lean forward, she pried off her boots and then kicked her feet up on the coffee table, stretching her toes.

Shelby and Sadie cast a worried look at her. She tried to smile to allay their concerns.

"Have you eaten anything?" Sadie asked.

"I ordered BBQ in the hopes that Jake would eat," Susannah said, pressing a hand to her tummy, "but neither of us could choke much down."

"How about I make you some toast? Jam or honey?" Sadie asked with steel in her voice. "It always makes you feel better."

Since the women in her family always fed people in crisis, she didn't waste the energy arguing. "Honey."

"All right,' Sadie said, nodding. "I'll get that while Shelby makes the tea. Do you want to come into the kitchen with us so we can keep you company?"

She almost laughed. When they were little kids, they hadn't liked to go into another room without each other. "It's only a few yards away."

Sadie worried her lip. "I can wait with you."

Shelby took her elbow. "The longer we spend dithering, the longer this tea and toast is going to take. Hustle it, Sadie. Holler if you need us, Susannah."

Left alone with her thoughts—well, out of earshot at least—she closed her eyes. The full weight of her hurt welled up in her heart, and she knew why it was so strong.

She'd fallen in love with Jake.

After all these years, she'd finally found someone she loved, someone she'd do anything for. And he was hurting. So much so, she didn't know if she could help him. But she'd be there just the same and do what she could. Surely her presence had soothed him today. What might have happened on the highway if she hadn't been with him? A couple of tears spilled down her cheeks despite herself.

"Hey now," Shelby said, her voice much more subdued than usual.

Susannah jumped a mile. "Good heavens! You could have told me you were in the room." In fact, her sister was standing right over her.

"I set the water to boil and came back out to check on you," Shelby said, sitting beside her. "I'm glad Mama called us to pray for you."

Yeah, Mama must have known she needed them. "Me too. Oh, Shel."

Her sister cuddled close. "It's okay, Suse," she said, using her nickname. "We're here for you."

The warmth of Shelby's embrace soothed her heart some. Whenever one of the McGuiness children had a bad day at school growing up, Mama would always ask everyone to hug that person. Her motto was that hugs made everything feel a little better. Susannah hadn't needed a hug like that in so long, but she welcomed it like a child welcomed her favorite teddy bear.

The teakettle whistle sounded, and she patted Shelby on the back after giving her a good squeeze.

"Go see to the tea," she said and then wiped her face. Heavens, if she had a trace of makeup on, she'd be astonished. Not that a little thing like makeup mattered in a crisis, but she was Southern enough to want to look her best at all times.

"I've got everything," Sadie announced from the doorway, carefully balancing a tray with a piece of toast, her red and gold flowered teapot, three mugs, a jar of Mrs. Janice's local honey, and a spoon.

Shelby cleared a spot on the coffee table while Sadie extended the plate to her.

"Eat," she ordered. "You look like a gust of wind could blow you over."

Her sisters shared another concerned look as she ate. Shelby left to retrieve some napkins and dropped one in her lap. The honey was sweet on her tongue—a comfort—and the toast warm and buttery. She closed her eyes and simply chewed.

She heard the rattle of the teapot, and soon a mug of tea was pressed in her hand. When she opened her eyes, her sisters were sitting on the floor between the couch and the coffee table. Both were touching her, which she appreciated.

When she finished her toast and drank as much tea as she could, she patted the sofa on either side of her. They jumped up and cuddled close after setting their own mugs aside.

"Okay," Sadie said in her practical voice. "Start from the beginning."

Recounting the day's events wasn't easy. A few of the words stuck in her craw, and she had to clear her throat to continue. By the end, tears were spilling down all their faces, and her sisters were clenching both her hands something fierce.

"You love him, don't you?" Shelby asked, studying her face.

She nodded and released a pent-up breath. "I even kissed him today. It seemed...the right thing to do."

Sadie's mouth dropped open, and Shelby gave her a stern glance.

"Then it's official," Shelby declared. "You've decided to be with him through all this."

They all knew Susannah didn't kiss men lightly. Maybe she was old-fashioned, but she saw it as a kind of commitment. If she liked a man enough to kiss him, then she thought he was good enough for her in the long run. Which was why she hadn't kissed a lot of men...

"Do you think Mama will give her blessing about y'all dating after today?" Sadie asked, shaking her brown hair free like Susannah's recitation had given her a tension headache.

"I don't know," Susannah said honestly, once again feeling the temptation to call her mama. This time she wanted answers more than comfort.

"I bet she'll agree," Shelby said. "You know how she always says connection is the source of healing."

"Well, you'll see tomorrow, won't you?" Sadie declared, squeezing her hand. "In the meantime, I think you did the best you could under the circumstances. I have to admit that I've always been a fan of Jake's because of his music and well...the whole package."

"Sadie!" Shelby gasped.

"I didn't mean *that* package," Sadie chided. "Good Lord, whose mind is in the gutter?"

Susannah felt her lips twitch. It felt good to hear them bicker like this; it felt normal.

"What I meant was..." she continued, giving Shelby the stink eye. "Now that I know about everything he's been through, I'm in awe of him. I would never have imagined he was that tortured."

"Me either," Shelby said, shaking her head. "He's lucky to have you, Susannah. There are so many horrible leeches out there looking to be a country music star's baby mama."

She winced. She hadn't thought of that, not that Jake would be interested in a woman of that ilk.

"Susannah," Shelby continued in a softer tone. "I know you love Jake, but as your sister I have to point out that ever since you were in high school, you told us you wanted to be with a man who was stable and dependable. Someone who wouldn't..."

Sadie gave an audible sigh. "Leave you. Like Daddy left all of us."

Tension built at the back of her neck. "I know what I said." Heck, she'd all but vowed it.

"I'm only saying this so you can be sure," Shelby said, her brow knit with concern. "I don't want you to get hurt."

Sadie nodded in agreement. "We like Jake, but we *love* you. You're our sister. We'll always put you first. Mama can help Jake apart from that if necessary."

Hadn't she considered much of what they were saying to her in the car on the way home? "He's a good man, and these troubles...he'll overcome them. I know he will. And I do love him, enough to be there for him."

"What about waiting a while?" Shelby asked. "I'm only playing devil's advocate."

No one played devil's advocate quite like Shelby. "I don't think waiting is the answer. Besides, he said our connection isn't a common occurrence for him either."

"But it shook him," Shelby said, "if today's events are any indication. He felt he had to protect you."

"It made him want me to leave," she said, remembering how much that had hurt. "I was afraid he might leave if I didn't."

"Maybe Daddy had PTSD," Sadie said suddenly, making everyone's head swivel to look at her.

"What in the world are you spouting off about?" Susannah found herself saying. "Daddy wasn't in a war, and he didn't have PTSD. I would remember."

"Don't be ugly to me just because he left when I was in diapers," Sadie said, her mouth tight now. "Why can't I tell myself that? It's a better story."

"Sadie? Do you think about Daddy leaving us a lot?" Shelby asked softly, a contrast to the intensity radiating from her eyes.

Their youngest sister nodded and hung her head. "I just want to know why sometimes or what happened to him. That's all. I don't...remember him."

"I don't either," Shelby said, fiddling with the couch's upholstery. "I was only two when he left."

How they had gotten to talking about Daddy, Susannah would never know. "Thinking about it doesn't change what happened. You know what Mama always says—"

"Yes, but there are things we deserve to know," Shelby interrupted. "Important things. Things like..."

There was a passion in her voice, one Susannah hadn't heard before.

"Things like his medical history and that of his family," Shelby continued. "Gail recently discovered she has a familial disorder, and it got me to thinking. I don't know anything about daddy's family's medical history. What if we have genetic things in our bodies that we don't even know about, ones that could be prevented beforehand?"

"Oh, my God, Shelby," Sadie cried out. "I never thought about that. Not once. Poor Gail. How is she?"

Susannah shared her concern. Gail was a wonderful woman if not a tad eccentric.

"She's on medication," Shelby said, "but she's angry she didn't know about her family's medical history. She outright suggested I find out for my own health—and that goes for all of us."

Susannah didn't like the sound of where this was going.

Her sisters had always been more curious about their daddy than Susannah felt was healthy for them. She wasn't sure she ever wanted to see him again because the hurt of him leaving had so weighed on her.

"Well, you can't ask Mama for it," Sadie said with a pronounced frown. "I've tried. She won't say a thing about his family."

"You tried?" Shelby asked, her hand loosening from Susannah's. "When?"

"I asked in high school when we had a class genealogy assignment. I had to make a family tree." She made a few squiggly motions in the air. "That was pretty much my tree. It was worse than the one in Charlie Brown's Christmas."

They were getting riled up, and for no good reason. "Well, you'll just have to trust that your health is good and that God and modern medicine will take care of anything that might come your way."

Shelby cast her eyes down, and Sadie's face had fallen.

Susannah felt a different hurt rise, the kind that always came when she thought about Daddy's abandonment. "The reasons Daddy left us were his own, and Mama always said speculating about them wouldn't change anything. They had nothing to do with us."

But even she wondered if that were true. Had the weight of raising and supporting four children been too much for him? Or were there other factors they didn't know about?

"It still sucks," Sadie whispered.

"Yes, it certainly does," Shelby said slowly. "I've...ah... been thinking of hiring a private investigator to see what... he might find out. Gail thought it was a good idea."

Susannah gasped in shock. The idea of hiring a private eye to find their daddy had never dawned on her. And if

Gail had seconded Shelby's notion...well, it would only make her sister more intent on this foolishness. "What? Why in the name of all heaven would you do that? Mama would be furious. Besides, nothing good would come from it. Nothing. Do you hear?"

Sadie and Shelby were looking at each other, and she could see a thread of solidarity developing between them.

"I think it's a good idea," Sadie confirmed.

How had they gone from comforting her about Jake to discussing hiring a private investigator to find their daddy? "Shelby. Sadie. Listen to me. This is *not* a good idea. It would hurt Mama, and it could hurt the rest of us too."

"I'm already hurt," Shelby said in a voice laced with anger. "We all are. Why not be hurt *and* have answers to the questions that have plagued us our whole lives?"

"J.P. would be against this idea if he knew," Susannah said, using her brother as a trump card. Everyone respected him. After all, he was the de facto head of the family. Mama hadn't married Dale until they were mostly grown up.

"You and J.P. are such fussbudgets," Sadie fired back. "And it's not nice to bring J.P. into a discussion he's not a part of."

She was overtired, and her anger was growing in leaps and bounds. "It *will* involve J.P. if Shelby goes ahead with this hare-brained scheme."

Her sister raised her head, and from the look in her brown eyes, Susannah could tell she had wounded her. "I'm sorry, Shelby. I'm...it's been a day."

Sadie finally pulled her hand away, and Susannah felt the absence profoundly. "We should go so you can get some sleep." With that, she rose and carried the tray into the kitchen.

Shelby swept up the crumbs from her toast with a

napkin and then balled it up and deposited it into the trash can in the corner.

"I'm sorry I got upset," Susannah said, not knowing how to make things right. "It's just...there's a lot of hurt with Daddy."

"I know," Shelby said, biting her lip. "I didn't mean to throw this at you after such a rough day. But when Sadie said that thing about Daddy... I thought it might be the sign I was hoping for. Well, it was as good as a rabbit hole, wasn't it?"

And they all knew where rabbit holes led, didn't they?

"I'll just help Sadie tidy up and then we'll head out," Shelby said and left the room.

Both of her sisters returned a few minutes later, and Susannah embraced them fiercely. They were upset now, and she hated that—especially after they had been so kind to her.

"Thanks for coming over," she said, trying to give them a smile. As it was, her mouth felt like it was weighted down by lead.

"You're welcome," they both said all polite-like.

"Talk to you tomorrow?" Susannah asked.

They answered, "But of course," but the words had a strain to them.

After they left, she forced herself to rummage in her purse for her cell phone. Jake might call her if he needed something tonight. Threads of emotion moved through her body. Fear? Excitement? It was hard to pinpoint her feelings. They were all jangled up—rather like she was with him.

When she picked her phone up, she read the texts all her siblings had sent her. Her heart warmed, but it was the one from her mama that brought tears to her eyes.

Sleep with the angels, darlin'. I'm praying for you and Jake.

And with those words to comfort her, she sought her bed, asking the angels to work overtime on all their behalf.

18

Since Jake had done more tossing and turning than sleeping, he greeted the dawn like J.P. had suggested and made a decision.

He was going to take the bull by the horns again. He would do anything to overcome his PTSD, anything to become totally balanced. Of course, the added incentive was that he got to see Susannah and be the kind of man she deserved. But he had to do it for himself first and foremost. He'd talked with way too many vets who had shown up for therapy at the behest of their wives, mothers, or girlfriends. It didn't seem to stick if it wasn't the person's choice one-hundred percent.

This was his choice, and since Louisa thought she could help him, he planned to let her.

The homework she'd given him was folded neatly in the pocket of his jeans. He'd struggled over it mightily.

The church parking lot was mostly empty when he arrived, what with it being so early. When he entered the office, the church secretary greeted him and ushered him in straight away.

He closed the door and tugged on the collar of his neatly pressed white shirt. "Louisa," he said by way of greeting.

She rose immediately and came around her desk to give him a hug. When he tried to pull back, she only held on tighter.

"Settle a minute," she said softly. "You look like you need a good hug this morning."

It was a little awkward, being held by her, but when she finally released him, she was smiling. He, on the other had, had broken out into a sweat.

"Seems you had a breakthrough yesterday," she said. And the unexpectedness of that pretty much made his mouth plop open.

"Ma'am?"

"I told you not to call me that, Jake. Come. Let's sit."

He took the couch, but mostly because he knew she preferred her chair. Leaning forward, he put his elbows on his knees. "A breakthrough?" he said slowly, wondering about her kind of counseling.

Her brow rose. "From what you said on the phone last night, things intensified again all of the sudden, didn't they?"

He finally noted that she was wearing a pale yellow suit coat, which seemed at odds with the darkness he was about to level on her. "That's a mild way to describe it. I had a full-blown episode. With your daughter. Ah...can I have some water?" he asked, his mouth suddenly bone dry.

"Absolutely," she replied, rising to pour him a glass.

After draining the whole glass—he couldn't seem to stop with a couple sips—he set it down on the end table, more than a little alarmed to see his hands were shaking. He decided to sit on them.

"When you were being counseled before, did your episodes ever intensify with your sessions?" she asked.

"Some of the exposure therapy made me throw up," he said, remembering how devastating that had been. He'd made sure not to eat at least four hours before a session, but the dry heaves hadn't heeded him.

"What happened yesterday was like that," she said, giving him an encouraging smile. "This isn't a backward step, Jake. It's called momentum."

He blew out a long breath. "Louisa, you do have a funny way of looking at things. My old therapists thought I was re-traumatizing myself."

"Perhaps what you were doing with them *did* re-traumatize you, but yesterday sounds different to me. From my perspective, two important things triggered it."

"All right," he said, bracing himself. "Let's hear it."

"The first was the young woman who asked for your autograph," she said, and then leaned forward. "Did you bring your homework, by the way?"

He gulped. "Yes."

"How did you find it?"

Shaking his head, he dug out the piece of paper and handed it to her. "Ah...well...I couldn't think of too many things, to be honest."

She opened the piece of paper and scanned it. "The only people *on this whole planet* whose lives have been changed by you being alive are your fans?"

His face reddened. "Well...yes. I mean...they tell me my music changes their lives. Well...some of them. Like Mary yesterday. Of course some can't stand it. But I doubt you meant the haters."

She folded up the paper and handed it back to him. "You didn't include your family."

"No ma'am...I mean, Louisa," he said immediately. They surely couldn't care one way or another.

"As a mother, I can tell you that despite your current relationship with your own mama, you *did* change her life."

He rubbed his forehead. "I agree that I changed it. I'm just not sure she would concur that I did so in a positive way."

"Ah..." she drew out. "Do you ever remember her loving you, Jake?"

Well, wasn't that question a punch to the gut? "I remember some nice birthdays when she made me my favorite cake and let a few of my friends come over."

"All right," she said, handing him another glass of water. "Let's leave your family aside for the moment."

His hands weren't shaking as much this time, he was comforted to see.

"You didn't mention any of the men you served with in the Army," she said.

He'd figured she would pick up on that. "There wasn't anyone I could rightly name. I mean Monty, Darren, and Randy didn't have their lives changed by knowing me. We're just friends." It wasn't like he was the only one who'd carried Monty to the Humvee after his leg was blown to bits. He sure as hell wasn't going to talk about Booker.

"Jake, I find that hard to believe," she said, leaning forward in her chair. "I've read all the press I could find about your military service. You received a Silver Star. Someone in the Army must have thought you warranted such distinction."

He grimaced. The article about the events that had led to him receiving that star had made him livid. He hadn't wanted anyone to know about it. "Any guy would have done what I did."

She shook her head, her silver hair bobbing around her ears. "And yet, you were the one who charged into a building to take out the sniper who had most of your unit pinned down, saving the lives of seventeen men. And you refused treatment for the bullet wound in your shoulder since so many of your men were down."

He shifted in his seat and broke eye contact. "I also got my butt chewed out by my commanding officer for going into that building without proper back-up," he told her. "The bottom line is, Louisa, none of us wanted to get shot."

"Does that make you a bad guy, in your eyes?" she asked him. "Deciding to do something because you didn't want to get shot?"

He could all but feel himself getting angry, and he knew he was starting to turn into that man he didn't like much. "It certainly doesn't make me heroic."

"Which is why it bothered you so much when that woman told you that you were a hero," she gently said. "Mary was her name, right?"

"Look," he said, grinding out the words. "I don't like anyone thinking I'm a hero. I've known heroes. I'm not one of them."

She tilted her head to the side. "What have those other men done that you haven't?"

"They save lives," he ground out. Why couldn't she understand? "I need to stand."

"Go ahead," she said, staying where she was. "So you've decided that you aren't a hero because you weren't able to save your best friend after you rescued all those other men by taking down that sniper."

Jake walked to the window to stare out the blinds. He was glad she hadn't drawn them. He hated having sessions without natural light. "I know what you're thinking..."

"Do you now?" she asked, and while it was said politely, he could hear the steel in her voice—much like he'd heard it in Susannah's yesterday.

"I've heard this all before," he said, stalking back to face her. "A hero isn't supposed to let anyone down. He's supposed to bring back everyone in his unit. I didn't do that."

"Jake, you set a pretty high prize for yourself. To me, it sounds unrealistic to think any soldier can save *every* man he serves with."

"You think I'm playing God again," he said, and then he heard the echo of J.P.'s voice in his head, and it made him pause. Last night, his friend's words had reached him, but today, his anger had blown them to bits. "Your son said the same thing."

"So you talked to my son about this?" she said, a smile spreading across her face. "What else did he say?"

"Pretty much the same thing you did," Jake said, stomping his foot. "Do you think I *want* to feel like this? Like a failure? And so angry I couldn't save Booker that I want to hit something? I wish it were as simple as y'all make it out to be, and sometimes the words make sense to me, but..."

"There's a lot of emotion balled up inside you," Louisa said. "That's why yesterday was a breakthrough. It's forcing its way out. It needs to come out, Jake."

"If that's what you consider a breakthrough..." he said, hanging his head. "It didn't feel good, and it was downright scary."

"Of course it was," she said. "The other reason you were triggered yesterday is because of Susannah."

His head shot up.

"You didn't like her hearing anyone say you were a hero,

and when you had your episode, you were terrified you'd fail her like you did Booker. I'll bet your protective instincts went into overdrive, didn't they?"

Pain shot through his temple, and he rubbed it. "I was scared I was going to kill her or get her killed in my truck. Louisa, I was paralyzed. I couldn't even change lanes and get to the shoulder."

"And yet you finally managed to do just that," she said softly.

"I don't think I would have without Susannah," he said, cracking his tense neck. "She's a lot like you. She looks like a flower, but she's got a spine of steel when she needs it."

Louisa chuckled. "I'm happy to hear that. But Jake, she's a positive force for you. That much we know. She helped you through your episode. Did you find her a comfort?"

Shifting on the couch, he looked away. She was more than a comfort. Her kisses had rocked his world and soothed his soul, but how was he supposed to tell her mama that? "Yes, she was a comfort."

"Good," she responded immediately. "Then you should definitely keep seeing her."

He met her searching gaze again. "You mean you still think it's all right for me to ask her out?"

She nodded. "I do. Her presence helped you through what happened yesterday. In my eyes, that kind of connection between humans provides the greatest opportunity for healing."

Hadn't J.P. said the same thing? "I'm...still not sure it's fair to her."

"I expect Susannah has already decided that for herself, no?"

Jeez, did she have some special sense that told her he'd

kissed her daughter? "She seems to have decided, yes." He'd awoken to a text from her at dawn, wishing him a good morning with her mama and saying she was praying for him. He was never going to delete that message.

"So what next?" he asked. "I pretty much disassociated yesterday and then got paralyzed on the road. Should I not drive your daughter anywhere when we go out together?" The thought had kept him awake last night. Maybe he wasn't safe to operate *any* heavy machinery around her.

"How long had it been since you had an episode like that?" she asked like her daughter had.

"A couple years," he answered, and just hearing the words out loud made him feel that he was probably over-reacting.

"Then take the lessons you can from it," Louisa said, folding her hands in her lap.

Lessons. Maybe he should write this down. "What would those be?"

"We've only met twice, but I think we need to focus more on you seeing yourself as someone who deserves love. You told me you concluded God doesn't love you anymore because He didn't answer your prayer to save Booker."

His chest tightened. "Among other things."

"Do you believe other people love you besides your fans?" she pressed.

The tension spreading across his temple intensified. "I'm not close to a whole lot of people anymore." This was getting embarrassing. "Guys...don't think about each other that way."

"Did you love Booker?" she flat out asked him.

For a moment, he couldn't breathe. "Yeah. But I never told him." He hung his head. "Not even when he was dying." Not that it had dawned on him to do so. Everything had happened so fast, it seemed, but when his mind played it back, it seemed like they'd been running through water.

"It's not easy for men, especially men in the military, to express their love for the people in their lives. But you express your love in your music."

He was able to draw in a full breath as he thought about his songs. Yeah, his work allowed him to talk about love. But he longed for it more than he had it.

"Maybe now you'll do the hard work of making yourself vulnerable. To have real connection with people, it's important to share how you feel."

"It's a little awkward, don't you think? You encouraging me to date your daughter."

She steepled her fingers. "Let's be clear. You want to date my daughter, and she wants to date you. It's important for this to be *your* choice. It is *not* a tool of counseling."

He almost cursed, which would have been wildly inappropriate. "Right. And let me be clear. I'm *not* using her as a tool to get better."

"I know that, Jake." Her hands rested again in her lap. "You seem tuckered out. How about we set a time for our next meeting before I give you more homework?"

Somehow he managed to suppress the groan. Hadn't he said he would do anything? "Does it involve walking over hot coals? Because I think I would be really good at that."

She laughed. "Most men would prefer to walk over hot coals. It satisfies the Alpha in them. I'd like to see you again this week if you have the time. How does this Friday sound?"

"I'm not on tour now, so my time is yours." Plus he'd committed himself to getting better—no matter what.

"Good," she said, rising to note it in her day planner.

"Now, for your homework. I want you to write a letter to God."

"A letter to..." He shook his head, gulping. "Seriously?"

"Yep," she said brightly. "I want you to tell Him how you feel."

Some voice in his mind shouted, *Dear God, You suck.*

"I'm not so sure that's a good idea," he drawled, thinking how short the 'suck' letter would be. What if part of him wanted to say other things like that? He would burn in hell for sure.

"Uncensored," she said, waggling her brows. "You can even call him bad names if you need to get them off your chest. I don't judge."

"Are you..." He stopped himself from saying crazy. "Louisa—"

"Trust me," she said, coming over and patting his arm. "You have a lot of anger stored up. Just let the words come and don't think too much about them."

In all his counseling sessions, no one had ever suggested something like this. "You do have some interesting ways about you, Louisa."

"I'll take that as a compliment," she said, embracing him.

This time he was better able to hug her back, but she still clutched him a little longer than he was comfortable.

"Now go ask my daughter out and have a good time," she said cheerily when she released him.

He found himself clearing his throat. "Yes, ma'am."

She didn't correct him as he left her office. His legs were heavy, and his chest pretty much felt crushed by a boulder. But when the sunlight hit his face, he found himself smiling.

Today he had permission to ask out the woman of his dreams, and that gave him hope more than anything.

19

S usannah had tried not to fret all morning, thinking about Jake meeting with her mama. She'd alternately prayed and paced back and forth in her kitchen, drinking tea and attempting to focus on some invoicing she hadn't completed this week. So when Jake texted her and asked if he could swing by her place, she immediately responded with her address.

After bussing her lips with some pink gloss, she stood by the window and waited for him to arrive. His truck parked on her street not long after, and she watched him carefully as he strode to her front door. His caramel-colored cowboy hat matched his leather jacket and boots. His mouth wasn't as grim as it had been yesterday, but his shoulders looked tense.

She made her way to the front door and opened it after waiting for him to knock. She'd been raised Southern enough not to appear *too* eager.

"Hi," she said immediately, wondering for a moment if she should hug him or kiss him in welcome.

"Hey," he said softly, making an attempt at a smile. "Thanks for letting me swing by."

His reserve made her unsure of herself, so she didn't move to embrace him. "You're always welcome. Of course, all I've been thinking of this morning is about you meeting with my mama and how you're doing. Come on in."

She stepped aside, and he entered, taking off his cowboy hat and resting it against his thigh.

"Here, let me take your hat," she said, but he seemed a little reluctant to hand it to her. Then she realized why. He was nervous. Deciding to take a chance, she stepped close to him and wrapped her arms around him.

"Whoa," he said, but then he gently returned her embrace.

She rested her head against his chest and felt his heart beating rapidly against her ear. His body was warm, and when she didn't release him, the tension holding him in place slowly seemed to dissolve.

"I have something I need to tell you," he said against her hair.

That sounded ominous. "Okay." Reluctantly, she stepped back, but she didn't want to lose the connection between them, so she took his hand in hers. "Would you like something to drink?"

He shook his head, keeping a hold of her hand. "No, I'd best get this out first."

There was something in his face, something that made her heart clutch. She led him to the couch and sat beside him.

Clearing his throat, he took a deep breath. "Your mama gave her blessing for us to see each other," he began, looking down at their hands. "If that's what you still want. But then I realized on my way over that I need to tell you...

Jesus, this is going to be hard. Sorry, I shouldn't take the Lord's name in vain in front of you."

She scooted closer and clutched his hand. "It's okay. Whatever you need to tell me...you tell it whichever way works best for you."

He let out a jagged breath. "I...ah...just need to say it."

Her heart felt like someone had stepped on it. "I can't imagine that happening, but why don't you let me be the judge of that?"

"All right...it's about my best friend in the Army." His thumb stroked the inside of her palm. "His name was Booker. I've never been able to stop dreaming about what happened..."

She watched his face, wishing he'd meet her eyes, but since he couldn't seem to, she simply listened.

"I dreamed about it...him...the night before you came to my house to decorate."

Her lungs seemed to stop working. She remembered how exhausted and beaten down he'd looked that day. Now she was finally about to learn why.

"I'm not proud of what I'm about to tell you, but it needs telling. We were on patrol in an alley..." he began.

As she listened to him describe what happened, she bit her lip—hard enough to taste blood. She couldn't imagine being in that kind of danger, let alone the horror of having your best friend shot right beside you. Her throat thickened, and she fought the urge to cry. When he talked about all the blood pouring out of his friend's wounds and how he'd applied pressure to keep him from bleeding out while asking God to save him, his voice broke.

Hearing that tortured sound coming from him, she could no longer hold back her tears. They streamed down her face unchecked. She squeezed his hand hard, sensing his friend had died. Jake swiped at his own eyes, still keeping his gaze averted from her.

He resumed his story, telling it almost mechanically. When he described seeing the combatant preparing to fire at him, she felt like she was in that alley too. All of her muscles locked in place, and she held her breath, waiting to hear the next part.

It took him a moment to continue, and when he did, a burst of anger rolled through her. She wasn't a violent person. She'd been raised to believe killing was wrong, but she was glad Jake had shot that man. Gladder than she'd ever imagined feeling about such a thing.

When Jake told her that Booker had died, she felt the depth of his agony. It was clear he blamed himself for his friend's death. And God.

"You had a right to know what happened," he said in a hoarse voice. "I'm no hero. Not like that woman yesterday thinks. Or anyone else for that matter. I let my best friend down when he needed me most. Sure, I prayed to God, and I'm mighty pissed He didn't answer me, but I had a role in it too. I could let you down like that, and if I did, it would finish me, Susannah."

"Don't say that," she whispered harshly, tears tracking down her face.

"I...care for you...more than I've cared for anyone in a long while." He finally met her gaze, and the sorrow etched across his face grabbed her heart like a fist. "It's not just that I have PTSD. That's not the full truth of things. I feel responsible for Booker's death, and deep down, I... You deserve better than me, Susannah."

Then he bowed his head like he was waiting for her to pronounce judgment over him. She did the only thing she knew to do—she raised up on her knees beside him and pressed a soft kiss to his cheek.

He jolted and looked at her. In his cobalt blue eyes was surprise—but there was longing too—a longing for love, a longing for absolution.

"I think you're a good man who was put in a horrible situation," she said quietly. "One I can't begin to imagine. I'm so sorry about your friend. More than I could say. But you're not to blame for his death. Truth be told, I'm glad you defended yourself. I wouldn't have wanted you to die too."

His face bunched up.

"I would never have had the blessing of knowing you, and you're pretty darn wonderful, if you ask me," she said, sniffing over her own tears.

He blinked rapidly as tears filled his eyes. "No one I've cared about...has...*ever* said that to me." The words seemed wrenched from his very soul.

Then he squeezed his eyes shut and bowed over. Feeling him lean into her, she nestled against him and let go of his hand so she could put her arms around him.

He reached for her and wrapped her in a fierce embrace. "Oh, God," he whispered harshly, and she could feel him fighting a storm of emotions. "Oh, God."

"It's okay," she said, stroking his back. "You can let go, Jake. Just let it all out."

He made an anguished sound, still clutching her tightly. And then he broke.

She held him while he cried, crying silently with him. He pressed his face into her shoulder, soaking her shirt.

It was gut-wrenching and beautiful all at once. After a time, his anguish lessened to harsh rasps. He leaned back against the couch, doing his best to take deep breaths, taking her with him.

"I can't imagine what you think of me...after all that," he whispered.

She cuddled close to him, trying to ease the shame he felt over crying in front of her. "I think you're incredibly brave, and that you needed to let that out." How much more was bottled up inside him?

She pressed another kiss to his cheek.

"Susannah," he whispered harshly.

"I'm right here, Jake." She waited with tears in her eyes to see what he would do.

He looked at her with his watery blue eyes, *really* looked at her. His hand touched her cheek.

"Your brother was right," he said in that same harsh tone. "You just might be my miracle."

A smile tugged at her mouth. "What you told me doesn't change how I feel about you. In fact, it only makes me care about you more."

He brought her closer to his body, and she fit perfectly —just like she already knew she did.

"Maybe you're my miracle too, Jake." And even though she qualified it, she knew it was true. The depth of this connection was a gift. She believed that. His trust in her only magnified her feelings. What must it cost him to tell her this story? But he had gone through the torture of it. Because he believed she deserved to know what haunted him.

"We haven't even had a real date yet," he said, stroking her hair, "but the way I feel about you...it's like I've been with you for years."

"Sometimes it works that way," she said against his chest.

"You have one last chance to change your mind," he said, and this time his voice sounded stronger. "I'm a mess. I have survivor's guilt and PTSD and a whole bunch of other disorders probably."

It wasn't like him to be dramatic, but she wasn't going to point it out. "I won't change my mind," she assured him and leaned back so he could see her face. "I want to be with you."

He let out a ragged breath. "I've...tried so hard to overcome my PTSD, but I never seem to snuff it all the way out. It's like those damn trick birthday candles. Just when you think you've blown them out, they relight. And you blow and blow again with all your might, but you can't stop them from coming back to life. It's a hell of a thing... It wears on me. I don't want it to wear you down. That would cut me deeper than anything."

She chose her words carefully. "I know things won't always be easy, but we'll face them together. Like we did yesterday. But I want your promise. You'll continue to let me help you."

His head fell back against the couch, and he stared at the ceiling. "You drive a hard bargain."

"Yes." She knew she had to press him on this point.

"I gave up making promises a long time ago," he said, meeting her gaze again, "but I'll let you have this one."

Her heart seemed to soar, hearing that. "Thank you."

He released another ragged breath. "You McGuiness women are fierce creatures, but it seems you work miracles because of it. Susannah...what I told you. Other than your mama, I've never told another woman in my life about Booker. Whenever people ask me about that song, 'Man Down,' I keep it general. I didn't even tell your brother the whole story when we wrote the song together. I need you to know that."

His trust in her humbled her. "I'm glad you told me."

He blew out a long breath. "I am too, although I wish I'd spared you my breakdown. I should have waited until at least our third date to lose it in front of you."

Her mouth twitched. "At least," she tried to joke.

"That reminds me," he said, leaning in and kissing her cheek. "I have something for you in my truck."

She let him rise and watched him head to the front door. Taking a moment to settle herself, she closed her eyes and offered up a simple prayer. *Thank you, God. And thanks for continuing to help us.* Jake might call it a breakdown, but to her, it had been a huge breakthrough—both for him and for *them.*

When he returned, he was holding a bouquet of flowers as massive as his chest. There were roses in red, yellow, and white, and a collection of exotic orchids mixed with pink snapdragons and purple gladiolas.

She pressed her hand to her heart. "Oh, my goodness..."

He lifted his shoulder sheepishly. "I stopped by a florist on the way...in case you didn't...ah...change your mind about me." Then he walked over and sat beside her on the couch, extending the bouquet to her.

Inhaling the sweet smell of the roses, she smiled up at him. "They're beautiful, Jake. Thank you."

"Susannah," he said, taking her hand. "Will you do me the great honor of having lunch and then dinner with me tonight? After all we've been through, I have some dates to make up for."

"Lunch sounds good," she told him with a laugh. "And dinner. Jake, I..." How could she express all that she was feeling right now? "I'd pretty much go anywhere with you."

An easy smile crossed his face, the kind she'd seen when he was performing. Her heart lightened at the sight of it.

"That's how I feel too," he said, "but I need to ask you something. If we go out in public, people might start talking, and we might not be left to ourselves."

Yes, she'd had a bird's eye view of how a public outing might go. People would likely press him for autographs and pictures. He was probably worn out from all the emotion. She certainly was. As for the talk, there was nothing she could do about it, so she wasn't going to fret.

"How about we get some take out?" she asked him. "We can set something up here."

He seemed relieved. "I want to take you somewhere fancy...but..."

"It's okay," she told him. "Another time. I'm just happy to be with you, Jake."

He plucked a rose out of the bouquet and traced her cheek. "I'm pretty happy to be with you too. Tonight, I promise you romance. I just...couldn't wait to see you, is all, which is why I asked you to lunch first."

She gave him a warm smile. "I'm glad you didn't wait."

Sliding the rose across her nose, he tapped it playfully. "You are so beautiful you take my breath away."

Oh, how those words softened everything inside her. "You're pretty handsome too. I could look at you all day."

His eyes locked on hers, and she saw the change in them. There was desire there now. Her belly tightened in response. He leaned in slowly, and she met him halfway. Their lips met, and at first, there was the sense of coming home. As their mouths continued to sip at each other, something stronger emerged. The current ran through her, and she set the flowers on the coffee table and nestled closer. His hand came up to cup her face as his tongue sought entrance. She opened to him without hesitation.

As he continued to kiss her and she him, she reveled in the knowledge that her whole life had changed.

20

Though they didn't go anywhere more fancy than her living room and didn't eat anything more elegant than pizza, lunch with Susannah was the best date of Jake's life. He could hardly believe this beautiful, smart, kind, and special woman wanted to be with him. Her smile could usher in world peace, if you asked him, and he didn't care if that made him sappy.

Now that she knew everything, Jake could admit to himself that he was in love with her. All the way. Love had not played a large role in his life, but he knew how it felt. Being with Susannah was like writing and playing a new song. *Magical.*

They'd arranged to meet at his house at seven for a special dinner, and Jake was determined he'd give her the kind of date she deserved. He actually called his manager for help—something he'd never done for personal matters —making sure to mention Susannah was capable of inspiring plenty of songs in him.

Before Susannah was due to arrive, he swept one final glance around the room. Hundreds of tealight candles illuminated the den while large white taper candles lined the entryway in hurricane glasses. Fire blazed in the hearth, adding to the warm glow in the room. A profusion of colorful flowers were arranged in large vases around the house. Susannah McGuiness was the kind of woman who deserved romance, and tonight, he was going to give it to her.

He took one final opportunity to check his appearance in the mirror. His tan dress shirt was the one he'd worn to his first Country Music Awards, and he had on the belt he'd commissioned for his first performance at the Grand Ole Opry. Fashioned in silver, it was engraved with an American flag. And his boots...well, he'd brought out his lucky pair, the brown leather ones he'd been wearing the night he was spotted by a talent scout in the Bluebird Café.

His jaw was clean-shaven because he planned to kiss her senseless again. He couldn't get enough of her mouth and the feel of her body under his hands. But he was going to be a gentleman too. Things were happening quickly between them after being on simmer for so long, and he didn't want to make assumptions.

When he opened the door, he stepped back to behold the vision before him. Her gorgeous brown hair spilled over her shoulders in glorious waves. Her eyes were a bit darker tonight and lined in charcoal. But her mouth... He couldn't stop looking at her mouth. She'd swiped it with a dark pink.

"Wow," he said, leaning in to kiss her cheek, not sure how she felt about him messing up her lipstick so early in the evening. "I didn't think you could get any more beautiful, but fancy me being wrong."

When her hand settled on his chest, he stilled. He became aware of his heart, the one that seemed to beat to a different cadence whenever she was around—like the opening chords of a love song.

His arms came around her. "I can't seem to help wanting to hold you and kiss you after waiting so long."

She returned his embrace, resting her head against his chest. "I know what you mean."

He nestled his head into her neck for a moment, inhaling her scent—exotic and floral all at the same time. "I even missed you after I left you," he whispered. "Is that crazy?"

"I missed you too," she said, burrowing even closer. "So I guess we're both crazy."

Jake pulled back so he could see her beautiful face. *Crazy in love,* he wanted to say, but he didn't want to make assumptions there either. The pace of their courtship hadn't been normal, and while he might know she was his true north, he didn't want to assume he was hers.

The wind blew around them, and Susannah shivered.

"Come in. I shouldn't have kept you in the doorway."

After he shut the door behind her, he helped her with her coat and the sight of her dress pretty much had his mouth going Saguaro-cactus dry. It was a red sheath of a thing that clung to her slender body in all the right places.

"Goodness me," he declared. "You leave me breathless."

The smile she gave him was so full of light he imagined the stars would be envious.

"That was the plan. This is a date, after all." Then she turned and gasped. "Oh, my heavens! You have candles. Where did those come from? Because I know we didn't buy them. And flowers!"

He put his arm around her waist because he could. "I had some help. Come see."

As he led her into the den, she reached for his hand and all but melted into his side. "You did all this? *Today?*"

"As I said, I had help."

She stopped in the center of the den, and the glow from the candles touched her face. "This is beautiful, Jake. More than I could have imagined."

He touched her face with his free hand. "I wanted our official first date to be special. You...deserve...well, hell, everything good in the world, Susannah. I want to be worthy of you."

She kissed his palm. "You are, darlin'."

Hearing her call him that made his legs a little unsteady, like they got when he won a music award. "Come see what someone else cooked up for dinner."

She laughed. "Hired out, did you?"

"I'm not terrible in the kitchen, but you deserved better tonight."

Leading her to the kitchen, he couldn't help but take pride in how much the house was transforming. Before Susannah, he'd barely had a frying pan to his name. Now he had everything a famous chef could ask for.

"Oh, you have appetizers," she gasped. "Good heavens! Is that lobster on those canapés?"

He lifted his shoulder. "When I asked the chef for fancy, he suggested lobster. I hope you like it."

"What's not to like?"

She raised his hand and spun in a circle, and he caught her to him and led her into a two-step. After seeing the tears she'd shed for him, it made him happy to see her this light-hearted.

"I forgot to put on some music," he said, pressing his cheek to hers as they danced.

"We seem to be doing okay." Her steps matched his

easily, and he led her into another turn. It was effortless. They danced like they'd been together for fifty years.

"I've pretty much fallen head over heels for you," he whispered against her ear, unable to keep the feelings in any longer. "I feel about you like I feel about one of my songs."

She pulled closer to him. "I feel the same way."

They danced a little while longer, and then he finally pulled away to serve her some food.

"You must be hungry," he said, handing her a plate.

"These all look so tempting," she said, studying the tray. "Besides the lobster, what else do we have here?"

"Gruyere cheese puffs and a honey and fig chutney over some kind of homemade cracker." He'd had the chef write down the menu in case he forgot.

She popped one of the puffy things in her mouth and made an *ummm* sound, which was erotic enough to make his ears go red...and for other things to happen. He grabbed a few onto his plate to distract himself, thinking he'd have to eat a truckload of these little things if they were the main meal. Thank God his appetite had returned.

"The chef prepared a cream of asparagus soup and a root vegetable salad for the first courses." He glanced over to where they sat on the counter. "I hope you don't mind us serving ourselves. I didn't want to have anyone in the way tonight."

"I'm glad there's no one else here. That would make me feel weird anyway. Let's get our plates filled and sit in front of the fire."

He glanced over at the dining room door. "I have a table prepared for us all date-like."

"Do you now?" she asked with an impish grin. "Let's go see."

When they entered the dining room, she turned and hugged him again. "Did you buy out the florist?"

"Pretty much," he said, not wanting to admit he'd actually bought out two of Nashville's finest.

She halfway skipped over to the three-foot-tall arrangement of roses in pink, red, and white displayed on the side board they'd found together. Plucking a pink rose out, she lifted it to her nose and inhaled deeply.

"You did that earlier," he said, stepping closer to her. "That's how I knew roses were your favorite."

"You're pretty observant," she commented, tapping the rose against his chest. "And handsome. Have I told you that tonight?"

His eyes dropped to her mouth. He couldn't help it. "No, but I like hearing I please you."

"You do," she said softly.

Their gazes met, and he lowered his mouth to hers and kissed her properly. "I've wanted to do that since I first saw you in the doorway. But I wasn't sure how you'd feel about me messing up your lipstick before our date started."

She played with one of the buttons on his shirt. "Don't wait next time. I wanted you to kiss me too, but I didn't know...well...how to tell you. I'm...this isn't my normal."

He lifted her chin so he could see those beautiful moss-green eyes. "It isn't mine either, Susannah. I know musicians have a bad rap, but I'm not one of those guys."

"I know that."

The steadiness in her voice assured him that she meant it. "Good. Now let's eat this fancy dinner."

They doled out the soup from the warmer, and Susannah dotted both of their bowls with the delicate greens the chef had left.

"This stuff looks like shamrocks to me," he said, hovering close to her because he couldn't stay away.

"Watercress," she said, sneaking a smile at his expense. "It's good for you."

"You'll probably say the root vegetable salad is too," he fired back with a drawl. "Back home, we only ate root vegetables when money was tight."

"We did too, growing up," she said, handing him his bowl. "But they're really popular now. Likely because they contain so many vitamins and minerals."

He made a show of rolling his eyes, falling into this easy, familiar rhythm of flirting with her.

"Take the soup bowls into the dining room, and I'll serve up the salad," she said.

"I don't want you to get food on your nice dress." He looked around for a towel, and seeing one, tied it around her waist.

"Oh, doesn't that look lovely," she said, gesturing to her front. "This is what my outfit was missing."

He couldn't resist giving her a peck on her cheek, and when he pulled back, her whole face seemed to glow like those tealights in the den.

Though he wanted to linger near her, he took the soup bowls into the dining room and positioned them on the dining room table. The dinner plates and silverware were his, but he certainly hadn't folded the fancy napkins into swans. That was a touch that had been added by the helper his manager had sent over. He grabbed the plates, thinking they would need them for dinner, and headed back into the kitchen.

"Someone turned our napkins into swans, and I have to admit, it makes me feel a little guilty," he said.

She glanced over from spooning out what looked like turnips. "Why is that?"

"We're eating grouse for our main course."

Her lips twitched. "Swans and grouse might be related."

"I know," he said, setting the plates down in the staging area. "I might have to unwrap those swans before we take the main course into the dining room. I'd hide them in the closet, but we need our napkins."

"Unwrap the poor guys," she said in a serious tone, earning her another kiss. "Come on. I have the salad."

"Yay," he mocked, but he took the salad plates from her. "This had better be good."

His manager had managed to hire one of the best personal chefs in Nashville on short notice, but still. Root vegetable salad?

To Jake's surprise, the salad wasn't terrible. The tangy vinaigrette cut the earthy chalkiness he always associated with them. The soup, however, was out of this world.

"I have to admit," he said, trying not to rest his elbows on the table like his mama had taught him was bad manners. "I think the watercress adds something."

"Me too," she said, taking another spoonful and sliding it into her luscious mouth. "Personally I love the salad more."

"On that, my dear, we will have to disagree." He pushed his half-eaten salad plate forward. "I'm holding out for the grouse."

"Shh..." she said softly. "Don't say that too loud. The swans might hear you."

Since the swans—or what had been the swans—were resting in their laps, he doubted it. "I'll whisper about the grouse into your sweet, soft ear next time."

She twirled her earring and gazed at him, and since he

knew the motion was meant to tempt him, he leaned forward and kissed her gently on the lips. Her eyes were alight when he pulled away.

"You can whisper into my ear anytime," she drawled.

When she resumed eating the root salad, he watched her. The delicate line of her jaw made his fingers itch to trace it. "I like you like this."

"Like what?"

"All relaxed and natural with me. It's...more than I imagined it would be, and I mean that in the best way possible."

She set her silverware on her plate. "Did you used to think about us like this? Together?"

A feeling of vulnerability washed over him before he remembered she'd seen him at his worst. "Yeah, I did," he choked out. "A lot."

Her hand rested on his forearm. "Me too. And you're right...it's even better. I'm glad I'm finally here, Jake. Like this."

"I'm glad too, Susannah."

And with that confession, he couldn't help but kiss her again. She didn't seem to be in any hurry to finish the rest of their meal, so he pulled her onto his lap and kept right on kissing her. Soon they were both breathing hard. He finally felt her push against his chest, and he immediately released her.

"We should probably finish dinner," she said softly, but there was a wrinkle between her eyes—one he didn't quite understand.

She rose and gathered up their plates before disappearing into the kitchen. He sat a moment, reviewing his steps. Had he done something wrong? She'd seemed to feel as eager as he did. Well, he couldn't read her mind. Best ask her outright. He followed her into the kitchen.

The roasting pan holding the grouse sat open before her, and she was brandishing a butcher knife. "Do you want me to do the carving or pick at it yourself?"

"Ah...I don't know," he said, hooking his thumbs into his jeans, unsure for the first time in the evening. "They don't look rightly big enough to carve, although the chef told me they were the finest grouse on the market. Ah...red grouse, I think. From Scotland. He said to chew carefully because the shot might still be in the bird."

Her horrified look might have made him laugh if these unwelcome nerves hadn't already formed a knot in his belly.

"Well...then we can just plate these as they are and hope neither of us has to make an emergency dentist appointment in the morning."

She turned back to the main course, arranging the grouse on the plates and then adding portions of wild rice and garlic spinach to each one. When she thrust the plates out at him, he took them, but only for a span of a second. He shook his head and set them aside. If he didn't say anything now, it would be like taking a step back, and that was the last thing he wanted to do with her.

"You and I seem to be pretty in tune with each other, so do you want to tell me why you have a line here—" he touched the spot between her brows playfully, "—after we kissed in there? And don't tell me it's because you're excited about the grouse."

She seemed to hold her breath for a moment before letting it out slowly. "Things are...well, moving fast between us. I didn't want you to have...any...oh, good heavens." She closed her eyes and pressed her finger to the very spot he'd touched moments ago.

"Surely after everything that's happened, you can tell me what's going on," he said softly. "Come on, now. Why don't you hold my hand? It can't be all that bad."

As they linked hands again, forming that now familiar but no less thrilling connection, he noticed the pale pink dotting her cheeks.

"I'm not sure if there's ever a good time or way to say this," she said, "but with the way things are heading between us...well, you need to know."

His body tightened like an over-strung guitar, trying to guess what in the world had her so riled up. "I'm listening."

"I'm..." She gave a nervous laugh. "I've been saving myself for marriage."

It took him a moment to comprehend what she was saying. Then he blinked. "*Oh...*"

"And...I know it makes me weird and old-fashioned in this day and age, but I still believe it's the best way for me."

He fought the urge to rock back on his heels. She was a virgin. Holy hell. He hadn't really thought about it, but he supposed he should have considered it a possibility. She was a church-going preacher's daughter. He knew what the Good Book said about pre-martial sex even though he didn't see what all the fuss was about. If two people cared about each other, he didn't see why they should be judged for having sex. But he respected other people's opinions. Right now, he especially respected hers.

"I don't think that makes you weird," he said, easing closer to her. "It might be a bit counter-cultural, but who the heck cares? Your values are your values. You should always do what you think is right."

She was biting her lip, gazing at him steadily. "But you understand what this means, right?"

He might have eaten turnips earlier, but he hadn't fallen off the turnip wagon. "Yes, I understand, and I won't press you."

Right now, he didn't rightly know how far their...intimate interactions could take them, but he figured she would tell him when the time came.

"You don't need to be concerned about it, honey," he said, raising her hand so he could kiss the back of it. "I'll never press you or make you uncomfortable. But you'll... ah...need to give me some parameters, I expect, from time to time."

She flushed prettily at that statement and looked away. "Ah...of course."

He took her into his arms without any pressure so she could relax again. Her shoulders looked as tense as his felt.

"It'll be fine," he said, rubbing her back.

"You don't mind? I mean...I was so afraid to tell you." She pushed her head against his chest. "I was afraid to disappoint you."

It was like someone was clutching his very heart. "Have you been worrying about this all afternoon? Susannah, you could *never* let me down. How could you even think it after everything we've been through?"

She blew out another deep breath and finally looked at him. "I thought you might want to...have sex tonight." Then her eyes rested on a place over his shoulder. "After today."

He let out a sigh and tipped her chin up to look at him. "I was going to let you set the pace. I care about you and how you feel. Your values...they make you who you are. That could never disappoint me, and I'd never want to change you."

"I'm glad you can understand," she said, although she still seemed to be struggling to breathe.

He kissed her softly on the lips. "Don't give it another thought. We'll figure it out."

"Good," she said, giving a shaky laugh. "Because I really like having you hold me and kiss me."

Yeah, so did he. He'd just have to restrain the urge to want more than that. Moving forward, he'd have to be even more sensitive to her moods and wishes when it came to touching her. There was no way he was going to hurt her or let her down by making her uncomfortable.

"I like that too. Now we should eat before that red Scottish grouse thing needs to be microwaved."

She nodded, and he let her grab the plates since she all but lunged for them. It was clear she was anxious for something to do with her hands.

And darn it all, he had to admit that part of him liked knowing she hadn't been with another man. He took a moment to dream that he might be worthy of marrying her one day. That he might be lucky enough to make love to her and be her one and only for the rest of her life.

Setting aside thoughts of the future, he followed her to the table, and they dug into the grouse. Truth be told, it was more like spearing the little guy. There wasn't much meat on it, but what was there tasted pretty good. There was a trace of game meat, but thankfully no shot. He polished off his sides in an effort to fill his belly, hoping dessert would be more robust.

She was still picking at her meat all delicate-like, and he took a moment to watch her.

"You eat fast," she commented with a slow smile.

Her nerves seemed to have faded away after their talk in the kitchen, and for that, he was grateful. "I always did.

Growing up, it meant more playtime after dinner before dark. And in the Army..." He let the sentence trail off, not wanting to introduce darkness to their night.

"I've always been a slow eater," she said, chewing a piece of meat thoughtfully. Suddenly her eyes widened. Her mouth stopped working, and she quickly turned her back to him, rummaging for her napkin.

"I see you found the shot that ended that bird," he commented with a chuckle.

"Oh, that is so gross! I'm going to have to wash my mouth out." She rose and darted out of the room.

He opened her napkin. The hunter had used an eight shot. Jake found himself holding his breath. He hadn't seen a bullet since his Army days. His mind conjured up images of ammunition shells on a dust-strewn street in Baghdad, so he forced himself to close the napkin. Sitting back in his chair, he breathed deeply and reached for composure. He wasn't in Baghdad anymore. He was here in Dare River with a beautiful woman.

He was not going to let the past ruin this moment.

But he couldn't close it out, so he rose and took the napkin into the kitchen and tossed the whole thing in the trash. The woman who'd come over to help him set up had left a few extra napkins on the kitchen counter, so he grabbed Susannah a fresh one.

When she returned, she shook her head. "Sorry about that. I realized as I ran out of here that I was making a fuss."

He forced a smile. "Make all the fuss you want. It's no bother to me."

"Well," she said, dropping into her seat. "That was a first. Usually, I don't think about how the animal I'm eating died."

"And yet that's what happens. Everything dies." Then

he bit back a curse. "Sorry, that was a horrible thing to say." And on their first date, no less.

Her gaze flew to his. "No. You're right. It's okay to say... whatever comes, Jake. You were more than understanding of me in the kitchen. I want to be the same way for you."

Somehow those words helped wash away the last of the residue clinging to him.

Noticing her new napkin, she dropped it into her lap. "Thanks for handling that for me."

"No bother," he said, clearing his throat. "I'm sorry it had to happen."

"How about we move on to dessert?" she suggested. "I'm assuming a fancy meal comes with dessert."

"It sure does," he said, rising and taking their plates this time. "I believe I told the chef that you have a thing for chocolate."

The delighted squeal behind him burned away any of the lingering ill ease he'd felt after seeing the shot. "You did? Oh, what did he make?"

"I believe he made you a triple chocolate cake with raspberry and espresso filling."

Another squeal erupted. "He did? If he were here, I'd have to thank him. Profusely. But since he's not, I guess I'll have to thank you."

"No thanks necessary," he said immediately. "Are you ready to behold the cake?"

He took the pastry box out of the refrigerator and flipped it open.

"*Good heavens!*" she exclaimed. "It looks delicious."

He had high hopes for this dessert after the grouse. "The chef also left one of those stainless steel makers that whips cream." Of course, he'd had some fantasies about other possible uses for the device, but he'd put them on the shelf for the moment. Her delight over the cake would have to be enough.

"All righty then," she said, taking the box from him. "Let's serve us up some cake."

After they were seated with their dessert, Jake found himself experiencing a new level of sexual torture. Watching Susannah eat chocolate could tempt a monk, but listening to Susannah eat chocolate...well, she could tempt a saint. He tried to focus on his own cake, but he couldn't maintain his composure.

No, not when she was uttering those adorable little moans beside him and fluttering her eyelids as she chewed.

"You're torturing me, you know," he drawled, glancing over at her.

She immediately stilled and stopped chewing. He'd meant it as a bit of a joke, no more than that, but the delight faded from her face. "Oh, I'm so sorry. I didn't think."

She was so upset, she dropped her fork. It clanged against the plate and fell onto the tablecloth, staining it with chocolate and whipped cream.

"Look what I did," she declared, dabbing her napkin in her water glass and wiping at the stain.

"Don't worry about it," he said, hating to see her upset. He should have kept his mouth shut. "It'll wash."

"No, I was clumsy."

He stopped her by putting his hand over hers. *"Susannah."*

The vulnerability in her eyes wrapped around his heart and squeezed.

"It's okay. Really. I didn't mean to make you uncomfortable."

She frowned. "I didn't mean to make you uncomfortable either."

"I know," he said, rising from the chair. "Let's finish eating our cake in front of the fire."

Maybe a change in scenery would help them relax together again. She nodded, and they both took their plates into the other room.

The tealights were still casting a romantic glow in the den, and since Jake had fed more logs into the fire, there was a nice blaze awaiting them. She sat on the couch beside him, but there was a new distance between them. He didn't like that. No, not one bit.

"Susannah," he said softly. "Just because we aren't going to make love doesn't mean we can't touch each other. Would you mind scooting over a little closer to me?"

"Sure." She inched over to him, but her body was as stiff as an old washboard.

Telling her to relax would only make her tighten up more, so he kicked his legs out and ate his cake, watching the fire, hoping she would settle. This time she didn't share her enjoyment. In fact, she didn't eat much more of her cake before setting it on the coffee table.

"I didn't mean to take away your pleasure in the cake," he said quietly over the crackle of the fire. "I was only... well...flirting with you. I'm sorry it was the wrong move."

She blew out a breath. "Our Sunday school teacher always said we needed not to be too enticing is all. That it was hard on men not to...have sex before marriage."

He set his plate aside and turned to face her. The delicacy of the topic was not lost on him. He needed to choose his words carefully. "I expect it can be hard on a woman as well."

Her eyes widened. "I hadn't really thought of that

before. But...I guess you're right. When you kiss me..." Her cheeks turned red. "Well, I shouldn't say."

He fought a smile; without trying to, she was being as alluring as she'd been with the chocolate. "Yeah, you'd best not say. At least not right now." Then he shook his head. "No, heck, I've changed my mind. I *want* you to tell me. We might not be able to make love, but at least we can be honest with each other. Perhaps we're approaching this all wrong. We're both adults. I want to make love to you, but I respect your decision. And I'm going to want you when I kiss you and hold you. There's nothing I can do about that, and I'm not sorry for it."

Her eyes darkened when he said those words, and he forced himself not to reach for her.

"That's how I'm made," he added. "I don't want that to make you uncomfortable, but the truth is that I want to kiss you and hold you and touch you as much as you're willing to let me. I'm not going to lie and say that my body is going to like not making love to you, but I'm not ruled by it."

"I'm glad you can be honest with me," she said softly, so softly he had to strain to hear her. "It was hard to tell you... and then things got all awkward. I don't want it to be that way either, Jake."

He held out his hand to her, which she took without any hesitation.

"You need to know something," she said, scooting closer to him. "I meant what I said the other day. I've never felt this way about anyone."

He fought the words resting on the tip of his tongue. It was only their first date. Sort of. She deserved more romance. And deep down he needed to see how things progressed before he told her how deep his feelings went.

"I've had feelings for other women," he confessed. "But

I've never felt for anyone what I feel for you. I felt it the first time I saw you. Then I held your hand that first time, and... well if I were writing a song, I'd say it was like coming home." He didn't mention he hadn't felt much of home in his life, which is what had made the sensation all the more jarring...and beautiful.

"Would you play a song for me?" she asked. "I...really love your voice."

"I'd love that," he said, feeling a smile spread across his face. "Music is a pretty special person in my life. She kind of saved me. Let me grab my guitar."

When he reached his studio, he selected the first guitar he'd bought after coming to Nashville. That guitar had held all his dreams in the beginning. And then those dreams had come true.

He had new dreams now, ones that involved a life with Susannah. Them raising a family together. Maybe his guitar could help bring those dreams to life as well.

He headed upstairs to sing to the woman who possessed his heart.

21

Shelby waited until nine o'clock to call Susannah and tell her that she and Sadie wanted to meet her for lunch. For a moment, she thought about asking Tammy and Amelia Ann to join them, but that might be too much for Susannah. Her sister was feeling delicate right now, so she and Sadie would have to be gentle.

Of course Shelby wasn't feeling all that gentle. She'd fretted and prayed something fierce over her sister and Jake, and she wanted a praise report, as their church called it. All she and Sadie knew was that their mama had given Susannah and Jake her blessing to be together, and so they'd...no surprise...had a date. Her sister had promised to give more details at lunch.

They met at Husk, one of their favorite places in Nashville. Sadie and Shelby arrived first, and when a waiter showed their sister to their table, Susannah's million-dollar smile said it all.

"Wow!" Sadie said, hugging her first. "You're practically glowing. Things *must* have gone well last night."

Yes, Susannah looked infused with sunshine, but Shelby

could tell it was happiness, not an afterglow. She knew Susannah was still waiting for marriage. Shelby herself had let that ship sail in college with the long-term boyfriend she'd thought she'd marry. They hadn't, which was for the best, but she'd had to forgive herself for feeling like she'd made a mistake.

Being a preacher's daughter, she well knew her mama's opinion on pre-marital sex. Louisa thought it was best to wait, but thankfully was open-minded when people...well, succumbed to the temptation. Shelby had come to believe it was okay to be with someone she cared about. But she didn't talk about it with her sisters, fearing they might judge her. And Sadie never talked about sex, so Shelby didn't know her feelings on the subject.

"It's good to see you so happy," Shelby said, hugging Susannah when it was her turn to greet her.

"It's good to *feel* this happy," her sister replied, shrugging out of her coat. "Oh, you've gotten bread already and that glorious honey butter they have."

They took their seats, and Susannah immediately reached for the food.

"So..." Sadie said, bouncing up and down in her chair. "Tell us about the date."

"Yes, tell, tell," Shelby encouraged.

"Oh, it was like a dream," she practically cooed. "Jake even hired a chef to make us a fancy meal."

She proceeded to describe the menu, which made Shelby reassess Jake some. She'd pegged him as more of a simple good ol' boy, as they'd say, being from Arkansas and all. But it seemed he was adventurous enough to hire a chef to make her sister a special meal.

"I'm impressed," Shelby said when Susannah finished

her story, "but it must have been so disgusting to chew on the shot in the grouse."

"And you had to spit out a bullet in front of Jake on your first date! You must have been so embarrassed." Sadie's eyes were wide as she grabbed more bread and buttered it as thick as a slab of bacon.

"I was mortified!" Susannah declared. "But he was so good about it. Heck, he was good about everything."

Shelby thought that might be code for Susannah having "the talk" with him, but she didn't ask. Sadie glanced at her, and she could tell her sister was thinking the same thing.

"That's great," Shelby said diplomatically. "I'm so happy it went well for y'all."

"We need more of this goodness." Susannah signaled the waiter and asked for more bread and butter.

"Absolutely!" Sadie said, shoving another piece in her mouth.

Shelby tore off a piece and ate it more delicately.

"Don't give me that look!" Sadie said, nudging her shoulder with her hand. "I didn't eat breakfast."

"I was too excited to eat," Susannah said. "Let me tell you about the candles and the flowers. There were hundreds of them."

"Hundreds?" Sadie asked with a gasp, reaching for another roll the moment the waiter set the basket down on the table.

Shelby thanked the poor man and told him they'd be ready to order in a few more minutes. From his expression, he obviously feared he was next if the bread ran out.

"Hundreds of tealights and candles in hurricane glasses lined the entryway to the den. And the flowers! You'll have to come over to my house for some. He piled my car up with so many vases I could barely see out of the back of my Audi."

"Really?" Sadie asked between bites.

"I'm glad Jake has a romantic side. You deserve it." Shelby didn't add "after everything," but there was no need.

Sadie nodded in agreement.

"He sang to me too," Susannah said, making circles in the condensation on her water glass with a dreamy smile.

"Shut the front door!" Sadie said, causing a few patrons to look over. "It was like you had a private concert. Personally I would have fainted dead away."

Sadie could be so dramatic sometimes. Not that Shelby wasn't the same way. They just weren't often dramatic at the same time. "Would you let Susannah continue, please?"

Her sister stuck her tongue out, and a woman at a nearby table gasped.

Shelby laughed. "If that woman's in Mama's church…"

"She's not," Sadie told her with an eye-roll. "I would know her. Can we order now? I'm hungry."

"No kidding," Shelby mused, raising her hand to signal the waiter. "The poor man is terrified of us."

Sadie's head immediately swiveled in his direction. "Why? We're just a bunch of beautiful women having lunch."

"I think it's the amount of bread and butter being consumed by our table," she commented, pointing to the second bread basket, which now sat empty.

The poor waiter didn't make eye contact as he took their order, and he all but grimaced as he asked if they'd like more bread.

Sadie immediately said, "Yes," and he scuttled off.

"So when are you and Jake seeing each other again, Susannah?" Shelby asked.

Her sister turned bright pink. "This afternoon. More guest bedroom pieces are arriving, and I want to be there to arrange things. Then we're having dinner again. I can't wait to see what he's got planned."

"Me either!" Sadie exclaimed, clapping her hands only once, thank God. "You'll have to call or text us to let us know how it goes."

Shelby shot her a glance. "You don't have to give us daily reports unless you want to."

"Thanks for clarifying," Susannah said with a trace of humor in her voice. "It's kind of nice to share this with y'all. I've...never really had it before. No date I've ever been on has prepared me for how it feels to be with Jake. I am so blessed."

"You *are* blessed, sugar," Sadie said, grabbing her hand. "Imagine. Dating Jake Lassiter! It's every woman's dream."

"It wouldn't matter to me if he was our busboy," Susannah declared. "He's a good man. Heck, he's more than good. He's wonderful, and he's been through so much to become who he is."

"We know you love him," Sadie said, twirling the ends of her hair. "Does Jake feel the same way?"

Leave it to Sadie to go for gold. The server appeared with their food, and they took a moment to thank him before he walked away.

"It's early yet," Susannah said, not denying her feelings. "He says he's never felt this way about anyone either."

"Wow!" Sadie exclaimed, biting into an asparagus spear. "You're so lucky, Susannah."

"I'm happy for you, sugar," Shelby said, digging into her sweet potato fries.

"Me too," she said, picking up her burger. "I only hope that between his strength, Mama's help, and my...well, love, he can move past all the things that have tortured him. He deserves happiness. More than anyone I know after all he's endured."

Yeah, that sounded a lot like love to Shelby. As happy as she was for both of them, she'd add another prayer to her list. She'd start praying Jake wouldn't break her sister's heart. There were still shadows tormenting him, and she could only hope he'd be strong enough to withstand them.

Susannah chatted on, telling them more about the house and her plans to paint a mural in the dining room. It sounded like Jake was a positive influence about her art, which eased Shelby's mind a little more.

When they finished their meal, they left the server a hefty tip and headed to the parking lot.

"Have fun with Jake," Sadie said, kissing and hugging Susannah something fierce.

"He's worried about taking me out in public because he doesn't want me to have to deal with the hassles of his life," Susannah said when she released her.

"That sounds reasonable for a while," Shelby said thoughtfully, "but it isn't practical in the long run."

"Yeah!" Sadie exclaimed. "If he keeps buying up that amount of flowers, there won't be any left in the entire city."

"I hope he keeps buying you flowers," Shelby said. "If you ask me, when a man stops doing the little things, the magic is lost."

Susannah opened the door to her Audi and threw her purse inside. "I have a feeling he's going to do fine."

"Me too," Sadie said, giving her another hug.

Shelby wrapped her arms around Susannah as soon as

Sadie let her go. "I'm happy he makes you happy, but if you ever need us like you did the other night, don't hesitate to call."

When Susannah pulled away enough to meet her eyes, some of her happy glow had dimmed. "I will. I'm hoping for the best."

She nodded and waited until Susannah had driven off before turning to Sadie. "Mama's right. She's going to need a lot of prayers."

Sadie swatted her. "Oh, you're always fretting. If Jake's anywhere near as happy as Susannah, he's well on his way to recovery."

"I sure hope so," Shelby said, rubbing her arms as the wind picked up. "I need to get back."

"Me too," Sadie said, "but I need to talk with you about something real quick."

Giving her sister her full attention, she crossed her arms to ward off the chill. She should have worn a thicker coat. "Okay, but hurry. I'm freezing my tail off out here."

"Are you serious about hiring a private investigator to try and find Daddy?" she asked. "I couldn't stop thinking about it after what you said about Gail and...well...I have to be honest. I don't want to try and find Daddy just to discover his medical history."

Shelby blinked a couple of times. "I don't either, but I've thought about it a lot since Susannah got all flustered. She's right about it hurting Mama, and that would kill me. It would open up a can of worms if we find Daddy." Which is why she'd turned the burner down for the moment.

"I agree," Sadie said, "which is why I think we should pray on it some more. If we still feel it's the right thing to do in a few weeks, let's talk to J.P."

Shelby frowned immediately.

"I know what you're thinking," Sadie said, holding up her hand, "but hear me out."

Since turning tail from Sadie and racing off in her car would be immature, she held her ground. "All right. Let's hear it."

"We both agree we don't want to hurt Mama—or anyone else for that matter."

Shelby nodded.

"If we explain our reasoning to J.P., I think he'll be an ally with Susannah and Mama, should we choose to go through with it. I've never known J.P. to forbid us to do anything, and I think he might remember some things about Daddy, what with him being older when he left."

"J.P. doesn't know why Daddy left any more than the rest of us do, Sadie." She fought off her frustration. "But you're right about him being more...open-minded than Susannah."

Sadie hugged her, and they swayed in place.

"So let's pray about it more and then see how we feel," her sister said, letting her go. "It's a big step."

"We may not find anything," Shelby told her. That truth had dug in deep like a burr.

"But we might," Sadie fired back. "All the more important for us to discuss this with everyone who's willing to talk about it. Our decision will affect the whole family, Shelby."

"It doesn't have to," Shelby said. "If people don't want to know what we discover, we won't tell them."

Sadie walked over to her car and unlocked it. "I need to run, but Shelby...if we find something, everyone will deserve to be told. Especially any medical stuff. But if we find him, I'd...I'd want to visit him and talk to him—even though I don't know what our reception would be."

Shivering at the thought, Shelby dug out her key fob. "So we pray on it a spell more," she agreed with a nod. She gave her sister a wave and headed over to her own car, unlocking it with the fob. Once inside, she rested her head on the steering wheel.

Sadie was right; her interest in finding their daddy was about so much more than learning about his medical history. Gail's recent news had only magnified her one true desire.

She wanted to find her daddy for real.

22

Over the next week, Susannah's life altered dramatically. She spent every day with Jake, either working on his house, which included beginning the mural, or simply being with him.

They went out to their first restaurant together, and the next day, sure enough, there was a picture of her and Jake holding hands all over social media. She didn't mind. It wasn't like they could hide away from the world forever, and now that they were officially dating, they didn't care who knew. Of course, it bothered her a touch to think some might suggest she was being less than professional, dating a client, but after all the strides they'd taken together, there was no way she was going to wait until his home was finished to be with him.

Her mama called, and they talked a good spell about how happy Jake made her. Her brother checked in with her too, and Tammy, Tory, and Amelia Ann insisted on taking her out to lunch. She delighted in sharing her joy with them over a scrumptious sausage and pepperoni pizza at DeSano Pizza Bakery. Tory had given her some tips about what it was like to be involved with a country music star. While she'd joked about using a frying pan on the more obnoxious photographers, she'd said to simply let the men do their thing. That's what the press wanted mostly anyway.

Truth be told, her expanding family was so interested in her business, she wouldn't have been surprised if Rye himself had called. Now, if Clayton had done so, she would have fallen off her chair.

When Sunday rolled around, she and Jake went to church together. They held hands going into the service, during, and pretty much throughout the fellowship afterward. Tongues wagged. People stared. Many flat-out congratulated her, saying it was about darn time she'd found a man. She was so happy, she didn't even mind. Much. Jake took it all in stride, telling everyone he was the luckiest man in the world.

She'd asked him to come to Sunday dinner, and he insisted on helping her make the blueberry pie she'd promised to bring as a contribution. All he really did was wash and stem the blueberries, but it felt so good to cook with him and bring something they'd made together.

When they arrived and joined everyone in the kitchen, where pots were simmering and meat was sizzling, she made sure to tell everyone Jake had helped with the baking.

Rye immediately slapped him on the back and said, "When you start baking pies with a woman, you're a lost cause. I know that from personal experience."

"You've never made a pie in your life, Rye Crenshaw," Tory said, giving him an arch look that made him smack a kiss on her cheek.

"I wash things," Rye said with that wicked drawl of his. "Sometimes."

"Don't listen to him, Jake." Tory picked up a clean spoon

and shook it at her husband. "That man likes to think that watching in the kitchen is helping." She thrust it into a bubbling pot of grits and stirred with a good amount of gusto.

"When the cook is so beautiful, I can't do anything *but* watch. I'd cut my hand with a knife or burn myself. I recall someone burning her hand taking out the cornbread once."

"You're impossible!" she said, shaking her head.

Everyone was laughing when Annabelle bolted into the house with a panting Barbie at her side.

"Jake!" she yelled, catapulting herself into his leg. "I was in the tree house with Rory. Mama radioed you were here."

"Radioed, huh?" he asked, sinking down to one knee to receive her little hug.

Susannah pretty much melted at the sweet sight of them together, and everyone else seemed to have the same reaction. Her mama sidled up to her and wrapped an arm around her waist.

"He looks happy," Mama said softly. "Like you."

"*Yeah*," was pretty much all she could say. "I love him, Mama." It felt so good to say the words, to give voice to this truth she knew in her heart.

"I know you do, sugar," Mama said with a squeeze. "And he loves you."

He hadn't said it yet, but she knew he did. Every time he looked at her...well, it was like she was the sun and the moon and the stars combined—which he told her pretty much every day. He'd even written it into a new song, he'd said, but he hadn't shared it with her yet. But she knew it was about her. About them. Talk about humbling and romantic.

"Are you happy with his progress?" she asked, keeping her voice to a whisper so no one would overhear.

"You know I can't say," Mama replied, resting her head on her shoulder. "He needs to tell you, sugar, but I think it's pretty obvious he's happy."

Jake did share some of the aspects of his sessions with Mama with her. He'd told her about Mama's assignment to write a letter to God, which had unsettled him but crystalized how he felt. This past week, he'd had two sessions, and he said he wanted to continue to give his PTSD the attention it needed. He hadn't experienced another episode, and his relief was obvious. She took it as evidence their prayers were helping. She continued to lift him up every time he came to mind, which was pretty often. Truth be told, it was probably a good thing he was her only client right now. She couldn't imagine trying to concentrate elsewhere.

"He's good with Annabelle," her mama said, and Susannah knew what she was suggesting.

He would be a good father. That thought had already struck her a couple times. She refused to feel bad about it.

Jake finally stood, and Annabelle took his hand. "Seems we're going to see the tree swing."

"We're not going to *see* it, Jake," Annabelle said in exasperation, looking so darling in her blue coat and pink stocking hat. "You're going to *push* me."

"Oh, right," he teased. "You'll have to remind me. I'm getting along in years."

"You're not that old," Annabelle told him, pulling him toward the back door. "But even old people can push me on the swing. Granddaddy does sometimes."

"Thanks so much, missy," Rye's daddy fired back. "She's a spitfire, that one."

"Yes, I am," Annabelle responded with a wink. "Come on, Jake."

He looked up at Susannah, and she felt a smile spread across her face.

"Seems I have a date," he drawled.

The moment he left, she could feel all eyes pinned on her. She lifted her shoulders and said, "So, we're pretty happy."

"We're not a bunch of mules," Rye said, crossing the room to tweak her nose. "He baked a pie with you, girl. That man is crazy about you."

"And I him," she responded with a grin.

"That's good," Rye said, two-stepping his way over to his wife's side. "When's dinner going to be ready, honey?"

"Do you ever think about anything but your next meal, Rye Crenshaw?" Tory asked him.

He snaked his hand around her as she was passing him and pulled her flush against his chest. "Yeah, darlin'. You and the baby. Now let's see what we can hunt up for snacks."

"I have them right here, Rye," Tammy said, pulling a large serving plate out of the refrigerator. "Eat away."

Rye plucked one of the pepper slices off the plate and popped it into his mouth, making Tory laugh.

"We really can't take him anywhere," she told everyone.

"He's incorrigible," Rory said, brightening up when his uncle handed him a slice of pepper. "Right, Aunt Tory?"

"Right," she agreed, ruffling his blond hair.

Tammy removed a few more dishes from the refrigerator and set them on the counter. "I made a spicy ranch dip for the vegetables. That should go well with the savory zucchini treats you made, Tory."

Susannah took a plate and filled it with a few pepper

slices and a dollop of ranch. Her sisters crowded in to do the same. Someone cleared their throat behind her, and she turned to see Amelia Ann. Her friend crooked a finger at her, so Susannah crossed the room to where she was standing with Clayton.

When she reached them, Amelia Ann kissed Clayton on the cheek. "Run along and find someone else to chat with for a bit. We have some girl talk to do."

Clayton leaned in and kissed her cheek. "I'll bet the topic begins with the capital J. Susannah, it's good to see you and Jake so happy."

"Thanks, Clayton." When he left, she turned to her friend. "You've worked wonders with that man. Before you, he'd pretty much rather chew gravel than have a civilized conversation."

"Don't I know it," Amelia Ann declared. "What can I say? I have the touch. Seems you do too. I know you told me how things were between you and Jake, but let me tell you, honey. Seeing is believing. That man is going to have a ring on your finger before you know it. Hand to God."

The way she was feeling, a ring sounded pretty wonderful. She might have daydreamed about it some. Besides, that way they could finally explore the passion between them. That part of their relationship...

Well, it was the only one filled with tension.

After another belly-stuffing dinner, Susannah watched Jake mingle with her expanding family. Everyone was more than welcoming. Now that he was with her... Well, they knew where things were heading.

When all the dishes were cleaned up, they settled into the den. Annabelle climbed onto Jake's lap again, which Susannah thought too sweet for words.

"Y'all look good together," she told them seriously. "Mama says."

Someone loudly cleared their throat, and Susannah looked up like everyone else.

J.P. walked into the center of the room, his hands crossed behind his back. "I have some good news to share..."

When Susannah saw Tammy stand up too, she reached for Jake's hand. Was it finally happening? Annabelle scooted off Jake's lap and ran over to clutch her mama's hand. Rory took J.P.'s. Then Tammy and J.P. reached for each other with their free hands.

"Tammy has finally agreed to marry me," he said, letting the most lop-sided grin she'd ever seen from him spread across his face.

Annabelle jumped in place. "Finally!"

Rory added, "Amen!"

Tammy cast them all an impish glance, and untucked the chain around her neck holding a diamond ring. "I told y'all I would eventually. Thanks for being patient with me."

"I would have waited decades for you to agree, honey," J.P. told her as he took the ring off its chain and slid it onto her finger.

"Thank God it didn't take decades," Rye announced, rising and hugging the whole group—the whole family— with his long arms. "I don't think I'll be able to dance the two-step at your wedding when I'm that old."

"I can dance all right at my age," Hampton Hollins informed his son as he pulled Tammy into a hug.

Margaret Hollins embraced the happy couple and the kids with a natural, wide-mouthed smile and then proceeded to hug everyone waiting in line to congratulate J.P. and Tammy—something more than shocking to Susannah, who remembered the woman's earlier reserve. My, how she had changed.

"My daughter is getting married!" she declared. "And to the best man imaginable."

Laughing from her Mama's fierce hug, Amelia Ann turned toward her sister with a sheen of tears in her eyes. "I'm so happy for you, Tammy. You deserve all the happiness in the world."

"Thank you, honey. We're getting married in June, sugar, when J.P.'s gardens will be in bloom," Tammy told her sister. "I hope you don't mind us getting married so closely to you and Clayton."

"Not a bit," her sister assured her. "I'm going to bring in May. You can round out June."

The congratulations continued, and someone popped a bottle of champagne. The kids became even more hyper, bouncing around and telling everyone how the chocolate fairies couldn't wait for them to live at J.P.'s house again.

"First a baby, and now two engagements," Louisa said beside her, a knowing look in her eye. "Our family is truly blessed."

Her mama couldn't have been more right, and Susannah was so happy she could share their blessings with Jake. Maybe someday they would share this kind of news with her family.

They weren't the first to announce they were leaving, but a couple of hours later, they exchanged a look and followed Amelia Ann and Clayton out the door.

Jake drove to his house since she'd parked her car there that morning. "I'm so glad Tammy finally agreed to marry J.P. That man has waited something fierce for that sweet woman."

"I know," Susannah agreed. "They deserve all the

happiness in the world after everything they've been through."

"I couldn't agree more," Jake murmured, taking her hand as he thundered down the road.

When they arrived at his house and parked, he leaned over and kissed her warmly on the lips. "I've been wanting to do that pretty much all day."

The garage door light was on, but little else, so there were shadows on his face. Somehow it only made him more beautiful. "It's the longest we've gone without kissing in days," she said.

"By my account, it's been at least five hours. I don't want to ever break that record."

"Me either," she agreed, turning in her seat and setting a hand lightly on his thigh.

"Want to come inside and kiss me some more?" he asked, his mouth turned up in the most flirtatious smile.

"I do," she said, equally flirtatious. "Thanks for asking."

He laughed and opened his door. She did the same and met him at the side door.

"It's early yet," he said as he let them inside the house. "Do you want to watch a movie?"

"I thought we were speaking of kissing," she said, smiling at him.

"We were. I imagined kissing you *while* we were watching a movie. Like a teenage date."

It did feel rather like they were teenagers sometimes. Their hands could only stray so far before they were forced to separate. Stopping the flow of passion between them was becoming increasingly difficult. Susannah had been struggling with her feelings. Was it wrong that she was doubting the wisdom of waiting after all these years? Jake made it *really* hard to want to wait. She knew it was wearing on him. By the end of the night, there was often a downright grimace on his face. Hers too.

"Okay, let's watch a movie," she agreed. "What sounds good to you?"

"I'm assuming action movies are out," he said, earning him a look.

"Why ever would you assume that? Just because I'm a girl, doesn't mean I don't like action." She flushed at the sight of his grin. "I didn't mean it that way."

"I know," he said, reaching for her hand. "Come on. We'll pick out something together."

They settled on *Casablanca* since it had both action and romance. Susannah had seen it many times, but watching it with Jake was different. After all, he'd actually been in a war. The thought made her worry—what if this set him off?

"Does this movie bother you?" she decided to ask, watching him out of the corner of her eye.

He immediately turned to look at her. "Why would it?"

"Well...it's about a war."

His laughter dissolved any tension in her belly. "Trust me, sugar. This movie is the furthest thing from my experience in Iraq."

"Good," she said, turning back to the TV.

Humphrey Bogart was wearing his iconic white suit while walking through Rick's Café, eyeing Ingrid Bergman with mistrust. Susannah tried to focus on the movie, but it was difficult with Jake's warm body next to hers. His thumb was making circles on the top of her hand, and it was swirling something inside her. Shifting closer, she settled her head against his shoulder. His breathing stilled, and she felt it: the slow, steady beat of desire rising between them.

Helpless to resist, she raised her head. His was already descending to kiss her. Their mouths met, and like usual, they both tried to keep it light. Soon it was impossible to deny the heat. Her mouth opened, and their kisses grew lusher. Wetter. She heard herself moan when he stroked her tongue with his. Rising so she could press both of her hands against his chest, she caressed the hard muscles there. So far, they'd kissed while clothed, but they hadn't taken it any further. Sure, Jake had run his hands over her body, but she knew he was waiting for a sign from her before pushing that boundary.

Tonight she was going to give him that sign.

When his hands slid up to hold her waist, caressing the indention there, she lifted her blue cashmere sweater. Their gazes met, and his eyes flashed with heat and desire. His hands stroked her bare skin and traveled up her ribcage until he was touching her breasts. His mouth found hers again, leading her in a deep, arousing dance while he showed her how sensitive her breasts actually were. She moaned into his mouth again, and he pulled back slowly.

"I want to take your bra off," he whispered against her cheek. "Is that okay?"

She nodded and felt his hands come around her back. The material went tight and then came loose. Holding her breath, she waited for his hands to touch her again. He slid them around, igniting all sorts of fires inside her. When he raised the bra slowly above her breasts, still keeping her sweater on, the sensations running through her were so intense she had to close her eyes.

He was watching her, she knew, and she almost felt too vulnerable. His fingers caressed her nipples, rubbing them, sending electricity straight down her belly and beyond. Oh, she liked this. She really liked this.

"Susannah," he said softly.

She opened her eyes and gazed into the deep cobalt blue of his own.

"I want to take your sweater off," he said, his jaw tight from tension. "I promise to stop when you tell me. Will you trust me?"

She raised her arms slowly in response. He slid the sweater off, and her bra too, and then settled back to look at her. The fire was warm, so she wasn't cold, but she found herself shivering all the same. Having him see her like this made her feel vulnerable and hopeful all at once. Trusting him with her body was big for her, and from the delicate way he was touching her, he knew it.

"You're beautiful," he whispered, tracing the mounds. "Everything about you is beautiful. I truly am the luckiest man in the world."

And then he lowered his mouth to her breasts and gave her a new taste of pleasure. He took his time, heightening her desire. The suction of his mouth became her sole focal point. When his hands gripped her waist to bring her closer to his mouth, she couldn't contain her moan.

"Oh, Jake," she breathed out.

He kissed her again, and she put her hand to his chest, wanting to touch him too.

"Would it be all right if you took your shirt off too?" she asked, her words as hesitant as her touch. "Or would that be too much?"

She was always worrying about making him too uncomfortable. She hated that her values made him feel so frustrated.

"Too much and not enough," he ground, immediately unbuttoning his shirt. He was shrugging out of it when he froze. "Ah...I have a scar. On my shoulder. From combat. It's why...I don't take my shirt off in public. I hope it doesn't bother you. I can keep it on if it does. I know it's not...pretty."

He'd been injured? Her breath seemed to freeze in her lungs. "I didn't know," she said, tracing his face.

"I'm glad you didn't find the article they published about it." His mouth flattened into a straight line. "It may have made events out to be bigger than they were. It's only a shoulder wound, but it's still...a sight."

While she wanted to know more about whatever bit of heroism he was underplaying, that could wait—right now she needed to touch him. Sliding her hands inside his shirt, she eased back the fabric and helped him remove it. His pectoral muscles were beautiful and defined, but he'd been right to warn her. The scar looked to be about four inches long.

"I was hit with a high-powered rifle," he told her, watching her carefully.

Leaning forward, she kissed the long ridge of that white line dotting his skin. *He could have been killed,* was all she could think.

"Oh, Susannah," he said, weaving his fingers into her hair with a groan. "I knew you were the sweetest girl in the world, but I never expected you to react like this."

She kissed the scar again, in benediction, and placed her hand over his warm chest, where his heart was racing. "I'm so glad you came home safe. It was like God was answering my prayers before I even knew to say them."

He expelled a rush of air from his chest, and she took the harsh sound as her invitation to kiss his wound again.

"I wondered for a long time why I made it back and Booker didn't, but right now, I think I made it back because I had to meet you."

She laid her forehead against his chest as those words

rolled over her. Then she raised her head and looked him in the eye. "I love you, Jake."

His face scrunched up, a sure sign he was fighting emotion. "I love you too. I've wanted to tell you all week."

Her lips trembled, and she made herself smile. "I wanted to tell you too, but I thought it was too soon."

He shook his head. "Love isn't dictated by time. So let's agree not to let time slow us down from expressing how we feel."

"That sounds mighty wise if you ask me," she said as the energy of their love filled her. She was expanding inside, her heart growing with each beat.

"Tell me again," he whispered, caressing the line of her cheek with his thumb.

"I love you," she said, the words strong and true.

"And I love you," he responded in that same sure tone. "Always and forever."

This time, when their mouths met, there was something new in their connection. The press of their lips seemed to be a bridge to something else, something permanent, something that could never be taken away.

They slowed down so they could be present for each touch of their lips, each dance of their tongues. His hands caressed her breasts while her fingers lovingly traced his scar, as if to erase all the pain and bad memories it held.

When their passion started to blaze out of control, Jake pressed back and kissed her cheek. She knew it was time to stop—although she wished otherwise. She made her hands fall away from his hot skin. As he shrugged into his shirt, she followed suit, dressing quickly. He didn't help her. Didn't touch her again. It was for the best, she knew. Though she wanted nothing more than for him to keep on touching her and her him, but she knew where that would lead.

"I'll be right back," he said, rising from the couch.

Every night he took off into the kitchen after they separated. She listened to the water run in the sink and knew he was putting a wet towel to the back of his neck. Usually his nape was damp when he returned to her with two glasses of ice water. He'd tried to joke about the ice before, but it had fallen flat. They were both too hungry for each other to laugh about it.

She waited for him, but he took longer than he had on previous nights. Her heart hurt for it. When he finally returned, there was tension around his eyes even though he gave her a smile.

"I'm sorry," she said again, something she found herself saying every night. "It's not fair to you."

He sat beside her after putting their glasses on the coffee table. While he didn't pull her close, he did situate his body next to hers.

"I've told you not to feel bad. Honey, it's just the way it is. I would rather be with you than anything else in the world, so don't give it another thought."

Not once had he ever tried to push her. Not once had he snarled at her out of frustration.

"Do you want me to go?" she asked quietly, noting that the movie credits were now rolling on the screen. The ending of the movie clearly hadn't captured their attention.

He took a hold of her hand. "No. Let's sit by the fire for a spell. Do you want me to sing?"

On a few other nights, he'd brought out his guitar after they'd cut their passion short, and she wondered if playing helped soothe him some. "I love to listen to you sing."

And so he sang to her with love in his eyes, as her mind ran through all the reasons why loving him with her body couldn't be a bad thing.

23

Jake found himself opening up more in his sessions with Louisa. He was the one who came up with the idea of flying his old Army buddies to town for a spontaneous get-together, but her encouragement was what helped him get there. She was all for the idea—she said something about how connecting his past with his present would be a powerful way to integrate the healing he was undergoing. He didn't know much about the integration part, but he was feeling happier each day—something he wanted to share with his old friends.

He called each of his friends and started off the same way: "I need y'all to meet my girl." Each time, he barely managed to finish the sentence before receiving the same response: "When?"

A week later, he picked his buddies up from the airport and drove them out to Redemption Ridge.

Monty was the first to exit the vehicle when he pulled to a stop out front. His shrill whistle made everyone rub their ears. "Holy shit, man. I thought your last place was nice, but these digs..."

"Your whistle still sounds like a missile getting ready to make impact," Darren said, rubbing his ear. The diamond earring he'd gotten after leaving the service twinkled in the sun. "This place is mighty fine, Jake."

Monty made the sound again, giving Jake the chills. The reason Monty had started making it as a joke in the first place was to relieve their tension during missile strikes by the enemy.

"That's not a sound a man can forget," Jake said, shaking his head.

"Yeah, it's just as impossible to forget how perfect Monty's hair always looks," Randy said with a snort, scanning the grounds with the other guys. "Although it's long enough to braid now."

"Bull-sheet," Monty said, running his hands through his dark curls. "The wife likes it. Trust me, Jake. If Susannah is the one for you, you'll do anything to make her happy."

Jake studied his friend some more. Monty walked to the back of the SUV to help Darren with their carry-ons, moving much more gracefully with his prosthetic than the last time Jake had seen him. His friend had been depressed for a long time following his injury, and he'd struggled with feeling like less than a man without his whole leg. Thank God his new wife seemed to have helped him see himself in a new light.

"Susannah *is* the one, I think," he told them, knowing it was true in his heart.

Darren patted his massive chest like he was imitating a heartbeat. "I've never seen you look so dopey-faced, Lassiter," he joked.

"Dopey?" Randy fired back, wrapping his arm around Jake's shoulder. "I'd say he looks like Dudley Do-Right."

"Not that again," Jake said, wincing. "You know I hate that nickname."

Monty twirled his carry-on in a dramatic circle. "But it's so true. Even the media calls you one of the most wholesome country singers out there."

He narrowed his eyes at them, which didn't dim the wattage of their teasing grins. This was the way they ragged on each other every time they were together. "And y'all are clucking like a bunch of hens. Best come on in and see the rest of the place before you lay an egg in my front yard."

The guys started clucking like chickens, of course, and they kept doing it sporadically as he led them around the house, the clucker sending the rest into gales of laughter . He caught them blinking a few times at the sheer expanse of his house, which didn't surprise him since they'd all come from modest upbringings. Darren had escaped one of the most dangerous Latino neighborhoods in Los Angeles by enlisting, while Randy had entered the Army to go to college, not wanting to join a Detroit gang like his older brother. Monty had seen the Army as his only way out of the small-town trailer park he'd grown up in outside of Mobile, Alabama.

Jake concluded the tour by passing out beers. They hunkered down in the den, and Jake turned to one of his most bittersweet tasks as host.

"To Booker and all the rest of our friends who didn't make it," he said, and they all clicked their beer bottles together.

They were quiet for a minute, but Monty broke the tension by cracking a joke about them all being no better than a bunch of women sniffling after a funeral. They kept the conversation light after that, shooting the shit and catching up. But the next time there was a lull in the conversation, Jake decided it was time to speak his mind.

"Reverend Louisa—Susannah's mama—has really been helping me deal with the stuff that's been coming up for me lately," he told them. "I'm...more hopeful than ever that I might be normal again."

"You know there's no such thing as normal, Jake," Monty said, gesturing to his leg. "We don't have the same experiences as most of the people around us, but that doesn't mean we're a lost cause. May shows me that each day."

"I'm glad she's making you so happy, man," Randy said, tipping his beer in Monty's direction. "No one deserves it more than you. Well, except for this asshole country singer over here."

Jake shook his head, knowing it was all good fun. "Asshole country singer? I'll have to tell my manager to use that headline for my next concert."

"So when are we meeting Susannah?" Darren asked, kicking his feet up on the footstool in front of the loveseat. "You've been your usual clam of a self when it comes to telling us about your lady. How hot is she?"

"Dudley Do-Right never tells," Monty said, chuckling. "But I'm happy to report that May is as hot as a five-alarm chili and then some."

"*Ooh,*" Darren and Randy called out.

"I can't believe you just compared your wife to chili, Monty," Jake said, nudging his good leg with the tip of his boot.

"Well, she's hot...and sweet," Monty said with a drawl. "Did I mention sweet?

After meeting May a few times, Jake had to concur.

"How's work going, Monty? Are you still using your magic to make cars run? Mine might need an oil change."

"Shee-et, bubba. I'll give you an oil change." Then he shrugged. "The garage is okay, I guess. My boss is an asshole, but it keeps me busy. There's always a car to fix. The money's not great, but May is working at a new restaurant where the tips are better. We're saving up to buy a house."

When people talked about struggling over money, Jake felt guilty for all he had. "If you need anything, man..."

"We're fine, Jake," Monty said crisply, taking a sip of his beer.

Jake went mute. He'd offered his help before, and while he knew it was a touchy subject, he couldn't help but offer. These guys were his friends, and he had more money than he could ever spend.

Randy shot him a glance, and he could all but hear the man telling him to back off. They were all a prideful lot when it came down to it. He had to respect that.

"Anyone up for some pool?" Jake asked, eager to get them back on easier ground. "As you might have noticed, my lovely lady found me a fabulous pool table for the game room."

"I'm game, haha," Darren said, cracking his enormous hands. "Can we put on some salsa music?" he asked, flawlessly executing a few dance steps.

"No!" they all immediately shouted.

"Your preoccupation with that music makes me worry about you, man," Randy teased him. "We should listen to country—for Jake."

He winced. "Let's not. Rap or hip-hop is fine with me, but no salsa. Maybe Monty can do one of his Eminem imitations."

Monty launched into "Lose Yourself," and Jake tipped back his beer and took a sip as his friend rapped out the famous song. Before his injury, Monty used to dance like Eminem while he rapped. Now, he bobbed from side to side carefully, moving his shoulders in time with the beat. Jake started to move in time with the rhythm, and soon they were all rapping the song like in the old days.

When they finally left to go to the game room, Jake hung back to walk more slowly with Monty. Darren and Randy were jogging down the steps to the lower level, already jawing each other about who had the better pool cue. Some things never changed.

Monty put his arm around Jake's shoulder. "How are the nightmares?"

"I haven't had one for over a month now, thank God," he answered, thinking back to how much his life had changed since that last dark night. "What about yours?"

Month gave a lopsided smile. "You know. They come and go. Sometimes I dream I still have my leg. That I'm dancing a two-step with May to one of your songs. Those ones are the worst."

Jake nudged him. "But you're happy, right? Getting married seems to have...I don't know...balanced you out more."

"May's a good influence, and she makes me happy. But I can't depend on her or anything else for that. I have to stand on my own two feet. Bad joke."

It was, but it was one he made often—Jake figured the levity helped him deal with his loss.

"You're standing and then some," he said, gripping his shoulder. "I'm only glad May's there to support you when you need it."

"Me too," Monty said, walking down the steps carefully. "I'm still going to one session a week. What about you?"

"I'm seeing Reverend Louisa more than that," Jake said as they entered the game room. "I wanted to give my recovery more attention now that I'm moving forward with Susannah. And it's easier since I'm not on tour right now."

Randy had already racked the balls, and seconds later, he sent multi-colored pool balls spinning willy-nilly across the green felt table.

"Solids," Randy called out as the red ball dropped into a corner pocket. He positioned his stick to shoot again. "Damn, I'm good."

"And annoying as always," Darren fired back, balancing his pool stick across his massive shoulders like an Aikido master.

"I guess we're watching you two yahoos play," Jake said, settling on the sofa with Monty.

From this vantage point, Jake had a good view of the decorations he and Susannah had chosen together—paintings of the Tennessee countryside and a display of his favorite classic country albums. This room had turned out well. Heck, all of the rooms were turning out well. The way she'd set up these rooms was further evidence that she saw him and what he needed almost better than he did himself. Susannah had even managed to find him an interior water feature for the den upstairs, and he couldn't wait for it to arrive.

"We look good playing, don't we?" Randy said, flexing a bicep, making Jake wish he had a pillow to toss at the man, but this was a game room. Pillow-free, he'd told Susannah.

"You look like y'all don't know which end to sit on," Monty called out, rubbing the line where his real leg ended and the prosthetic began. Jake studied his face. Monty's mouth was tense, something he hadn't noticed before.

"Is your leg bothering you from the traveling? I can grab a footstool from upstairs." He hadn't thought to add one to the room. Maybe he and Susannah could look for one.

"The pressure on the plane always makes the area around the prosthetic swell. It'll be fine in a few hours."

Jake might have his own issues, but one thing he did have was a completely healthy body. He took a moment to be grateful for it. "I'll get that stool."

When he returned, Monty elevated his foot and leaned back with a sigh.

"When are we meeting Susannah?" Monty asked.

"Tonight," he answered. "She's coming for supper."

"After everything you've told me about her, she sounds too good to be true."

Jake didn't know about that. But as he watched his friends play pool and listened to their familiar interplay, he realized he'd never been able to enjoy being with them this much because he felt more present and happier now than he had in the past. And Susannah was playing a big role in making him feel that way.

24

Susannah found herself oddly nervous when she arrived at Redemption Ridge to meet Jake's Army buddies. She'd purposely dressed casual in jeans, boots, and a blue cotton shirt. His friends would be her best window to what Jake had been like in the Army, and she wanted them to like her.

The door swung open before she could even knock, and Jake grabbed her to him and gave her a hard, urgent kiss. She put her hands on his chest and all but melted before he set her away from him.

"I had to do that quick," he told her with a grin. "The guys are here. I ran up when I heard your car."

She cast a look around his body, but didn't see anyone else. "Where are they?"

"Finishing up a game of pool," Jake told her, taking her hand. "It's been a non-stop contest for a couple hours now. Randy and Darren have been long-time pool rivals, and Monty is egging them on. I've told them to watch their language around you, but I can't guarantee they won't slip."

Her mouth twitched. She couldn't help it. "I doubt I'll faint, Jake. You don't cuss much now. Did you when you were in the military?"

"Like a sailor," he said, laughing. "It didn't jive with who I became when I left the service, but I still slip up around the guys some since it's how we used to talk. I'll do my best not to drop the f-bomb around you."

She couldn't imagine Jake ever dropping the f-bomb. "That's mighty kind of you," she said in a teasing voice. "Let's go meet your friends."

The moment she and Jake entered the game room, three men whirled around to give them their attention. The one who'd been sitting on the couch quickly got up. They were a motley crew for sure, and all of them were giants. Especially the one with the diamond earring.

"Guys," Jake said, putting his hand to her back. "This is Susannah. Honey, the tall one over there who still has a military crew cut—God help us—is Randy. He's currently beating Darren, who mentioned showing you his salsa moves later, something I told him was *never* going to happen."

From the charming smile he shot her way, she expected he was used to showing women his...ahem...moves frequently.

"Hey, Susannah," Darren said, using his pool stick to make a fake lunge at Randy, who blocked it with scary efficiency. His quick response made Susannah wonder what kind of training they must have gone through in the military. Both of them set down their pool cues.

"Do we at least get to hug her?" Darren asked Jake, an eyebrow winging up.

Jake rolled his eyes. "You might ask her."

She eyed the massive hand Darren had thrust out to

her. His body seemed to fit his size. Jake towered over her, but Darren was like a tall tree.

"A hug might be nice if you promise not to crush me," she said, stepping into his arms hesitantly.

"I won't crush you none," Darren said, giving her a gentle back pat. "Jake would crush my balls. Woops. Forget I said that."

"Don't mind him," Randy said, pulling the man back by the arm. "Darren doesn't know how to act around nice ladies like you."

"Ouch," Darren said, placing his hand on his heart dramatically.

"And you do?" she asked Randy, fighting a smile.

"Yes, ma'am, I do," he answered, giving her a playful wink. "But not like this one over here who's crazy about you. Did Jake tell you about our nickname for him?"

She heard a groan and looked over.

"Don't do it, man," Jake said, narrowing his eyes. "Payback is hell."

"I'm shaking," Randy said and then gave a good imitation of the motion, making all the men snicker. "We call him Dudley Do-Right."

Putting a hand over her mouth to cover her smile, Susannah took a moment to compose herself. Jake was watching her carefully for her reaction.

"In a certain light, I can see the resemblance," she teased, playing along.

Darren hooted, and Randy shoved Jake hard in the chest, making him fall back a few steps. The man still standing by the sofa took a few steps toward her. There was a slight hitch in his walk, which tracked with what Jake had told her. Monty wasn't as muscular as the rest of the others, but he was tall. She imagined they must have looked like a pretty intimidating group when they were in the Army, and they'd undoubtedly turned a lot of heads in their uniforms.

"I'm Monty," he said, taking her hand, but not shaking it. "Don't listen to any of these guys—except for Jake. He's the only one who doesn't tell tales or talk out of school."

"You don't either now that you're married, Monty," Randy said with a pointed glance.

"You'll know why when you get married yourself, Randy. If any woman ever decides to take pity on your sorry ass."

"Oohhh," Darren cried out, dancing back a few steps, grabbing Jake, who was laughing.

"Jake, I said 'ass.'" Monty turned back to look at him. "Is that a swear word?"

"If you have to ask..." Jake said in an aggrieved tone, but he was smiling. "Ready to run yet, honey?"

She shook her head. Sure, they were giants. But they were Jake's giants. "I don't intimidate easily. Besides, they're your friends, and I hope that makes them mine."

There was an odd light in Jake's eyes when their gazes met.

"She's an angel," Monty said, finally dropping her hand. "Just like you said, Jake."

"She sure is," Jake replied. "Why don't you yahoos finish your game? Then we can go eat. What can I get you to drink, sugar? White wine? I was so excited to have you meet the guys, I forgot to ask upstairs."

"I'll have a beer to show my solidarity with y'all," she told him, earning her a kiss on the cheek from the man she loved.

"I'll run and get it," he told her and hurried off.

Everyone was looking at her, so she smiled at them, resisting the urge to fuss with her shirt. "Please go back to your game," she told Darren and Randy, who grinned and picked up their pool sticks, brandishing them like *Star Wars* Jedis for a beat before resuming their contest.

"You might want to stay out of their way," Monty told her. "I was sitting on the couch if you'd like to join me."

She followed him to the couch and took a seat beside him. "I'm so glad y'all could come out on such short notice. It means the world to Jake to have you here."

"He's a good guy," Monty said, rubbing the skin above his prosthetic.

Susannah debated whether to ask him if he needed anything. "Jake tells me you've been married almost a year now," she said instead.

"Yes, to another angel named May," Monty said, the corners of his mouth tipping up. "I'm pretty lucky. After I left the Army, I wasn't sure I'd find someone who wanted to end up with me. I mean I'm handsome and all, but the prosthetic is a mood killer."

He was being self-deprecating, but Susannah sensed raw pain underlying his words. "You *are* handsome," she said, not knowing how else to respond.

"Aren't you smart for noticing?" Monty gave her a playful wink, and for a moment, he looked years younger. "Jake mentioned you decorated this behemoth of a house. It looks real good. Nothing like that last lady."

She blinked.

"Jake texted us photos of that train wreck. The dead deer? I'm only from a small town in Alabama, but even I know that's not classy. Sure as shi...hell ain't classy enough for Jake now that he's made it big. I couldn't be happier for him. And now he has you. Seems like good fortune is finally starting to become his friend. For a while...we all wondered how life would turn out."

"Did you know what you wanted to do when you left the Army?"

Monty gripped his pant leg, and her heart clenched in on itself. She wished, belatedly, that she could take back what she'd said.

"When I got out of the hospital, I didn't have a clue. All I knew was that I had a lot of rehab ahead of me. People kept telling me how lucky I was to have made it. I owe these guys my life—although I wasn't too grateful at first."

Her breath seemed to have stopped in her chest. "Jake and the others..."

"Dragged me back to the Humvee after I stepped on that landmine," he said, his voice harsh. "If they had gotten me to a medic any later, I would have died."

Her throat thickened. "I can't imagine what that must have been like for you."

"Bless your heart for saying so," he told her, patting her knee. "Some people have no trouble telling me they know what I'm going through. I usually want to punch them in the face."

His sidelong glance was filled with wry humor, but once again, she could sense something simmering beneath it. "People can be stupid sometimes."

He gave a quiet laugh. "But I'm married now and have a decent job working as a mechanic. The only thing I was ever good at—besides being in the Army—was fixing things. When I was in high school, my baby brother and I rebuilt a '64 Mustang we found in a junkyard some thirty miles out of our town. Man, that baby could run."

"Do you still have her?" she asked.

He shook his head. "Nah. I had to sell her to pay some of my medical bills. The VA didn't cover everything, if you can believe it."

Even though Susannah had heard horror stories about veterans' medical bills on the news and from her mama, it still shocked her. "I don't understand how that could be allowed to happen."

"Bureaucracy," Monty said, looking up. "Lover boy is coming back. It's good to see him so happy. I don't know that we've ever seen him quite like this."

Jake sauntered forward with an enormous grin on his face—the one she was used to seeing.

"Like what?" Jake asked, handing her a beer.

"Sappy," Monty said, lifting his bottle. "Happy. Look, I rhyme like a rapper."

Jake raised his brow and reached for his beer. "To being happy and to the women who help remind us to smile," he said, extending the bottle.

"To being happy and the rest," Monty repeated and clicked his beer bottle with Jake's before turning to do the same with Susannah.

The men shared a look, and Susannah's breath caught. It was like watching two retired warriors making a pledge. She felt honored to witness it, knowing it was yet another bond these men were forging, on top of many more.

25

For the next couple weeks, Jake felt like he was walking on a cloud even though he kept an eye out for rain. With each passing day, Susannah was buoying him with hope. Being with her and expressing his feelings for her hadn't triggered another episode and neither had the visit from his friends. He wasn't naïve enough to believe he was completely cured, but he felt more balanced.

She was a stabilizing force, there was no doubt. And their love...well, it could move mountains. That he believed.

It was time to move another mountain, and today he planned to discuss his idea with Louisa. He was a permanent member of her church now, and while he hadn't completely made his peace with God, he wasn't as angry as he'd been.

During fellowship every Sunday, Louisa had been introducing him to other people living through hardships. One family in particular, the Hendersons, seemed to have everything—good jobs for the parents and three beautiful kids. But their five-year-old son had recently been diagnosed with a brain tumor. Since the boy was a big fan of Jake's, Louisa had asked if he'd be willing to meet him. He'd ultimately spent over twenty minutes talking to Frankie. While it had tugged mightily at his heart, it had helped remind him that he wasn't the only person who'd struggled. This little boy was fighting for his life, and he'd done nothing to deserve that. Jake still didn't understand why bad things happened, but meeting Frankie had helped Louisa drive home a particular point. God hadn't been punishing Frankie or him or Booker or anyone else.

For the moment at least, he'd stopped asking The Big Why. And he felt more peaceful for it.

Like always, Louisa gave him a warm hug when he arrived for his session. "Each time I see you, you look even happier than before."

He was like one of the songs he was writing. With every new lyric added to his life, he became more complete. Love was making him complete. He was too much of an artist to dismiss the notion as corny.

"You were right. Love changes everything."

"I'm glad," she said, gesturing to the couch for him to sit. "How did your homework go?"

He unfolded the piece of paper after removing it from his denim jacket. "Good. You wanted me to think about the top three things I want most in my life. Let me read them in reverse order."

He gave her a smile since these items had been pretty easy for him. She responded with a wink.

"Number three. I really believe in the music I'm writing right now. I think it's going to resonate with a lot of people about hard times, redemption, and changing their lives." Rather like he was doing. "I want to win the CMA for Best Album of the Year next year." Before his music had been real and soulful, but it hadn't been filled with a lot of hope.

But now, between Susannah, Louisa, and these sessions, he was seeing the world differently. For a long, long time, he'd been asking the wrong questions. Rather than ask why bad things happened in the world, he would ask how more good things could happen from them. That revelation had unlocked something deep inside him. He wanted to help make more positive things happen both in his life and in the lives of others.

"That sounds like a wonderful goal. From all I've heard of your music, I think it's only a matter of time until that happens. What's next?"

"I want to help more people. Once we finish today, I'd appreciate you giving me Frankie's phone number. I'd like to send him to Disney World or somewhere of his choice before he...while he's able." His brain tumor was inoperable and too far gone for chemotherapy.

She gave him a beaming smile. "I expect that would mean the world to him and his family. I have a few other people who need some help if you're interested."

The knowledge that he could make a difference filled him with light. He might have originally believed the only lives he'd changed by being alive were his fans, but now he knew better. A purpose in life wasn't something you *had*. It was something you gave to the world.

"Just give me a list, and we'll get it done."

She looked about as happy as she did around her family, and he was thrilled to be the cause. He hoped that would continue when he told her his final wish.

"You've got it. And the last?"

He took a deep breath, striving for calm. "I want to have a family. Truth be told, I want to have one with your daughter." He checked to see how she was taking the news, but her smile hadn't dimmed, which encouraged him. "I know we haven't been together long, but she's home for me. I don't want to be with anyone else, and quite frankly, I don't want to wait. I love her, and she loves me. Louisa, I'll abide by your thoughts, but I'm asking for your permission to marry your daughter."

She pressed a hand to her heart. "I was hoping you weren't going to draw that out. I think y'all getting married is a wonderful idea."

His breath whooshed out. "You do? You don't think I need to wait any longer to see if I'm okay?"

She shook her head. "Jake, how many times do I have to tell you that you're not broken? You have PTSD, but you're managing it. Yes, you have things you're still working through, but the less you lock yourself away in some self-imposed tower, the happier you feel. Am I right? Deciding to love my daughter has been one of the biggest decisions of your life. You have chosen life for yourself."

He *had* chosen life. It still amazed him how much that decision had changed everything.

"I'm so glad you approve," he said, wanting to pretty much grab her and hug her. "Louisa...I can't tell you how grateful I am for everything you've done."

She rose and held out her arms. "Come here."

Embracing her got him all emotional. He was going to marry Susannah. He could hardly believe it. "You're the best. Do you know that?"

"You're pretty wonderful too, sugar," she said, giving him a final squeeze. "It's going to be a joy to have you as a son."

Crap. Now he was really choked up. "I couldn't think of a finer mother-in-law."

"This doesn't change anything about what we're doing here, though," she told him, stepping away to pour them both some water. "We keep plugging away. Talking about what comes up. Getting married tends to bring up other types of issues."

She must have seen something in his face because she immediately added, "For *everyone*, Jake. Getting married is a big deal. But for you and Susannah...well, it seems like something you've both been moving toward all your lives."

She understood him so well. "I couldn't have said it better. I might have to use that in a song."

"Imagine that!" She laughed. "One of my comments in a song."

"I plan to talk to J.P. too. About marrying Susannah." It was only right.

"I suspect I know what he's going to say," she said, her mouth twitching.

All that mattered was what Susannah was going to say. He'd bet his whole career that she felt the same way he did. It was becoming increasingly difficult to keep from making love. They'd been pushing the boundaries a bit, but she seemed to want him as much as he wanted her. He couldn't wait to remove that final obstacle between them.

"I'd like you to do your pre-marital counseling with a preacher friend of mine," she told him.

Yeah, it would be weird to have those discussions with her. "Thanks for suggesting someone."

"It's not someone Susannah knows well either," she said drinking her water. "It'll be less awkward that way."

He didn't know what pre-martial counseling entailed, but he was all for it. Thinking about all the counseling he'd had recently, it was almost humorous. "It sounds like I'll be in counseling three times a week now."

Her shoulders shook. "We'll call you an enlightened man because you're taking the time to know and love yourself."

He almost blushed at that, and he wasn't the blushing kind. "I just want to continue to feel good and be the kind of man I want to be." Because Jake was doing all of this for him. Susannah was important, but it couldn't be only because of her.

"I think you're doing great," she said, shaking her finger at him. "Never doubt it."

"Thanks, Louisa. That means a lot." He stood. "Well, I'd best let you get on. I'm going to visit your son."

She hugged him again. "I won't tell you to give him a kiss for me."

Jake made a face. "I'll give him your best."

"I'll see you in a couple of days, Jake."

He left her office with hope burning bright in his chest. When he arrived at J.P.'s house, his friend met him on the porch. Charleston, J.P.'s red setter, nuzzled his hand.

"Good to see you, bubba," J.P. said, giving him a man hug. "I'm glad you called. I was about to take Charleston here on a walk to Dare River. You up for that?"

"That sounds fine with me," he said, watching as the dog pranced ahead.

The weather was in the high forties, but the sun shone down on them while they made their way through the gardens Tammy had designed. Most of the flower beds were fallow like his were, but there were a few bushes with bright red berries on them. Jake tucked his hands in his jacket as they strolled down the path.

When they entered the woods to Dare River, Jake turned to J.P. "As part of my homework, your mama asked me to list the three things I most want in the world going forward. Having a family topped the list. I told your mama this morning that I want to marry your sister, and she gave me her blessing. Since you're her older brother and my friend, I wanted to ask for yours as well."

J.P. stopped and put his hand on Jake's shoulder, turning him so he could meet his gaze. "You have it. Welcome to the family."

He blinked. "That's it? You're not going to grill me or give me a speech?"

"Have I ever?" his friend asked with a chuckle. "I told you that love changes things. As far as I'm concerned, why put off what you want? No need for you to wait as long as Tammy and me."

Jake heard the thread in J.P.'s voice. "I'm glad she finally agreed."

"Me too, Jake, although I wish we didn't have to wait until June," the man said, bending down and picking up a stick. "You ready, boy?"

Charleston nodded his head, watching the stick and then took off in the direction J.P. hurled it. The dog bounded into the brush.

"I hope Susannah won't insist on a long engagement," J.P. said.

"We agree there." Especially given how badly he wanted her. "Do you think I should ask your sisters to help me pick out a ring?"

J.P. snorted, taking the stick from Charleston and hurling it again. "If you want to become their favorite brother-in-law straight away, that would be a good plan."

"But I'll be their only..." Then he broke off, realizing his friend's joke. "Ah...I see. Did they help you pick out Tammy's?"

"I picked it out with Rory and Annabelle," J.P. said with

a smile. "They needed to be involved, although Annabelle was pretty pushy about me getting her mama a chocolate diamond. Don't ask."

There were chocolate diamonds now? He could barely imagine trying to pick out a plain one out of the thousands of them out there. He definitely needed help. "Can you give me your sisters' numbers?"

"I'll text them to you when we get back to the house," J.P. said. "I can come along out of solidarity. Shelby doesn't watch you like a demented fan girl anymore, but I've still caught Sadie doing it every now and again."

"I like the idea of you coming, anyway," Jake said. "I think Susannah would like knowing all her siblings helped me."

J.P. nodded, scratching Charleston behind the ears.

"Do you think I should ask Tammy, Amelia Ann, and Tory too?" Jake asked.

"Heck, bubba, if you're thinking that big, you might as well invite Rye and Clayton." J.P. laughed. "I would keep it small for the moment, although I have a feeling Rye would probably have more thoughts about the ring than the women. He was practically a maniac when he took Clayton and me shopping for Tory's. I've never seen the man fret so much."

Jake joined in with his laughter. "Only the McGuiness siblings then."

They made their way down to Dare River, and the scene reminded him of the mural Susannah was painting on his dining room wall. He'd asked for a deer in the patch of woods and a boat in the water, coming home, the owner's dock within sight. The rest he had left up to her. She was half-finished, and he liked to pretend he was working on his new song while she painted in her sexy white smock. In fact, that's probably what she was doing right now at his house.

She had a key now and his spare garage door opener. He'd given them to her two weeks ago. He loved coming home and seeing her car in his garage. Slowly but surely, she was becoming as much of a part of his home as all of the furnishings they'd selected together. No, that wasn't quite right. *She* was the one who made it a home. He would go back to sleeping on a mattress on the floor if it was the only way he could have her. Not that he would. She liked to have things around her, and he found he did too. They meant he had a home, something that was his, something that reflected who he was.

It was almost like God had a plan all along for them. From the beginning, they'd worked together to make his house on Dare River a home. Now she was going to be living there with him. Together they would raise a family on that land.

While he wasn't praying perhaps as often as he should, he took a moment to give thanks whenever he was feeling grateful. As J.P. tugged on the stick with an excited Charleston, Jake bowed his head and took a moment.

When they returned from their walk, J.P. gave him Shelby and Sadie's numbers. He called Shelby first at J.P.'s suggestion and got her voicemail. He didn't want to make such a large request in a message, so he simply asked her to call him when she got the chance because he needed her help.

He and J.P. were picking up their guitars—he'd thrown one in his truck that morning in the anticipation that he'd see his friend if the meeting with Louisa went right—when Shelby called him back. She was a little too cheery in her greeting. Apparently, they were both feeling a little weird, what with this being their first conversation on the phone. He asked if she might have time to help him select a ring for her sister, and she pretty much squealed on the phone. Then she added, "Of course, I'd be happy to help." When he asked if she could talk to Sadie for him, she assured him she would do so the minute they hung up.

"She's excited," he told a chuckling J.P.

"I could tell," the man said, strumming an intriguing melody. "Wait until Sadie hears the news. It's best that Shelby offered to call her. Her scream might have deafened you in one ear."

Thank God for that. Screaming women—even ones at his concert—never failed to embarrass him. His music was good, he knew, but the screaming... He wasn't sure it was because of the music.

Five minutes later, Shelby called him again. J.P. fought a smile and continued to play the guitar.

Jake picked it up. "Hey, Shelby."

"Hi!" she said louder than normal, but this time he was prepared.

He was holding the phone away from his ear.

J.P. snorted. "Hey, Shelby," he called out.

"Is that J.P.?" she asked.

"Yes. I came over here. To ask his blessing." He felt his face grow a little hot. "After asking for your mama's."

"I figured you must have done that, but Sadie and I wanted to ask you."

There was something in her tone. "I promise to be good to her, Shelby."

"I know you will be, Jake," she immediately said, but he wondered if she was thinking things were progressing a little too fast.

Well, that was her opinion, and she was entitled to it.

Jake had already sought out the opinions that were most critical to him.

"Sadie is going to take off early today, and I think I can swing it. Where shall we meet you?"

Today? He hadn't thought much past talking to Louisa and J.P. But why wait a moment longer? If he found a ring, he could ask Susannah tonight. Heck, it was only going on eleven o'clock since he'd had an early meeting with Louisa. His manager could help him set up another romantic dinner at his house.

"That sounds great. I've...ah...never bought a woman jewelry before." Okay, now he was really embarrassed. "Where does one go in Nashville?"

Now J.P.'s shoulders were really shaking, but he continued to play his guitar quietly in the background.

"We'll start at Tiffany's at Green Hills," she told him. "And if we can't find something there—unlikely—we'll go to Village Jewelers or Genesis."

"Do you know her ring size?" he asked, feeling like a complete idiot now.

"I have a tape measure," J.P. said.

Jake muted the phone so Shelby wouldn't hear. "You're not helping."

All he received was a chuckle.

Shaking his head, Jake unmuted the phone. "That sounds like a good list."

"You might have your manager call ahead to Tiffany's to see if we can have a private viewing. They do that for stars."

Right. If he went in there looking for rings without arranging something like that, it would be all over the papers.

"Actually, what am I thinking?" she said. "Have your

manager call and ask them to send out a selection of rings for you to look at. Duh! I'm thinking like a normal person."

He didn't like being reminded that he wasn't "normal" anymore, but she wasn't wrong on this point. "I'll have him make the call. Does Susannah want a diamond, do you think? She...ah...strikes me as a traditional kind of woman."

"Diamond. Princess cut."

"Got it." He'd heard most women had an idea in mind. "Thanks, Shelby."

"Give me a holler when you have a time from Tiffany's. I'm sure they'll hustle someone out for you today."

That wasn't something he liked to assume. He didn't like to make people jump simply because he was a star. "I'll see what my manager can do."

They would need to discuss a potential statement for the press once Susannah agreed to marry him. Or maybe they shouldn't announce it. Maybe they should simply pretend to have a party or something and then get married there. That way the press wouldn't be stalking them at every turn. He didn't want their day soured by all that madness. That tactic had worked for other stars, but he'd leave it to Susannah to tell him what she preferred.

"I'll call you when I know more," he told Shelby. "Thanks for your help."

"It's no bother," she said, "no bother at all. We'd do anything for Susannah."

He almost said, *So would I,* but he simply said goodbye and hung up.

"Need a beer?" J.P. asked. "Or a whiskey? I changed my mind. Maybe we *should* invite Rye over. You're going to need more testosterone once my sisters show up."

"I need to get back to the house for a while," he said,

eyeing the clock. "Susannah is painting my dining room, and we were going to have lunch."

"How about you call your manager and get him going?" J.P. suggested, setting his guitar aside. "You aren't going to be able to do much thinking today, I have a feeling. This way you can go and see Susannah and send her home at some point. We can meet you at your house when the jeweler arrives."

"Ah..." His brain had pretty much exploded after discussing the princess cut.

J.P. grabbed his phone and handed it to him. "Call your manager."

He did and bumbled his way through the conversation after receiving the man's congratulations. As soon as he set the phone down, J.P. put a beer in his hand.

"One won't hurt," his friend said.

Twenty minutes later, his manager called to convey that he had scheduled Tiffany's for four o'clock at Jake's house. J.P., God bless him, took over the task of calling his sisters.

"Now, go home and be with my sister, but try and act normal, or she'll know something is up."

He pressed the space between his eyebrows. "I don't know why I'm all stirred up."

"Don't you?" J.P. asked, laughing. "You'll do fine, bubba. All this flash is because our women like it. In the end, what truly matters is that you love each other. No ring is bigger than that truth. Remember that."

As he drove back to his house, he breathed deep and remembered his friend's words.

Susannah met him at the door and threw her arms around his neck. "I missed you. I expected you a couple of hours ago. Did you get caught up?"

"I...um...stopped by to see your brother," he said, sticking with the truth and trying to keep his face straight.

"Oh," she muttered, and before she could ask why, he took her hand.

"Show me what you've accomplished this morning while I was out."

They walked to the dining room, and like always, she was shuffling her feet a little like she was bashful. "I don't know how much I accomplished. You can decide."

When he passed through the doorway, he stilled. She'd painted the back of a man sitting on the dock, his feet dangling in the water. Jake knew it was him. He turned to her.

She was watching his face. "You...well...you *had* to be there. It's your land. Your strip of the river."

He was so moved by the reality of all his dreams coming true that he brought her against his chest. "I love you. Do you have any idea how much?"

Her arms came around him. "I was a little worried you wouldn't like it."

"I love it," he said, and after she agreed to marry him, he'd ask her to add herself to the mural too. "It's beautiful, Susannah. You have a gift."

"You tell me that every day," she said, shrugging and giving him a quirky smile.

"And I mean it. Every day." Shaking off the double-punch of emotions, he took her hand. "Let's grab some lunch, and then I need to send you off for a bit. My manager called and told me I have a meeting this afternoon."

"Oh. I can leave now if you need."

"No," he said, stopping to kiss her on the mouth. "We have plenty of time for lunch." Plenty of time in fact for everything, he thought, now that their whole life stretched out before them.

"Okay. If you're sure. How about we make some sandwiches and sit by the fire?"

Sitting by the fire had become their favorite thing to do together. Well, besides kissing and touching. He veered his mind away from those thoughts. He didn't need any more distractions. His brain was already doing back handsprings thinking about choosing the best princess cut later.

But he shouldn't have worried about that. Ultimately he didn't even need the McGuiness siblings' help. He knew it was the perfect ring the instant he laid eyes on it. Out of the ten gorgeous rings the jeweler had laid out, it was the only one he could envision on her hand.

"She's going to love it!" Sadie declared with grand enthusiasm. "And it's already the right ring size. It's a sign."

Shelby studied him carefully. "You already seem to know her."

"That might be the finest compliment I've ever received," he said humbly. "J.P., any thoughts?"

His friend leaned over and peered at the ring he held. "I think it'll fit."

Shelby playfully socked him in the arm while Sadie heaved a dramatic sigh.

After Jake handled the payment and showed the salesman out, he stared at the blue box in his hand like an idiot. He couldn't seem to help it. He was proposing. To Susannah! Tonight.

One of the sisters cleared her throat, and he looked up to see Shelby and Sadie watching him like two women who had something important on their minds. Sadie elbowed her sister. J.P. let out a groan behind him.

"Okay, now that you've settled all that," Shelby said, putting her hands on her hips. "Run us through your plan."

"Plan?" he asked.

Sadie's mouth twisted. Shelby narrowed her eyes.

"*The plan* for how you're going to ask her to marry you?" Sadie said with a hint of exasperation.

He gulped, grateful she hadn't called him an imbecile. "I was...going to ask her over dinner. My manager is setting something up at my house."

Sadie made a sound that reminded him of a game show buzzer when someone gave the wrong answer.

"Be nice to the man, Sadie," J.P. warned gently. "He's doing his best here."

"A woman wants her wedding proposal to be romantic," Shelby said, giving Sadie a nudge to the ribs.

All he could do was nod. "What do you suggest?"

Sadie crossed her arms across her chest. "You're going to need a boat."

26

Susannah made sure to check her make-up in the rearview mirror before getting out of her car. Jake had called her more than a little ruffled around five-thirty and asked if there was any way she could accompany him to a fancy dinner with one of his record company executives at seven-thirty on a private boat. Apparently it was a last-minute arrangement that had arisen from his afternoon meeting.

The poor guy hadn't sounded like himself, and while she was rather dreading this dinner, she wanted to support him. Was something happening with his new album? He was working on it nearly every day, fine-tuning the songs he'd written. She thought they were terrific, but had they?

When she exited her car, she saw Jake striding down the gangplank. From the looks of it, his recording company had rented—or owned perhaps—a luxury boat. She didn't know a thing about boats except that she liked sailing on them. This certainly was the way to go, but she wouldn't expect them to treat Jake with anything but the utmost respect.

The Cumberland River seemed a little stirred up because the boat was bobbing in the harsh glow of the marina's fluorescent lights. The brass work was buffed to a glow, and she caught sight of the boat's name: Destiny.

"Hey," Jake said, kissing her on the cheek. "Thanks so much for coming."

She put her hand on his chest. He was wearing a gray suit with a white dress shirt. Was that a purple tie? Good heavens! It was the most dressed up she'd ever seen him. She was glad she'd worn her go-to black cocktail dress.

"What's going on, Jake?" she asked, more than a little alarmed. "Can you tell me?"

"Everything's mostly fine," he said with a tight smile. "This all came together at the last minute. I don't have time to explain. We need to get aboard."

"Okay," she said, taking his hand and letting him lead her up the gangplank.

She pasted on a smile, determined to win over the record company executives—even if they were giving him a hard time for whatever reason. They passed a few crew members on the way to a large stateroom. The furniture was decorated in a rich cream. Champagne was chilling in the ice bucket on a glass coffee table. Two crystal glasses sparkled in the candlelight. Above the stateroom was a dining room set for two. Large bouquets of roses were sprinkled throughout the connected rooms, filling the air with a delightful fragrance.

Then she noticed no one else was around. "Are we the first to arrive?"

He smiled at her—it was a genuine smile now—and all she could do was smile back. The way he was looking at her was so heartbreakingly sweet.

"No," he said, and then he dropped to one knee before her, keeping ahold of her hand.

Her mouth dropped open. "Oh, my God." Was he? "*Oh, my God!*"

"Susannah McGuiness. The first time I held your hand, I knew I'd come home. I love you more than I can show you, but I promise to do my best."

He paused, and she pretty much had to put a hand on his shoulder so her knees wouldn't give out.

"Will you marry me?" he asked in that deep baritone voice she so loved.

"Oh, Jake," she said, running her hands through his hair, looking deep into those beautiful cobalt eyes. "Yes! Of course I will. Yes!"

"Good!" he said, laughing, and then he fumbled with his suit jacket. "I'm sorry. I did it wrong. I was supposed to present you with the ring as I proposed."

"It's okay," she said as he pulled out the most recognizable blue box in the whole world. *Tiffany's!* She had to fight the impulse to dance in place.

"You'd think I would have gotten it right after all the drilling Shelby and Sadie did on me."

Her eyes were latched onto the box he was opening. "My sisters?" And then she saw the ring. Had she been given the choice of any ring in the world, this is the one she would have selected. It was the perfect princess-cut diamond. "Oh, my God! You have my ring."

"Of course I have a ring," he said, sliding it on her finger. "And it fits. Thank God."

She clutched her hand to her chest, feeling the imprint of the diamond. "No, *my* ring. This is the one I would have picked out myself. Did Sadie and Shelby tell you?"

A dopey smile appeared on his face—one she found more than endearing. "No, I did, but they approved."

Somehow that made it so much more special.

"I love it!" She held her hand out and watched rainbows burst to life in the stone. "The promise of rainbows... I have rainbows in my ring." Of course she did. This man was her rainbow.

"Rainbows, huh?" he asked, peering closer, still on his knees. "I'm not going to be upset that I can't see them. So I did okay, then?"

She launched herself at him, and he caught her against his chest as she almost overbalanced him onto the floor. "You did great!"

Laughing, he framed her face with his hands. She was half sitting on his lap, and her smile was probably even dopier than his.

"I love you," he said, caressing her cheek. "Thanks for saying yes."

Her heart seemed to rise out of her chest like it was tied to a dozen balloons. "I couldn't have said anything else. I love you! So much I... Oh, Jake, I'm so grateful for you." Then a thought hit her. "You said Shelby and Sadie..."

His eyes narrowed at her tone. "Yes?"

"My sisters know you were going to propose?" She let out an unladylike squeal. "I have to call them."

"I talked to your mama and your brother too," he told her, helping them both stand. "I hope that's okay. I wanted to ask for their blessing...and I wanted to make sure your mama was okay with it for other reasons."

He didn't need to say which ones. "You're fine," she told him, pressing her cheek against his. "We both are. This is meant to happen. *We're* meant to happen."

He kissed her neck. "I wanted to make sure... I would never hurt you. Not for anything."

She wrapped her arms around him and looked into his eyes. "I know that, Jake. We're good. We're so good!"

Leaning closer, she kissed him. His lips softened under hers, and she closed her eyes, awash in the feeling of love and joy coursing through her veins. She felt like a one-hundred-person Gospel choir was singing inside her, and as she poured herself into that kiss, sending up a prayer of thanks to God for finally answering her prayers and sending her a good man to marry.

With the seal of their new commitment on her finger, something changed inside her. She felt an urgency rise up, one she couldn't deny herself or him anymore. She thrust her tongue into his mouth, and he groaned, angling his head to take the kiss deeper. Inching her fingers between them, she flicked open his suit jacket and set to work on the buttons she could reach. She fitted her hands in the opening and ran her fingers across his bare chest.

"You're playing with fire tonight, honey," he said, pulling back just enough so she could feel his ragged breath on her lips.

"I can't seem to help myself tonight," she whispered, feeling the hard line of his arousal pressed against her.

"Me either," he said, clenching his eyes shut as she traced the defined muscles of his chest. "We can do this for a bit, but I'm not going to be able to stand too much. You'd best leave your clothes on unless you're ready to break another barrier tonight."

She felt the beautiful press of her ring on her finger and made the decision she'd been struggling with since their first kiss.

"I don't want to wait anymore," she whispered, awash in the heat of his hands on her skin.

He edged back and looked directly into her eyes. His cobalt eyes shone brightly, and she could see his pulse beating hard in his neck. "What? Are you sure? You wanted to wait."

She *had* wanted to wait. She'd wanted to wait for the right man, for that magical day when they became man and wife. "We both love each other, and we're getting married. As far as I'm concerned, I said yes to you tonight." She hoped God would understand.

His hands tightened on her waist. "I am going to marry you. There's no question about that. And I want to make love with you, but if this is going to cause you a moment's regret, I'd rather wait for our wedding night."

For years, she'd dreamed about her wedding night. In some of her fantasies, her husband would carry her across the threshold in her wedding dress and then slowly slide it off her as he kissed his way across her shoulders. In others, she prepared for him in the bathroom, anointing herself with an exotic perfume and slipping on a white nightgown before coming into the bedroom to find him waiting for her. None of those fantasies had made her shiver quite like the feeling of Jake's awed gaze and the sensation of his strong hands on her body.

"We're engaged," she said softly, feeling the certainty of her decision fill her. "I have to do what's right for me. For us. I don't want to withhold something beautiful from either of us. Not for one second longer."

The corner of his mouth tipped up. "It *will* be beautiful, honey. That I can promise you."

"I know it will," she said, even though she was a little

scared now that she'd admitted what she wanted. "I want to please you."

This time he tilted his head to the side, a soft smile on his face. "You light up my life by simply being you. Don't worry for a moment about pleasing me. We'll take this slow. Do it together."

Her mouth was so dry now. "I'm being silly, I know. It's only because I've never made love with anyone before."

He brought her hand to his mouth and kissed the palm. "How about this? You've never made love to me, and I've never made love to you. It's a first for both of us."

Those words washed away the rest of her fear. "I like thinking of it that way."

His smile was soft and warm, and oh, how it made her belly churn like cream being transformed into custard.

"It's the truth. I'm a little nervous too. I want to make it good for you." Then he laughed. "I *will* make it good for you."

"I know you will," she whispered.

Somehow their hands touched. "It seems like every time we take another step together we always hold hands."

"I'll always hold your hand," he said. "As often as you want, until you or I breathe our last."

She didn't like to think about that final moment, but it was true that their path together stretched out before them now. They were committed to each other for as long as they lived. As she looked at his face, she wondered how he'd age. Would he develop laugh lines around his eyes? Would his hair gray? Would he grow bald? She couldn't help laughing softly.

"What are you thinking?" he asked, raising her hands to his mouth and kissing them.

"About whether you're going to lose your hair."

He shook his head. "I guess it's a good thing we're getting married now if that concerns you."

"I didn't mean it that way," she said immediately, kissing him on the mouth to soften the words.

"I know you didn't. Well...a thought just struck me." He inclined his head to the adjoining room. "We have a fine dinner prepared and a crew that's thankfully following my orders not to interrupt us. And we're on a boat."

Perhaps he was as giddy as she was if he'd forgotten that. "Yes, we're on a boat."

"It cast off as soon as we came aboard." He gave her a look. "I don't want to make love to you for the first time on a boat. Or in earshot of anyone."

"Oh," she said, looking over her shoulder. *"Oh."*

He chuckled. "So this is what I propose. I'll go talk to the captain and ask him to head back to the marina. We can't be too far out."

Now she heard the quiet rumbling of the engine underneath them and felt the soft sway of the ship moving over the water. In all the excitement, she'd been oblivious. "How far had you told him to go?"

"I thought a couple hours on the Cumberland with the moon shining above us might be nice. I'd intended to wrap my arms around you as we drank champagne on deck."

That plan certainly bore the mark of Shelby and Sadie. God bless her sisters. "We can still do that if you'd like. I don't want to ruin the night you planned."

His shoulders shook. "Honey, you can't expect a healthy living and breathing man to want to keep going down a river when the woman he wants like crazy has just agreed to marry him and make love to him for the first time. Even I don't have that much strength."

No, and he'd waited so patiently for her. "We could swim to shore," she said in a teasing voice.

"Imp," he said, kissing her on the mouth. "I'll go talk to the captain. Start on the appetizers so the crew feels appreciated."

He was the only thing she really wanted, but the meal they'd set out did look appetizing now that he'd drawn her attention to it. The rack of lamb and bacon-dressed fingerling potatoes were especially inviting.

When he returned, he told her they were only thirty minutes out. They made quick work of the meal, and by the time the crew had secured the boat to the dock, they were ready to disembark.

They raced away from the boat, and he pulled her to his truck. "We can get your car tomorrow."

She didn't argue, awash in a sea of excitement. They were rushing off to make love, and if she'd drunk more than one glass of champagne, she would have thought she was giddy from it.

"Just so you know," he said as he pulled onto the highway. "I'm going to speed a bit more than my usual, if that's all right."

"Speed away," she said, laughing.

When they reached his house, they both shot out of the car and raced to the side door in the garage. He paused to turn on lights to illuminate their way. When they reached the stairs, they raced down the hallway—both of them knowing their ultimate destination.

At the door, they skidded to a halt. She was breathless, and so was he. But both of them were smiling.

Slowly, his smile faded, and he cupped her face. "I love you, and I'm going to be the best husband you could hope for. That I promise you. And I'm going to be the best lover you've ever imagined."

She shivered at those words. "And I promise to be a good wife to you. To always love you and support you. And I'll be the lover you always wanted. Just tell me how."

All of the stars of the heavens seemed to shine in his eyes as he gazed at her, and she felt the presence of something bigger than both of them.

"We'll both tell each other how," he said, leaning in to kiss her gently on the lips. "It's like writing a song and then adding the lyrics. You have to take it slow and listen to what makes the best melody. Experiment with what makes the best music. For me, that part is as fun as playing the final melody."

Her belly tightened with sheer lust. She almost had to fan herself. Experiment? She hadn't thought of it that way. It sounded fun and forbidden all at the same time.

"Let's experiment then," she whispered and felt her cheeks flush.

"You're adorable when you blush," he said, tracing that heated flesh. "I'm going to enjoy making you blush even more."

She did blush more. This was really going to happen. "Shall we go further into your bedroom? We seem to be hovering in the doorway."

"Last chance. Is this really what you want?"

That he would ask her again humbled her and only confirmed her decision. "Yes."

His laugh was husky. "I've been imagining you in that bed since we first picked it out together, but I imagined making love to you well before that."

"Me too," she admitted, and the daring of that admission made her feel a little breathless again.

He raised her left hand to his mouth and kissed the back of it and then pressed a kiss to her ring. "If we could get away with it, I would hire a plane and take us to Vegas tonight so we could get married." He instantly blanched. "Not that I'm suggesting you don't deserve a church wedding. Because you do. I only—"

"I know," she interrupted.

He took a deep breath then, and she could feel the change in him.

"Let's think for a moment about how we can make this as special as it deserves to be," he said in a husky voice. "When a man and woman come together for the first time —especially when they just got engaged—it's a moment to commemorate. I would have been better prepared if I'd known your feelings on the subject were going to change."

"Can we light some candles?" she asked.

If she was going to meet him as an equal partner in love, she had to voice what she wanted. Even if it made her blush. Not that the candle request was blush worthy. But there would be other requests, and darn it all, she was going to make them.

He leaned in to kiss her on the cheek. "I have candles. Lots of them since I've met you."

Her mouth tipped up a little at that. "I know you've bought some things for the house just because I like them. Are you finally going to tell me which ones?"

His hand slid down her arm in the most arousing caress imaginable. He could turn her body into a long line of wild-fire merely by touching her.

"I think I'll draw it out a bit," he said, stroking the inside of her wrist. "I'll tell you a few, and you can guess the rest. When you're right, you get to claim a prize."

Those cobalt eyes of his were filled with mischief, and

she could well imagine the kind of prizes he had in mind. "That sounds like a fun game."

The smile he flashed made her own smile all the wider. Her nerves fluttered away, mixed with the potent love and friendship that had grown between them. Oh, and desire. She couldn't forget about that.

"Why don't we go light those candles?" he asked, raising her hand to his mouth and kissing the inside of her wrist.

Who knew that part of her body could be so sensitive? She wondered what parts of his body would surprise her like that.

"They're downstairs," she said, wishing they'd had the foresight to bring them up on their mad dash to the bedroom.

"I'll grab some. Do you want some more champagne?"

She took their joined hands and held them against her heart. "Go find some candles. I don't want any more to drink."

He stood and pulled her slowly to him. She wrapped her arms around him, and they just stood there for a moment, holding each other. Reveling in their connection.

"I love you," she whispered. "So much."

Stroking her back, he kissed the top of her head. "I love you too. More than I could ever show you."

"Then show me," she said, caressing his jaw. "I'll endeavor to show you too."

"You do, darlin'. Every day. I'll grab some candles. I'll even make us a fire."

She eyed the fireplace on the side wall, stocked with wood but to date unused. "It's not cold enough for a fire tonight."

His wink was downright endearing. "It is when you turn the air conditioner on. I'm going to get those candles."

He returned with his arms so full of candles she wouldn't be surprised if he'd left a trail of them up the stairs. She laughed as she helped him arrange them around the room.

"I'll get the candles lit," she said and walked over to the box of matches she'd laid on the mantle. The box was decorated with the American flag. My, how delighted she'd been to find patriotic matchbooks. They'd joked that it was a much subtler way to honor his military service than the old decorator's choices.

Sulfur tickled her nose when the match fired, and she set about lighting the candles throughout the room. He quickly balled up newspaper and added it to the grate. As she laid the matches next to him, he tugged her to his side.

"Where do you think you're going?" he asked in a husky tone, nuzzling her ear.

"You aren't going to be able to light that fire if you're kissing me." Her voice was so husky, it was almost unrecognizable to her own ears.

"I can do more than one thing at a time," he answered, running his nose down her nape. "I have skills."

She shivered like bed sheets hanging on a clothesline in a gentle breeze.

"You might have noticed I can even play my guitar and sing at the same time," he drawled.

"I might have noticed that," she said. Deciding that she wanted to entice him too, she slid her hand down his back. He shivered beneath her touch, although the way a man shivered was different than a woman. His muscles were locked with tension and seemed to vibrate like the earth's aftershocks from an earthquake.

"You're right," he said with a groan. "I won't get the fire lit."

She released him and gave him some room, looking around. The tree bed was freshly made, all the more inviting for the whimsical throw pillows she'd added. It touched her that he arranged them on the bed each morning after he woke. She'd noticed from the few times she'd peeked into his bedroom while she was over here.

"You agreed to the pillows because I wanted them," she said.

"I sure did," he responded, adding wood to the fire. "But I kinda like them now. The bed is more comfortable with them."

"I wanted to take away all your memories of the bare-bones barracks," she said softly. "You deserve comfort and beauty, Jake. I wanted to give that to you."

"Why don't you get comfortable on that deer skin rug you arranged in front of the hearth?"

She sat down with her knees drawn up and watched as he gathered more wood from the discreet wood box in the corner of the room and laid the logs in teepee fashion.

As she watched him light the paper so the fire caught, all she could think about was Jake stripping off her clothes and making love to her. Did he want her to take his clothes off too? She jumped when his hands settled on her shoulders. He was kneeling before her now, the fire cracking and popping behind him.

"Whoa there," he said, giving her a sweet smile. "You're thinking too much all of a sudden. People have been coming together since the dawn of time. We're going to be fine."

When he put it that way, her nerves seemed silly. "I love you."

"I love you too," he said, sliding his arms around her. "Now come here and let me make you mine. And I'll become yours."

His head lowered, and he took her mouth in a slow, drugging kiss. He kept kissing her until her grip on his suit jacket loosened and her shoulders relaxed. Then he continued until she gave a quiet moan. Running his tongue over her bottom lip, he took the kiss deeper. She pressed against him. Oh, how that man could kiss.

When his hands slid down her back and cupped her hips, she could feel the hard line of his desire. He broke their kiss to trail his lips down her neck, and she settled more firmly against him, allowing herself to touch the defined muscles of his back through his jacket.

"I haven't really told you this before," she said as she tilted her head to the side to give him better access, "but I love your body. I want to run my hands all over it."

He straightened, and his smile was infectious. "I'm glad." He hastily stripped off his suit jacket and tie and unbuttoned his shirt.

She could only watch as he tossed them all on the floor. Confronted with the beauty of his massive chest, her mouth went dry.

"Everything I am is yours now," he told her, loosely wrapping his hand around her wrist and drawing her fingertips up to rest against his pecs. "Touch me anywhere you want."

She did, gently at first, and with more hesitation than he probably wished. Before, she'd been careful not to go too far. They both had been.

"Am I touching you okay?" she finally asked.

"You can touch me however you want, honey," he said in a husky voice, rubbing his fingers along her waistline.

"I'm so darn happy to have your hands on me and to know we don't have to stop."

When she met his eyes, the cobalt blue was the same color as the blue flames in the fire he'd lit. The room was too warm—like her. "Show me, Jake."

He took her hand and pressed it hard against his chest. His skin was hot, and she wondered if hers was too. His fingers guided her touch in slow passes up and down those defined muscles. The power he represented as a man made her breathless.

She leaned forward to press her lips to his chest, and the muscles jumped. His breathing changed to a harsh rasp.

"Too much?"

"Not nearly," he drawled, helping her to her feet. "How about we get you out of that fabulous black dress. I *really* want to touch you, Susannah."

Her lungs filled with more air at his words, and then she exhaled deeply. She wanted him to touch her too, but she was in a dress, which meant she was going to be standing before him in her underwear. Well, they were going to end up naked, so what in the world was she dithering about?

Before she could lose her nerve, she turned around and lifted her hair over her shoulder. "Would you unzip me?"

"It would be my pleasure," he drawled, and so he did.

The zipper went down as slowly as a drop of honey down the honey jar. He pressed kisses against each inch of skin he exposed, sending pulses of heat through her body. When her dress dropped to her waist, she forced herself to push it the rest of the way over her hips. It pooled at her feet, and she stepped out of it and kicked off her heels. For a moment, she was afraid to turn around. Then Jake's hands settled on the roundness of her hips, and she knew he was looking his fill.

"You are so beautiful," he said, kissing her shoulder blades.

Right now, she could only be grateful she'd chosen a matching bra and panties. Then his hands slid around her front, settling against her stomach as he pressed the hard, hot line of his body against her own.

Every muscle south of the Mason-Dixon line tightened and then became liquid. His mouth settled against her neck and lit a trail of fire there.

"How does that feel?" he asked.

"Like heaven," she answered with complete honesty.

"Good," he said, nipping her nape. "Let's see if we can expand on that."

She wasn't sure how to expand on heaven, but when his hands slid up her belly to cup her breasts, she decided she needed a new word. He ran his thumbs over the gentle rise of her cleavage, and she shivered. Suddenly, she was desperate to have his hands on her bare flesh. The strength and insistence of the urge shocked her.

"You can take off my bra, if you'd like," she said softly.

He kissed her neck. "I was planning on getting to that in a little while."

A little while seemed too far away. "Why wait?"

"Well, now," he said, kissing her neck. "Music to my ears."

Her bra tightened as he undid the back clasp and then she tugged it down her arms and let it slide to the floor by her dress. His hands slid up her ribcage, and she held her breath until his hands settled over her bare breasts. For some reason, his hands seemed even hotter than before. And then he rubbed her nipples with his fingers, and her head fell back against his chest.

She bit her lip to hold back a moan, but the sound

emerged despite her efforts when he executed a delicate tugging motion.

"Don't hold back from me," he whispered against her ear. "I want to hear everything you're feeling when I touch you. I promise to let you hear me too. Let's make some music together, Susannah."

She hadn't thought about the musical quality of lovemaking before, but it immediately made sense to her. There would be different notes of passion from bass to alto, and the underlying beat of their hearts would serve as the percussion.

"I want that too. Touch me, Jake."

He turned her around, and she met his gaze. His eyes lowered so he could take in her body. Suddenly she felt self-conscious, but his hand was gentle and worshipping as it ran down her chest to the top of her underwear. Her breath froze, and he looked up.

"I want to touch you here," he said, rubbing his fingers over the waistband.

She gulped. He'd always stayed away from that level of intimacy before. "Then do."

Without taking his eyes off her face, he cupped her. Her breath shattered at the sensation his hand created. The shiver she gave this time came from deep within her.

He sank to his knees in front of her, and she pretty much stopped breathing. His hands cupped her hips, and he pressed a kiss to her belly. Another quiver rippled through her, and he raised his head to look at her again. On his face was the most beautiful smile she'd ever seen.

"You have no idea how much I want you. But we should probably discuss something important before we get too... ah...are you okay with me using condoms? I didn't want to assume you were on birth control. You being a virgin and all."

Good Lord. She was an idiot. How in the world could she have forgotten something as important as that?

"Unless you want to start a family right away?" he asked, watching her face closely. "I want a family with you. I want it more than anything. But I...want us to have our time, and if I'm being honest, I want more time to work on my issues."

The edge in his voice told her how much courage it must have taken for him to propose to her. He was still worried about his PTSD, but he'd decided not to let it dictate his happiness.

"I'd like us to have our time too," she assured him. And truth be told, she didn't want to be pregnant on her wedding day. "We can start our family when we're both ready."

He let out the breath he was holding, and she put her arms around him and waited for him to settle. When he did, he cupped her face and kissed her long and sweet.

"Let me grab some condoms," he said, his blue eyes darker now.

Condoms? Plural? She shivered. She could barely think past this first time. It was like the old adage. Once she opened the barn door...

When he returned, he held out his hand to her. "Come, my beautiful fiancée. Let me love you by the fire."

The fire's glow touched her skin as she lay down beside it. Jake sank onto the rug with her, and they were both on their sides. Her back was to the fire, and she felt the heat from the flames tickling her. Then she realized it was his fingertips running playfully across her bare skin. He kissed her again, and she kissed him, letting the last of her nerves float away like the fragrant smoke from the fire.

An urgency was building inside her, and she finally gave herself permission to surrender to it.

"Why don't you take your slacks off?" she whispered against his mouth.

He rolled onto his back and made quick work of them. The soft glow of firelight played against his broad, muscular body, revealing his briefs and the more than adequate bulge in them. The heat in her body seemed to radiate out from deep inside her.

"You're so handsome," she said, staring at the muscles rippling as he stretched out beside her. "Sometimes I can't believe how gorgeous you are."

His finger playfully tapped her nose. "I feel that way about you. You take my breath away, and seeing you like this, all bare and soft and beautiful with the fire touching your skin...I still can't believe you're mine."

Because she wanted to—or, really, because she couldn't help herself—she laid her hand on the smooth expanse of his muscled thigh. "Make me yours, Jake."

"Oh, honey," he said in a husky voice. "Let me show you how good it's going to be between us."

She took his hand and pressed it between her legs in a bold move, giving him permission to take things further. "Let's take these off."

His eyes flickered to hers. "Mind if I help?"

"Please." And this time she did gulp as she rose up on her knees and helped him lower the panties down her thighs. It was a bit awkward, untangling them from that position, but she managed.

"How do you feel about me taking off my briefs?" he asked when she lay back down on her side.

Being bare in front of him made her feel vulnerable. But where there was true love, there were no barriers.

"I think that's a good idea," she said in a voice she didn't recognize.

The corner of his mouth turned up, and he made quick work of freeing himself. His erection was huge and awe inspiring, if she were being honest. He let her look her fill, not speaking until her eyes darted to his.

"It's not going to hurt you," he said softly. "Except maybe at first. I hope not much."

Now she really was being a ninny. "I know. I've just never..." Jeez. How was she supposed to admit this? "I've never seen one...like this...in person."

She could tell he was fighting a smile. "It only wants to please you, like I do. Remember that." Then his eyes darkened. "If you need us to slow down, say the word. We have all night."

They did. And they were engaged. She'd agreed to marry him, and they were going to make love tonight. She needed to buck up. "I love being with you. Show me how much I'm going to love this."

His smile returned, bold and bright in the firelight. "You really are going to love this, honey. That much I can promise you."

Then he leaned down and took her right nipple in his mouth until she writhed against him. He lowered her to her back and switched to the other breast. Her back arched, and when it did, his hand slid between her legs and parted her thighs. The first pass of his fingers against the intimate part of her was a shock, but heavens, it felt so good she was helpless to do anything but utter a moan when he showed her how her body was made to respond. Between the press of his mouth and his hand, she grew more urgent. Downright needy in fact.

There was something here, something waiting for her. That much she knew. She pressed her head back into the floor and moaned, long and deep.

He rose up and took her mouth in a drugging kiss, increasing the press of his hand between her thighs. "Show me what you're feeling, Susannah. Let me feel all of it."

Her eyes squeezed shut as he increased the pressure of his hand and mouth on the parts of her body that wanted him the most. Something was rising inside her, something strong and beautiful.

"Oh, God!" she cried out, awash in a divine magic more powerful than any she'd ever known.

"Come for me," he whispered, raining sensual kisses across her skin now.

The pulse of her body rose until all she felt was that incessant throbbing. And then it broke free. She exploded in a long rush of sensation, moaning with abandon now, completely out of control.

She heard the tear of a wrapper and then felt Jake open her legs wider. She was too awash in the glorious sensations running through her to open her eyes. Something pressed between her thighs—and she knew it was him, seeking entrance.

Struggling to the surface, she forced her eyes open. He was gazing at her with an intensity that made her skin feel tight all over again. His pulse beat hard in his neck.

"I need you," he whispered harshly.

Oh, those words. She raised her shaking hands to his shoulders, trying to soothe him as he had her. There was a press of strange flesh inside her, and she winced a little.

"Sorry, honey," he said, kissing her cheek. "I promise it's going to get better."

It took some time for that to be true. He seemed too large, and her body too small. Her earlier passion evaporated like water on hot sand. But then he kissed her and her breasts, and she felt the urgency inside her return.

There was still discomfort, but the last vestiges of pain faded away. A flash of heat raced through her belly. Her hips surged to him, her muscles tightening around him.

There was a hiss of his breath. Her gaze shot to his face. The tension in his jaw looked agonizing.

"I'm sorry," she whispered, running a hand over the tightness there.

He turned his head to press a hard kiss to her palm. "Don't be. This is the good stuff."

When he pressed deeper inside her, she didn't think she could take it. Suddenly she couldn't keep her eyes open. *"Oh, God!"*

"Come with me now," he said, kissing her mouth.

The slow slide of him retreating and then surging back inside her redefined any concept of pleasure. Every time he moved, the friction of their flesh meeting seemed to burn through her.

His movements grew more urgent, as if he too couldn't hold back the tide. Her hips started to rise to his instinctively. She pushed back at him, not to press him away, but because she needed a stronger connection to him amidst all the wildness inside her. He rose onto his knees and increased the power and depth of his thrusts until she was panting and crying out, unable to hold back.

The line of tension in her body snapped suddenly, and she cried out, surging into him like a stormy sea finding its home against the jagged cliff face of the shore.

He froze over her and called her name in the most beautiful voice she'd ever heard utter the word: *"Susannah."*

She floated on a sea of pleasure greater than she'd ever known. The very heavens seemed to surround her. When Jake folded over her, his heart racing against her own, she wrapped her arms around him and surrendered to the love between them. She knew she was his, and he was hers. The knowledge seemed eternal.

He managed to roll to his back and bring her onto his chest. She rested her cheek against his hot skin and sighed. Life seemed so much bigger, and their life together... Well, it was forever. She knew that in a new way now.

"I love you," he whispered, kissing the top of her head. "More than I ever imagined loving anyone."

Nestling closer, she pressed a kiss to his heart. "Me too." In that moment, she knew she'd made the right decision.

He was the husband of her heart, and their bodies had forged the vows of their love.

27

Awakening next to Susannah filled Jake with a contentment and joy he'd never known. He'd made love to her in the middle of the night again, and the magic between them had only increased. She was warm and curious and more than generous.

She was sleeping on her side facing him with her hands tucked under her head. There was a pillow crease on the side of her face when she rolled onto her back, and he leaned in to kiss the mark. How was he supposed to resist? Her skin was as soft as goose feathers, and he placed gentle kisses along her jaw. Then he saw the smile.

"So, you *are* awake," he said huskily.

"Yes. Again," she replied, turning her head at him on the pillow. "Isn't it funny how we both woke up at the same time in the middle of the night? I didn't tell you before, but I was dreaming you were making love to me. And then I turned to you."

"And I woke up, wanting you too," he admitted, kissing her nose and then her chin. "I can't keep my hands off you."

"Me either," she concurred, sliding even closer.

"How did you sleep after we made love again?" he asked, kissing his way down her neck.

"I was out," she said, lifting her chin so he could kiss the underside. "What about you?"

"Truth be told, I didn't sleep much," he said, loving the scent of her this morning, a combination of flowers from her perfume and their passion—the sexiest fragrance in the world.

"Why didn't you sleep?" she asked, turning onto her side to face him.

Her big moss-green eyes were a little puffy, and without a stitch of makeup on, she looked even more beautiful than usual.

"I was too happy," he answered, wrapping his arm around her waist. "We got engaged *and* made love for the first time last night. It was a red-letter day."

He hadn't been afraid to fall asleep with her next to him, although the thought had crossed his mind. But only once. Old fears died hard, he supposed. He hadn't felt comfortable sleeping with a woman since leaving the Army.

"I feel like I've crossed into the Promised Land," he told her, knowing she'd appreciate the biblical reference. Nothing could take him back to the darkness. He was going to climb this light with all his strength.

"The Promised Land is a pretty good way to describe what's between us if you ask me."

She pressed herself against his body, and the feel of her warm, soft curves inflamed his senses. "How sore are you this morning?"

From the way she was stroking the muscles of his chest, he thought she might be thinking the same thing he was.

"Umm...I don't rightly know," she said in a hushed voice, pink in the face.

"Well, how about we test the waters? If you're too sore, we can enjoy each other another way."

Her eyes were a bit wide as he pressed her into the mattress and leaned over her. She was such an innocent. Sure, she knew things. She'd admitted she'd read magazine articles and books, but the doing of them was a heck of a lot different.

"Trust me a little more," he said, caressing her cheek. "I won't do anything you don't like. I promise."

The smile she gave him was brave and sweet all at once. "I know you won't. Honestly, I don't think you could do anything I don't like. I just...this is still new to me. Even after last night. I don't mean to get flustered. I...only wondered if you meant what I thought you meant."

It was hard not to smile, but he managed even though his lips were twitching. "If you're wondering if I can pleasure you without being inside you, then you're on the right track. Same for me."

"You'll have to show me how...to help you."

Her voice was low, and goodness if she wasn't beet red in the face now. Bless her heart.

"Don't worry. It'll be fun. If we don't end up doing it now, we will sometime."

He wanted to do everything imaginable with her. Well, everything except that *Fifty Shades of Grey* stuff. He had no desire to truss her up like some chicken, and that was messed up if you asked him.

Her trust in him paid off, and they were both pretty much giddy as they showered. He washed her hair for her, and she found more boldness and washed the expanse of his body, her lips lingering on new areas of his skin, delighting him.

As she made them coffee later, she smiled at him over

her mug. "I need to call my family and tell them the news. They're probably wondering why they didn't hear from me last night. Although knowing my sisters, I bet they called and texted me like crazy. I purposely didn't check my phone once we got here."

No, they'd been pretty occupied. He planned to call his Army buddies to share the news of their engagement later.

"Good heavens! Do you think they're going to know we had sex? That would be mortifying."

He set his coffee aside and pulled her into his arms. "I'm sorry that bothers you so." And it did. Though he felt no regret, seeing her distress felt as painful as salt in an open wound.

"I'm being stupid," she said, shaking her head. "I don't want anyone to think less of me. Especially Mama."

"If there's one thing I am certain about, it's that your mama would never think less of you. She loves you, and I have a feeling..." Did he dare say it? "I hope you don't mind me saying so, but I have a feeling she knows J.P. and Tammy have...gone down that road."

He pressed back so he could look into her eyes. Surely she had noticed the intimacy between her brother and Tammy.

She bit her lip. "It's different with J.P. He's...well...never mind."

"What can I do to help you with this?" he asked, not daring to ask why J.P. was different. Better to distract her.

"Can we get married right away?" she asked, brightening up immediately. "I mean...I don't really want to wait to live with you anyway. It would make things easier all around."

"Music to my ears, honey," he said, kissing her on the mouth. "I want you here too."

"How much of a miracle can your manager pull off?" she asked, fire in her eyes.

"My manager is the king of making miracles happen. I'll give Garth a raise."

Her mouth twitched. "Your manager is named Garth?"

"Yes," he said, his shoulders shaking. "His mama named him well before Garth Brooks took the stage. You'll have to meet him and the rest of my team. And my band. Now that we're all official-like." With their relationship being so new, he'd wanted to keep her to himself.

"I'd love to meet the people who matter to you," she said, kissing his cheek.

"I don't want the press to get wind of our wedding, or it will be a circus. How about we hold a party and make it a surprise?" The idea had sat with him awhile now, and the more he thought about it, the more he liked it.

"A housewarming party," she said, her smile reaching across her face. "How many people do you want to invite?"

"Only close friends for me," he told her, thinking it through. "We can hold a bigger party after we get married for people in the industry. If that's all right." Now that they were committed to a future together, he would have to get used to making decisions with her—an idea that sat rather well with him.

"I only want to have my family and close friends there too." After leaning in to kiss him, she grabbed the legal pad she kept on the kitchen counter for her design notes and tore off a couple of sheets. Sliding a blank page and a pen in front of him, she said, "Start writing down your names. Let's see how many people we have between us. Then we can call my family. I think we should invite them to dinner tonight and tell everyone at once. And I want to invite our extended family too. Is that okay with you?"

"I think it's a wonderful idea," he said, thinking it would be easier that way.

"We can call one of the local BBQ joints and order take-out," she said, scribbling furiously now.

Jake started on his list, and soon they had an initial guest list.

"Saying it's only close friends and family makes it easier," she told him as she texted her family about dinner.

Her phone immediately buzzed. "That would be Shelby calling." She picked up the phone, and immediately said, "I'm not saying a single word until tonight. Tell Sadie the same. I'll see y'all at seven."

Then she hung up.

"That was...kind of bold," he said, loving to see how she and her siblings interacted. The realization that he was now part of it—part of a real family—just about floored him.

"If I don't draw the line, I'll be on the phone all afternoon. Plus we have things to do. Do you want to call your Army buddies now?"

"I can wait a spell." He was used to seeing her focused —hadn't she scanned all those showroom floors like a hawk for him? But never like this. "I find you wildly hot right now."

Her brow crinkled. "Shut the front door." And then she shook her head. "*No.* I'm still sore, and we have some planning to do."

He was laughing as she picked up her guest list and shook it. "Focus, Jake. Getting married quickly is going to make things so much easier. If we waited six months and did something big, I'd have to invite Mama's church friends. Not all of them have been kind to me about being unmarried."

He had the urge to call them some pretty ugly names.

No one was going to treat her like that again if he had any say about it. "We're *never* going to invite anyone who's ugly to us to our home. I have to put up with haters as an artist, but I don't need them in my inner circle."

She laid a hand on his arm. "It's hard to imagine anyone saying bad things about you."

"It's their problem," he said, but felt compelled to continue. "The worst are the ones who say I was better off serving my country than being some famous singer. They sound like my father."

Her eyes became troubled. "Do you want to invite your parents to the wedding? I...wasn't sure what to say when I didn't see them or your brother on the guest list."

A tight feeling wedged in his diaphragm, and he wanted to curse it for ruining his happiness. Hadn't he just said he didn't want to invite anyone like that into their home? But somewhere inside he wasn't fully ready to give up on them. "It won't make a difference if I do invite them. Daddy won't change his mind, and neither will my brother. I...don't even know if they'd come."

"Shall we try and extend an olive branch to them?" she asked, rubbing his back in soothing motions. "You don't have to talk a lot to them, but..."

"If I don't invite them, I close the door forever." He could see her logic.

"I've seen people soften their stances as they get older," she said softly. "And...when grandchildren appear."

Grandchildren. Lord have mercy. They'd used condoms last night, but at some point they would start a family. He had to admit to himself that the thought still scared him. It was one thing to have Susannah agree to stand by him if and when he had another episode, but an innocent child? All he could do was assure himself he was going to be well enough to have kids someday. He wasn't going to let doubt creep in.

"All right," he said with a heavy heart. "We can invite them and leave the decision in their hands." Louisa talked about forgiveness all the time, and Jake knew he had to work on forgiving his family for not accepting him. He'd get there somehow.

The rest of the afternoon was a blur. Susannah talked him into setting their wedding date for the third Saturday in March, a little over three weeks away. She asked if her mama could marry them, and it made her laugh when he replied, "Who else would marry us? Rye?"

He called Garth and told him to move heaven and earth to make his wedding the best day of their lives. Without missing a beat, his manager said he was going to hire a couple extra assistants with event planning experience who'd help make it happen. It made it easier that they'd be using Jake's home as the venue. Between Garth's efforts and Susannah's, Jake knew it would be a perfect day.

Before he knew it, Susannah was already showing him color combinations for their wedding.

He ended up liking a pairing of deep purple and hot pink the best, though he expected the guys would rag on him something fierce about having pink as a wedding color. Especially Darren, Monty, and Randy—whom he stepped out to call briefly to share his news. His old buddies were overjoyed for him, but not surprised after seeing Susannah and Jake together. All of them promised to make it to the wedding.

The family came over that night, and pretty much everyone walked in with a knowing smile. There were a few exaggerated nods in his direction, and he saw more than one person whisper in Susannah's ear.

Jake saw to the drinks, and when every member of his expanding family had finally arrived, Susannah reached for his hand.

"So this won't surprise most of you, but...Jake and I are getting married."

A collective cheer went up, and some people even clapped their hands.

Annabelle and Rory jumped up and down like a couple of escaped ping pong balls, the little girl exclaiming, "Yay! Jake is going to be part of our family for real. Now he can be with us forever."

When Annabelle ran over, Jake swept her up in his arms and swung her around. "Forever and ever." He gave her a kiss on the cheek and set her down.

"I was tempted to send a hit man after you when you hung up on me this afternoon, Susannah," Shelby said, bustling up to Susannah. Sadie was trailing only a foot behind her.

"Yeah," Sadie said, wrapping Susannah into a hug. "And after all the help we gave Jake in picking out the proper ring and orchestrating a proper proposal."

Jake felt a warm hand touch his arm, and he knew who it was before he even looked to the side. The power of Louisa's touch was well known to him.

"Hey, sugar," she said, embracing him. "I'm so happy for y'all. It's the answer to one of my greatest prayers."

Jake got all choked up. "You had a lot to do with it. Thank you. The words don't seem like they're enough, but they're all I have."

"Oh, they're enough all right," she said, and then stepped back to let the others offer their congratulations.

J.P. gave him a bear hug and said, "It'll be nice to have someone else help with the McGuiness girls."

Just then, Shelby and Sadie let out ear-piercing squeals. "Three weeks!" Shelby yelled.

Amelia Ann, Tory, and Tammy all rushed over, and he watched as Susannah gestured with her hands, probably filling them in on the news.

"I like a man who doesn't dither," Rye said, slapping him on the back. "If you ask me, Tory and I did way too much of that. Sure, she was finishing her doctorate and all that jazz, but I would have whisked her off to Vegas in a heartbeat."

"And been permanently prevented from ever having children," Clayton said, shaking his hand. "Congratulations, Jake. I know you and Susannah are going to be very happy."

He knew they were too, and as he made his way through the rest of the evening, he felt like his life was finally coming together.

28

Finding a wedding dress for one woman was tough enough, but finding three wedding dresses in one *day* was the looniest notion ever, if you asked Shelby. And yet, somehow, Susannah, Tammy, and Amelia Ann managed to do just that on a blustery day in Nashville with all of the women from their extended family in tow.

Eight hours after their shopping trip had begun, Shelby's feet were aching from all the bridal shops they'd visited. The restaurant they'd chosen to celebrate their shopping success was warmly lit, quiet, and it boasted some of the best drinks in Nashville.

"I love my dress," Amelia Ann cooed out, awash in what Shelby termed "the bridal glow." If she hadn't suspected the others would judge her, she'd have said it rivaled afterglow.

"The organdy looks gorgeous on you, honey," Tammy exclaimed, sipping her champagne cocktail. "Clayton will be a puddle on the ground when he sees you."

"And J.P. too, sugar, when he sees you in that silk A-line," Amelia Ann said, tapping their glasses together in a toast. "It's classic."

Shelby eyed Susannah, who was busy texting.

"Are you waxing poetic about your dress to your fiancé, honey?" Shelby drawled, trying to bring her sister back to the group. "If I weren't so happy for you, I'd be tempted to put an ice cube down your shirt to help you focus."

Usually Susannah stowed her phone when they got together, but she and Jake couldn't bear to be apart without sending near-constant texts.

"Thank you for your restraint," her sister said, her bridal glow only dimming a couple watts as she put her phone away. "I was seeing what he's up to, is all. Why ever would I say anything about my dress? But he'll go crazy when he sees what I'm wearing. Don't you think I look like a fairy princess in it, Mama?"

"That and more," Louisa said, holding a sleepy Annabelle against her side.

They hadn't had the heart to make the little girl stay home with her brother, whom Dale was watching. Not when there was this much special shopping to do. Annabelle had been extra helpful picking out Tammy's wedding dress, and she'd promised more than once not to tell anyone—including Rory—what any of the dresses looked like. Now she was all tuckered out, the poor thing.

"We should get this little one home," Tammy said, rising and picking Annabelle up. "I feel like a bad mama, bringing her to a cocktail bar."

"It's a restaurant, Tammy," Margaret informed her daughter. "Don't worry your pretty little head about that."

Shelby signaled for the check, but Margaret shook her head.

"This is on me," she said, giving Tammy and Amelia

Ann a warm smile. "I'm so grateful to be here to share in this special occasion with my two beautiful daughters. I'm...I love you both...so much."

Knowing how much animosity had existed between Margaret and her daughters for much of their lives, Shelby felt herself tear up a bit at the emotion in the woman's voice.

After they paid the bill, they bundled into the two cars they'd taken for the excursion. When they arrived at Rye's house—mission central—they said their goodbyes and took off for their separate cars.

Sadie stopped Shelby with a hand on her arm before she could open her BMW.

"What?"

Her sister heaved out a breath. "I've prayed on it some, and after hearing Susannah talk about having J.P. take her down the aisle, I've decided I want to talk to our brother about looking for Daddy."

She'd also had thoughts of their daddy today. Tammy and Amelia Ann would be shepherded down the aisle by Hampton, but Susannah was going to have to have J.P. do the honors. If they had tried to make contact with him long ago, back when Shelby had first thought about it, maybe their daddy would have been the one...

"Did you see the look on Mama's face when Susannah mentioned it?" Shelby asked.

"Yes," Sadie answered with an emphatic nod. "I wanted to ask Mama what she knew right then and there. So much so I was afraid I'd scream."

Okay, now she was being overdramatic, but that was Sadie. "Do we have to do this *now*?"

"J.P. is going to be in a good mood, what with knowing

that Tammy bought her wedding dress today. He's likely to be more receptive."

She couldn't disagree with her sister's logic.

"All right," Shelby said, "but you're going to have to swear not to get too dramatic or maudlin. He hates that."

"Me? I don't know who you're talking about."

Her tone suggested she was truly clueless. "I'll meet you at his house."

"Dale was taking care of Rory, so he should be alone," Sadie informed her. "Tammy took Annabelle home for a nap."

"Unless one of the guys went over," Shelby finished. "Let me text him."

Since she was dreading this conversation, she rather hoped he might be hanging with the boys. But no, he fired a text right back with an invitation for them to swing on over.

"See you there," she said.

"Drive slowly, so I can follow you," Sadie called out. "I want to arrive with you."

She got in her car, shaking her head. What did her sister think she was going to do? Spill the beans before she arrived?

They made it there five minutes later than Shelby normally would because Sadie was the most law-abiding citizen on the planet.

"You drive like an old maid," Shelby informed her as they walked to J.P.'s front porch.

"Don't call me an old maid," Sadie said, nudging her in the ribs. "I'm already fit to be tied, thinking about talking to J.P. about this."

"Me too," she said, and they reached for each other's hands as their brother answered the door.

"Somehow I expected to see more joy on your faces," he

said, kissing both their cheeks. "I take that to mean there was no luck in the dress department. Tammy only mentioned she was going with y'all to look."

"Ah..." Shelby said, casting Sadie a glance. "Then mum's the word on this end."

"That's not why we're here," her sister added.

J.P.'s brow knit as he studied them closer. "Best come on in. Can I get y'all something to drink?"

If Shelby hadn't already consumed a cocktail, she would have asked for a glass of wine. "Sweet tea would be lovely."

"For me too," Sadie agreed, releasing their handhold to give Charleston a good rubbing behind the ears.

"I'll fetch us some," their brother said and headed to the kitchen.

"Do you want to tell him?" Sadie asked in a harsh whisper, "or shall I? I think you should start with Gail's news. J.P. respects her."

Gail had only asked her once if she'd come to a decision about contacting a private investigator. One of the many things Shelby valued about her was that she knew when to be pushy and when not. "I'll kick it off. You add your two cents."

"What are the two of you whispering about?" J.P. asked. "Y'all are worrying me."

Their brother stood in the doorway, three glasses in hand, eyeing them with concern. Charleston must have sensed it because he went over and nudged J.P. in the leg.

Shelby and Sadie took their glasses from him, but suddenly the tea didn't seem like a good idea. She set hers aside, and Sadie did the same.

J.P.'s eyes narrowed as he placed his glass on the end table by theirs. "If sweet tea can't make this better, I'm beyond worried now. Let's have it."

Shelby offered up a silent prayer and then asked, "Have you ever thought about finding Daddy?" she blurted out.

His face blanched, and since he was the steadiest force on the planet, Shelby felt immediate regret.

"Where's all this interest coming from?" he asked, crossing his arms over his chest.

Considering the change in his body language, Shelby worried he was more closed to the conversation than Sadie had thought.

"We've been thinking about it a spell," Sadie interjected, wringing her hands. "But truth be told, I've been wondering about Daddy my whole life. You were supposed to tell him about Gail first, Shelby."

"I...forgot," she said lamely. Somehow saying those words to her brother had shorted her brain.

Her brother took a moment to rub Charleston behind the ears. "Let's sit a spell, shall we?"

They took up their sweet tea and walked into the music room. Shelby spotted one of Annabelle's dolls sitting on the window seat. She clutched a pillow to her chest when she and Sadie sat on the couch. J.P. took an adjoining chair. All the sweet teas were arranged on the table, still untasted.

"Best start from the beginning," he said calmly, but Shelby noticed his hands had fisted in his lap. "Let's start with what Gail has to do with this."

Shelby summarized her discussion with Gail, and then Sadie proceeded to tell him what Shelby would have called the long version of events, even going back to her high school genealogy project. Good heavens. Shelby let her talk, but each time she got a little dramatic, she'd put a hand on her thigh. Her sister took her cue and dialed it back.

J.P. listened the whole time, not interrupting once.

"And then there was all the talk about you walking Susannah down the aisle today..."

Sadie trailed off, and J.P. made a humming sound.

"I can see how that might have gotten you to thinking," their brother said. "What about you, Shelby? How long have you been thinking about this?"

"For a long time as well," she said simply.

"We know this would hurt Mama," Sadie said, their shoulders touching now, mostly out of comfort.

"It would, but I can see why Gail's news and the planning for Susannah's wedding stirred you up," J.P. said softly. "Have y'all decided to hire a private investigator?"

"We wanted to talk with you first," Sadie said. "You're..."

"I'm?" he asked, looking at her intently.

She bit her lip, which looked to be wobbling all the sudden. "Well...you're rather like our brother and daddy all wrapped up in one."

His mouth flattened and then he stood. "Come here, you two."

They flew off the couch and into his arms. He wrapped them up and kissed them both on the head.

"Susannah got so mad at us when we mentioned it," Sadie said, crying softly. "We don't want to hurt anyone, J.P., I swear. We just want to know what happened to him and if he's still alive."

"And although I want to know about his family's medical history, that's not the only reason I want to look for him," Shelby felt compelled to admit.

His chest rose with a deep breath, and then he set them both back so he could look at them. "I don't know what you might find if you look. You know everything I know. I'm sorry you haven't made your peace with it, but I understand where you're coming from."

"Have you really made your peace with it, J.P.?" Shelby asked.

"Mostly," he said after a time. "I have some moments that creep up on me, but they don't come too often anymore."

"I'm happy for you," she told him. "But we don't have that same peace. If we decide to look for Daddy, it might give us that."

Sadie nodded in solidarity.

"And it might not," he said and sat back down. "He's been gone decades."

Shelby had thought of that. "I realize that. Do you know if Mama ever looked for him?"

"She did," he told them. "She was as confused as everyone else."

Her belly quivered. "Did the...did she ever contact the police?"

He leaned forward and put his hands on his knees. "What are you suggesting, Shelby? That there was foul play?"

"There could have been," Sadie shot out, rushing to her defense. "That's the point. We don't know. All I keep doing is imagining. I want the truth. Darn it all, we *deserve* the truth."

More silence followed as J.P. folded his hands in his lap. Shelby knew he was praying for guidance.

"If you want the truth, then you should do what your heart tells you to do." He stroked Charleston, who had taken up sentry duty by his side. "But you need to understand what could come out of this. It might be nothing, or it might be something. Both could hurt."

"We already hurt, J.P.," Sadie said, her voice breaking, which made Shelby take her hand again.

"If we move forward, we don't have to tell you what we find if you don't want to know," Shelby said. "Same goes for Susannah."

Their brother stewed a time more. "And Mama? If you discover something, what will you do about her?"

She and Sadie shared a look, and she could all but feel her sister's heart being pinched right alongside hers.

"Do you think we should tell her what we're planning?" Shelby asked quietly.

"No!" Sadie said, jerking her hand away. "She never wants to talk about this. Why stir her up when we don't know if anything will come of it?"

Shelby kept her gaze on J.P.'s. "Well?" she prodded.

"I don't think you should tell her about hiring someone," he said, rising and grabbing his sweet tea, which he downed in three gulps. "As for later...I honestly don't know."

Since her mouth was dry, she reached out for her sweet tea. Sadie did the same, her eyes troubled.

"Maybe we should pray on it some more then," Sadie concluded, clutching her glass to her chest. "I would hate to hurt Mama."

"But you're hurting too," J.P. said, proving yet again that he was the best brother out there.

"Do you think we should go through with it then?" Shelby asked, all of the pros and cons swirling in her mind.

"Are you going to be able to stop thinking about him? Susannah's wedding is likely to stir it up more. And what happens when it's your time to walk down the aisle?" He looked at them with gentle eyes. "You don't want this to weigh on you on your wedding day."

"I hadn't thought that far ahead," Shelby declared. Her own wedding? It seemed light-years away.

"Me either," Sadie said, "but he's right. I will be thinking about it on my wedding day, and I don't want to be crying about it."

On that they agreed.

"So we'll look into hiring someone," Shelby concluded, and Sadie nodded. "Gail recommended someone she's used in the past."

J.P. studied his boots thoughtfully, and Shelby waited to hear what he was working out in his mind.

"Wait until Susannah is married a spell," J.P. said in a grave voice. "We've gone a long while without knowing anything; a little more time won't hurt. I don't want any news of Daddy to mar her happiness."

J.P. was right. "We can do that."

"It's only reasonable," Sadie agreed. Then a thought struck her. "You're getting married too. Do you want us to wait for you as well?"

His face softened and he shook his head. "That's mighty sweet of you, but I'll manage. Besides, I don't think you could wait that long."

"We would for you," Sadie echoed.

"I know, and I'm glad you trusted me enough to talk to me about this," their brother said, walking over and putting his hands on both of their shoulders. "It couldn't have been easy."

"Heavens no," Sadie said, getting up to give him a good hug.

"We trust you," Shelby said as she stood and put her arms around both her siblings.

They rocked in place for a spell, and when they broke

apart, Shelby felt more grounded. J.P.'s support for their plan meant the world.

"Do you want to be a part of things?" Shelby asked him. "The hiring and the...um...process."

He crossed his hands behind his back and didn't answer all at once. "I don't know. When the time comes, ask me again. I'll pray about it in the meantime."

They all would, in their own way, she guessed.

"We'd best be going," Sadie said, picking up their glasses and taking them to the kitchen.

Left alone with J.P., Shelby leaned in and hugged him again. When she was little, his hugs were the best comfort in the whole world. That hadn't changed much.

"I know it was hard on you," she said, "seeing our side of things."

He chuckled. "And yet it's my biggest life lesson. You took me to a new level of listening and openness tonight. For a moment, I wanted to tell y'all to let it go."

"So you have moments of weakness like the rest of us," she teased gently.

"As if there was any doubt," J.P. said and released her when Sadie returned.

They embraced again, and Sadie brushed away more tears as he walked them to the door.

"You're still the best brother ever," Shelby told him as she stepped outside.

"Yeah, the best," Sadie agreed.

"Goodnight, girls," he said and closed the door.

They walked to their cars, and when they reached them, Sadie opened her purse and took out her wallet. "I thought about it long and hard and... I want to contribute to hiring the P.I. Here's some money. I'll give you what I can."

She felt blind-sided. "But—"

"I know I don't make as much money as you do, working at a craft store and all, but he's my daddy too. I want to help you find him. Gosh, that sounds all film-noir-like. What did Gail tell you about the one she recommended?"

Shelby's mind flashed to Vander immediately. "Not much, but I can ask her for more information. He has endorsements from some pretty big names, I can tell you."

"Excellent!" Sadie said, giving her another hug. "I know this won't be easy, but I feel oddly at peace about it now that we've decided. I love you, Shelby."

"Love you too," she answered, holding her tight before releasing her.

Her sister headed off to her Honda.

"Sadie!" she called out. There was a funny tightness in her chest. "Thanks for not letting me do this alone."

Sadie gave her a smile over her shoulder. "It's what sisters do."

But Susannah felt differently, and she was their sister too. J.P. had been wise to ask them to wait until all Susannah's wedding business was behind them before looking for their daddy.

Who knew what they were ultimately going to find?

29

If you asked Jake, the three weeks flew by faster than a speeding bullet. Susannah worked with the team Garth had hired, and he mostly said, "Um-hum," a lot when it came to agreeing to flowers, food, decorations, and other wedding-like stuff. The details boggled the mind, and he wondered how weddings had become so complicated.

But Susannah thrived on the details, and her gift was arranging things to make them beautiful. He would have supported her if she'd wanted to release hundreds of butterflies at the wedding. He'd heard of people doing that kind of thing. Normally he would say people who bought insects for show should probably be put on the front porch for a spell, but he would do anything for her.

By the time their wedding day arrived, he was as eager and nervous as he'd been before performing his first concert. Susannah felt the same. They'd moved her things into his house—their home—early in the week, and then she'd spent the rest of the week fussing with everything. As far as he was concerned, she could fuss away in their home for the rest of her life. His nightmares had continued to stay away, and he figured that was because Susannah mostly slept beside him now.

As he eyed the den, he was hard pressed to believe the room belonged in his house. White lights hung from the ceiling like strands of snowflakes, and hot pink roses tied together with decorative purple ribbons perfumed the air. Only fifty people would be in attendance for the wedding— all of whom they trusted not to breathe a word to anyone— while another fifty had been invited to the reception, which they'd billed as Jake's housewarming party.

"Looks pretty good if you ask me, bubba," Rye said, slapping him on the back. "I still question you agreeing to all this pink and purple, though. You lost your man-card on that one, my friend."

"I like the purple, Uncle Rye," Rory said, tweaking his purple bow tie. "Aunt Shelby said I look smashing in purple."

Rye plucked him up and lifted him over his head. "Rory, son, never *ever* let a woman tell you that you look good in purple. No matter how pretty she is."

The little boy laughed as Rye tossed him in the air before setting him down on the ground.

"Take it from an old pro like me. Don't put that girly stuff on until right before the wedding."

"Not all of us can get away with that," J.P. said, pulling out Rye's bow tie, which he'd stuffed into his handkerchief pocket.

"The wedding planner tried to make me put it on, bless her heart," Rye said, "but she gave up when she saw that ain't happening."

A number of the guests were already seated. His parents

weren't in attendance, although his mama had sent her apologies along with a gift of his and hers Razorback sweaters—which was at least a gesture of sorts. His brother hadn't responded at all to the invite.

But those he cared about were here, and that was all that mattered. His manager was chatting animatedly with his record producer, likely about his new album. His agent was present with wife number three, and his band members... Well, they had their legs stretched out in front of them like they'd tied one over after the rehearsal dinner last night. Jake hadn't wanted to be tired or hung over on his wedding day, so he'd declined their request to join them. The bachelor party they'd thrown him on Thursday had been enough.

Jake caught sight of Randy and Darren coming into the den. He looked around to see if Monty was trailing behind. His old Army buddies hadn't been able to make it in for his bachelor party last minute, so he was eager to catch up with them. "Excuse me for a moment."

He strode over to his friends, waving to a few people sitting in the back. But the moment his buddies caught sight of him, they halted in place.

The usual spring in Darren's step was missing, and he didn't look like he'd be ready to salsa to the number Jake had insisted they put on the DJ's list for the reception. Randy's massive shoulders were set in an angle suggesting he wanted to go nine rounds with someone. Jake's gut burned fast and hard. *Something's wrong,* he thought. He knew these guys. Had learned to read their body language when it meant life and death.

"Hey, guys." He gave each of them a one-armed hug. "Thanks so much for coming. I know it's a long flight from out West. I was sorry y'all couldn't make it for the bachelor party, but you're here now, and that's what counts."

"Yeah, man," Darren said, putting his arm on Jake's shoulder and gripping it hard. "We're really sorry we missed it. Work stuff, you know."

It had surprised him a little when Darren texted at the last minute to say they could only come in for the wedding, not the bachelor party. Sure they lived in different states, but something was off and he knew it. Best ease into it.

"I thought Monty would be with you guys," he said. "Did you leave him at the hotel because he was taking too long sprucing his hair?"

"Monty ended up not being able to make it," Randy said, but there was something in his voice. A strange hitch. "I'm sure he'd want us to give you his best. Everything looks set up for a great wedding."

"Yeah, man," Darren said, pulling on his diamond earring. "Your bride outdid herself."

If Monty had cancelled his trip, he would have texted Jake, right? They'd gone through too much together for him to cancel without telling him man to man. He couldn't ignore his gut any longer, so he put his hands on his hips and stared at his friends.

"What's wrong? Don't tell me something isn't up."

Randy tensed up, but Darren shook his head. "Nothing, man. You should go make yourself pretty for your bride. We can find our seats."

When Randy tried to sidle by, Jake stepped out in front of him. "Don't bullshit me, man. What happened?" The other conversations in the room seemed to cut off, and he realized he'd been loud—loud enough to attract attention.

Randy paused for a moment and then put his hand on

Jake's shoulder. "This isn't the time. It's your wedding day. We'll tell you later."

Jake stopped breathing, barely noticing that people were staring. "Tell me right now, or we're going to have words."

"Get yourself married, Jake," Darren commanded, narrowing his eyes. "Then go on your honeymoon. There's nothing to be done about it."

Jake's fear and frustration only mounted. He fisted his hands by his sides. "You'd better fucking tell me. And I mean *right* now."

He knew he shouldn't be cussing. Least of all in the room where he was about to be married, but he couldn't stop himself. He could all but feel something steal over him, something old and dark and strong.

Randy and Darren shared a look, and Jake almost changed his mind. Suddenly he wanted to turn his back on his friends and run away.

"It's going to upset you, man," Darren said heavily. "Won't you trust us on this?"

Jake shook his head. Whatever it was, he needed to face it. There was no way this news wasn't going to be pressing on his mind for the rest of the day. "Tell me."

His buddies shared a look, their jawlines tense as granite.

"Let's find a more private place," Randy said, rubbing his crew cut like his head hurt.

"We'll go out back," Jake said and led them outside.

Rain had been coming down all morning, but Jake brought them to stand under the eaves. Dare River was rushing in the distance, as powerful and unstoppable a force as always. Today, the view of his land didn't given him an ounce of peace. Not when his old friends stood in front of him with a demeanor more suited to a funeral than a wedding. And that's when he knew someone was dead, someone they'd served with. His mind started reaching for who it might be, who was still active.

He braced himself. "Let's hear it."

Randy and Darren shared a look again, and they might as well have been drawing straws.

Darren's mouth bunched. "It's Monty, man. He...he killed himself."

"What?" Jake's mind went blank. He stumbled back a few steps as the shock grabbed him by the throat and sunk in its teeth. "No. That's impossible. We just saw him. He was happy."

"I know," Randy said, kicking at the ground, his anger visible now. "He got fired last week and didn't tell May. We can only guess the rest since he didn't leave a note."

"Jesus," Jake said as the truth rolled through him. "So he lost his job. He could have found another one. Dammit! Why didn't he call us? I would have helped him out."

"We all would have." Randy hissed out a breath. "It came as a complete shock to May. Fucking broke her, man."

"When did this happen?" "Jake asked, starting to pace.

"Wednesday," Randy said, gripping his shoulder to stop him from pacing. "Don't be mad, man. May asked us what we thought she should do. She didn't want to ruin your wedding. So, Randy and I decided not to come to your bachelor party. We were afraid you'd pick up on the vibe."

"You were always sensitive, Jake," Darren muttered, tugging on his tie like it was choking him. "Dammit! Maybe we shouldn't have come today, but we just couldn't miss your wedding. We couldn't let you down like that."

Jake pressed his fingers to his forehead as pain flashed

through his temples. Monty was dead. No, he'd *killed* himself.

"We were going to wait to tell you until after your honeymoon," Darren said. "This kind of news..." He didn't have to finish his sentence.

"The funeral is on Tuesday," Randy continued. "Shit, man, we thought Monty would rather have you be on your honeymoon than at his funeral."

Darren's jaw clenched, and Jake knew that look. His friend was spoiling for a fight. Jake understood. He wanted to rip something apart.

Jake thrust his fist into the air. "Losing a job shouldn't have made him want to kill himself."

"It must have triggered him bad, Jake," Darren ground out, rubbing the back of his neck. "When does suicide ever fucking make sense?"

They heard a rap on the glass door to the house and all jumped and swung around, ready to fight. The wedding planner stuck her head out, giving them a startled look.

"Ah...Jake...we need you inside."

Oh, how he wanted to yell at her for interrupting them, but he bit the words back and inclined his head. The look on his face must have terrified her, because she disappeared as quickly as she'd arrived. He distantly wondered if she was running off for help.

"Come on, man," Randy said, putting a hand on his back. "I'm really sorry to lay this on you, but you're so fucking tenacious. We didn't want to ruin your day."

"We really didn't," Darren added, bracing his meaty hands on his waist. "What can we do?"

"Stick that ugly chin of yours out and let him hit it," Randy suggested. "Then you can let me knock it back in its place."

His friends laughed harshly. How many times had they joked like this while inwardly reeling from bitter news? Jokes about how they'd hook up with so-and-so's sister if they got out alive or how they'd siphon all the gas out of so-and-so's car, forcing him to hitch a ride in his uniform.

Jake couldn't laugh with them. All he could think about was how Monty had been triggered so bad he'd decided to end his life. Why hadn't he asked for help? Jake just couldn't understand it. Monty's life hadn't been perfect, but he'd had so much to live for.

"I need a few moments to collect myself," Jake told his buddies, wishing his head would stop pounding.

He was so wrapped up in his thoughts, his fist came up to swing when someone put a hand on his shoulder. His punch was effectively blocked.

"Hey!" Randy called out, holding Jake's fist in his hand. "Come on, man. Let's get you inside with your friends and calm you down."

"We shouldn't have told him," Darren said, shaking his head.

"He didn't give us a choice," Randy said. "Come inside with us, Jake. We'll get you a bourbon."

"No, dammit!" Jake yelled, pushing Randy back. "I need a fucking minute alone. You can't drop this bombshell on me and expect me to just walk back in there with a smile on my face. Monty was my friend."

He was panting, and when he felt a bead of sweat run down his temple, he swiped it away with one hand. He was losing it. He could feel it. And he couldn't seem to stop it from happening.

"He was our friend too," Darren said in a slow and steady voice, one that confirmed Jake was losing it completely.

"I'm going for a walk," Jake muttered, feeling the urge to run. "Tell them... Fuck... Tell them I need a goddamn minute."

He heard his voice say the words, but someone else was talking. The enraged, out-of-control man inside him. Jake strode out into the rain and heard Darren and Randy calling his name.

He swiveled around and watched them striding after him. "Didn't you hear me? Leave me the fuck alone."

They both halted in the rain. The back door opened, and J.P. and Rye came outside. His friends strode over to them, and Jake watched them talk in hushed voices.

They're talking about me, the voice in his head insisted.

His heart was pounding so hard he couldn't breathe. He bent over at the waist. "Oh, Jesus."

J.P. was suddenly beside him. "Jake. Let me help you, man."

When his friend put an arm around him, Jake pushed it away. "Leave me alone for a goddamn minute, okay? I just... I just got some bad news. Oh, God. Monty."

The blackness was swallowing him up now. The rain was soaking him, he realized, and he felt the chill of it deep in his bones.

"Rye is getting my mama," J.P. told him. "Just hang on. We'll talk this through."

Jake put his hands on his thighs, panting, feeling light-headed. *Don't throw up. Don't throw up.* "Monty was doing so great. It was just a fucking job. Why would he kill himself? Dammit! Why?"

"I don't know," J.P. said, crouching down on one knee in the wet grass beside him. "I'm sorry about your friend. You take all the time you need."

"I thought he was happy. And then he fucking does this. *What if I end up doing this?*"

His voice had turned hysterical, and the pain in his head reached crushing proportions. Monty wouldn't have gotten married if he'd known this would happen. Didn't that mean it could happen to anyone?

"What if I end up doing this to Susannah?" Her face flashed in his mind, and he stumbled, falling in the grass. "When I hit a rough patch?"

"Jake." J.P. put his hand on his shoulder. "Listen to me. You wouldn't do that. I know you, man. You're getting the help you need. I know this is a horrible shock, but don't let it cloud your own progress."

Thunder cracked, and Jake felt the reverberation from head to toe. God, the noise! It was too loud, louder than the pounding in his head. "You don't understand. There are *no* guarantees I'm ever going to get better."

God, he'd been such a fool to think he was past this.

"Monty couldn't do it." The logic of it all was playing out in his fractured mind. "And bad things happen all the time."

"Come back inside, Jake," J.P. said in a steady voice again, extending his hand.

His head was pounding so hard the needles of pain radiated out of his neck. "I can't! I can't marry your sister. I can't risk it."

"Don't say that," J.P. said calmly, helping him stand. "You *aren't* Monty, man. You're Jake Lassiter, and you're the strongest man I know. Just hang on here. You can talk all this out with my mama."

Then he heard someone shout his name. Pain seared his head as he turned to look at them. Louisa was coming through the back door with Rye holding an umbrella for her.

Jake pressed his hands on either side of his skull, as if he could crush the pain. "I...can't."

He sprinted to his SUV, which had been parked so that he and Susannah could easily get out later—and sped off down the lane.

The dark whispers in his mind were his only soundtrack.

30

Susannah was shaking out the train of her wedding dress one final time with Shelby and Sadie's help when her mama returned to the room. Rye had led her off a little while earlier to ask her opinion on something.

"Girls," her mama said quietly. "Could you give me a few moments alone with Susannah, please?"

Her sisters stopped fluffing the dress, and they all turned and looked at Louisa. There was no longer a radiant smile on her face.

"Mama?" she asked, feeling nerves swirl in her belly. "Is something wrong?"

Without saying a word, Tammy took Annabelle's little hand and led her to the door. Amelia Ann followed.

"You too, Sadie and Shelby," Mama said, her voice a quiet order. Her sisters exchanged a look and then left the room too, clutching each other's hands.

Susannah sank back onto the chair. "What is it?" she asked as her mama came forward and put both hands on her shoulders.

"Jake had some bad news, honey," Mama said, her eyes filled with concern. "You remember his friend, Monty, don't you?"

She nodded, feeling a sense of foreboding. "Of course. I just met him a few weeks ago. He's a sweetheart."

"Jake just learned that Monty committed suicide a few days ago."

"*Oh, Mama*," she said, rising out of the chair. "But...*why*?"

"No one seems to know much except that he lost his job recently," her mama said, helping her stand. "The news hit Jake hard, honey. Darren and Randy didn't want to tell him today, but he could tell something was wrong."

Of course he could. No wonder his friends hadn't come to his bachelor party. Jake had tried to play it off, but he'd been hurt by their absence, and it had surprised her too after seeing their bond.

"He must be devastated. They all must be." She remembered them teasing each other like brothers around her.

Her mama could only nod, tears in her eyes.

Susannah took off the veil her sisters had arranged since the pins were now digging into her skull. "Where are they? I don't care that I'm in my wedding dress. I need to go to Jake and his friends." He would need the comfort. They all would.

Mama rubbed her arm gently. "He is upset, honey. So upset, in fact, that he had another episode."

Her stomach sunk. "Oh, no."

When she made a move toward the door, her mama stopped her. "Susannah, I need you to listen to me."

She shivered at the underlying edge in her mama's voice. "What happened?" she asked, imagining the worst.

Had he barricaded himself in a room? Was he paralyzed again?

"We don't know as of yet, but J.P. and Rye and his friends are out looking for him."

"What do you mean?" She stared blankly at her mama. "He left?"

"He took off in his SUV," Mama told her. "The guys couldn't stop him."

Panic rose inside her. She'd seen him this upset before, but for him to leave her on their wedding day...

"I need to go look for him too." There was no telling what he might do.

"I'm not so sure that's a good idea, sugar," her mama said, pulling her in for a hug.

Her heart broke clean in two. "Why would you say that? *Mama*. What happened?"

"Honey, he's all awash in old fears right now. He's afraid to marry you."

She finally understood, and the pain of it buffeted her heart like hail. "He's afraid he'll do what his friend did, isn't he? But that's crazy. Jake would never take his life. *Never*." Of course she'd never have imagined Monty would do such a thing. Not for one minute.

"I don't think so either," her mama said quietly.

Susannah looked out the window. "It's storming. He shouldn't be driving. I saw how he can get. I need to go after him." Lunging for her phone, she tried to call him. But he didn't answer.

"It's no use calling him. He gave Rye his phone to hold during the ceremony. Honey, we're going to find him. And then I'll talk to him. We'll sort this all out."

Sort it out? "But what if he doesn't change his mind? Oh, my gosh. All the people downstairs..."

"We're going to give it a while longer before we say anything," her mama said. "His manager announced there was going to be a delay due to the storm."

That wasn't a lie, at least. A storm was raging fiercely outside. Lightning pierced menacing gray clouds, and thunder shook the window panes.

"I can't just stay here and wait. He's out there all upset. He needs me. Mama, he needs you too. He can't pull through this alone." She was more terrified than she'd ever felt in her life.

Mama pulled her into her arms, rocking her back and forth. "He's not alone, honey. Right now, we have to trust in God to help him and for the men to find him."

She clutched her tightly. "Mama. Can we pray for him?"

"You know we can, honey," she said, and stepping back, they gripped each other's hands and bowed their heads.

When they finished, Mama left her to tell her sisters and the rest of the women what was going on. Sadie and Shelby came inside and hugged her fiercely, followed by Amelia Ann, Tammy, Annabelle, and Rory.

Fear lodged under her ribcage when J.P. called and asked if she knew of any places Jake would go when he was upset. After beating her brain, she mentioned the couple that came to mind. J.P. said he and the guys had already checked them—with no luck—on the recommendation of Garth and his band members.

Then she remembered his cabin, the cabin where they were supposed to spend a few days for their honeymoon before flying off to the resort in Puerto Rico.

"I'm going to Jake's cabin," she told her brother. "Y'all let me know the minute you find him."

When she hung up, she grabbed her purse. "Shelby and

Sadie, would you please go to my townhouse and wait there? I know J.P. said they checked it, but he might go there later. Mama, you stay here in case Jake comes home."

They all nodded.

"He might go to the cabin if he wants somewhere to think. If his last full-blown episode is any indication, the noise from the storm will bother him. He might want a quiet place to settle." Please, God, let that be true.

"I'll go with you," Amelia Ann volunteered, her face knit with worry like everyone else's.

"No, you stay here," she said, wanting to face Jake alone. "I'll call y'all if he comes to the cabin, and expect you to do the same if you see him first. I'll be fine."

As she left the room and hurried down the back steps to the garage where her car was parked, she realized she'd be better off changing her dress. But maybe it would calm Jake to see her in it—to show him the strength of her commitment. Didn't every married man say he never forgot the first glance of his bride in her wedding gown?

She managed to make it to the cabin in a little over forty minutes. When she opened her car door, the first tears finally broke free. There weren't any vehicles parked in the drive, but someone had lined the path with hot-pink rose petals. Rain continued to pound the earth, so she did her best to step around them and headed inside. The entry was carpeted with rose petals too, and she followed them to the master bedroom. More rose petals covered the bed. The white sheets were turned down invitingly, and a whole assortment of candles were scattered around the room, waiting to be lit. Fresh wood was laid out in the fireplace.

They were supposed to make love in this room after saying their vows and celebrating with those they loved surrounding them. Now, she wondered if that would ever happen. Sinking to the bed, she put her face in her hands and cried, unable to suppress her emotions.

Even though he had a good reason, the man she loved—a good man—had made her greatest fear come true.

He'd captured her heart, and then he'd abandoned her.

31

Jake drove aimlessly in the rain as his inner demons raged like the storm outside his windows. His mind kept playing images of Monty from their recent get-together. His friend had seemed so happy...

Now Monty was dead by his own hand, and his final act had stripped Jake of all hope.

Jake wanted to beat his fist to the sky again. How could something like this have happened? It wasn't fair. It wasn't fucking fair.

He'd lost his bearings a while back, but he continued to speed down the country road he was on. Rain pelted his windshield, and over the pain in his head, he wondered if he should pull over and wait out the storm.

The pain in his head had lessened to a medium throbbing, and while he couldn't draw a full breath yet, he wasn't panting like he'd been doing after he left the house.

The full import of what he'd done finally dawned on him as he squinted through the windshield wipers.

He'd walked away from Susannah on their wedding day. He was despicable. A coward. She was more than better off without him. Especially since he couldn't guarantee her that he wouldn't end up like his friend.

His chest felt as empty as if someone had filled it with bullets from an AK-47.

The sound of his wheels hitting the rumble strip on the road filled the car. He jerked on the steering wheel to re-center the SUV and felt the wheels skid. He slowed down and pulled over to the side, realizing it would be safer if he stopped.

There was a fenced-off field beside him, and he turned off the car, breathing deep. He was sweating, and he felt like he was about to have a heart attack. He tapped a pressure point on his hand—a method of easing anxiety introduced to him by one of his doctors—and closed his eyes.

Help me. Please. Some part of him prayed as he inhaled deep gusts of oxygen. The more he breathed, the more the pain in his head lessened. And so he filled his lungs, calling back his tools of mindfulness, focusing on his body sitting in the chair.

I need help. Really bad. I messed everything up.

He continued the litany, not knowing what else to do. Part of him wondered if this was how Monty had felt in his last moments. The darkness seemed to be swallowing him up.

Tears filled his eyes, and he hung his head. *I'm sorry. I'm so sorry. I don't know what to do.*

Warmth touched his shoulder, and it took him a moment to realize there was a bright light behind his eyes where before there had been only darkness. He opened them and squinted at the sunlight reflecting off the rain-washed road. It was bright enough to be blinding, but as his eyes adjusted, he took in the scene before him.

Half of the land was covered in darkness, and from the

blur up ahead, he could tell it was still raining in the west. But the other half... The sun had broken out of the thick, gray clouds and was shining on everything in its path. The green of the grass on a nearby hill was brilliant, and the blue, eastern sky looked like the waters of the Caribbean. And it wasn't raining on him. Not anymore. Then he saw a shimmer of color in the blue sky and squinted to make it out. But whatever it was had disappeared. Seconds later, there was another flash. He tilted his head, searching the sky, but it still eluded him.

He got out of the car with an urgency. There was something there, something important, and he had to see it.

As he stood in the blaze of sun on the wet pavement, the shimmer converged again, and this time stayed. Lines of red, blue, purple, yellow, and green appeared in the sky.

Jake stumbled back, leaning against his car. *A rainbow,* he thought. *A great, big giant of a rainbow.* It stretched across the sky and grew in size as the sun melted away the dark clouds in the west. The rain seemed to stop mid-drop. Everything around him seemed to still, as if all of nature was watching, listening.

The quiet of the moment rolled over him as he stared at that rainbow.

There's always the promise of rainbows, he remembered Susannah saying on her first visit to his home.

His heart had stopped racing in his chest, he realized, and his head didn't hurt anymore. The numbness he'd felt had been replaced with warmth, and it wasn't from the sunlight. Then he realized what it was. That feeling was grace, the kind Louisa had preached about months ago. The kind he felt when he was sitting in front of the fire along-side Susannah, singing her one of his songs.

The rainbow captured his attention, and on the quiet

country road, he felt something powerful growing inside him. It seemed to fill his whole body, and he finally realized it *was* himself. He was coming back to himself, and all he felt was peace.

In his whole life, he'd never once seen a rainbow.

Today, in one of the worst moments of his life, that rare beauty of nature had finally appeared in the sky over *his* head.

It was a sign.

He had to go back. Had to face Susannah and beg for her forgiveness. He hoped she could forgive him, but regardless of what she chose, he would continue to be relentless about his therapy. Although he didn't judge his friend for the choice he'd made, he would *not* end up like him.

Louisa had once told him the reason his life was improving was because he had chosen life. It seemed he had to choose it again, and if he had to keep choosing it again and again, well, he would. Life was a gift. Being with Susannah, playing his music, and helping people had taught him that.

The news about Monty had almost made him lose sight of that, but God had saved him from the abyss so he could make this choice yet again.

His life did matter. It mattered to him, and because he shared himself with the world, it mattered to a whole lot of people. Susannah and Louisa flashed to mind. Then Frankie, who'd gone to Disney World with his family a couple of weeks back. And the waitress in Sweetwater and her brother, who thought he was a hero.

He stayed until the rainbow faded, and after casting up another thank you to the blue sky above, he got into his SUV and started down the road. At a roadside gas station, he asked the attendant if he could use their phone since he'd left the house without one. Jake knew how he must look in his wet groom's suit, but the older man thankfully didn't say a word.

He called J.P. first, not knowing if Susannah would welcome his call just yet. His friend assured him she was deeply worried and that she'd gone to the cabin in the hopes she would find him there.

He got back in his truck and drove there immediately.

Susannah's car was parked on the gravel driveway when Jake arrived at the cabin. He firmed his shoulders as he stepped out of his truck, throwing his damp tuxedo jacket over his shoulder. Patting down his wet hair, he scanned the two-story cabin. There were no lights on inside, which concerned him.

Susannah loved the light.

He'd brought the darkness to her again, brought it to her on their wedding day. Burning with shame now, he started down the flagstone path to the front door.

Halfway there, he spotted a couple of pink rose petals. Pausing, he picked one up. He'd asked Shelby to line their bridal path with Susannah's favorite flower, but only a few of the petals were left. Had Susannah swept them up as she'd waited to see if he'd return?

His heart broke. What must she have felt to arrive here alone and see what was supposed to have been a romantic gesture? Devastated, he imagined, as his mind filled with the image of her sweeping those rose petals into a dust pan in the rain.

The front door was unlocked, so he stepped inside. Her purse was on the coffee table in the den with her key chain lying beside it. When he spotted the key to his house—their home—he flushed with shame.

"Susannah?" he called out.

No reply came.

Tracing his way through the house, he found their bags in the master bedroom. Again, the rose petals were missing from the bed. Her bags were still zipped, and he didn't see her wedding dress in the closet when he looked. Heading to the kitchen, he spied a wine opener and a half-dyed cork lying on the counter. He picked it up. She was drinking red wine tonight. She wouldn't touch the champagne he had chilling in the fridge.

The luxury cabin didn't have many rooms, so it didn't take long to determine she wasn't in the house. He walked to the French doors leading down to the covered outdoor area by the river, which he'd built to be shady year round. He eyed a flickering light in the twilight and knew it could only be her. She brought the light with her wherever she went.

Jake opened the door and walked down the stone path to the water, squinting until his eyes adjusted to the night. From the gentle rush of the water, it looked as though the rain had been lighter here.

When he reached the end of the path, his whole chest tightened. From the soft glow of the fire in the stone fire pit, he could see Susannah sitting on one of the cushioned sofas arranged in a half-circle facing the river. Her wool coat covered part of her wedding dress, and in her left hand was a glass of wine. Her engagement ring winked in the light as she raised her glass and drained it.

He took courage from seeing she hadn't removed the ring, but his heart clenched as he watched her raise her knees to her chest and lower her head to rest on her poofy skirt.

This was what he'd done. He'd reduced his bride to a picture of misery on her wedding day.

He walked toward her and—not wanting to scare her—sat down on the adjacent sofa. As a soldier, he'd learned how to be quiet, and she was so wrapped up in her own world, her head nestled on her knees, she neither saw nor heard him. His hands itched to rub her back or cuddle her close. Instead, he waited for her to become aware of him.

In the soft glow of the lamp, he watched her. Her long hair was frizzier now from the humidity of the air. She'd left it down instead of putting it up in some elaborate coif. Her perfume surrounded him, and when he heard her sniff, he almost reached for her. God, he'd made her cry. Of course, he'd made her cry. It was her wedding day.

She raised her head to look out over the river. Tears shimmered in her eyes in the firelight. He could bear the silence no longer.

"Susannah," he called softly.

She jumped in place. The wine glass she'd been holding slipped from her hand, but thankfully it was empty. He took the glass and set it aside.

She stared at him with veiled eyes, as if assessing his condition. "J.P. said you were coming. I've been praying nonstop. Oh, Jake... I'm so glad you're safe. I was so worried. I thought you might want a fire...and to sit by the river. The house...I...wasn't sure what to do to help you."

He realized now why she'd cleaned up the rose petals; she must have worried that the reminder of what was supposed to happen today would make him more ill at ease. "I don't know what to say to you. There aren't enough ways in the English language to say 'I'm sorry' to make up for leaving you on our wedding day and breaking my promise to you to never go off like that. But I am sorry. More than I could ever say. Will you let me explain?"

The weight of her every hurt and fear welled in her

moss-green eyes. "I know about Monty," she whispered, resting her cheek on her knees. "Oh, Jake, I'm so sorry. He seemed so happy when he visited."

He felt himself rock in place. "I thought so too. He was a good man. He...I don't know how he could have done this."

"Neither can I," she said quietly. "His poor wife."

Jake nodded, unable to imagine what that sweet woman was going through. "When I heard the news today...I spiraled out of control. I couldn't seem to stop it from happening. Susannah...I was afraid that if Monty could do that to himself, what if I ended up doing that to myself—and ultimately, to you." His voice broke, and he bit the inside of his cheek to keep control.

"Oh, Jake." Tears rolled down her face.

"I thought working with your mama and loving you would cure me. The love I have for you, Susannah... Well, it's bigger than any I've ever known—even for music—and your love for me...well, it pretty much redefines the word for me."

Her lips trembled, and this time she wiped the tears streaming down her face. He waited to see if she would speak, but she remained silent.

"The love between us made me feel like we'd move the mountain that had been weighing me down for years."

"I thought it would too," she whispered finally.

The agony in her voice called to something fierce inside him, and he felt tears gather in the corners of his eyes. Had she given up hope on him?

"I walked out on you the day of our wedding, and I don't know if I can ever make up for that. I don't even know if this is a weight you want to carry. Susannah, I felt more broken today than I ever have, and it scared me to my core."

She reached her hand out tentatively, almost like she

was scared to touch him, and laid it on his arm. That hesitation squeezed his heart.

"You're not broken, Jake. I know this episode was bad, but it's nothing you can't overcome. I believe that."

His whole chest lifted at her words. "I broke my promise to you about stepping back."

Fresh tears welled in her eyes and spilled over. "Yes, you did. And it hurt me, Jake, even though I know you didn't mean to."

"I'm so sorry, honey," he said hoarsely, covering the hand she rested on his arm. "Can you ever forgive me?"

"Of course I forgive you," she said immediately.

How could he believe she'd do anything different? She believed in the importance of forgiveness. "I'm humbled by that. More than I could ever tell you. I want to be worthy of you and your love, Susannah."

"You are," she whispered.

He wanted to caress her cheek, but he was afraid it was too soon to touch her like that.

"Let me tell you what happened after I left."

She nodded, and he opened the palm of his hand to her, inviting her to hold it. For a moment, she studied it. Then she slowly put her hand in his.

Breathing a huge sigh of relief, he continued, "I drove. I didn't know which direction I was going. I just...drove. I found myself on a country road in the middle of farm land. The storm had been going something fierce, and the sun suddenly broke through the clouds. Half the sky turned a brilliant blue while the other half continued on storming in darkness. I saw a line of colors shimmer in the distance. At first I didn't know what it was..."

"It was a *rainbow,*" she said in a hushed tone, tears falling unchecked down her face again.

371

His throat closed with the memory. "Yes. I stopped the truck, and as I watched, that rainbow sailed across the sky. The half that had been storming seemed to fade in the face of all that brilliant light—almost like it was no match for it. That rainbow finally stretched across the whole sky. I knew it was a sign, a sign for me to come back. That God was helping me. That there was hope for me yet."

"Didn't I tell you?" Her lips were trembling now. "There's always the promise of rainbows."

He clutched her hand. "I was filled with such peace. I knew what I wanted again. I wanted to live. I *wanted* to be married to you. I wanted to make my life with you, Susannah. I love you. *God knows how much!*"

He knuckled away the tears rolling down his face. A cool hand touched his jaw, and he met her gaze.

"I love you too," she whispered hoarsely.

Closing his eyes, he let that simple benediction roll over him. "You need to know that I don't want to be a victim to this regardless of what happened today, but if it's given you pause... I totally understand." Even though it would break his heart all the more.

She clutched his hand, forcing him to meet her gaze.

"I don't think I could ever stop loving you," she said in a tear-clogged voice. "The words in those wedding vows I planned to say today...*every* word is from my heart, just like the ones I told you the first night we made love. Those vows are a promise. Right now, they feel like a promise of rainbows, like the one God gave you today. I believe in us, Jake. Even after today. And I always will."

He lowered his head and pinched the bridge of his nose hard, trying to control his emotions. Her love for him... He'd come to believe it truly was a miracle, but he was so humbled in the face of it. "Susannah, I want to give you rainbows and babies and laughter, and I always want to give you my best. I'm...just not sure I always can. Today showed me I still have a long way to go."

He felt her scoot closer. "So, you keep working at it. Jake, I won't leave you to do this alone."

The rainbow might have filled him with peace, but her love filled him with new hope. "I want to promise you that this won't happen again, but I can't."

Her face fell, and he rushed to continue, "What I can promise you is that I will continue to choose life. I wasn't tempted to hurt myself—like Monty." He had to take a moment as the knife of those words pierced his throat. "Living isn't simply existing. Your mama helped me see that. It's being present and being engaged with the people around you. I want you to pray with me that God continues to help me with that." After seeing the rainbow today, he didn't simply know he had heaven's support. He believed it.

"I always pray for you something fierce, Jake Lassiter," she said, "and I won't lie and say today didn't scare me to my core. But that rainbow today... Jake, it was more than a sign. It was a miracle, and I have to trust God to help you more than I ever could."

He nodded, seeing the light of that rainbow in his mind. Peace filled him again, and it became easier to draw breath. "When I decided to marry you, I was making a stand against all that shit."

She let out a shaky sigh. "You need to know that I don't blame you. But you also need to know that you leaving today brought back all that stuff from when my daddy left us."

"Oh, honey," he said, lowering his head until their foreheads touched. "I'm so sorry. I didn't even think." And how selfish was that? He'd been totally caught up in his own problems.

"I only told you because you need to know how I feel too. We're partners now—in good times and in bad." She made a valiant effort at a smile.

"I think today redefines bad," he said, rubbing his head against hers in comfort.

"Moments ago you said my love redefined the word for you. Maybe you need to trust that."

Maybe he did. "I don't doubt your love for me, and I don't want you to doubt my love for you. But I...hate weighing you down. Susannah, it's dark shit. Pardon my French."

"I'm not most people." She rushed into his arms, the embodiment of every promise, every loving word she'd said to him.

"Don't I know it, and that makes me the luckiest man in the whole world. Susannah, I'm going to want you until I fall asleep and meet my Maker."

She was crying softly now.

"And when I meet Him," Jake continued, "I'm going to thank Him for giving me the best woman in the world to love."

"Oh, Jake, I love you," she breathed over his skin like a potent benediction.

As he held her against his heart, he felt her love begin to heal the hollow parts inside him.

32

Susannah stood in the wings as Rye Crenshaw finished his opening set for Jake's charity concert for veterans suffering from post-traumatic stress. Jake already had his guitar resting against his chest.

They were holding hands, and he was playing with the diamond ring he'd put on her finger only three weeks ago at their small, private wedding. This time, they'd planned an even smaller wedding than their first aborted one, and it had been perfect in every way.

Her mama came up beside them, smiling, and gave Jake a warm hug. "I just finished having a long talk with Booker and Monty's widows. They're lovely women. You were right to invite them to the pre-concert party in your dressing room. I know it was hard on y'all, but it's the way healing works."

Jake was the one who'd arranged for his old Army buddies to attend the concert with other veterans, one of whom was the brother of that waitress from Sweetwater. Jake had specially requested that Howard be present, and given all the attention the media was giving this concert, the Army had agreed to arrange it. It felt right for him to be here tonight, almost like they were coming full circle from that first episode Susannah had experienced with Jake, an episode that had only strengthened their bond.

But it was at Mama's gentle urging that Jake had included Booker and Monty's widows. The fear that they might deny his gesture had weighed on him something mighty. He'd cried in Susannah's arms after receiving their RSVPs.

"I'm glad they came," Jake said, rubbing his eyes. "I wasn't sure May would so soon after...Monty's death, but Diane...well, that was a total surprise. She said she doesn't blame me anymore, and I...God, I needed to hear that."

That revelation had reduced him to tears. He'd excused himself after talking with the sad-eyed woman, and Susannah had followed him and held him through the storm.

"You're doing a wonderful thing here, Jake," Mama told him, patting his chest in comfort. "Not just for others but for yourself."

"Thanks, Louisa. You're an angel," he added, and as far as Susannah was concerned, Mama had more than earned her wings, helping Jake like she had.

She and Jake had gone from two sessions a week to three after his last episode. Often Susannah would come home to find him working diligently on the homework Mama had given him. He'd only had one nightmare, which he'd told her about in the dark of night after being sick in the bathroom.

Her heart had shattered to see him that way, but she'd listened to him and held him until he once again fell back to sleep. She was learning how to be his helpmate each day, and he was doing the same for her by being present when they were together and sharing how he felt even when he had trouble putting it into words. His continued healing was awe-inspiring and humbling, and she felt God's hand guiding them every step of the way.

"You're going to do great, honey," Susannah assured him.

"Right," he said, breathing out deeply. "I'm trying to remember that."

"Can Scout and me come closer to the stage, Jake?" a sweet little voice suddenly interrupted. "He can't see very well from back there."

Susannah looked down to see the little girl tugging on Jake's shirt. It was hard not to smile, particularly since Annabelle was holding the pink leash for the new labradoodle she'd insisted on choosing as a wedding present for Jake and Susannah. Jake hadn't been ready for the puppy yet. He'd spent so much time delving into the past and trying to heal lately that he was still feeling too raw to add another new element to his life. So he'd asked Annabelle to take care of Scout until he was ready to take on the responsibility, to which she'd responded, "I'm pretty responsible."

"Scout can't see, huh?" Jake asked crouching down and petting the cream-colored puppy. "Are you sure he won't bark? I'm going to be singing in a few minutes."

Susannah shared a look with her mama. Her mouth was twitching like hers was.

"He won't!" she assured him with an emphatic nod. "I promise. We had a talk in the car like Uncle Rye does with his dogs. He wouldn't dare misbehave. Scout knows tonight is *really* important for his family."

The puppy wagged his tail like he completely understood every word Annabelle had said, and after seeing the little girl work her magic, Susannah wasn't the least bit surprised.

"Okay then," Jake said, tapping her on the nose and making her laugh. "Y'all can stay here with Susannah and Louisa."

Susannah looked over her shoulder and gave her brother a nod that she had everything in hand. He wasn't the kind to bolt forward and drag the little girl back like some daddy's might.

"Get ready, Jake," one of the stage hands called out.

Rye finished strumming his guitar in a dramatic sweep and lifted the instrument overhead and thrust it into the air. The crowd went wild.

Jake tucked her hair behind her ear and then kissed her lightly on the mouth. "I love you."

"I love you too," she whispered.

"Y'all are so cute," Annabelle said, making them both laugh.

Susannah watched as Jake joined Rye onstage. The two men hugged, and Rye pretended to lift him off the ground. Susannah knew he was helping Jake with his nerves. After waving to the crowd, Rye walked off stage and crouched down beside Annabelle and Scout.

"Good evening, folks," Jake called out, sitting on the bar stool in the center of the stage. "Thanks so much for coming out tonight. I've done a lot of concerts—some of them celebrating the incredible men who are currently serving or have served our country—but tonight I'm talking about something a little closer to home. I'm talking about post-traumatic stress, something I'm still struggling with. Something many of our service men and women struggle with."

The crowd was sitting down now, and the entire arena had gone from cheering and screaming to quietly intent.

"I haven't talked about it much because I was ashamed of it. People say I'm a hero for serving, but honestly, you feel anything but heroic when you're struggling with PTSD."

He cleared his throat, and she clutched her hands, silently praying God would help him find the words to make this easier for him.

"You see, a friend of mine recently committed suicide."

Her gaze tracked to May, who was sitting in the audience. Tears were already running down her face, and Susannah's heart went out to her.

"We'd served together, and while he'd gotten help for his PTSD, he...just couldn't make it. No one really knows what he was thinking in those final moments, but if it's anything like some of the things I've felt, I can kind of understand it. He felt broken. Like he'd never get better. Like nothing he could do would ever fix him."

The spotlight illuminated the tears in the corners of his eyes, and Susannah prayed he could keep it together enough to continue.

"Many of you may be surprised to hear that the suicide rate among veterans is fifty percent higher than among non-military people. That's something I hope we can change by being more open about this horrible disorder affecting so many of our vets."

Jake patted his guitar and bowed his head.

"I'd like to take a moment of silence for my friend, Monty, and for all the service men and women who have taken their lives."

A picture of Jake and Monty flashed onto the screen, and Susannah held her breath, seeing Jake in his Army uniform. Monty looked young and handsome, and it hurt her heart to think about him taking his life in quiet desperation.

Susannah lowered her head, and she felt her mama take her hand. Someone took her other hand, and she noticed Shelby had sidled up beside her with Sadie on the other side. A large hand came and rested on her shoulder, and she looked behind her and saw J.P with Rye and Annabelle. Her family had formed a unit around her, and they prayed with the rest of the audience.

Susannah felt grace wrap around her and fill the entire arena, so much so that chill bumps broke out across her skin. God was here. She could feel it. And she added a prayer of thanks. She and Jake wouldn't be together if not for God's help, and she knew it was grace that would keep them together.

"Thank you," Jake said quietly. "You might have heard that I recently married the most beautiful and loving woman in the world."

When he looked over, she couldn't keep the smile from spreading across her face. "I love you," she mouthed.

He mouthed it right back. "I've been doing therapy for my PTSD for five years now, on and off, but I can tell you that being loved by the sweetest woman alive and loving her has simply changed my life forever. And I'm grateful. My mother-in-law, Reverend Louisa, has a saying that God always brings us a miracle when we need it the most. Well, I needed a miracle, and God brought me my Susannah. But he also brought me a rainbow in my greatest moment of despair, and that's the song I want to sing y'all tonight. It's called 'The Promise of Rainbows.'"

He strummed his guitar, and even though Jake had played the song for her before, she felt tears track down her cheeks as he started to sing the words he'd written from his heart.

I came home broke.
I came home afraid.

I laughed less.
Barely said a word.

I didn't trust myself.
I didn't trust God.
I lost my dreams.
I lost myself.

But I picked up my guitar,
And I started to strum.
A melody flowed, and words gathered some.

I found my voice.
The promise of rainbows was in the clear blue sky again.

But I was still lost.
Still afraid.
I held my head up high during the day.
But at night, I kept a light on.

The past loomed too large.
There was no safety.
No loving voice to tell me I was okay.

I thought I'd fallen from grace,
Thought I'd never be forgiven for the things I'd done.

But love found me.
Healed me.
Saved me.

The promise of rainbows was in the clear, blue sky again.

I'm not broke.
I never was.
I was only lost, adrift in this crushing pain.

I trust love now.
I trust myself.

I know who I am.
I am a good man.
And I'll be a good husband,
And a fine daddy some day.

I'll love the woman God made for me.
And I'll love the sons and daughters she gives to me.

I was saved by grace.
Healed by love.

Life's magic is all around me.
I'm a blessed man.

The promise of rainbows is in the clear blue sky again.

When Jake finished the song, silence hung in the arena —a living, breathing sound. Her heart was warm and huge in her chest as Jake hugged his guitar to his chest, tears sparkling in his eyes.

And then people started to clap. The roar of the crowd spread across the arena like grace had earlier. People rose to their feet, cheering now. Susannah could see thousands of people wiping their eyes like she and her family were.

Her eyes fell to Monty's widow again in the front row. May was weeping silently, and Randy had his arm around her in comfort. Darren was on the other side, brushing away his own tears. Susannah knew it was going to take a long time for the pain of Monty's loss to lessen.

"Thank you, friends," Jake said in a hoarse voice. "Thank you so very much."

He took off his guitar and walked across the stage to her. J.P. stepped forward to take his guitar, and then she was crushed in his arms.

"I love you," he whispered fiercely against her neck.

"I love you too," she said back, clutching him to her.

Then he stepped back and framed her face. Their gazes locked and held.

"No matter what," he reaffirmed, speaking of his vow to always choose life, to always choose connection.

"No matter what," she repeated.

That simple phrase was their vow to each other, their mantra, as he coped with his PTSD every day.

As Jake stepped back onstage to the crowd's cheers, rainbow prisms flashed around him. They covered his whole body, and when he looked up, his face held both shock and awe.

J.P. whispered in her ear, "The rainbows were Rye's idea. We didn't tell Jake."

She watched as Jake let his head fall back and stared above. She could all but feel him praying, and so she joined him.

Thank you, God, for the promise of rainbows.

Love The Promise of Rainbows? Treat yourself to the audiobook! Narrated by the acclaimed Em Eldridge.

Are you wondering about Shelby and her quest to find their daddy? Dive into The Fountain Of Infinite Wishes now, or keeping reading for a sneak peek.

THE FOUNTAIN OF INFINITE WISHES

DARE RIVER ★ BOOK 5

CHAPTER ONE

Finding your daddy was a scary proposition.

Especially when he'd abandoned you as a child. Shelby McGuiness was glad one of her sisters, Sadie, was joining her to kick off the search.

Hiring a private investigator was an equally scary proposition.

Shelby walked into the brass and glass lobby where Vander Montgomery's office was located in downtown Nashville. She'd purposely scheduled the meeting for Friday afternoon so she'd have the weekend to work through her emotions. Thank goodness for that—they weren't even in the P.I.'s office yet, and she'd had to forsake her morning cappuccino because her tummy was so upset.

Now that the family wedding season—three in three months—was behind them all, she and Sadie had decided it was time to move forward with their search. Their elder sister, Susannah, was well settled with her new husband, Jake; their brother, J.P., and his new wife, Tammy, already acted like they'd been married for years; and Tammy's sister, Amelia Ann, and her husband, Clayton, couldn't seem to get enough of each other. J.P. had given his blessing for the search, asking only to be informed of their progress, while Susannah had been dead set against it.

Their mama didn't know about their search for Daddy —something they'd all agreed was necessary, not that it washed away the guilt. J.P. was prepared to play peacemaker if everything went south. The McGuiness women could get riled up, especially when they didn't see eye to eye.

During their siblings' wedding preparations, Shelby had found herself wondering if their daddy would end up walking her down the aisle. Sadie had admitted she'd had the same thought. Of course, there was no telling if they'd even find Daddy. Shelby sure as shooting didn't know if he was sorry he'd abandoned them. But hope loomed large in her heart. What if they could form a real father/daughter relationship?

She and Sadie finally spotted each other in the crowd of worker bees meandering through the lobby. Her sister hurried over. She was a picture-perfect snapshot of summer in her white blouse and yellow skirt with navy wedges. Shelby had never been so happy to see anyone in her whole life. Her sister must have felt the same way, because her hug was more like a clutch. Shelby clutched her right back.

"Are you ready for this?" Sadie asked in a rush.

"Yes," Shelby told her, releasing a long breath. "As we agreed, we can always decide Vander's not the right private investigator or pull the plug at any time."

Not that Shelby thought Vander could be the wrong

choice. Her boss, Gail Hardcrew, had raved about the man after using him herself.

"I keep telling myself that," her sister said, locking arms with her. Together, they walked to the front desk and signed in with security. As if by silent agreement, they didn't loosen their clasp one bit until they reached the elevator.

While the car glided upward, Shelby said conversationally, "His office sure is located in a nice building." Southerners liked to be conversational when they were as nervous as a new soul approaching the gates of Hades.

"Yes, it's lovely," Sadie responded, following the cue. "Only a successful P.I. could afford rent in a place like this. I can't even imagine what he pays per month."

Working as Gail's accountant, Shelby had a pretty good idea what his rent went for. One of her boss' two restaurants was down the street. "It's pricy, that's for sure."

There were a few record companies located in this tony building as well, but that made sense to Shelby after reading some of Vander's endorsements. He ran background checks for country music stars. It was a sad fact that country singers had to delve into the backgrounds of those closest to them, but it was part of stardom. When J.P. had been in the business for a short time as a singer, his manager had handled such matters for him. And certainly mega-star Rye Crenshaw, J.P.'s best friend and Tammy's brother, did the same.

On the seventh floor, she let go of Sadie's arm as they exited the elevator and traversed the navy-carpeted hallway to the mahogany door bearing the brass nameplate of Montgomery Associates. The door clicked when Shelby opened it. The little touches of a high-class firm were everywhere, from the bold modern art on the walls to the plush furnishings Shelby knew cost an arm and a leg.

A woman stood from behind a sleek metal reception desk as they walked through the door. She was mid-thirties, blonde, and drop-dead gorgeous—the perfect counterpoint to the smoldering picture of Vander that Shelby had seen on his website. This was a pretty people's private investigation firm, Shelby decided. No wonder Gail had liked him. Her boss preferred her associates to be wicked smart *and* good-looking if at all possible, and she was bold enough to admit it out loud.

"You must be Shelby and Sadie McGuiness," the woman said with a genuine smile. "Welcome. Can I get you anything to drink?"

"Nothing for me," Shelby answered, wishing she could rub her jumping tummy without looking like a ninny.

"Water would be nice," Sadie said, and even to Shelby's ears, her sister's voice sounded raspy.

The receptionist disappeared and returned with her water—in a Waterford crystal glass. Shelby had a hunch she could have asked for that cappuccino, and the woman would have reappeared just as quickly. "Please follow me."

They passed by three other offices. One woman was on the phone, her syrupy drawl audible, while the other two were hunched over their computers, picking at their keyboards like they were keying in numbers. Shelby knew that sound. It was the same one she made while doing Gail's accounting, different than the more fluid melody of composing emails.

Sadie reached for her hand, but Shelby gave her a look. Holding hands on the walk here was one thing, but they were both women in their twenties. Not little girls. They needed to stand tall as they did this.

Even if this monumental step made them both feel like scared girls all over again.

The woman opened the double mahogany door at the end of the hall and ushered them inside, discreetly closing the door behind her as she left. Vander looked up immediately and smiled at them.

Even though Shelby had seen his picture on the Internet, she wasn't prepared for the punch of attraction she felt. His eyes were as dark-lashed as they looked in his photo, and heavens if they weren't a brilliant aquamarine. His black hair seemed curlier somehow—almost as though he'd tamed it for the professional photo. But his suit was as crisply tailored as the one he'd been wearing in the shot and looked to be Italian, if she had to guess.

"Please come in, ladies," he told them, rising from his desk and coming around to greet them. The crisp way he shaped his consonants and vowels in that baritone voice of his pegged him as a Yankee. "I promise I don't bite."

Shelby wasn't too sure about that, but she held out her hand. Goodness, he was a tall man—she had to crane her neck to meet his steady gaze. "I'm Shelby McGuiness."

He shook her hand firmly, professionally, but she had to work hard to block the ping that fired up her arm from that brief contact. "Vander Montgomery. And that would make you Sadie." He immediately turned to her sister and shook Sadie's hand as perfunctorily as he'd shaken her own, giving Shelby time to pull herself together.

"Yes. That's me. It's good to meet you, Mr. Montgomery."

"Vander, please," he said, gesturing for them to take the two black leather chairs with decorative gold arms in front of his desk.

Shelby traced the leaf motif on the arm of the chair,

taking in his office. He had expensive taste, but everything in the room was elegant. His desk was a sturdy Hepplewhite mahogany. A couple Montblanc pens in gold and red lay on his desk beside a day planner engraved in gold. A view of Nashville and the Cumberland River stretched out behind him. It all painted a picture that was as obvious as a tick on a hound dog. He was a powerful man who liked to make an impression, but who also felt comfortable working in a powerful setting.

As Vander resumed his seat behind the desk, Shelby's eyes lingered on the more inviting setup in the far corner of the room—a side table with gold-upholstered chairs. She wondered if he only met with clients there after they had officially hired him.

"You mentioned when we made this appointment that you're interested in locating your father," he said. "Tell me about him."

"His name is Preston McGuiness," Shelby said, clearing her throat when it seemed to fail her. "We don't know much about him. He left when we were children."

"How old were you both when that happened?" he asked, not bothering to offer his condolences, she noted.

"I was only two, and Sadie..." She gestured to her sister, wanting to include her in the conversation.

"I was a baby," her sister said, clutching her hands in her lap.

"And why are you interested in finding him now?" he asked. His posture was neither slouchy nor ramrod, but he still exuded an intense interest she found compelling.

"We...ah...I..." Shelby was babbling and shut her mouth to compose herself.

"There's his medical history for one," Sadie blurted out

with a huge gust of a breath. "You know, for family diseases and such."

He gave her a kind smile, and Shelby slowly blew her own breath out. Heaven help her, she hadn't expected to get this emotional.

"It's all right to be nervous," Vander said. "Looking for a father who left you over twenty years ago is a big deal."

Shelby nodded.

"The biggest!" Sadie blurted out. "Our other sister, Susannah, got married a few months back, which got us both to thinking. Our brother...you see...well, he escorted her down the aisle. She likely would have asked him to do it anyway—J.P.'s the best big brother there is—but she didn't have a choice."

Vander was still smiling, holding that steady gaze. "Congratulations. I hope your sister and her husband are very happy."

Her sister relaxed more in her chair. "They are. Thank you. And then there's...Shelby, you should tell him the rest."

That easy smile didn't alter as he turned it toward her.

"Well...we don't know why he left...or where he is." Shelby's heart was beating like one of those wind-up monkeys was pounding on it from the inside. "We don't even know if he's still alive."

"I see," Vander said, nodding. "Is your mother still alive?"

"Oh, yes!" Sadie said immediately. "Very much so. But she...doesn't like to talk about him."

He took their measure again. "You mentioned a brother and your sister, Susannah."

He earned at least ten points for remembering those facts after one casual mention. "Susannah doesn't approve of my wish," Shelby blurted out. "Our wish. Sorry, Sadie. She thinks it will open a can of worms and..." Gosh, it was awkward to tell someone their personal business like this. "She's afraid it will hurt Mama. I mean...we are too, but we want to know."

"J.P. is aware of our plans though," Sadie blurted out. "J.P.'s our big brother. He's given us his blessing, and that's...well, it means the world."

Vander smiled again at Sadie. "Thanks for clarifying that, Sadie. What do you think will happen when and if I find your father?"

"Ah—" Sadie exclaimed, looking at her for an answer.

"Is that question really necessary?" Shelby asked. "We're obviously here, and we want to hire you."

"I'm sorry if the questions seem personal," he said in that same even Yankee tone. "I know this must be hard for you. But in order for me to do my job to the highest standard, I need to know my clients' goals."

"It's simple," Shelby said with an edge in her voice. "We want to find our father. That's our goal."

Sadie looked over at her and shook her head as if to chide Shelby for being harsh. She couldn't help it. Questions like that might talk them right out of wanting to find Daddy. It was hard enough to dig into the past without considering the many ways in which it could go wrong.

"This is difficult for us," Sadie said, looking back at Vander. "I'm sorry Shelby was short with you."

"I can apologize for myself if it's needed," she said tersely, crossing her arms over her chest. She knew she was being difficult, but all of a sudden, she couldn't seem to help herself. Anger was pouring into her like water in a leaky boat—even though she knew it was misdirected.

"You don't need to apologize for anything," Vander said, rising and coming around his desk.

Shelby knew he meant it, and she released a pent-up breath. "I seem to be...emotional. I *am* sorry."

"Again, there's nothing to be sorry about," he said, sitting on the edge of his desk. "As I said before, kicking off a search like this is tough. It would be for anyone. I'm here to help you. We don't know each other yet, but if you agree to move forward with me, we will. I'll need to know everything you can remember about your father. Since you were so little when he left, most of what you know likely comes from other people. Am I correct?"

They both nodded.

"Most cases that involve an absence of this many years require a little more legwork. The databases I usually use to find someone only go back about twenty or twenty-five years—around when computers became mainstream. Your daddy disappeared on the cusp of that time if I've judged your ages right."

"You have," Sadie said. "I hadn't thought about the computer thing. Oh, goodness."

"It makes sense to me," Shelby said. "I didn't expect it to be easy. I've done my own Google searches and the like, and I'm pretty good at finding things out. I couldn't find anything."

"You seem incredibly smart...and brave," Vander said, gazing at her intently. "But I have access to information you wouldn't. We may get lucky with your father. We may input his name and last known address some twenty years back and get a hit."

"But you don't think it's likely?" Sadie asked, glancing Shelby's way, tension around her mouth.

"I have a gut feeling it might not be that easy," Vander said, resting his hand on his knee. "Otherwise, your mother wouldn't be so unwilling to discuss why he left or where he went."

."You think our mama might know all of that?" Sadie asked, blinking rapidly.

"Sometimes a parent keeps that kind of information a secret to protect her children."

That was impossible. "Our mama isn't secretive," Shelby told him, her mind spinning now. "She's a preacher."

His face didn't change, but Shelby thought his eyes crinkled a fraction. "Was she a preacher when your father left?"

"No," Sadie said slowly, like she was thinking things over, "but both of them were good church-goin' people."

And yet, their daddy had up and left his wife and four children, Shelby could almost hear Vander thinking.

"What more can you tell me about your father and your family?" he asked.

Shelby let Sadie paint her version of the story, and while Vander kept his focus on her sister, she felt him glance her way every once in a while to take stock of her reaction.

"Is that how you remember things?" he asked her finally, shifting his large frame on the desk to give her his full attention.

"Sure...I mean...as you said, most of what we know is from J.P. and Susannah since we were so young." Truth be told, she and Sadie didn't really have their own memories of Daddy, and that bothered her more than she wanted to say.

"All right," Vander said. "I think I have a clear picture of things. Let me tell you what my services include. As I said, I'll use all the resources available to me to discover your father's whereabouts. Obviously, the greater the difficulty, the more resources I'll need to use, but I promise you, if you want me to, I will pursue every lead available. We won't know whether it will be easy or difficult to locate him until we start the search."

They both nodded. He pushed off the desk and walked around to sit in his office chair.

"Depending on how things go and what we find, we'll be in constant communication. If you need to reach me, I'm pretty much available day or night. Lucky for me, I don't need much sleep."

The thoughts that came into Shelby's head had nothing to do with Vander working a case to find their daddy. She imagined showing up at his front door in nothing but a trench coat. Goodness gracious, she really needed to stop watching murder mystery romances on TV. When she came back to the conversation, Vander was looking at her with that quiet intensity of his. Her mouth parted, and for a moment, she could have sworn he'd read her mind. Then he shifted his attention back to Sadie.

"And how much do you charge?" Sadie asked.

"Two hundred dollars an hour, plus expenses if there are any," he told them, handing them each a sheet of paper. "Here's my fee schedule so we're all on the same page."

His presentation was simple and flawless. Shelby felt Sadie waiting for her to make eye contact and knew her sister was worried about the money. Even though Sadie worked at a craft store and lived simply, she'd wanted to contribute to the cause. Shelby had agreed, but would be covering the lion's share.

"If you'd like to confer a moment," Vander said, standing again. "I can give you a few minutes."

Shelby suppressed her surprise. He obviously didn't have anything confidential in his office, or he'd never have offered to leave them alone here. Or maybe he had them pegged for trustworthy people. Most people assumed so, with their mama being a preacher and all. Then again, he might have a camera in his office. He was a P.I., after all. Gracious, she was overthinking things.

"Thank you for the offer to confer," Shelby said, knowing Sadie would do better if they chatted. "A moment would be *lovely.*"

He gave them that killer smile of his, as if he'd enjoyed every drop of sugar she'd poured into her Southern drawl. "Ladies, would you like anything else to drink?"

"No thank you, Vander," Sadie said, smiling at him as he turned and left them alone.

"I can handle his fees, Sadie," Shelby told her the moment the door closed.

"I didn't expect it to be so expensive," her sister said. "I guess I should have if Gail and all those politicians and celebrities use him. He's really nice, don't you think? I didn't expect that."

For some reason, Shelby hadn't either. She'd known he was handsome and successful, but Vander Montgomery also knew how to listen and manage client relationships better than many of the professionals she worked with. It only made him more attractive in her eyes.

"Do you think he can find Daddy?" Sadie asked.

Shelby took in the restrained power emanating from the room and nodded. "If anyone can, he can. But I think we're asking the wrong question. I rather hate admitting it, but Vander was right to press us about what we expect to find. Are we really prepared to learn things we're better off not knowing? I got mad at him, but really I...just got mad, is all. I feel like I'm poking a stick in my own hornet's nest, you know?"

"I know exactly what you mean," Sadie said softly. "I get angry, but it also makes me sad."

Suddenly Shelby wasn't sure what they should do. Vander had dredged up all the anger she'd shoved into a box a long time ago. Their daddy had abandoned their family. Their mama hadn't really ever explained it satisfactorily. Maybe she couldn't. But maybe Vander was right. Maybe Mama was being secretive to protect them.

"We were taught that pursuing the truth is always the best course of action." Sadie made a face. "Even though we weren't given that truth."

"Maybe Mama doesn't really know why Daddy left," Shelby said, as much to convince herself as her younger sister. "Maybe this would help her find closure too."

"She must suspect *something*," Sadie said, her voice raising. "A good man doesn't just up and leave his family without a word."

"No, you're right." That part of the puzzle had never made sense. If Mama had said he'd had a drinking problem or been in trouble with the law, Shelby might have understood. But no excuse had ever been given. He had been there one day, gone the next. That was all they knew.

"I sure wish Mama would answer our questions," Sadie said in exasperation. "It would save us a lot of money and heartache."

"But Mama hasn't said a word about him in all these years, even though she knows it's caused us heartache." Shelby felt her diaphragm tighten. "I don't see that changing."

"Neither do I," Sadie said. "And that scares me. Mama preaches about talking about things so they can heal, and all her silence has done is allow this hurt to fester and grow."

Truer words had never been spoken. Shelby didn't like to think about what it must cost their Mama not to live her values. Or why. In fact, it scared her spitless.

"What do we do if Susannah asks us about this again?" Sadie looked over her shoulder at the door to see if Vander had returned. "I'm terrible at hiding things."

"She's too happy with Jake to ask," Shelby said. "Besides, I think she's going to be an ostrich about this."

"But what if we find something?" Sadie asked, tears filling her eyes. "What if we find Daddy? Don't we have to tell her?"

Shelby's heartbeat ramped up, and she pressed her hand to her chest, taking deep breaths to quell its urgency.

"We'll tell J.P. first and see what he thinks is the best course of action," she said when she was able to speak. "Like we agreed."

"And Mama?" Sadie asked, wringing her hands now.

"If we all agree—and I mean even Susannah—we tell Mama we love her, but we needed answers."

Sadie got a little more teary-eyed at that. "I'm just going to pray God can soften this whole situation. We don't need any more hurt coming up from the past."

Yet, they both needed to find out the truth—or at least try to—in order to move forward with their lives. "So we hire Vander."

Her sister reached for her hand. "Yes. I still want to contribute what I can."

"You really don't need to," Shelby said, patting her hand. "You know Gail pays me well."

"He's my daddy too," Sadie said with a stern nod. "I want to contribute *something*."

Since Shelby knew better than to hurt anyone's pride—

especially her sister's—she smiled. "I'll take them in baked goods and crafts."

"I can make you a quilt!" The corners of her sister's mouth tipped up.

"Sadie, you're always giving your quilts away. You should keep one for yourself." In fact, her sister usually thought of others before herself, just like Mama had taught them they should.

"I know you're right, but there's always someone who could use a quilt. Besides, the only reason I got good at them was because I made so many for the people at church. Now, I get to sell them at the craft shop. It's a blessing. Every quilt I make is stitched together with love."

Yes, every swatch her sister selected was done with intention. Her quilts were all the more special for it.

"I can make you peach jam too since we're just coming up on peach season," Sadie continued. J.P.'s wedding had been three weeks ago on the first Saturday of June, but because Tammy loved peaches so much, he'd found some early Eastern ones and asked Sadie to make a peach pie for the rehearsal dinner. It had been delicious.

Out of all of them, Sadie was the homiest. She'd even grown tomatoes for salsa last summer, and as if that hadn't been effort enough, she'd packaged jars for everyone in the family with hand-written labels and artful bows. She was a good sister to have around.

"Done," Shelby said, and they shook on it.

They hugged each other. The door opened, causing them to break apart.

Vander stuck his head inside. "Are you finished conferring?"

"Yes," Sadie said brightly as he walked toward them.

He sat on the edge of his desk again and gave them

that compelling smile. Her reaction to him was completely normal, she decided—the man was a chick magnet. His charm must come in handy with his job. People talked to nice, well-dressed handsome men—especially women.

"We'd like to hire you," Shelby said, giving him what she hoped was also a professional smile. "Thank you for letting us talk it through."

"This is a big decision. I want you to be one hundred percent sure you want to move forward."

"We do," Sadie said, nodding.

He gave them a measured look. "Let's go ahead and sign a service agreement so I can get started. You can tell me your father's last known address so I can include it at the bottom."

Sitting down at his desk, he typed for a minute, prompting Shelby when he needed the address, and then printed off the service agreement. He handed it to her when he was finished. Sure enough, their family's last address together loomed large at the bottom of the page.

They'd lived in that house for only a few more months after their daddy's abandonment, because Mama hadn't been able to afford the mortgage on her own. Shelby had been too young when they'd moved to miss the house on Meadow Grove Street, but she'd driven by it multiple times as an adult. It was something she'd never shared with her siblings, but every time she did it, she imagined what their life might have been if they'd remained whole. How she'd imagine Daddy pushing her on the tire swing. Or J.P. playing in a sandbox as a more carefree little boy.

Shelby wished she had more real memories of that simple white colonial house with the black front door and matching black shutters, but like everything else from that time in her life, she only knew it from pictures and her flights of imagination.

Sadie rummaged in her purse. "Do you need a photo of Daddy?" she asked, handing him the one of their family taken two months before he'd left.

Vander took the photo and studied it. "You have his likeness, Shelby." Then he locked gazes with her. "The eyebrow line is the same. And the mouth. Your bottom lip is...full...like his."

"Is it?" she asked, a little breathless. "I mean, do I...look like him?"

Sadie shot her a look, which she ignored. She needed to pull it together, but since no one ever talked about their daddy or so much as brought out a picture, she'd never been told she resembled him. J.P. resembled him more than the rest of them, not that the McGuiness siblings talked about it much. In fact, this photo was the only one they had of that time. Sadie had snuck it out of a photo album when she was a junior in high school and put it in her bedside stand. If Mama ever knew, she'd never said anything.

It rattled the heck out of Shelby to hear she looked like Daddy. Besides, Vander was staring at her with such intensity. Talking about her full bottom lip...

"You do. From this photo, Sadie takes more after your mother."

"Yes," her sister agreed, and Shelby wondered if she was longing to hear if any of her features resembled their daddy too. Those physical attributes were all they had of him— so far.

"The database I start with doesn't have any photos," Vander said. "I'll just plug in your father's name and last known address and see where things go from there. Sometimes I can use the local tax office to trace someone, but that's another step. If I end up needing to do some door-to-door visits at former residences, the photo might come in handy, although he's older now."

How many residences had their daddy had in the last twenty-plus years? There was so much they didn't know.

"This is a pretty precious photo, I imagine," Vander said. "You two have a beautiful family. Would you like to keep it with you until I need it? Copies of photos aren't as effective in the field as originals. People tend to be more receptive and less suspicious if it's a real photo."

Sadie's lip trembled, and Shelby reached for her hand. She knew how important that photo was to her sister.

"You can keep it," Sadie said softly. "Maybe it will help inspire you...to see what he used to look like. Goodness, I... wonder if he even looks the same. It's been a long time, hasn't it?"

Vander nodded, and despite his polished façade, Shelby could feel the compassion in him. He might be a powerful man, but he had heart. Her interest in him was only building, and she wondered about him, personal things like where he'd gotten that accent, how he'd come to Nashville to be a P.I., and why in the world his parents had named him Vander.

"I promise I'll take good care of it, Sadie," he said, carefully laying the photo down on his desk. "Thank you for entrusting it to me."

Her sister gave him a teary smile, and Shelby knew they'd better hustle. Vander didn't need to see Sadie's waterworks during their first meeting.

"I'm happy to sign the agreement," Shelby said, taking out a pen from her purse.

When she looked up, Vander was handing Sadie a box of tissues.

"You go ahead and cry if you need to," he said quietly, still sitting on the edge of his desk. "Lots of people come into my office with difficult stories. You can't ruffle me, I promise."

The first tear slid down Sadie's face. Shelby had half a mind to shush her or stop her, but she knew better. When Sadie was like this, it was best if she let it out.

"You can leave us alone another spell if you'd like," she told Vander, taking her sister's hand and squeezing it.

He only spared her a quick glance. "No need. I told you. It doesn't bother me."

And he seemed to mean it. Vander sat across from Sadie as she let loose a waterfall of tears, and Shelby busied herself with reading and signing the service agreement.

"Sadie," she said as she handed the signed agreement to Vander. "Let's let this poor man get on with his day and find you a cup of tea."

The look Vander shot her rooted her in her chair. His aquamarine eyes didn't look like calm waters now. There was heat—the kind that would scorch.

"Take all the time you need, Sadie," he said gently. *Don't listen to your sister*, Shelby all but heard him say, and if that didn't shame her...

"No, Shelby's right," her sister said, rising from her seat and handing him the box of tissues, which he set aside. "I'm sorry for that display."

"Pay it no mind," Vander said. "If you need to express your emotions at any time during this process, you just go right ahead. I have a broad shoulder. Sadie, I'd like you to sign our agreement too. Seems only right."

He shot Shelby a look that served as a silent message.

"But Shelby is...ah...paying for things," Sadie said.

"Payment is different," Vander said. "You're both my clients. He's your father too."

Sadie gave him a tremulous smile and signed it.

"When I have any news about your father," Vander said, setting the agreement aside, "I'll give you a call."

"I'll be your main point of contact," Shelby said, deciding it would be more efficient.

Sadie glanced her way, and there was hurt in her eyes.

Vander didn't respond immediately. "How about I text you both, and if you're able, we can set up a face-to-face? Once I confirm whether this is going to be easy or a little more challenging, we'll need to agree on next steps. I'll ask for your sign-off before I move ahead. Both of you."

He'd done it again. Impressed her with his ability to manage his clients. Everything he did and said was carefully calibrated to ensure neither of them felt left out. Then she wondered if two people in the same family might develop different opinions during a process like this. That thought made her tummy burn. Surely she and Sadie would stay on the same page?

"That's fine," Shelby said, putting her arm around Sadie's shoulders to ensure he knew she cared about her sister.

"You've been wonderful, Vander," her sister said. "I'm...grateful."

"It's been a pleasure, Sadie," Vander said with that smile of his. "Shelby, it was good to meet you as well. I'll be in touch."

He gave her his total focus as he shook her hand, and she was firmer in her shake than she normally would have been. He didn't blink once, as if daring her to soften. She left his office quickly, determined not to quail.

Her sister hurried to keep up with her, and in the elevator, she didn't say a word. When they reached the parking lot, Sadie turned to her. "I know you're attracted to him."

Shelby didn't bother to deny it.

"I won't tell you what to do," her sister said, unlocking her older Honda. "I can't tell if he likes you or not. But he strikes me as a professional. I know you are too. Let's not make him...uncomfortable. We want him to find Daddy."

That hot anger rose up again, and Shelby took a moment before responding. Otherwise, she'd spew flames, and that wouldn't help anyone. "I won't make him uncomfortable. Besides, I got the distinct impression he didn't much like me."

It didn't matter, though.

She knew he wasn't the kind of man who would let anything affect his work.

CHAPTER TWO

Vander Montgomery walked to the window after closing the door behind his new clients. The view of the Cumberland River didn't calm him. Neither did the reminder that he'd earned this killer view of Nashville.

Every time a client hired him to find their father, he got all stirred up.

It didn't matter that he was thirty-five, and his father had been murdered twenty-five years ago this August. Part of what haunted him was that the crime remained unsolved after everything he'd done to find out who had murdered his father, Nashville detective Jed Montgomery. It didn't help that he was now the same age his father had been when he was murdered. He had no model for how a man was supposed to live past this age, and it bothered him. Acutely.

He shrugged out of his suit jacket, feeling constricted.

Vander had poured everything he had and was into finding his father's killer, until he'd been forced to face the conclusion there was nothing more he could do to find the man. After that, he'd poured himself into creating his detective agency and helping the people his father had served. That was something he'd succeeded at, *excelled* at. But it was no longer a challenge.

What was he supposed to pour himself into now?

Being a thirty-five-year-old successful bachelor in the South, he had plenty of people telling him it was time to find a good woman, settle down, and have a family. He'd never had much interest in that. After all, client after client had given him ample evidence that marriage and family didn't work out for everyone. It hadn't worked out for his parents either.

But work wasn't enough anymore. He knew how to deal with clients and handle their cases. Nothing felt like much of a challenge, except there was something about Shelby McGuiness...

As a P.I., Vander sized people up immediately—it was his gift and a key component of his success—but the man in him had sized her up as well when she'd sauntered into his office in her pale pink designer dress suit and sparkly chandelier earrings. She was as classic Southern as pecan pie, but with a modern edge. Her rose perfume dotted with a pinch of peony and musk suited her to a T, and her silky light-brown hair and whiskey-colored eyes had stirred something in him. Cream-colored Jimmy Choos with straps that wrapped up her calves like vines had showcased her knockout legs. He was a leg man, and he appreciated a woman who wore sexy heels. Sue him.

He'd even liked her strong and determined attitude

until she'd turned it on her sister. Regardless of that fact, she'd fired something up inside him only his father's case and his business had fired up before.

He was going to need to keep a tight rein on himself while he worked on this case. It was counter to his personal code to show anything other than a professional interest in his clients. The curse word he uttered didn't ease his agitation.

A discreet knock sounded behind him, and Vander cursed again. He knew it was Charlie, coming to check on him. She was his number two, with the official title of vice president. He'd hired her for her sixth sense, but he hated it when she turned that uncanny perception of hers on him.

The door opened, but Vander didn't bother to turn around. "I won't tell you to go back to work."

She snorted. "You know I'm too tenacious for that. Besides, I had those Southern belles pegged for a missing father the minute they walked into reception."

"It's a waste of company hours for you to monitor new client arrivals," he told her for the hundredth time.

"It's my way of testing my sixth sense," she answered like she always did. "Need to make sure it's one-hundred-percent accurate."

"It usually is," Vander said as she came up beside him, clad in simple black pants, low heels for running after people if needed, and a white button-down shirt.

All the detectives who worked for him were the best out there—he'd made sure of that. Gage Farris was an ex-cop who'd retired young, fed up with the bureaucracy and politics in Atlanta. Lawrence Patterson had run his own private detective outfit until he'd gotten tired of the paperwork and management and come to work for his biggest competitor —Vander. Then there was the support staff that Montgomery Associates used for the more routine work of background checks, something they had a slew of from their country singer celebrity and politician clients.

But Charlie was special. Somehow she'd become his best friend. It helped that they weren't remotely each other's type.

"Why don't you pass this case off to me?" Charlie asked him, putting her hands on her hips. "Give yourself a break for once. It's the twenty-fifth anniversary of your dad's death. I know it's on your mind more than usual."

It was. The thirtieth of August lived large in his mind. His nightmares had returned too. The ones where his mom told him his daddy had been hurt by a bad man and wouldn't be coming home ever again. Then there was the new dream that shook him to the core, where his dad's wounded corpse rose out of the morgue and asked him, *What are you going to do with the rest of your life, son?* before vanishing.

Vander tightened his muscles to fight off the shiver that wanted to run through his body. He cleared his throat. "You know I can't do that, Charlie."

There was ultimately no choice for him. He'd returned to Nashville to go to Vanderbilt, where his parents had met and the place after which he'd been named, in the hopes of solving his father's murder one day. But while he'd failed himself, at least he could find other people's fathers—or mothers—or learn why they had been killed or had gone missing. It was the only redemption he'd found.

"You're a stubborn son of a bitch, Vander," Charlie said, frowning darkly.

"Don't I know it."

He had resigned himself to never knowing why his father had been left for dead in a downtown alley a stone's throw from one of Nashville's bottom-feeder music venues, the kind of place where washed out, hopeless musicians went to play and drink themselves to death, bemoaning their lost dreams.

The police report suggested his father had been undercover, looking into the selling of illegal substances onsite, and had been discovered somehow. No witnesses had ever surfaced. No prints were found on or around the body. And the murder weapon—a GLOCK 17—was never recovered.

"I was afraid you'd say that."

He was always reassuring her, but part of him liked that she cared enough to worry. Neither one of them had had much of that growing up.

"The girls were pretty," Charlie said in that practical way of hers.

"Were they?" he bluffed and immediately realized his mistake.

Before he could even register it, she was moving, and her hands were on his shoulders, turning him toward her. Her strength always surprised him since she was five foot nothing and weighed a mere one hundred and ten pounds, mostly muscle.

"Holy shit!" she said, staring into his eyes. "You're *attracted* to one of them. You really need to give me the case now."

He frowned at her.

"The slightly older one, right? I'd peg them for Irish twins, but there's still an older/younger sister thing going on."

What the hell was he supposed to say? He'd felt that pull as soon as Shelby came striding through the door, trying to act like their appointment was just another business meeting.

"*Vander.*"

"Fine, she's hot," he said, brushing his shoulder. "But it's *not* a problem. Charlie, you know me. I wouldn't take the case otherwise. Shelby might be gorgeous, but I didn't like her much."

"Why not?" Charlie asked, studying him.

"Do you always have to ask so many questions?" he asked her in exasperation. "Forget I said that. Of course you do. It's your job." He'd best say it before she did.

"You're really riled up," she said, trying not to laugh. "What did this Shelby do to make you dislike her? Besides igniting some weird male attraction in you. Yuck. I think I need to wash my mouth out for saying that."

"Ditto for hearing it." But he decided to answer. "The younger sister, Sadie, has a soft heart, and I didn't like how Shelby treated her."

"Sadie cried, didn't she?"

"Yes, she did," he said, remembering how bravely the woman had tried to hide it in the beginning.

It pissed him off that Shelby had tried to stop her. The pain of losing a father was immeasurable, and his mother hadn't done him any favors by telling him to keep it locked up inside like his hurt heart was a bank vault. Her way of dealing with grief was to pretend none of it had happened. She'd moved them back to her rich family in Boston, who hadn't approved of her marrying a Nashville native, especially one who'd decided to go into law enforcement over the law.

His mother had soon fallen back into his grandparents' mentality and had done everything in her power to beat the Southern out of him, even going as far as to make him take voice classes until all trace of his accent was eradicated.

For years, he'd fought the anger and the fathomless

sorrow, but he'd erupted in high school, running wild, flirting with the law, all but daring his mother to throw him out like he felt she'd done emotionally.

It had taken his social studies teacher—also his lacrosse coach—pretty much busting his balls to get him back on track. Ruining his life wouldn't bring back his father, Mr. Hawkins had told him. Nor would it make his father happy if he was in heaven like people said. Why not position himself for a better life, so he could make his own choices once he turned eighteen? That advice had finally penetrated Vander's thick skull.

He'd stopped partying with the rough crowd, turned around his failing grades, and gotten into Vanderbilt University as a way to reconnect with his father and his roots. His mother and grandparents had been violently opposed to his return to Nashville, even more so the direction he'd taken with his studies, and it had been the last break in their already strained relationship.

Vander hadn't wanted to be a cop like his father, but he'd loved the idea of investigating things and uncovering secrets, so he'd majored in criminal justice. Becoming a private investigator had seemed the best course, and he'd pursued it wholeheartedly. He'd opened his own private investigation company in Nashville after securing his license, serving the same community his father had.

"Of the two sisters, *Shelby* looks more polished and tougher, although I bet they'd both still run in the opposite direction if I so much as said boo to them," Charlie said, leaving his side to open up the mini-fridge disguised as a cabinet.

She was tough, it was true, but something told him that Charlie might be wrong about the McGuiness sisters—or at least the older one.

"I'm not convinced Shelby would back down," Vander told her, following in her wake. "It took guts to come here. The mother doesn't know about their interest in finding their father, and their other sister is against it. The brother sounds like he's supportive."

"But he wasn't here today." Charlie handed him a bottle of Perrier—sue him, he liked the fizzy water—and grabbed a regular bottle of water for herself.

"No, he wasn't." And Vander wondered about that too.

"What's your gut tell you about this case?" Charlie asked.

"Home troubles, I'd bet," he told her, running through what little he knew of the case so far. "The mother is currently a preacher. Sounds like they all went to church together like a good Southern family before their father cut out on them."

"Going to church disguises a lot of deadbeats," Charlie said in that jaded tone of hers. "Foul play doesn't feel right to me."

"Me either," Vander said, and truth was, he could usually smell violence on a case before he had the facts to support it. "The reason isn't as important as the amount of time he's been gone. He went missing when Shelby was two, and from my guess of her age—"

"That was twenty-six years ago," Charlie told him with a smirk. "I looked up her driver's license."

"Of course you did, even though we're not supposed to use databases to look up our clients unless we suspect them of something," he said, rolling his eyes, doing the math. Shelby was seven years younger than him. Not that he had any business calculating things like that.

"Shelby Marie McGuiness also likes to speed," Charlie continued. "She got a ticket for doing eighty-eight on I-64 last month in a new white BMW convertible licensed to her and her alone."

The car suited her understated elegance. He ignored Charlie's additional confirmation that Shelby wasn't married. Neither woman wore a wedding ring. Besides, any husband worth his chops would have been holding his wife's hand during an appointment as big as this one.

"I'm surprised she didn't talk her way out of it."

Charlie's smirk widened. "The officer was female."

"*Ah*," was all he said.

"I'll run the father's name today," Vander said, taking a sip of his water. He hated to make clients wait on a case like this.

Charlie shook her head. "I already did."

"Dammit, Charlie! You didn't even have confirmation it was a lost father case."

"*Please.* You're insulting me. I always know. What was the use in waiting? It's a dead end, Vander. There are no records of any addresses or credit cards for Preston Matthias McGuiness after he left the Dare River area. He dropped off the face of the earth. He clearly didn't want to be found."

"You don't need to do my job for me, Charlie," Vander said, setting his water on the edge of his desk. "You have plenty of your own cases."

"Yes, but I knew those two were going to be trouble for you the minute they walked in," she told him, crossing her arms and staring at him with those determined hazel eyes of hers. "I'm going to help with this one, Vander, and you're not going to stop me. You need a friend right now more than ever with August 30th approaching, and since you're such a stubborn son of a bitch, I'm your best bet."

He cursed fluently, which only made her laugh.

"You can change your mind and give me the case," Charlie said, lifting her shoulder. "I promise to be gentle with the soft-hearted one."

This time he scoffed. "You couldn't be gentle with a koala bear. Dammit, you know I can't give up this case."

"I do," she told him, patting his shoulder before walking to the door. "Aren't you lucky I'm your best friend and don't listen to you when you're being a doofus?"

He didn't rise to the bait. "I'll let the McGuiness women know we want to take a look into his family and see whether they're up for it."

"I'll sit in on the next meeting with you," Charlie said, not posing it as a question.

The door closed behind her petite frame before he could respond—just like she'd intended. It looked like he was going to have a partner on this one. Of course, the sisters might decide not to move ahead after learning the official trail was a dead end. But something in Shelby's eyes told him she was ready to pursue the truth about her father as doggedly as he had tried to solve his own father's case. After meeting her and her sister, he had to admit he was pretty happy to have Charlie's support.

Not that he'd ever tell her that.

Continue reading *The Fountain Of Infinite Wishes*...

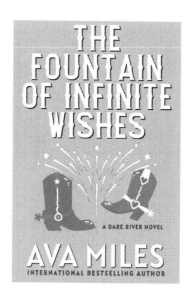

The Fountain of Infinite Wishes
Dare River ★ Book 5

A gripping and emotional tale about believing in wishes coming true and searching for love—no matter where it leads.

Scan to dive into *The Fountain of Infinite Wishes* now!

MORE RECIPES? MORE RYE?

Love Tori's recipes and want some of Ava's home cooking? Grab Country Heaven Cookbook.

"Delicious, simple recipes... Comfort food, at its best."

— FIRE UP THE OVEN BLOG

Want more Rye Crenshaw in your life? If you haven't read The Dare Valley series where Rye pops in now and again, check it out. It begins with Nora Roberts Land, a #1 National Bestseller and Best Book of the Year!

Did you know Ava also writes nonfiction books? Check out more of her trademark unforgettable inspiration on living a happy and fulfilling life.

ABOUT THE AUTHOR

Millions of readers have discovered International Bestselling Author Ava Miles and her powerful fiction and non-fiction books about love, happiness, and transformation. Her novels have received praise and accolades from *USA Today*, *Publisher's Weekly*, and *People Magazine* in addition to being chosen as Best Books of the Year and Top Editor's picks. Translated into multiple languages, Ava's strongest praise comes directly from her readers, who call her books and characters unforgettable.

Ava is a former chef, worked as a long-time conflict expert rebuilding warzones to foster peaceful and prosperous communities, and has helped people live their best life as a life coach, energy healer, and self-help expert. She is never happier than when she's formulating skin care and wellness products, gardening, or creating a new work of art. Hanging with her friends and loved ones is pretty great too.

After years of residing in the States, she decided to follow her dream of living in Europe. She recently finished a magical stint in Ireland where she was inspired to write her acclaimed Unexpected Prince Charming series. Now, she's splitting her time between Paris and Provence, learning to speak French, immersing herself in cooking *à la provençal*, and planning more page-turning novels for readers to binge.

Visit Ava on social media:

 facebook.com/AuthorAvaMiles

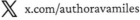 x.com/authoravamiles

 instagram.com/avamiles

 bookbub.com/authors/ava-miles

 pinterest.com/authoravamiles

DON'T FORGET...
SIGN UP FOR AVA'S NEWSLETTER.

More great books? Check.
Fun facts? Check.
Recipes? Check.
General frivolity? DOUBLE CHECK.

https://avamiles.com/newsletter/